Johnnie Stark was a
product of the Gorbals.
Tall, broad-chested, and
with dark, sullen eyes he
looked like a fighter – and he
was.

Johnnie liked women –
and women liked him. For
their sake, and for any
other reason that seemed
good to him, Johnnie was
ready to fight. There were no
Queensbury Rules in the
Gorbals, and when violence
erupted, any weapon was
used . . .

No Mean City

A. McArthur and
H. Kingsley Long

CORGI BOOKS

NO MEAN CITY
A CORGI BOOK : 9780552075831

Originally published in Great Britain by
Neville Spearman Ltd.

PRINTING HISTORY
Neville Spearman edition published 1956
Corgi edition published 1957

40

Set in 10/11¼pt Linotype Times by
Kestrel Data, Exeter.

Corgi Books are published by Transworld Publishers,
61–63 Uxbridge Road, London W5 5SA,
A Random House Group Company.

Addresses for Random House Group Ltd companies outside the UK
can be found at: www.randomhouse.co.uk
The Random House Group Ltd Reg. No. 954009.

Penguin Random House is committed to a sustainable future for
our business, our readers and our planet. This book is made from
Forest Stewardship Council® certified paper.

Printed and bound in Great Britain by Clays Ltd, Elcograf S.p.A.

Contents

CHAPTER I

RENT MUST BE PAID

In the thick and stagnant darkness John Stark lay wide awake. His wife slept beside him and their youngest child whimpered in the crook of her arm. The door of the cavity bed was barely ajar, for the night was cold and the children had opened the window which gave upon the street. Stark was so accustomed to the sour stench of the "hoose" that he preferred to lie there in a sort of cupboard, stiflingly close, but warm with the heat of their three bodies.

Cavity beds are so common a feature of the Glasgow slums even to this day that the tenement dwellers take them for granted. The ordinary "room-and-kitchen" apartment, and even the one-roomed "single end", always include a cavity bed or beds. These beds are no more than windowless closets – little tombs about five feet by five by three and a half. The door of each closes against the side of the bed and flush with the wall of the room itself.

Stark's discarded trousers lay on the top of the blankets. The baby had bronchitis and was likely to be sick again if it started coughing. He did not want to wake the child or his wife, and so his hand moved stealthily inch by inch to the pocket which contained all that was left of his week's money. He did not take the money out; he counted it up by the feel of each separate coin, reaching the same total again and again. Then, very, very softly, he whispered blasphemies.

For he was a shilling short of the rent. The Factor would call in the morning and demand seven and elevenpence. He wouldn't say very much at having to wait for a day or two because the Starks were good tenants. But he would certainly call again before the week was out.

"Ay," thought John Stark bitterly, "and the bliddy auld bastard will be standing on the stair-heid again next Friday if we canny pay him before. That will be fifteen and tenpence and we can fill oor bellies on what's left."

Stark had drunk beer that day; not enough to affect his sobriety, not enough even to quench his thirst, but still enough to leave him short of his rent money. His mouth was dry and he wanted to relieve himself, but he was afraid to get out of bed.

" 'Executors of Hell-knows-who, deceased,' " he mused, "an' the Factor tell me the auld man died before I was born! I wonder who gets wer rents now. Seven and eleven for this hoose; seven and eleven for the one opposite, an' six shillings for the single end between. That'll be about twenty-one shillings for the landing, and four landings to the stair. I'd like fine to own this bliddy tenement."

The call had now become imperative. Stark pushed wide the door, which concealed the cavity bed in the day-time, and thrust a hairy leg to the old chair, from which he stepped down to the floor. Cautiously he re-fixed the blankets and at last stepped out into the living-room with its faintly perceptible square of window at the far end.

He was a big man and strong, but, although there were "eleven of a family" in that two-roomed apartment a draught came from the open window and he shivered as he stood there in his grey flannel shirt. It was in his mind to cross the room to the front door four steps away and thus to gain access to the closet on the stairway landing outside which served all three "houses" on that floor, but the cold and an angry knowledge that the landing might be wet to his bare feet deterred him.

"I'll just make do wi' the sink," he decided, and tiptoed at once into the kitchen. The door between the two rooms was seldom closed and there was no-one sleeping on the kitchen floor. Two small daughters and a niece shared the second cavity bed, but they would not wake and it would not matter if they did. Stark satisfied his need and let the tap run for a moment or two. Then he crept back to his bed as cautiously as he had left it.

"If it hadny been for the rent money being short," he reflected, "I wid have spoken to the Factor the morn. I telt the O'Learys I wid. It's six days now since their closet was stopped up and it's a bliddy disgrace, eviction or no eviction."

He hoped that when the Factor called the overflow might be "rinnin' doon the stair" as it so often was. "He'll no' mind the stink," Stark chuckled "but he's awfu' parteeclar aboot his boots. Ay, and rinnin' drains is bad for the property."

The probability was, though, that the O'Learys would clean the stair before the Factor arrived. They were always behind with their rent and so they dared not complain of small matters like defective drains. With the rent paid up to date, they would have made a fuss fast enough. Now their only fear was that some tenant on a lower floor, like Stark, for instance, would raise hell on his own account. Then, of course, the drains would be repaired, but the O'Learys would almost certainly be evicted, for they were always a month in arrears. They had never been able to catch up since Dan O'Leary had been put on short time six months before.

"Ach, tae hell wi' the whole lot o' them!" muttered John Stark. "Whit wad I no' give for a glass of whisky!"

Blending with the other smells of the house was the reek of paraffin. It was particularly strong in the cavity bed when the door was shut, for the woodwork was infested with bugs and Stark's wife conscientiously tried to keep them under by smearing every crack with oil.

And yet, even in her sleep, he could feel her scratching. The movements of her arm exasperated him almost beyond endurance. He would have shaken her and told her to lie still if it had not been for the baby, not yet six months old.

Being out of work and on the dole as he was, another child was not a financial burden. Two shillings was allowed for the baby and it scarcely cost as much as that. But as he lay there in the darkness he wondered grimly how it was that all the women in the slums seemed to want kids, even Annie, over forty and with seven living.

He supposed it was his fault as much as hers. They slept together and had long since ceased to love. Still . . . sharing the same three-foot bed, what could one expect?

"But there'll be nae more breadsnappers if I can help it," he resolved grimly. "Kids are all very well for a woman, but they're a bliddy nuisance to a man."

John Stark began to feel drowsy. He could hear his dead brother's daughter, Maggie, snoring in the "shake-doon" beyond the fireplace. The girl always slept with her mouth wide open and her nose was small, with pinched nostrils. She ought to have been sent to the hospital when she was young. Still, she was bringing in three-and-sixpence a week now from the carpet factory.

He thought of his neighbours, the Hurleys, who had recently found a good lodger. The Hurleys were almost as crowded as the Starks, but they were lucky, because their lodger was a night-worker and so there was always a bed free for him in the day. Besides, they had only one baby in the "hoose".

"There'll be no night-working lodger for us," he reflected gloomily; "no' wi' all oor bairns yammering and scrabbling aroon' a' day long."

And then sleep was very near. He began to think of horses that would run in the three-o'clock race next day. There was one of them, an outsider, that "owed him money". What was the name of it? Ah, "Shining Knight".

John Stark chuckled into the darkness.

"Shining Knight," he repeated softly, "an' a good name too on a bliddy, shining, stinking night like this!"

Stark breakfasted in a sullen silence which neither his wife nor the younger children dared to break. Maggie, the orphan niece, was already away to "the toil" in the carpet factory, and young Johnnie, the eldest of his own children, had also started work that week as a coalman's boy. The tea in the big enamelled pot was stewed from long standing, and the children gazed enviously at the kipper on their father's plate. Stark ate a mouthful and then pushed the plate away from him with a grunt.

Mrs Stark stared at him anxiously. She seemed about to speak, but thought better of it. Instead she took the kipper and spread the meat on slices of bread to make sandwiches for the children. Stark looked on indifferently. He was not really hungry, but he would have liked to eat the kipper himself. Some mornings he would have done so.

He did not wait for the children to finish their sandwiches but picked up his cap. He knew his wife wanted to ask him about the rent money, and that, fearing the truth, she did not dare. He left her without a word.

Soon Mrs Stark was alone in the "hoose". Making a playground of every street, swarming in and out of the close-mouths, clattering up and down the stairs, moving in gangs from court to court, the children of the Gorbals made the most of a sunny day. Only the women and the sleeping night-workers and, here and there, a sick man, remained in the tenements.

There was "Auld" James Hurley, for instance, in the house across the landing. He lay wide awake, his fingers restless on the blanket edge, his eyes fixed upon a crack in the wall which oozed vermin.

But "Auld James", who was only forty-six, was in a poor way. He had been "acting queer" ever since his "bad leg" got so bad that the proprietor of the corner fish shop had been obliged to sack him. Stark, who had married on eighteen shillings a week as a labourer in a Gorbals distillery, was slightly contemptuous of James, who had never known how to spend his money like a man even when he was in work and earning thirty shillings.

Joining friends at the street corner, Stark settled down to a study of the *Noon Record*'s racing form and tips. When the Queen's Head opened its doors they all trooped into the bar and went on arguing about horses over their first beer. Stark had decided to back Shining Knight, but one horse was not enough for him. Betting in threepences as he did, "long shots" were necessary – "doubles" and "trebles" which hardly ever turned up. That day he finally picked two other outsiders, grouped them with Shining Knight in a treble, and handed his "line" to one of the runners employed by Arthur Ross, the street bookie of that district. And all three horses won.

That was an unlucky win for Stark and several other people. It did nobody any good except Ross, a fat, stocky little man with bright eyes, who paid out his limit and got a great deal more than thirty-eight shillings' worth of publicity.

Arthur Ross was "well put on". He wore a neat blue suit and a bowler hat and there was a silk scarf round his neck. The Gorbals respected him as a man with enough brains to make money without working for it. A shilling was a large bet in Ross's book, for many of his clients were "on the dole", and to all of them in Rose Street and Waddell Street and Spring Lane and South Wellington Street anything more than sixpence was a plunge. But hundreds of men and women and not a few of the older children backed their fancies with Ross or his runners. The odds were always a little pinched because a bookmaker naturally ignores small fractions on penny bets, and many an individual backer, even when he did pull off a long shot, never got his money at all.

Ross would swear that the line was wrongly made out or handed in too late – any lie would serve. But he never welshed all his clients at once, and, when the book was good and a little advertisement worth paying for, then he would even settle a limit bet. The Gorbals, not trusting him an inch, never sure of their winnings until they had actually collected them, admired him all the more for his astuteness and success. They went on betting with him for this reason – and because all the other bookies were just the same.

That Saturday afternoon when they learned at the Queen's Head that John Stark's third horse had won, his friends were betting – but not in Stark's hearing – that he would never touch the money.

"Ross'll no' pay him," said Rob Matthews bluntly. "It widny be worth his while, for Stark canny lose all that dough back to him in months – no' at thruppence a day!"

Rob was mistaken. At seven o'clock in the "single end", or one-roomed apartment, that was Arthur Ross's paying-out office, John Stark drew his thirty-eight shillings limit in full.

"Ross," he said with solemn gratitude, "I always said you were no' a bad bookie. When you've finished your business I'll be at the Queen's Head. Will I be seeing you there?"

"Ay, likely," said the bookmaker, grinning. "If you can still see."

By nine o'clock, when the pubs closed, John Stark had started upon a drunk of the first magnitude. His legs were still steady under him, but he took half a bottle of whisky away in his hip pocket and two bottles of beer in his jacket. It did not even occur to him to return home. He went instead to a "kipshop" where, for three shillings, he could share a bed with a lass of eighteen. And he went on drinking.

Young Johnnie Stark, with a bullet head very like his father's, was also "awa' oot o' the hoose" all that Saturday, except when he came back from work to the midday meal. He was a big lad, exceptionally strong for his fifteen years. His mouth was hard and sullen, his eyes dark and his complexion sallow. A thick crop of black hair was brushed back from his broad, rather low forehead. He looked like a young fighter and, indeed, he could lick any lad in the school he had so recently left.

Johnnie had just drawn his first week's pay – three shillings and sixpence – from the coalman. He gave his mother two shillings, and then, ignoring the rabble of his younger brothers and sisters, he set out to flaunt his new independence round the town.

He changed a shilling to buy a twopenny packet of cigarettes and walked out of the shop letting his remaining ten coppers and sixpenny piece run through his fingers in his trousers pocket. The mood was on him to explore new territory, and he did no more than fling a surly nod at those acquaintances he passed, until one lad of his own age, a fair young fellow slighter and taller than Johnnie himself, stopped him with a direct greeting.

"Whaur are ye going, Johnnie?" he asked. "I was wanting to see you, for I'm going to the toil myself on Monday."

Johnnie looked at Bobbie Hurley with a kind of contemptuous interest.

"I widny think there wis much you could dae, Bobbie," he said. "What have ye got, and what'll they be peyin' ye?"

"Ach, it's no' a job like yours, Johnnie. I'm just to

14

be soap-boy in Graham's barber's shop. But I'm to get three shillings a week certain and mebbe another shilling in tips."

"Away and take a runnin' jump at yerself! There'll be nae tips for a soap-boy – no bliddy likely."

Bobbie Hurley flushed, but his manner was apologetic.

"That's what they telt me, all the same," he protested. "Auld Graham's red-heided assistant said I'd get a tip now and again for kerrying a line to the bookie or fetchin' a paper for the men who are waiting their turn. But I'm no' counting on it, Johnnie. I know it's no' the same thing as being a coal-boy."

"Too true, it's no'!" said Johnnie, mollified. "It's hard work shifting bags on the kert (coal-waggon). But that's no' aw Ah dae: I'm awa' up the stair-heid collecting the tick and bawling oot tae the auld weemin who'll no' pay. An Geordie telt me yesterday I'm doing fine for him and he'll mebbe gi'e me a rise in a month or two. Here – have a fag."

He extended the paper packet with impressive nonchalance and his friend accepted a cigarette gratefully. They went over the Albert Bridge into the Saltmarket, their hands in their pockets, swaggering, each secretly comparing himself with the other.

Stark thought that although work was scarce, he would stand a better chance of earning a living than Hurley, whom he regarded as unfit for hard manual labour. Hurley, on the other hand, was confident that his personal appearance would stand him in good stead, whilst Stark's strength of body and limb would avail him little in Glasgow. Friends of a kind, yet at heart they despised each other.

They boasted amiably as they walked; not of their families, for that would have been absurd even to them, but of their ambitions and of their confidence that one day they would get "a good, clean home" with a pretty young wife to look after it. That is the common ambition of young men in the slums. Few of them can imagine anything much beyond it.

They were back in the Gorbals now and talking of success and the way to achieve it.

"After all," said Bobbie, "there's no harm in trying to get educated, eh?"

Stark's laugh was so derisive that Hurley flushed.

"I know it's daft thinking things like that," he went on hurriedly, "but do you no' sometimes wish you could get awa' oot o' the slums awthegither?"

"Some hope! The Gorbals was good enough for better men than you an' me an' aw! Wishing's nae use and Ah'm no' caring onyway."

Just at that moment a girl, carrying a violin-case, came running into Cumberland Street from Abbotsford Place closely pursued by four jeering youths. She wore a hat and was neatly dressed, but her skirt was rather longer than the prevailing fashion and she ran awkwardly, being a little bandy-legged.

"Hey! See yon lassie carryin' the fiddle?" shouted Johnnie excitedly. "That's Lizzie Ramsay. Come on, Bobbie, let's run. Be a sticker and don't let those bastards get away w' it."

Johnnie was pounding along the street before his friend knew what was happening. Bobbie ran after him, however, lagging a little when he saw that the four youths were "tough". He thought they came from the Plantation district.

The fact that Lizzie Ramsay was from Gorbals, while the four young men were not, was enough for Johnnie. His actions always ran ahead of his thoughts, and when he saw one of the four stopping Lizzie and beginning to twist the violin-case out of her hands, he was enraged and ready to "stick" for all he was worth.

"Nit the jorrie (Leave the girl alone)!" he yelled. "Nark it! nark it!"

16

Astonished by this intervention, the biggest of the four youths let go the violin-case and greeted Johnnie with a blasphemous obscenity.

". . . To hell wi' you and your feedlin', stair-heid bit stuff," he finished through his uneven teeth.

Johnnie grinned and charged. He dodged the tripping foot of one of the big lad's companions, ducked his bullet head, and hit his enemy hard in the stomach. His knee jerked up to meet the toppling head. He grunted under the flail blows of an assailant in the rear, drove his heavy boot downward against a shin bone and heard a shout of pain.

The fight was over almost before it had begun. Bobbie Hurley came up as Johnnie broke clear, but the Plantation boys had had enough. Two of them picked up their leader, dazed by the knee blow to the chin, and the fourth was already limping away down the street.

"Ye're no' a great runner, Bobbie!" said Johnnie contemptuously.

Lizzie Ramsay, the cause of this battle, gazed at her rescuer in almost speechless admiration. She was not a real Gorbals "slummy". Her father was a commissionaire at a picture palace, and the Ramsays were well-doing for slum people. Geographically, they belonged to Gorbals, but they lived in one of the better streets, with only five of them in a palatial three-roomed dwelling.

"Whaur are ye goin' wi' your fiddle?" Johnnie asked her roughly, flushing in spite of himself.

"Ah'm gaun for ma weekly lesson in the music-room yonder," she returned, and there was pride in her voice as well as gratitude.

Johnnie made a rude sound.

"Away ye go to your scrapin'!" he sneered. "They'll be thinkin' someone's kilt the cat, and nae wunner."

"You'll be Johnnie Stark?" said the girl more humbly.

"Ay, that's me."

"It wis a sight tae watch they Plantation boys running

17

away. They'd have broken my violin mebbe if you hadny come up when ye did."

She would have given a great deal to say "thank you", but she dared not risk his ridicule. She was seventeen, two years older than Johnnie, but she thought him a grand fellow.

Bobbie was staring at both of them and Johnnie Stark caught his friend's eye.

"Come on away," he said savagely. "And you'd best be gaun to your lesson, Lizzie Ramsay. If they'd been Gorbal lads I widny have cared if they *had* broke your violin."

He turned and went swaggering up the street, Bobbie at his elbow. The girl stood where they had left her, a fair-haired lass shaping into womanhood. She wore her unfashionable long skirt to simply hide her legs, which would have been shapely enough if they had only been straight.

Johnnie, already anxious to clear himself of any suspicion of gallantry to a girl like Lizzie, turned and looked back at her.

"Away to your fiddlin', Bandy!" he shouted.

She coloured hotly and hurried on to the music-room.

"She's no' sae bandy as aw that," said Bobbie Hurley with mild reproach as his gaze followed her.

"Ach, tae hell wi' her! I've nae time for lassies like her," was Johnnie's contemptuous retort.

Presently they were nearing their own tenement again. In Rose Street, outside the corner public house, a little group had collected, and Bobbie Hurley's step quickened as he heard the sound of a mouth organ.

"That'll be a clabber jigging, Johnnie," he exclaimed. "Come along an' have a deck (look)."

Dancing was then, in 1921, and still is, the most popular sport in Glasgow's slumland. And some fine dancers have been bred in the tenements, though nearly all of them began on the pavement with the clabber jiggings. Outside

18

the Rose Street pub there were only two couples dancing, a young man and his girl and two other girls waltzing together. A ragged, bleary-eyed old fellow, lamentably undrunk, was playing his mouth organ like an artist: many a vaudeville musician might have envied him his talent.

"Wull we split that couple?" said Bobbie to his friend.

Johnnie laughed and did not answer. When the girls whirled within reach, he stepped forward neatly and took the bigger of the two round the waist. Bobbie caught the other and waltzed away with her so that the step was never broken.

At the conclusion of that dance someone gave the mouth-organ player a penny. He changed from "The Merry Widow" to a one-step. Johnnie danced that and then gave his partner the go-by, but Bobbie and the smaller girl went on dancing until the "orchestra" stopped playing. A considerable crowd had gathered, whistling the tunes and clapping their hands to the beat of the music. Bobbie and his partner were good. The Gorbals pavement critics approved of them.

"We'll be seeing you at the jiggings yet, Bobbie Hurley," came a voice from the crowd.

"Ay, and Lily wi' him, likely," shrilled a woman.

The young couple broke away from one another somewhat sheepishly and Bobbie rejoined his friend.

"It's a fact," said Johnnie dispassionately. "I've seen worse dancers than you and Lily McKay at the jiggings. Ah'm gaun up to the hoose for ma tea."

When he reached home his mother, a faded, silent woman, was spreading slices of bread with margarine for the younger children.

"You're back then, Johnnie," she said mildly.

"Ay," he said, "but Ah'm gaun oot again. Where's the auld man?"

Four or five voices joined in an excited chorus to tell Johnnie that Father had landed a limit bet. "And

19

ye know what that means," said Peter Stark bitterly.

"Haud your tongue, Peter," said his mother urgently. "He'll likely be coming up the stairs and hear ye."

Johnnie laughed harshly. "No bliddy fears, Mother!" he said. "The auld man'll no' trouble us the night. If it's right he's drawn a limit bet, he'll no' darken the hoose till Monday."

When Johnnie came back from the pictures that night, the "hoose" was in darkness.

He sniffed the tainted air with faint, familiar disgust. He took off his boots and socks, his jacket and trousers, and then wearing only his shirt, crept beneath the blanket beside his brother Peter in the "shake-doon" by the window.

"Push over, you fat little bastard!" he snarled. "I've not got any room."

Peter stirred in his sleep. Johnnie lay wakeful with his hands under his head. He thought of the American gangster hero who had shot his way through half a dozen big fights in the big picture, only to be riddled by a "Tommy gun" in his turn.

"Yon's a grand life!" meditated Johnnie Stark.

He thought, a little uneasily, of his mother, whose heavy breathing he could clearly distinguish on the other side of the room. He wondered when his father would come home and half hoped, half feared, that he would be in the house when that happened. "Let the auld man wait two years," he thought savagely, "and I'll no' be feart of him. Ay, and I'll bash him if he bashes Mither, the poor auld lady."

He thought, drowsily, of Lizzie Ramsay and her violin. He grinned in the darkness and silently his lips formed the one word: "Bandy".

He turned over on his side and his eyes closed. "I'm in work," he thought contentedly, "and tomorrow it's me for the long lie."

And then he too slept, a slum lad bred and born,

with his lips firmly closed over strong teeth never brushed, his youthfully powerful limbs relaxed, his breath drawn and expelled regularly and gently through wide nostrils, a miracle of health defying its environment.

CHAPTER II

A WORKER TAKES A LONG LIE

Night brings no kindly silence to the tenement dwellers of the Empire's second city. The wide streets are deserted; the courtyards are empty; here and there the close-mouths may shelter shadowy figures, but each box dwelling is sealed by its own front door. The tenements themselves are never silent. There are sick children who wail and healthy ones who get restless; half-drunken men who snore and mutter; half-sober ones who quarrel with their wives. In the "hoose" next door, or in some other "hoose" on the landing above or below, there may be a party in progress which will last for forty-eight hours. And ever and anon front doors will open to allow some hurrying figure to reach the single landing closet which serves three households.

And yet sleep falls upon the slum dwellers. It is a depressing fact that men and women can get used to almost anything – to stench and vermin and over-crowding that is close to physical discomfort. They get used very easily to noise. They are conditioned by their environment to shut it out. But sometimes, when they are ill, it assails them like an enemy.

"Auld" James Hurley was ill. His bad leg worried him like a subdued toothache. Drink and malnutrition had brought chronic stomach trouble in their train. He had lost his job and his wife constantly reproached him. She lay beside him in the darkness, asleep and breathing heavily.

Hurley's eldest son, Bobbie, was dreaming of the day when he would be a star dancer. Hurley's youngest child was cutting its teeth and whimpering fitfully. An elder sister, using the vilest language in the gentlest tone, soothed it into silences as fitful.

"Auld" James's fingers were never still upon the edge of the blanket. His eyes were wide open, staring into the dark. From the "hoose" next door there came the sound of a gramophone playing and the shuffling of dancing feet. A woman's high-pitched slum laugh cut into that night of lesser noises like a sword. The sick man jerked violently into a sitting position and his lips began to tremble.

His children were "Catholic" like his wife, but he himself was a Protestant. He had not been to church since his wedding, but his mother, born on a Lowland farm, had clung, even in the Gorbals, to the grim Calvinism of her childhood and had quoted texts to her bairns, which were the more terrifying when she was the more in drink.

He began to repeat texts now in a whisper that did not wake his family.

"Babylon is fallen, is fallen, that great city, because she made all nations drink of the wine of the wrath of her fornication . . ."

The gramophone next door was playing an old record: "Swanee, Swanee! How I love you! How I love you!" And the woman laughed again.

"Auld" James got out of his bed and his wife woke up. She could see him, a lean silhouette against the window frame with his arms raised above his head and his fists clenched.

"Whit's the matter wi' ye, ye auld deevil?" she called querulously, and then, on a new note of sudden alarm: "Hey, James, wheesht! Ah'm comin' tae ye."

Mrs Hurley stumbled across the floor to her husband's side and laid a restraining arm upon his shoulder. He turned his distorted face in her direction and struck her back-handedly across the lips. She clutched and tore his

23

shirt as she fell and the household of eight was startled into wakefulness.

"Tormented with fire and brimstone!" shouted "Auld" James Hurley. He ran to the door, threw it open and stood laughing like a madman on the landing. Then he tore down the stairs shouting texts once more. The police picked him up near the river an hour later, a crazy figure in a torn shirt. They took him to the infirmary and from there he was transferred to the asylum in which he died some years later. The doctors regarded the case as one of acute nervous exhaustion. The Gorbals said more simply and without surprise that the slums had driven "Auld" James mad. Men did go off their heads like that, sometimes, when they were sick and the everlasting noise and worry got on their nerves.

It made very little difference to the Hurley family. They were "on the Parish" in any case, and their neighbours agreed that they would be "likely better off wi'oot the auld man than wi' him". It made no difference at all to the general life of the tenements and the incident would scarcely have been remembered if it had not occurred almost at the same time as the much more exciting happening in the house of the Starks, who lived in the same tenement on the opposite side of the same landing.

There was actually an interval of several hours between the one tragedy and the other.

Young Johnnie Stark, eager to be up and out on a fine Sunday morning, was having the "long lie" to which his position as a wage-earner entitled him. He drove his brother Peter out of their "shake-doon" at an early hour. Someone brought him a cup of tea where he lay, his hands beneath his head, staring at the ceiling with lordly indolence. The younger children were soon out of the house playing on the stairs or in the court. His mother, holding a string bag in one hand, stood over him for a moment before she left the apartment in her turn.

"Ay, Johnnie," she said, with a wistful mixture of pride and apprehension, "so you'll be taking your long lie the day?"

He grunted and his lips softened into the suggestion of a smile.

The old woman hesitated. "Ah'm worrit, Johnnie," she went on apologetically. "Your father will be hame likely ony time noo."

"Ay, mebbee. An' you're gaun oot wi' the old bag to get in twa-three bottles o' beer, Mither, against his coming? Ah widna say it wisny thoughtful o' ye. He'll be needing it."

"Do you no' think it wad be better if you an' Maggie wis to be awa oot the day?"

Johnnie glanced across to the other shake-down by the window where his cousin still lay, a shape beneath the blankets and a tousled mop of curls on the pillow. There were only the three of them left in the room by that time.

"Maggie's *always* better oot o' the hoose," he sniffed disdainfully, "an she wad be away oot noo if there was ever a lad wad look at her twice. But never worry for me, Mither. Ah'm no scaired o' the auld man. Mebbe I'll hae some beer with him if he comes in; though, mind ye, Ah'm no' expectin' him till the morn."

Mrs Stark still hesitated. Her lips moved as though there had been something she wanted to say. But she thought better of it and the front door closed behind her.

It had scarcely done so before Maggie Stark flung her blankets aside and scrambled to her feet, an unkempt figure in blue woollen knickers and vest. Her feet and legs were dirty. On her arms were many red, slightly swollen marks, caused by vermin.

"I heard what you said, Johnnie," she flashed, "an' what wad ye say if I telt ye I *had* a fellah of my own?"

"I wad say ye were a liar, Maggie, or else maybe it's daft Geordie that was biting your neck on the stair-heid the other night."

She flamed into anger and cursed him for an over-grown bairn that thought himself a man. He laughed at her, sat up ostentatiously to light a cigarette and then turned away, lying on his elbows with his face to the wall.

Maggie Stark went bitterly into the kitchen, leaving the door open. She began to rinse her face at the sink, but it was a Sunday morning and the thought crossed her mind that she might make a more extensive toilet. She looked at the open door and at the back of Johnnie's bullet head. Then she shrugged her shoulders angrily, flushed a little, and pulled her vest down to her waist.

She had rinsed away the soap from face and neck and shoulders, but her eyes were still tight closed as she groped for the roller towel. Johnnie's voice came to her close at her elbow.

"Ye're no' a bad built lassie, Maggie," it jeered amiably. "Ay, an' you're a big girl and aw!"

She opened her eyes wide to face him and threw back her head. If his gaze had mocked her then, she would have fought him and taken the inevitable hiding. But there was a sparkle in his eyes that was not unfriendly, and suddenly Maggie found herself trembling and afraid. She held the towel awkwardly to her chest.

"Ye're kiddin' me, Johnnie," she whispered.

"Ah'm no' kiddin'. You're right bonny the noo, Maggie."

The boy was not quite sixteen and the girl only two years older, but they stared at each other with eyes that had been wide open to all the facts of sex since early childhood. The jargon of the psychoanalysts may be unknown in the Gorbals, but Maggie Stark, undesired in her eighteenth year, was the victim of an inferiority complex peculiar to the daughters of the slums. And now, as the colour flooded her sallow cheeks, she saw release and triumph and self-assertion in her cousin's eyes.

And with a little cry, she flung her arms round his neck.

Johnnie's mother found them together on the "shake-doon" a little later. She stood tongue-tied in the doorway, her free hand clapped to her lips in a gesture of consternation. Her grey hair was untidy and the string bag was weighted with four bottles of beer she had bought in one of the many shebeens.

Maggie snatched the blankets about her, but Johnnie sat up and grinned defiantly at his mother.

"Wheesh!" he said awkwardly, "there's nae harm done. Maggie an' me can look efter oorsel's."

Then Mrs Stark screamed. She put the bottles of beer on the floor and ran across to the girl. Her hands closed upon Maggie's mop of hair and tugged savagely until the sullen face was lifted to meet her own.

"You dirty little bitch," she stormed. "You canny get a man ootside, an' so you wad tak' ma Johnnie."

With her free hand she hit the girl savagely across the mouth and Maggie, shrieking in her turn, tried to wrench her head free from the detaining hand.

Johnnie laughed. He watched his mother with a kind of admiration and it was not until she had slapped Maggie's face again and again that he stopped laughing and took Mrs Stark firmly by the shoulders.

"Stop it, ye auld fule," he said, still without heat. "Stop it, or aw the neebors will be coming to the stair-heid. Have I no' telt ye that there's nae harm done?"

Maggie was weeping noisily and, freed from the older woman's grasp, she began to storm at her in a voice which rose to a scream.

"Haud your tongue," said Johnnie angrily, enforcing the command with an ungentle, flat-handed blow. The whole affair was becoming a nuisance to him. He was terribly afraid of the neighbours, but of their laughter, not of their indignation. He did not know how he would "haud up his heid" if whispers should follow him and he should guess that people were saying: "Hey, hey! That'll be young Johnnie Stark. His mither caught him in bed

27

wi' his cousin that canny get a man, and skelpit the pair of them."

But there were never any whispers of quite that kind, for at that moment John Stark senior came home and gave the Gorbals something else to talk about.

Johnnie's father was then in the most dangerous phase of his big "drunk". He had sobered up after sleep and drunk more whisky to pull himself together. His woman companion of the night before had left him in a shebeen – an illicit drinking-den – and they were to have met again a little later on. But he discovered after she had gone that she had picked his pocket. With murder in his heart, he left the shebeen to find her, and then his thirst took hold of him again. He came home for money with which to buy more liquor.

His eyes were red-rimmed and his chin dark with stubble as he stood on the threshold trying to take in the scene which confronted him. Both women, his wife and his niece, were stricken into panic silence and immobility. Young Johnnie's heart was beating hard with a terror he could not quite control and he clenched his fists in desperation. For several moments nobody said a word.

Mrs Stark broke the silence. She picked up the string bag containing the beer bottles and held it out towards her husband.

"John," she quavered, "Ah wis thinking you wad be glad o' a drink o' beer."

"That's whit you wis thinking?" he said. "Ay, an' it's no' a bad thought. Gie me one o' they bottles."

He took a bottle from the bag, and stood swaying a little.

"Whit bliddy game's been gaun on here?" he asked in almost conversational tones. "Whit for is Maggie greeting and standing aboot, wi' next to naething on, like a wee lassie? Whit for did ye hit her, Johnnie?"

Nobody spoke. Johnnie backed away a little closer to

the wall, his fists clenched and his eyes desperate and wary.

The older man took one step forward and caught his wife by the shoulder.

"Whit's gaun on here?" he asked again, his voice rising to a shout. "If there's any bashing tae be done, you can leave that to me. Ye'll no' speak, eh?"

He loosed his hold and struck his wife in the mouth with his clenched fist so that she reeled away from him and fell, with the blood streaming from her lips.

"Jesus!" said young Johnnie, his face working with hate and fear.

His father paid no attention to him. He advanced with slow steps and terrible deliberation upon his niece. Before he reached her she began to scream at the top of her voice.

"Ye'll no' talk?" he said. "Ay, but you can bawl, and before you're hurtit! Do you think Ah'm a mug, Maggie Stark? Do you think when Ah find ma brither's daughter half naked in the hoose wi' ma son still in his shirt Ah'm gaun tae believe ye've been havin' a prayer meetin' thegither? No bliddy fears! Ah'll look after you first for the hoor you are, and then I'll attend to the boy."

He had unbuckled his leather belt as he spoke and now he laughed, a horrible, anticipatory laugh.

"Johnnie, JOHNNIE," the girl screamed. "Don't let him bash me!"

But Johnnie, who could lick any fellow of his own age, was not quite sixteen. And his father was a big man and in drink. The boy made no move, but his face was hideous.

Stark senior flung his niece to the floor and began to flog her with the belt. Her shrieks were scarcely human under that urgency of terror and agony. Young Johnnie was uttering blasphemies in quick succession without knowing what he said. Suddenly he picked up a chair and aimed a crashing blow at his father's head. The older man raised his left arm just in time and then, with a roar like a wild beast, he sprang at his son. A terrible blow took the boy between the eyes and stretched him senseless. John Stark, no longer sane in his drunken frenzy, thrashed and thrashed at the fallen body.

And then the mother intervened. She flung herself upon her husband's uplifted arm, and clung to it, an elderly woman, not strong, but roused to the final defiance.

The beer bottle which John Stark had dropped when he advanced upon his niece was now lying on the floor at his feet. He stooped with his free hand to take it by the neck. Then he struck his wife on the head with the full bottle. The blow made little noise, but it stretched Mrs Stark like a dead woman beside her unconscious son.

Maggie lay sobbing and whimpering where Stark had left her. He stood stupidly with the bottle in his hand. He stooped and shook his wife by the shoulder. Her body was limp under his hand. Stark blinked, opened the bottle and drank. Then some foggy memory returned to him of the girl who had cheated him of his limit bet.

He looked round the room and his glance came to rest upon the clock over the mantelpiece. It was the only article of any value in the house. He walked over and placed the clock under his arm. Then he went back to the front door and as he opened it there was the scurry of feet on the landing and on the stairs and the slamming of other doors. The women of the tenement had heard the screaming and the blows. One or two of them had run to fetch their men. But Stark left his "hoose" and gained the street unmolested. He was arrested in a shebeen some hours later, drinking whisky bought with the money for which he had pawned the clock.

It is unlikely that anybody would have called the police at all if it had not been that Mrs Stark was taken to the infirmary with a fractured skull. For a long while they thought that she would die, but she recovered and refused to give evidence against her husband.

For once the neighbours were ready to supply that. They agreed that he had come home drunk and "bashed" the family. There was no word said of motive. Young Johnnie swore sullenly that he did not know what it was all about. The old man was just fighting mad and he, Johnnie, got "knocked doon" and could remember nothing else. Maggie vindictively confirmed the bashings but was also silent as to motive. Her evidence was conclusive. Stark, stubbornly mute in the dock, was sentenced to three years' imprisonment. His family never forgave Maggie and afterwards she left the Gorbals altogether and went to live with a friend in Bridgeton.

Stark did not live to serve his sentence. He died in jail from some obscure internal complaint about eighteen months later. Johnnie by that time had definitely become the head of the family, and in his eighteenth year he was earning eighteen shillings a week. People said that the whole affair had made a man of him.

Young Bobbie Hurley, his friend, was still lather-boy in the barber's shop at that time, but he was already a well-known performer in the cheaper dancing halls.

The two young men did not often meet. Their work and their pleasure lay apart. Johnnie spent most of his spare time in the open-air gymnasium on the Green or in the billiards halls and pubs. He was on the fringe of the gangs. Bobbie was dancing mad.

One day Johnnie walked into Graham's barber's shop for a shave and grinned contemptuously while his friend lathered his chin.

"Ah'll be oot of this shop pretty soon noo," said Bobbie in a whisper. "Lily and me are doing fine at the jiggings. We're the leaders off noo."

"Ay. I always telt ye ye were no' a bad dancer. You'll reach the Palais yet, maybe; that's if you don't go the way of your auld man."

"He's no' exactly daft," returned Bobbie defensively. "The doctors say it was a nairvous breakdoon."

Johnnie laughed.

"You can call it that, Bobbie," said he amiably. "An' Ah'm no quarrelling wi' ye. Efter aw, madhoose or jail, there's no sae much to choose between them. But *my* faither was a fighting man. Your auld man had a 'nairvous breakdoon'. These kind of things, mind ye, they run in the family."

CHAPTER III

A QUESTION OF HATS

Just across the Clyde from the Gorbals lies Glasgow Green, the city's most frequented park. There, in a triangular patch on the bend of the river between the King's Street and St Andrew's bridges, is an open-air gymnasium much frequented by the youth of the slums and, occasionally, the battle ground of conflicting gangs.

Johnnie Stark was exercising on the parallel bars. He sank his body until the shoulder-blades met and only the elbows and heels were above the bars. Slowly and smoothly he raised himself to rigid, full arms' length. He rose and sank again and again, counting silently until he had reached his regulation fifty movements. Then his feet swung free of the bars and he vaulted cleanly to the ground. There were several other young men there of about his own age. They watched him respectfully as he resumed his neat blue jacket. He flung a nod at them and walked away with a little swagger.

Vanity is as much a dominant motive in the slums as outside them. Johnnie had little to be proud of except his strong body and reckless spirit. He spent a lot of his leisure at the Green Gym, and much of his money on his clothes. He was not ill-looking and in the Gorbals men and women too are very much judged by their appearance. A good suit of clothes wins a certain respect for the wearer. Johnnie wore "a whole suit" – that is to say, the coat and trousers were of the same navy blue cloth and had been sold together *as* a suit. His shoes were well polished, a bright "tony-red". In the language of the Gorbals, he was "well put on" and proud of his "paraffin". There was actually a paraffin dressing on his sleek black hair, and, perhaps there may be some association of ideas between slumland's passion for smoothed and glistening crops and its general term for a smart appearance.

But Johnnie would never have worried his head about the derivation of words. At school he had not even secured his "merit certificate", that minimum standard of education which the Council had set. His failure to do so meant thirty evenings at night school when, by reason of his age, his normal "schuling" was at an end. Even a diligent lad can't contrive to learn a great deal in thirty evenings. Johnnie, utterly bored, endured the night school as so much detention and learned nothing at all. He could read the racing papers and the football reports and he could do simple sums and he was satisfied that this was an adequate equipment for all practical purposes.

On the way back from the gym, Johnnie ran into Mary Hay, who had been at school with his cousin Maggie.

They had met on previous occasions with scarcely a word exchanged. Johnnie would have thought it beneath his dignity to waste time on a girl whom he remembered as a little scrub. Now, suddenly and startlingly, he realized that Mary was grown up. She came from a home as poor as his own and she wore no hat, but her blue skirt was neatly cut and her white blouse was both unsoiled and well filled. She smiled at him to show attractive white teeth.

"Where are ye gaun, Mary?" he asked.

"An' whit's that tae you?" she retorted pertly. "If you must know Ah'm gaun for ma supper to the fish shop at the corner."

"Are you? Then we'll go thegither. Ah cud dae wi' some fish an' chips masel'."

He fell into step beside her, and Mary, pleased and

flattered, turned her head this way and that, hoping that other people might see her with her escort. Presently they were seated opposite one another, their elbows on the white-scrubbed table beneath the electric light. Between them was a single plate heaped with fried fish and steaming chips, for the shared supper is not uncommon in the Gorbals.

"I mind of you," Johnny said thoughtfully, "when you were at the school." It was on the tip of his tongue to say "with Maggie", but he held the words back. He looked at Mary with a slanting mistrust, wondering whether she would have the hardihood to mention his cousin's name or recall the old scandal which had been suffocated in its infancy by other and more sensational events.

Her blue eyes met his own frankly enough. If she thought at all of Maggie, who had left the Gorbals, she was careful not to say so.

"Ay," she agreed simply. "I was at Camden Street School till I was thirteen, an' no' the school Bobbie Hurley was at! Bobbie—'

Johnnie shrugged his shoulders. "Ach, him!" he said vaguely. "He's barberin' the noo. But he's no' a bad dancer."

"He's the best dancer of the Sooth Side, is he no'?"

"He's a great dancer, aw right, but Ah'm no' that bad masel', Mary."

The tone was almost pleading and Mary flushed at its intimacy.

"I'd say you were right in his class," she conceded. "There's no' much in it."

Johnnie laughed and surveyed the girl with a deliberate stare which passed like a challenge closely under his eyebrows and beneath the peak of his cap. He prodded with his fork at a thick, white, flaky piece of fish and pushed it in the girl's direction.

"Ah'm no' so good as Bobbie, and you know it," he

said slowly. "But Hurley's a Catholic all the same, Mary. You and me are Prodisants."

"Too bliddy true, we are!" she agreed fervently. "Catholics are aw right, but it's best to settle doon wi' one of your ain kind. Dae ye no' think so, Johnnie?"

He did not miss the significance of that question. He considered her with calculating eyes; her eager sallow face with its big bright eyes, the aggressive thrust of the young breasts under the white linen blouse, the small hands that supported the sharp chin.

"Wull we dance the night?" he said with assumed indifference. "Ah'll take ye to the National, and Ah'm paying."

She was delighted. She would have paid for him almost as gladly, but it was no small achievement to go to any dance as Johnnie Stark's "bit of stuff". For Johnnie was known in the Gorbals as not yet taking any interest in women. Some of the younger men even quoted his contemptuous comments on the folly of marriage and the unwisdom of getting tied down when lassies "ready to oblige" were ten a penny.

Johnnie was no more than a dancer with natural ability of whom there are thousands in the tenements. Mary Hay was an expert amateur who might have become a star had she so chosen. But they made a good couple on the National's crowded floor, and they left the hall about eleven o'clock in excellent conceit of themselves.

He took her arm as they neared home. The semi-embrace was significant among young people of their class. Mary's family was "on the buroo". She herself had never worked for a boss and had no mind to do so. She wanted nothing better than to find some young man to marry and to settle down with. Johnnie's vaguely rumoured episode with his cousin Maggie did not affect her in the least, or, if it did, it merely left her with the impression that Maggie must have been a fool not to hold him. She knew Johnnie was not yet earning much

36

with the coal cart, but she thought he would soon be drawing a man's full wage. She knew he was "well put on" and rather looked up to among the lads of his own age. She knew, above all, that if she could catch him she would be making something of a social success. And her own arm was warmly responsive to the pressure of his.

In spite of her formal protests he took her into a "shebeen", a "hoose" where whiskies and beer were obtainable at any hour. She could drink her whisky as composedly as he himself, but she protested that she was not used to it. He studied her meditatively, noting her pale lips innocent of all make-up and the orderly waves of her hair that had never been confined beneath a hat.

If Mary Hay had used rouge and lipstick; if she had polished her nails instead of merely trimming them; if indeed, she had sported a slightly superior "paraffin" she would have proclaimed herself, coming as she did from a poor class tenement, as a prostitute – amateur if not professional. But she did none of these things. She was, quite definitely, "one of the hairy" – a hatless slum girl conscious of her station in life.

But he thought her extraordinarily pretty. He stared at her white blouse with its two clearly defined points. He noticed, with approval, that her neck was clean and that her teeth were quite exceptionally white when she showed them in a smile. And suddenly that desire of woman, which was dormant within him but had been repressed, took hold of him again.

He paid for the drinks and led Mary out of the pub, holding her arm tighter than ever.

"Do you know, Mary," he said, "that you were about the best dancer at the National the night? And you a Prodisant, the same as me."

"Ach! Ye're just kiddin'!" she repeated defensively. "There's lots of good Catholic dancers too. Still . . . I widny feel that I was right married unless a minister did the marrying and aw that, wid you, Johnnie?"

The switch of ideas was too obvious to escape his notice. "Aw, I widna care who mairrit me as long as I wis mairrit," he assured her.

"Ah, no' me! I wid want a minister."

"Plenty get mairrit by the sheriff. You know that?"

"Ay, I know it aw right, but that doesny mean to say that I wid fancy it masel'."

They had arrived by this time at the close-mouth which gave access to Mary Hay's stairway. The streets were for the moment deserted and the two young people paused in a queer unspoken crisis of nervous antagonism.

"I wonder where Nan will be now?" said Mary. Nan was a friend of hers whom they had met at the National with her boy. Mary did not care in the least what had happened to her. She simply asked the question for something to say.

"In her bed, likely," said Johnnie curtly. "She's just the sort to hurry awa' back to the hoose even when a fellow goes home wi' her . . . I hope it's no' like that wi' you, Mary?"

She stared at him anxiously. "I'll no' rin away'," she said.

He gave her a cigarette and for some moments they smoked in silence. Then they walked together into the dark tunnel mouth of the close and towards the foot of the stairs.

Mary Hay was feeling nervous, for Johnnie's arm was urgent within her own. She threw back her head and emitted the loud and strident and excruciating slum laugh – a high cackle that ends in a kind of wail.

In spite of himself, Johnnie started. He thought, but only for a second, that she was mocking him. The cold dark close seemed to echo her laugh eerily. Johnnie caught her by the shoulders, twisted her out of the shadow into the moonlight, and pressed his own mouth ardently against the girl's pale lips.

"You stay up the stair, don't you, Mary?" he demanded hotly.

"Sure," she said weakly, "I stay up the stair."

"Come on up, then. I've got something to say to you."

"Aw right," she whispered, "but let me go, Johnnie: I'll no' rin awa'."

He released her shoulders reluctantly, but he followed hard behind her, his body almost touching her own until they paused on the third landing. It was cold and most of the panes of glass in the landing window were broken.

"Christ!" said Johnnie Stark. "It's no' very comfortable up here the night."

"It's no worse than ither places!" she retorted loudly and on a defiant note.

"Who said it was?" Johnnie spoke through lips which scarcely moved and his right arm closed about her, tugging her towards the open door of the landing closet. She struggled desperately, but in silence.

"No, no, Johnnie!" she implored as she lost ground. His intentions were beyond possibility of doubt. But she did not scream. She knew that if she did it would turn out the worse for her in the long run. She realized that she had brought this ordeal upon herself and that the Gorbals would have no sympathy for a lass who had egged on a smart young fellow like Johnnie Stark only to insult him. And, in her turn, she would have been cruelly insulted and even disappointed had he yielded to her protests. And so the struggle lasted for several minutes – a wordless fight in the moonshot darkness of the "stair-heid".

Long afterwards, when it was all over and Mary was clinging tearfully to her lover, pleading with him and threatening by turns, Johnnie consoled her with a gruff promise.

"Don't worry yersel'," said he roughly. "There'll be nothin' aboot it. And if there should – well, we'll get married wi' a minister an aw!"

He kissed her and began to walk down the stairway.

"Come here a minute, wull you?" she wailed.

Johnnie ran back to her with a little thrill of triumph at the heart. She flung her arms round his neck and embraced him passionately.

"Aw, Johnnie!" she choked. "Johnnie, ye'll no' leave me?"

Johnnie Stark walked home very thoughtfully that night. The thought of marriage worried him a good deal. Unlike most of the Gorbals lads he had, at that time, no wish for a wife and home of his own.

But his heart was proud with conquest. He squared his broad shoulders and thrust his strong chin forward at a defiant angle.

"Ah'm no' caring," said he in a whisper. "She's aboot the best bit of stuff I've seen home from any of the halls yet. An' if anything does happen I might do worse than marry Mary Hay."

Every class of society constantly makes the mistake of supposing that every other class is regulated by its own taboos. It is not so. In the Gorbals, for instance, seduction – that is to say, the chance intimacy of two young people – may be a matter of gossip but is certainly not, in itself, a matter of scandal. And in this instance the affair between Johnnie Stark and Mary Hay might not have been known at all if the girl herself had not taken the utmost pains to advertise it.

She wanted quite definitely to boast of her triumph. To have caught young Johnnie Stark was an achievement for a girl of her class. If she had simply told her friends that he was courting her she would not have been believed. She preferred to tell them the true and much more plausible story that he had taken her home and been intimate with her. She did this, not, perhaps, in so many words but with traitor flushes and unmistakable innuendo. She "mouthed" the news to every friend who was certain to pass it on.

Within two days Rose Street and, broadly speaking, all the Gorbals, had heard that Johnnie was going with Mary and that, if what was only to be expected did happen, he meant to marry her "with a minister an aw!"

Johnnie's own family heard the story as soon as the rest of the world, but he was so much the head of the house at that time that none of them dared to comment on it. His mother, indeed, said with wistful timidity that she had always liked "yon lass o' the Hays", but Johnnie only grunted and would not meet this opening. Mrs Stark looked at him, sighed, and picked up her string shopping-bag.

And Johnnie went to the billiards-room in Rutherglen Road, smirking at the new respect and interest which was clearly caused by his arrival. "Not many of them," he thought triumphantly, "cud get awa' wi' a bit of stuff like Mary Hay."

He wished, all the same, that she had not made quite such a song about it. He did not want to be tied down quite so definitely. He was determined that, if nothing did come of his adventure, there was going to be no marriage. Meanwhile, since things had come to this pass in spite of himself, he was prepared to make the most of his new reputation as a Don Juan. He told his friends, including Bobbie Hurley, then paying one of his rare visits to "the billiards" that he was going to take Mary to the Masonic Hall the following week and that she was going to dance with him alone.

They were impressed and envious, for Mary was "talent" of more than ordinary charm.

"She's fairly coming on at the burlin'," he boasted. "She's a pure treat at the one-steps an' aw. An' at the half-settin'. It's aw right dancin' wi' one bit of stuff aw night, is it no'? Especially when you're to get aw you want after the dancin'!"

They were all impressed and envious, even Bobbie Hurley, who was already a dancer of semi-professional quality. He hastened to explain, what everybody there knew already, that he and Lily McKay always danced together, and he hinted that he too was "getting his rights" until such time as they should be married.

But the men playing billiards soon got tired of dancing talk, and after a while Johnnie and Bobbie left the hall. They had scarcely reached the corner of Rutherglen Road before Bobbie caught his friend's arm, drawing his attention to two girls on the opposite pavement.

"There's yon two bits of stuff we met a week or two ago in the Baronial Rooms," he said excitedly.

"Cripes! So it is," Johnnie agreed, "an' they're looking hellova well too, aren't they?" He raised his voice so that the girls, who came from Graigie Hall Street in the Plantation, should hear him. They did, and giggled loudly.

The Plantation lassies were smartly dressed and they both wore hats. In Glasgow, as in Rome, the hat is a badge of feminine quality. These girls were clearly a little above "the likes of Mary Hay", but they were neither of them in the least above a flirtation with the two young men.

The conversation turned, naturally enough, to dancing and the discussion of the various halls. The girls listened to Bobbie's opinions with some respect, for his reputation was known, but they paid less heed to Johnnie Stark's less expert comments.

"There's a lot of good dancers go to the Grove, dain't they, Polly?" said one of the girls to her friend. "I think it's better than the Baronial."

"Ay; there's nane of the hairy at the Grove."

"The hairy are aw right," Johnnie found himself saying angrily, although he knew that the Plantation girls could not have heard about him and Mary Hay. "There's some of them as good as the well-dressed talent."

"Dae ye think so?" said Polly contemptuously. "Well, I don't. Do you, Betty?"

"Don't fancy yourselves, for God's sake!" he retorted hotly.

"We don't need tae fancy oorsel's just because we don't like the bliddy hairy, dae we, Betty?"

A few months later it would not have been safe for any woman to answer Johnnie Stark back in that way, but this was before he had won his fame. He merely scowled and thrust his hands deep into his pockets.

"You can think whit you like," he said defiantly, "but I'll be along with one o' the hairy masel' on Monday next at the Masonic."

'That's where we're gaun to!" exclaimed Polly.

"We'll see you baith there," echoed her friend sarcastically, "wullent we, Polly?"

It was then that Bobby intervened in the conversation.

"Ah'm telling you," he said to the two girls, "this bit of stuff that Johnnie's got can dance. At the one-steps and everything there's few to touch her. You'll have to give in to that."

"Ay," said Johnnie gratefully, "an' she's a sentimental wee lassie an' aw! She thinks she widny be right married unless she was married by a minister."

All he meant to convey was the impression that his girl, although she might be one of the hairy, was as particular and refined as the Plantation girls themselves, but they took him quite seriously without realizing the implication.

"Christ!" exclaimed Betty, "we're aw alike if it comes to *that*! It widny do to be married to just anybody."

"Well, it's the same with the hairy," grinned Johnnie, as though he had scored a point.

"Mebbe, but *we're* middle-class," said Polly defensively, "there's a lot of difference between them an' us."

"A hellova difference!" echoed her friend, breaking suddenly into a laugh that seemed the very echo of Mary Hay's.

Johnnie flushed almost as though he had been struck.

43

CHAPTER IV

THE ROAD TO KINGSHIP

Sooner or later Johnnie Stark would have gravitated to the gangs in any case. He was already on the fringe of them in his eighteenth year, for he was strong and ready to fight. Other young men eyed him warily before they spoke but things had been rather quiet in the Gorbals since the last big street battle and no one ruffian had yet been acclaimed as leader in succession to Jock Sinclair who had been permanently crippled in that affray.

Battles and sex are the only free diversions in slum life. Couple them with drink, which costs money, and you have the three principal outlets for that escape complex which is for ever working in the tenement dweller's subconscious mind. Johnnie Stark would not have realized that the "hoose" he lived in drove him to the streets or that poverty and sheer monotony drove him in their turn into the pubs and the dance halls or into affairs like the one he was having with Mary Hay. But then, the slums as a whole do not realize that they are living an abnormal life in abnormal conditions. They are fatalistic and the world outside the tenements is scarcely more real to them than the fantastic fairy-tale world of the pictures.

Fighting is truly one of the amusements of the tenements. Nearly all the young people join in, if not as fighters themselves, at least as spectators and cheering supporters. Johnnie, with his weak mentality and powerful physique, was simply destined to be a battler, but he might have remained in the rank and file if chance and

Mary Hay together had not turned him into a Razor King.

Johnnie had not begun to carry razors in his waistcoat pockets at that time that he and Mary went to the memorable dance at the Masonic Hall. He rather regretted having told her about his encounter with the Plantation girls, but it "couldny be helped", for, as he had surmised, the story was already current gossip in the Gorbals. And he was uncomfortably afraid that behind his back men were laughing at him.

Actually the current of popular opinion had set in a somewhat different direction. There were other young men who thought that they had been slighted by "the Plantation talent". That very evening there was a group of them gathered in the Queen's Head and drinking heavily while they discussed the need for teaching some of these stuck-up lassies a lesson.

"I'm holding," one of them, Big Mourn, remarked in the crisp local phrase. "What's it to be?"

It was, as usual, a measure of special whisky all round and another half-pint of beer. Mourn paid for the drinks with a pound note and, leaving the change on the counter, he issued a challenge to the company.

"See this money here?" he said. "Well, I'll tell you whit I'll dae wi' it: if I don't get level with those Plantation bastards the night, you can all have it atween you. How's that for a wager, eh?"

Sweeny, darker and smaller and a little older than Mourn, spoke up at once. "I'll match your money," he said, "an I'll get up wi' the Plantation talent the same as you do. That's supposing they come along to the Masonic to-night."

"Ay, they'll *come*," laughed Bobbie Hurley, and actually they were all confident that the girls would come. There were two other rounds of whisky and beer before the party felt ready to set out for the Masonic Hall. Even then someone suggested that they should whip round for

45

a half bottle of Scotch and a screw-stoppered bottle of beer each to take with them.

"Ay, we'll do that," agreed Sweeny, "but Ah'm tellin' ye that everybody'll spot the screw-tops in oor jackets."

"Who the hell cares?" chorused the company, and soon they trooped out of the pub, red-faced and with bulging jackets.

Johnnie and Mary were naturally unaware of these preparations, just as the Gorbals lads were unaware that the Plantation lassies had secured a powerful escort for themselves in the person of Fighting Gus MacLean. Gus was rather sweet on Polly and, as she was paying, he did not mind going along to the jiggings with her and her friends, although he did not profess to be a dancing man.

The Masonic Hall in Parish Terrace was a square building with a floor that would take some two hundred couples. Near the main entrance was a recess where the young men gathered between dances. Round the walls of the hall itself were many chairs and wooden benches, some occupied by girls who had no partners and some by mere spectators.

Johnnie and Mary arrived just after eight o'clock and separated for a few moments while the girl went to the ladies' cloakroom to leave her coat. The young men who dance in the jiggings do not need any such preparation. By immemorial custom they fold their caps and slip them into their jacket pockets so that the peak protrudes from the opening in the tightly buttoned coat.

Mary rejoined her escort in the recess and found him scowling at two girls who were dancing together, looking, and no doubt feeling, in a class by themselves. Their faces were made up; they wore cheaply pretty dresses instead of the usual skirt and blouse, and they smirked self-consciously as they passed beneath the electric light.

"That's the two Plantation talent, Mary," said Johnnie as the two of them threaded their way to the floor.

"Ah've seen them before," she said contemptuously, "and by Cripes they're nothing startlin'!"

At that moment Mourn and Sweeny and the rest of the boys from the Queen's Head entered the hall. Their jackets bulged with beer bottles as well as the traditional cap. They shouted a greeting to their friends.

The band had now struck up again and the Plantation group at the far end was chattering loudly and in the best of spirits. But the floor was comparatively empty and there were many girls sitting on the benches and forms along the walls.

Sweeny, more resolute when it came to action than the bigger Irishman, walked the length of the hall straight up to Polly Gamble and asked her to dance. Although she glanced towards the door, she stood up at once and danced away with him.

"I think I'll go and have Betty Barker," murmured Mourn, encouraged, but not too confident. The other lads followed him, each determined to dance with a Plantation lass.

At their approach, however, Betty and three other girls immediately got up and began to dance with one another. This was a direct insult to Mourn and company and would have been so regarded in any other popular dance hall. It was quite impossible for a young man of spirit, thus obviously refused, to ask any other girl to dance with him. The Gorbals boys never hesitated.

"We'll have to split them," sang out Mourn in a loud voice now that the trouble had actually started.

"Sure thing," agreed Downie Williams. "You take Betty and I'll take her china (friend)."

"We'll take the other pair," shouted a man named Stewart with another of the Gorbals group.

All the other dancers contrived to keep clear of the Plantation girls and the manager hovered anxiously by the bandstand awaiting developments. He had to refund admission money to girls who refused to dance with young men and see them off the premises. The rule is strict in the jiggings and the manager hated to refund anything. Moreover, he knew Mourn and all the Gorbals lads and he did not want to "lose" any of them unless he was absolutely obliged to do so.

In any case, while he was hesitating, things happened very quickly. Big Mourn caught Betty Barker by the shoulders and broke her roughly from her friend's embrace. Downie caught the other girl as roughly.

"What the hell are you getting at?" shouted Betty. Her head only reached Mourn's top waistcoat button and she found herself dancing with him in spite of herself.

"None of your palaver," he snarled, "or I'll get you and your china thrown out, so I wull!"

The friend in Downie's arms was too terrified to protest, but the second couple of Plantation girls refused to be split.

Without a moment's hesitation Stewart dealt one of the girls a blow between the eyes with his clenched fist. She screamed so loudly as she fell that every couple on the floor stopped still and even the band checked in its tune. The other girl was knocked down with a brutal kick in the back. And pandemonium broke loose.

It is of some importance to realize that sympathies, on an occasion of this kind, may be very much divided in any Glasgow jiggings. There is a recognized etiquette in all societies, and in the dance halls there is normally scant sympathy for any young woman who ignores the local rules and insults a young man by refusing to dance with him. It is felt that she has asked for any trouble that results.

In this instance, however, the atmosphere of the hall was surcharged with excitement. All the young men and women had felt the storm coming. This was a gang feud and not a private quarrel. It was the Gorbals against the Plantation and the neutrals were eager to take sides.

Some one in that throng – not one of the Gorbals lads,

but a fellow with a beer bottle in his pocket just the same – sprang at Stewart from behind and felled him with a blow to the skull. Mourn, letting go of Betty Barker, drove his right boot with such force into the lower part of this man's body that he collapsed with a roar of agony. And Betty called: "Gus! GUS MACLEAN!" in a most piercing scream.

Johnnie and Mary were now on the fringe of a furious general fight. Sweeny fell staggering at their feet, his cheek laid open by a broken bottle.

"Oh, good Christ!" screamed Mary, and tore at the assailant's throat with clawing hands.

Her body got between Johnnie and the other man. He wrenched her free and grunted as he drove home fist and boot. Then, as though driven by a wind, the crowd stampeded left and right at the far end of the hall to leave the way clear for Gus MacLean, shouting curses and brandishing a razor in either hand.

MacLean had been "awa' oot to get a wee drink" while all the trouble was brewing. He had come back just at the psychological moment to hear Betty's scream. And now the worst, or best, fighter in the Plantation was charging into battle with flashing weapons.

One man, unarmed, stands little chance against a razor fighter, but Johnnie Stark was fighting mad and bayonets would not have given him pause. He ran three or four steps and then leaped clear off the floor at big Gus. They fell together with a crash that shook the floor, but Johnnie was on top. Quick as a cat, he regained his feet and kicked, and kicked again with iron-shod boot, against a defenceless head. Gus lay quite still.

Every bottle brought into that hall was smashed during the fight, which ended only with the arrival of the police – three or four of them swinging drawn batons. Dancers, fighters, men and women, everybody able to run, made a wild rush for the exits, and most of them, including Johnnie and Mary, got away.

But Gus MacLean and three other men were taken to the infirmary and detained. The Plantation fighter, indeed, suffering from severe concussion, was an in-patient for several weeks and was never the same man again. Officially nobody ever learned the name of his assailant. As usual, the police did not press their inquiries very closely. For one thing, the manager of the hall made it clear to them that he did not want too much fuss made about the whole affair. And, for another, they knew from long experience that evidence about a "rammy" is always conflicting, never reliable and frequently perjured. They knew, for instance, that a genuine "fighter" like Gus himself, even should he know the name of his assailant, would deny this knowledge upon oath to his last gasp.

And therefore they simply acted in accordance with precedent and tradition, making such arrests as they could among the wounded and those who were obviously mixed up in the riot. Stewart and Downie, both rather badly hurt, got six months each. Two women, neither of them directly concerned in the riot at all, were each fined two guineas. One other young fellow, who couldn't remember in the least how he came to lose three front teeth, went down for a month, being treated leniently as a first offender. And the Masonic was open for dancing again on the following night.

Johnnie Stark did not go to his "toil" for several days after that dance. His mother took much pains to mend a clean, six-inch cut in the sleeve of a blue jacket that never looked the same after the blood had been washed out of it.

When Johnnie went abroad at last he seemed very cautious of his left arm and kept it stiffly at his side. Women's heads turned to follow him as he walked and men were eager to bid him "Good day". And upon his next entry into the Queen's Head, a moment's hush fell upon the company, followed by a chorus of invitations to drink. Johnnie stood upon the threshold with his thumbs in the armholes of his waistcoat, forcing the jacket wide open. The handles of two brand new "weapons" projected from the upper pockets.

"Who is this, eh?" exclaimed a young gangster in awed admiration. "Look at him, boys! The Razor King!"

CHAPTER V

THE SHERRICKING OF THE KING

Vanity is an underrated vice. In the Glasgow slums at all events it is the very core of ruffianism. Many a young gangster, not yet lost to all decent feeling, deliberately hardens his heart, as he hardens his muscles. His vanity compels him to be brutal. There must be nothing soft about a "razor king". And it is exceedingly difficult to be tough only in spots.

The slum girls foster the vanity of the slum men. They shine in the reflected glory of their protectors' ruffianism. And Mary Hay, who was not at all sure of Johnnie's fidelity, still did all she could to establish his reputation in the Gorbals after the great "rammy" in the Masonic Hall. Johnnie had fought like a tiger that evening, but, in fact, after he had kicked Gus MacLean into unconsciousness and then battled his way out of the scrimmage, he and Mary were glad enough to make their escape from the hall. At that time he was not at all minded to try conclusions with the police.

It was Mary who spread the story that Johnnie had taken MacLean's razors away from him, hacked his way out of the mob and even driven two policemen into the street before his flashing weapons. To all and sundry she gave glowing descriptions of his fearsome prowess, winding up with a high laugh as she told of the way in which he had flung the razors away from him after the battle because he would not "lower himself" to keep so poor a champion's weapons.

Her tales came back to Johnnie himself and he glowed with pride. He knew that they were wild exaggerations and yet he was grateful to her. He made no comment. He took the drinks that the other lads were now so ready to pay for and wore a ferocious scowl, acting a part like any small boy playing at pirates and strutting an imaginary quarter-deck.

And yet he resolved in his heart that he would not marry Mary Hay. It is true, of course, that he had never loved her. She was just an attractive "wee bit stuff", a well-made, pretty girl of his own class who might have made him as good a wife as any other lass. Ay, but no wife for a razor king! He was making a name for himself now. He had but to wait a little, confirm his reputation, and then he would be able to pick and choose. He would not need to marry one of "the hairy".

This resolve did not become fixed in his mind for some weeks. He had to fight against a kind of tenderness for Mary. He admired her pluck. He knew how staunch she was and what a little hell-cat she could be in battle. Above all, he was uneasy in the knowledge that she was going to have a baby. He had promised her that if that happened she need not worry, for they would "get married wi' a minister an' aw". Well, it *had* happened and Mary didn't hesitate to remind him of his promise.

Perhaps she reminded him too often. He was moody and savage in her company, and at home not even his mother dared to speak to him about Mary Hay. Peter, his younger brother, kept out of Johnnie's way after taking a hiding for one laugh in the wrong place. Johnnie couldn't bear to be laughed at. Peter was cleverer than he. He said things that one could not take hold of. There was the faintest sarcasm in the tone of innocent words. He got his hiding because, just once, the words were clear. Mrs Stark was cutting bread and butter and handed a slice to Peter, who was nearest to her. That was when he laughed and passed it on to Johnnie, saying no more than, "the King first!" And, though all the family knew

53

that people outside were calling Johnnie "The Razor King" none had yet referred to this new title.

It is at least possible that if Mary Hay had been a girl of rather less spirit she would have held Johnnie to his promise in spite of everything. If she had put up with his neglect without reproach and his sulky and glowering company without resentment; if she had been content to be meek and to appeal timidly to his better nature; he might easily have softened and married her in the end.

She did nothing of the sort. She became shrill in her reproaches and once, as he flung away from her after another quarrel, a threat followed him: "*Jist you wait, Johnnie Stark!*" He did not turn his head, but in that moment he was decided to force a crisis.

The young men and women of their set followed the course of these events with amused interest. Johnnie was at the height of his early popularity as a razor king, and, though there were some who felt rather sorry for Mary Hay, all were agreed that she had very little to worry about because, if she did lose Johnnie, it would still be easy enough for her to get some other husband.

Big Mourn, an addition to the crowd that now surrounded Johnnie, expressed this feeling in a single sentence. "Being Razor King's girl wull get Mary a man, all right," he said. "Any amount of them wull be glad to take her!"

Everyone at the bar concurred. For that is the way things happen in Gorbals. The mistress of a razor king has become a somebody. She has been lifted out of the rank and file. There will always be some obscure fellow flattered to wed the great man's cast-off.

There was, indeed, one such man in that company. Joe Kendles, an ex-serviceman with an artificial leg, was doomed to obscurity. He was thirty-two and unmarried, and his disability pension, small though it was, gave him the standing of an independent income in that society. But he had had no luck with the lassies. Perhaps it was because of his wooden leg, or because he was weedy and ill-favoured, with a head that was bald in patches. With his money he could, of course, have found a wife of sorts, but not a girl like Mary Hay, a good-looker whom he had long desired and who would do him credit.

Joe made no comment but he was inwardly excited. He did not go about with any particular gang, but he was tolerated everywhere as a harmless fellow with money. In addition to his pension he had a light job in a large tobacco factory. He lived in a room-and-kitchen house with his father and mother, his three brothers and two older sisters, but he could well afford to set up a home of his own. And his heart swelled at the thought of marrying Mary Hay if, indeed, Razor King should discard her.

"Likely there'll be trouble first," he thought calmly. "Mary's no' the sort to be turned off wi'oot showing Johnnie Stark up. And if I stand up for her I'll likely get razored. And Ah'm no' caring."

Events played into this unlikely suitor's hands. Johnnie, with Mary's threat clear in his memory, knew just what he was risking when he began to frequent dance halls and picture palaces and public houses with Ella McBride, a dark, vivid girl of nineteen. He had no more idea of marrying Ella than of marrying Mary herself. She, too, was one of "the hairy", and her parents were even poorer than the Hays. But she knew her place. She loved to be seen with the Razor King and fully realized that she could expect nothing from him but his temporary favour and protection.

She came to him, indeed, at the call of a finger. They met on a Friday evening at one of the local picture houses – a night and a place where young folk were in the habit of meeting to pair off, perhaps for a night, perhaps for weeks, or months, or even the whole of life's journey.

Ella sat with a girl friend seeking adventure. And when

the lights went up between pictures Johnnie caught sight of her, her cheeks flushed, her eyes shining, her pretty, impudent face lit up with laughter and invitation. He raised a hand and beckoned twice with one finger. The seat next to him was empty and she came to him at once. Before the lights were lowered he had his arm about her and her head was against his shoulder.

They had never spoken until that evening, but Johnnie knew her name and everybody knew Razor King.

"Ah'm finished wi' Mary Hay," he said simply. "You and me wull go thegither now. Ah'm only doing Mary a good turn by letting her go. She's in the betting now. Somebody else'll marry her, wullent they, when they know Ah'm finished wi' her?"

Ella didn't attempt to dispute that, but she was a little uneasy in her mind as to what would happen to her if she, too, should happen to have a baby by Razor King. "But I'll be no worse off than Mary," she thought, and squeezed Johnnie's hand.

"Maybe Mary'll no' like anybody else as she likes you," she said astutely. Johnnie laughed in the dark and his left hand closed upon Ella's knee.

"It's what you like that Ah'm interested in," he said. "You and me can go thegither and chuck one another whenever we like, and nae sherrickin' or anything like that, eh?"

The word was out and Ella shivered in spite of herself. For a "sherricking" is a public showing-up of which none can foretell the consequences. And if Ella went with Johnnie Stark, she would be in it, too. His fingers tightened about her knee and she gave a little scream that was half a giggle.

"Mary'll no' have the heart," she said, "to give *you* a sherrickin', Razor King."

Her use of his new title stirred Johnnie more than he would have admitted. Her head nestled against his shoulder and her body quivered at his touch. He *knew* that Ella was his to do what he liked with. He felt magnificently masterful.

"Don't you fret," said he. "Anybody who tried to sherrick *me* – along wi' a big division like this – would need a big heart, eh, Ella?"

She lifted her head and looked round her, peering through the gloom, to which her eyes were now well accustomed. Near by were many lads of Johnnie's gang ready to fight at a word or a mere nod. Most of them were cuddling their own girls or staring at the screen. They were careful not to look at Johnnie and her. She sighed and leaned her head back against his shoulder.

"Ah'm no' worrying," she said. "You'd look after me, Johnnie!"

She lay against him, small and soft and enticing, so that he could savour her abandon and know the thrill of it. His arms went round her in a bear's hug and her lips were hot against his own. He pulled her roughly on to his knees.

"Ella McBride," he whispered, "I'll look efter ye. If yon Mary Hay lass so much as lifts her haun' tae ye, Ah'll dae her in. Ay; her an' any mug that tries to stick by her!"

She believed him. She was sure that he would win in a fight, but she would have liked it far better if no fight had threatened. There were dozens of girls in the big balcony sitting by that time on their lovers' knees. Ella was proud that the Razor King had chosen her.

Not that she loved him. For those who have been bred outside Gorbals it is not easy to understand the mentality of a girl like Ella McBride. She was less than innocent because her mind was fouled by knowledge. And yet, physically, she was inexperienced and well aware that Johnnie would not be satisfied with less than all he wanted. Already his arm was close about her waist, his breath hot on her cheeks, his whole embrace urgent with desire. All round her there were sighs and laughter and

57

faint protest. She was frightened as well as excited, but her mind was quite made up.

If she could have put her thoughts into words she might have said: "Better Johnnie than any ither lad. It's no' many lassies can catch a razor king, an' Ah'm no' *wantin'* tae keep him. Some ways I'd sooner have George. An' Ah wull, tae!"

For Ella was half in love with George Smith, a young man earning a fairly good weekly wage by "lifting lines" – or acting as runner – to a bookmaker in Bridgeton. She had no illusions about George and she was pleased that he was not very intelligent and not in the least moral. When it got about that she was going with Razor King it would just tip the scale in her favour as far as George was concerned. Sooner or later she meant to marry him. So far he hadn't been so much for marriage. Now he would realize that Ella must be something out of the ordinary. She would let him take her out during the day when Johnnie was at work and she would be "kinder" to him than she had ever been before. And in the end, when Johnnie was finished with her, he'd be glad enough to have her.

The show ended, and as the lights went up there was a prolonged rustle of couples scrambling apart. But Johnnie was contemptuous of appearances.

"Sit still, Ella," he commanded, "and don't be plummy (dull)."

He spoke in a loud voice and there was admiring laughter among his companions. Ella giggled and struggled, but he held her fast, and, except for his own gang, the balcony was nearly empty before he gave her a final kiss and told her cheerfully to get to hell off his knees.

Standing up and straightening his cap on his head, he announced aloud that he had something to tell them all when they got outside.

"Wait for me before you all go to the closes wi' your

partners," he said. "It's about me and Ella and that old blade of mine, Mary Hay."

There was a stir of interest and Ella was deeply thrilled by this public acknowledgement. She pulled up her stockings, displaying ostentatiously a bare, and none too clean thigh, but the other lads were too interested in Razor King to pay much attention to her.

Outside the picture palace they gathered about him. Johnnie, hiding his own excitement, kept them waiting while he lit a cigarette.

"This is what Ah've got to say," he announced at last. "Ah'm finished wi' the Mary Hay lassie. I've nothing against her, or anything like that, but Ah'm *finished* wi' her. Anybody that likes can go wi' her. She might no' just take anybody, for she's a great bit stuff for a hairy, an' she's been hellova good tae me. Ah'm tellin' ye this in case she tries to sherrick me. Ella an' me don't want any sherrickin'. So now ye know and ye can all go and have a good bliddy game tae yersel's."

Nobody in that group made the slightest protest. On the contrary, there was loud laughter, so loud that it might have been heard by the few men and women across the Clyde on the Glasgow Green. Many of them knew Mary Hay and liked her. But "the king" had spoken. They admired his cynicism. They laughed and, in their hearts, they all hoped that Mary would try something – just to see what happened; just to see what Razor King would do about it.

Johnnie took Ella's arm. "Come on," he said, "you an' me've got a lot to tell each other."

Ella called "Good night!" over her shoulder, but Johnnie did not turn his head. With a few words on the way, he took her to her own stair-head on the first storey of a dilapidated yellow tenement in Errol Street in the very heart of Gorbals slums. The place was so sordid that even Johnnie, hardened as he was, sniffed disgustedly. Bluntly he told her that she would do well, *when he was finished with her*, to marry anybody at all in order to get out of such a place. She laughed nervously and threw her arms round his neck. He was none too gentle with her.

And in the weeks that followed, this story – if it may be so-called – went all over Gorbals and was quoted with sardonic relish.

It was understood in the slums that Johnnie had issued an ultimatum outside the picture palace and eager "friends" of both parties were swift to bear word of it to Mary Hay herself. They were disappointed if they expected her to make a scene there and then. She said little, but her eyes were stormy.

Mary had no illusions about her fellow "slummies". She did not look for much support. All of them would be eager to see what happened; very few would care to get mixed up in the trouble. She herself had no hope of changing Johnnie's mind. She only wanted revenge.

For a slum lass in such case there is little hope of revenge except by a "sherricking". Occasionally it is true, she may have a fighting brother – or even a fighting father – ready to do battle in her cause and able, perhaps, to give the faithless lover such a thrashing as will discredit him for ever.

But Mary Hay had no champion of this kind. She had to fall back on that strange and wild appeal to crowd justice and crowd sympathy which Glasgow describes as a "sherricking".

For some weeks she held her hand – weeks in which Johnnie and Ella were flaunting their love affair in the dance halls and the picture palaces and the pubs. But at last, on a bright August evening at the mouth of her own close near the end of the long, gaunt, dirty tenement in which she lived, Mary loosed her emotions in a spate of words.

Joe Kendles was one of the small group who gathered about her.

"When Razor King comes out of the dance hall with

yon bitch the night, Ah'm gaun tae sherrick him!" she wailed. Her eyes were bright and her face pale with excitement. One could see that she was keyed up to a pitch of sheer desperation.

"Ah might be a hairy," she continued, still on that same wailing note, "but Ah'm no' gaun to be a doormat awthegither. Ah'm no' feart o' him. Ah'll tell him what he is, and if he does razor me, they'll all know what he did it for, so they wull!"

Kendles, leaning on his thick stick, flushed as he watched Mary standing there with her bosom high and her eyes flashing. His jaw muscles stood out in his lean face. He looked much more like the soldier he once had been. But he hid the wild elation in his heart. To himself he was saying: "Good old Razor King! Good old Razor King! You're a bliddy bastard, but you're giving me my chance." He was almost fond of Stark in that moment.

Aloud he spoke very differently.

"If Razor King, or whatever the hell they ca' him, lays a haun' on Mary Hay," he said, "Ah'll get into him masel', so Ah wull, with this stick if nothing else!"

No-one paid much attention to him. Even Mary, if she heard what he said, did not seem to take it in at the time. The actual drama was too close to bother about threats. Mary set off for the dance hall and her listeners followed her. Soon a dozen other people, some who knew her, some who were strangers, had joined the group, all of them eager to see the fun or the fight, or the "showing up", or whatever should come of it all.

Outside the hall Mary stood a little forward from this contingent, her fists clenched, panting with excitement. Young men and women, coming out of the building, in couples, in threes, or fours, or even larger groups, saw her standing there and, instead of dispersing, stood about the pavement or loitered in doorways, not talking to her, but forcing laughter and conversation among themselves. They were waiting for the "sherricking", thrilled, curious, eager, callous, not caring what came of it, greedy of sensation for its own sake.

True to the tradition of the slums, Mary was dressed for the occasion. She was wearing her best white shawl and, though she was bare-headed as usual, her hair was well combed, her face and neck were well washed, her shoes were shining and her stockings were neat under the short skirt, showing how well built she was in "the prams" (legs). It vexed her that her condition was not more apparent, if only to make it obvious that she was carrying Johnnie's child.

At last he came out with Ella McBride clinging to his arm and Bobbie Hurley and Lily McKay and others close behind him. Bobbie and Lily had been leading off the dance that night and Johnnie had stayed behind to congratulate them with lofty patronage. The two dancers were far better dressed than the rest of the company. Lily, in a smart blue coat and hat, actually carried her dancing-shoes in a brand new leather case, and Bobbie was wearing a bowler hat. Even Johnnie was impressed by this evidence of their rise in the world. His contempt for his old school friend was mixed with admiration. Lily was certainly the "smartest bit stuff" in the hall, but she had eyes for none but her partner.

The groups stood for a moment on the threshold and Lily, well aware of many admiring glances, asked Bobbie in a loud voice if he knew which side of that main street they must go to catch their tram. Everybody there knew quite well that she and Bobbie lived within easy walking distance. This talk of the tram was pure "swank", but they admired her for it. They admired her for being able to afford tram-rides nowadays even when they weren't necessary.

But she held their attention only for a moment before Mary Hay came running towards Johnnie and his girl.

She caught Ella by the hair with one hand and with the other ripped open her coat, tore her blouse down to the waist and then struck her in the mouth. "Ah'm no a dirty whore like you!" she screamed.

The attack was so swift and savage that all this was done before Razor King could intervene. Now he caught Mary's wrist and shouted: "Let her go, yuh bliddy fool, wull yuh?"

Mary did let her go instantly. She caught Johnnie by the lapels of his jacket and butted his face with her head, bringing the blood from his nose in streams and loosening a tooth. Her speed and fury thrilled the crowd and even Lily McKay, forgetting her elegance, stood and gaped, fascinated like every other slummie by a sherricking of the first class.

With an oath Johnnie wrenched himself free of Mary's hold and drove a blow at her more to ward her off than to hurt. But he hit lower than he meant to do, making her gasp and clasp her hands to her stomach.

"Yuh dirty pig!" she shrieked. "Yuh'd try and murder what's in therr, wid ye?"

There was a murmur in the crowd, an odd uncertain murmur, half of resentment, half of sheer excitement.

Johnnie stepped forward and hit Mary flat-handed across the face, a hard blow that sent her reeling back a step or two. But she was undaunted.

"He's only a liberty taker!" she shouted. "A dirty liberty taker. Don't let any wee lassies frae schule get near him, the bliddy swine!"

Johnnie's face had gone very white, but his lips and chin were streaked with blood. Swiftly though all had happened, thought can always outstrip action. In one flash of revelation he was aware of the uncertain temper of the crowd, of Mary's maddened and quite reckless face; of Joe Kendles limping and shouldering his way towards him, of Ella frightened and elated, at his side, and even of Lily and Bobbie, seen out of the corner of his eye, hesitating and fascinated, too. He could remember other "sherrickings" at which he had been merely an onlooker – one in particular, where a soft-hearted fellow had held his hand and was suddenly overwhelmed by the mob and beaten and kicked almost to death.

Johnnie didn't *want* to hurt Mary Hay. In that moment he actually admired her – the little hell-cat spitting at him there in the gutter. He didn't *want* to hurt that damned crazy cripple, Kendles. But he knew that his whole career was in the balance; that the faintest trace of "softness" in that crisis would forever destroy his reputation.

All these thoughts and many others passed across the screen of his consciousness with the speed of light. And his lips tightened into a harder line and his black brows drew closer together and he darted forward and struck Mary Hay under the chin, using his clenched fist this time, so that her head went back and she fell huddled on to the kerb.

Johnnie raised his boot to her fallen body and none observed the sudden change of balance that made the kick scarcely more than a prod. But Joe Kendles was on him then and he scarcely warded off the swinging blow of the cripple's heavy stick, deflecting it, indeed, from his head, but taking a heavy welt across the shoulder.

It was all that was necessary to steel Johnnie's spirit. Rage took hold of him like an enemy. His razors flashed from his pockets and with two lightning lunges he marked Kendles for life. The unfortunate cripple gave an unearthly shriek and raised a bleeding arm to an ear that hung backwards upon his cheek. Johnnie kicked him in the groin and he fell backwards across Mary Hay's prostrate body.

Lily McKay came to herself with this development.

"Come on away, Bobbie!" she screamed, taking Hurley's arm, in no doubt now as to what tram they should get or where they ought to go. "Come on away! The police'll be here in a minute and they'll be in the jail, some of them, before hellish long. They're no use tae *us*!"

Bobbie needed no second bidding. The pair of them went running down the street and the crowd scarcely noticed them. There were some, it is true, who edged away when the razors appeared, but the main body was too fascinated to move. It was a moment of intense suspense. The least faltering by the Razor King would have turned the spectators into a pack of wolves. Now most of them were equally ready to acclaim his triumph.

One young man, and one alone, sprang cursing at Johnnie's throat. Johnnie side-stepped and slashed his assailant across the neck. His eyes were alight and his lips were parted in a bloody grin. And suddenly the mob was all on his side, all shouting applause of the Razor King.

On the outskirts of the crowd someone raised the cry: "The police! The police!" and at once everyone was running. Johnnie ran with them, Ella clinging to his hand. And when the constables arrived on the scene – the street was empty except for the two injured men and the senseless girl.

Johnnie did not even throw away his razors. He was lost in the running crowd that hurried towards the South Side. Within half an hour he had washed and dried his weapons and concealed them under the stinking cavity bed of one of his "stickers", Alan Burr, a shifty-eyed desperado with thin brown hair.

Mary Hay was only stunned and allowed to go home after questions to which she returned no answers. Kendles and the other man who had been slashed were taken to the Royal Infirmary and both of them swore most stubbornly that their assailant was unknown to them. The slummie is like that: whatever his grievance, he will not tell the police anything.

And the "sherricking" was over. There is an etiquette in these things. Mary's "honour" was satisfied. The crowd had not taken her side and she could do no more. It might have happened differently. If Johnnie had shown any weakness he would have been bashed and kicked and trampled almost to death and, had he recovered from his injuries, he would scarcely have dared to show his face in Gorbals again.

Instead he had behaved as a razor king was expected to behave. He had vindicated his character by sheer, desperate ferocity. Far from damaging his reputation, the "sherricking" had confirmed and established it. He walked abroad like a king, indeed, and other young men coveted his surly nod of recognition.

Only in his own home did the whole episode pass almost without comment. Peter said nothing at all, having learned his lesson, but his dark eyes were contemptuous and his avoidance of his brother's company more marked.

Whenever he was in "the hoose", Johnnie felt his mother's eyes upon him, puzzled eyes, anxious, questioning and timidly disapproving. But she never said anything to him and he kept out of her way.

In course of time, after he had recovered from his wounds, Joe Kendles called on Mary Hay in her own home and offered her marriage in simple terms.

"You know I like you, Mary," he said. "Well, now that dirty rat, Razor King, has left you an' has no intention of marrying you or daeing onything for you, what about me an' you getting married?

"The kid wid get ma name," he went on, as though that were a matter of no great consequence but worth mentioning as an added inducement, "an' you'll never need to starve wi' me, Mary."

Her father and mother were drinking the whisky which Joe had sent them with promise of more to come. They told Mary she "couldny dae better for herself noo". Mary stared at her new suitor with a contempt which she did not attempt to conceal. Then she laughed harshly, poured

66

whisky into a tumbler, and drank with them all to her coming marriage.

And married they were in a Gorbals church, and before a minister too. Johnnie was home when his mother heard the news.

"Eh, the poor lassie!" she said, and looked at him.

He snatched up his cap and went out into the street.

But Gorbals society was frankly amused, the more so as this marriage was speedily followed by that of Ella McBride, who had been much more shaken by the "sherricking" than any of the others. Johnnie made no effort to keep her once he saw that she wanted to be free of him. She had served her turn, and he shrugged contemptuous shoulders when she tried to "break the news" of her coming match with George Smith, the Bridgeton line-lifter.

"What the hell should *I* care who you marry," he sneered. "Ah've had all I want from you, Ella, an' so bliddy good luck tae you!"

She was suitably grateful and humble, and George, as she had anticipated, now found her infinitely desirable. Both of them "had many a good laugh" at the thought of Mary Hay, who had fancied herself, taking such a man as crippled Joe for a husband in the end.

In the billiards hall, among his own cronies and lieutenants, Johnnie declared magnificently that he was through with women for a while. "As for they ithers," he sneered, "they're as well married, or half-married, as dead." And the sneer was followed by the expected tribute of their sniggers.

Lily McKay, growing more refined every day, thought both marriages were "disgusting". She and Bobbie had no intention of marrying yet awhile. They had just secured a permanent job as leaders-off at one of the better-class dance halls in Gorbals with a fixed weekly wage of four pounds ten between them.

Razor King heard of their success and shrugged his

shoulders. "Ah'm no' jealous of them, anyway," he observed disdainfully, "they're well enough in their way, Bobbie and Lily, whatever the guttersnipes may say."

"Guttersnipes" was the word he actually used.

CHAPTER VI

"ON THE BUROO"

Definitely established as "Razor King", Johnnie Stark was not quite nineteen when he went "on the buroo" in the late autumn of 1923. It did not make much difference to his pocket, for he had never earned a proper man's wage, but, for a little while, it touched his pride. His coalman employer gave him the sack one Saturday when work was finished for the weekend.

"It's becos Ah canny pey ye that Ah'm peying ye aff," said the coalman. He and Johnnie were alone in the stable at the time and the elder man was slightly apologetic.

"Ah wid hae kept ye on a while," he went on, "if Ah coulda peyed ye. You being a razor king wid ha' suited me fine; ye know that. It wid ha' been the goods for the tick. Ay, there's many who can find the money they're owing when it's you do the askin', Johnnie. But Ah'm peying ye eighteen shillings a week now an' that's too much for too little. Ah don't need a man for ma round an' you're too auld noo for a boy's job. So Ah've got a boy to start wi' me on Monday. You should go in for work of some other kind, noo. Ah wid try something else if Ah wis you."

There was a kind of deference about this explanation so that Johnnie scarcely knew whether to feel flattered or angry. He pocketed his money and lit a cigarette with an air of unconcern. His employer was gazing at him curiously and Johnnie, sticking his thumbs in the armholes of his waistcoat, walked away without saying anything. It was a little humiliating to feel that he was out of work. It galled him to think that Peter, nearly two years his junior, was not only in work but doing well. He wondered vaguely whether things had been so much different before the War, and his scowl grew blacker at the thought. It annoyed him to hear older people talk about their blasted war. He was barely fourteen when the Armistice was signed, but still old enough to remember the fantastic wages which had been earned by the workers in shipyards and munition factories during the war years. He shared the general impression that the men who joined the Army were "bliddy fools" if they went voluntarily and "plain daft" if they had been unable to avoid conscription. There was no hero-worship for the men who came back and never a trace of reproach for the sensible ones who had stayed at home.

Communism, of a sort, was preached at many a street corner, but the Gorbals jeered at the politicians. They did not believe in any of them. They thought them all a lot of grafters, scrambling for office, glib of promise, empty of performance. Voting "Red" because the offered bribe was bigger, they sneered as they made their crosses on the ballot papers. They cared for nothing – literally nothing – except the rate of outdoor relief and the faint hope of a reduction in the rent or a bigger allowance to meet this burden.

Some of the slum dwellers were "Prodisants" and the others "Catholics", but not one in ten thought of his religion as anything but a label or a banner to fight under. They were contemptuous alike of God and their fellow men. They despised their own City Council more than they despised Westminster. The Glasgow Municipal Buildings were commonly known among them as the "Chamber of Horrors" or the "House of Corruption". They told each other with the utmost relish of new Council houses whose tenants complained, either with malice or with truth, that they were verminous before ever they were inhabited! "Ay," they would say delightedly. "So-and-so must have made a grand profit out of yon – the clever deevil!"

Johnnie turned into a public house as it opened its doors and took a long time over one bottle of beer in the hope that some of his followers might come in and buy him further drinks. But none of them did and he paid up sullenly at last. The family were at tea when at last he reached home. He grunted a wordless greeting and drew up a chair.

Peter looked up at his elder brother and looked down again quickly at his plate. He thought resentfully that Johnnie was almost as much a damper on their spirits as their father had been. His mind was gloomy with fore-boding. He hated his brother's "success" as Razor King. It even spoiled his friendship with Isobel McGilvery and that counted for a great deal in his life just then.

Isobel lived with her father and mother, an older sister and a younger brother, in a room and kitchen home in Rutherglen Road, near Mathieson Street. They were quiet, well-doing people, and Peter knew that they did not like the thought of his being related to a hooligan like Razor King.

He glanced across at his brother with a sudden disgust. Johnnie was picking a herring from its bones with his thick fingers and Peter wondered why he had never before paid much attention to the unpleasantness of the spectacle. Perhaps it was because Isobel's family didn't eat like that. He had not done so himself for a long time now. Nor did their mother. She wasn't very well that night and he thought how old and tired she looked, sitting by the fire with her worn hands still in her lap.

Of his sisters, Peter scarcely thought at all. They were attractive enough to get men, he supposed, and they must know that that was the best thing for them to do. Sooner or later they would marry and not care for much outside their own "families". After that they wouldn't bother him nor he them. Perhaps they would be glad if he did well

71

for himself, but, on the other hand, he knew they wouldn't worry very much if he never won out of the Gorbals, never achieved the kind of respectable home-life he had set his heart upon, never escaped at all from the dreary contentment of mass failure.

They were not ambitious, but he was, by God! Johnnie, too, but in a different way, worse luck!

The faintest smile – a scarcely perceptible lift of the lips and a contraction of the brows that went with it – lit Peter's face and left it blank and sullen. Though he did not put his thought into words he was thinking that Johnnie was a complete failure at school and *yet* ambitious. He was thinking that, if there *had* been any other way to lift himself out of the ruck – to make himself different from the ruck – Johnnie would have taken it. The girls were content: that was the difference. They would do what the other Gorbals lassies did. Yes; but he and Johnnie were *not* content. They had to come to the surface. They *had* to be different, whether by razor slashing or by hard work.

"I wish tae God," thought Peter Stark moodily, "that Johnnie wad be half-way content with being ordinary! It's no' the same wi' me. For Ahm *no*' ordinary! Ah'm only a message-boy noo; but one day Ah'll be a traveller and one day Ah'll be sales manager. Ah can do it. Ah've got the brains. Ah'm wullin' tae work. They canny stop me."

Even in that surge of youthful ambition and boyish self-confidence, Peter Stark never fooled himself that he would be able to set up in business on his own account. He was a rebel, but his environment limited even his own rebellious ambition. That he should become an employer and a capitalist was a dream simply beyond the range of his imagination. All he wanted – all he ever sought – was a safe "collar-and-tie job", a guaranteed position of respectability and relative affluence.

Boys of seventeen don't carry dreams to their logical

conclusions. Peter, for instance, could imagine himself married to Isobel and living, not in the tenements, but in some "nice sma' hoose" right away from Gorbals. He could imagine shelves of books in the parlour and good clothes for himself and Isobel to wear. He could imagine, without any difficulty at all, the kind of home that would overawe Johnnie with its respectability and its evidence of prosperity, but he couldn't – or wouldn't – push this dream to the limit of including his mother in it or excluding her from it. Obscurely, almost subconsciously, he loved his mother. And yet he was ashamed of her. She would not fit into the framework of his ultimate ambitions. But she could not, like his sisters, be excluded from it.

Peter was at this time employed as messenger-boy in a "warehouse", or big general shop near Glasgow Cross. He had left school with a good character and some tiny reputation as a scholar. He used some of his spare time for reading and studying. Isobel was a young person of similar ambition. She was working in a laundry out in Rutherglen, but she was clever too.

Even her friends could scarcely have called her pretty. Her features were somewhat sharp and her brown eyes a little too prominent. Freckles marred the purity of her pale complexion. She carried herself well, but there was no denying that her legs were thin and that gave her solid, water-tight shoes an undue prominence. One would have supposed her feet disproportionately large, which they were not. The truth was that she had been growing too fast. She was too thin for her height. Even her face was pinched at that time when her sixteenth birthday was close behind her.

Peter, munching bread and butter, now that his herring was finished, couldn't analyse Isobel. He thought how her teeth flashed when she smiled; he thought of her rather thin arm warm within his own and he thought of how they had clung just once breast to breast and lip to

73

lip. And his cheek flushed and his heart thrilled at that recollection.

Johnnie interrupted his brother's reverie. He pushed back his chair and picked his teeth with a small fish bone. Then he grinned at Peter and leant across to him.

"Eh, Peter," said he, "are ye gaun oot wi' that skinny bit o' stuff the night?"

Everybody round the table, and Mrs Stark sitting in her chair by the fire, bent their eyes upon Peter after this question. He tried to force a laugh. He hated his brother then, but feared more than he hated. "She's no' sae skinny!" was all he had the nerve to say.

Johnnie laughed. Everybody laughed with him, uproariously, except Mrs Stark silent by the fire.

"You'd better watch oot," said Johnnie. "Isobel might slip intae a mangle some day and when she cam oot you'd no' be able to see her, Peter."

The younger brother's face paled and there was a glint in his dark eyes. His fists were clenched and his breathing came hard. He glowered at Razor King and rose to his feet.

"Ah think Ah'll awa oot," he murmured hoarsely.

Mrs Stark intervened quietly from her folded-up bedchair. "Finish yer tea first, Peter," she said, "and never mind they ithers."

Peter hesitated. Then he resumed his seat, but his cheeks were very red. One of his sisters giggled and then gulped tea noisily.

Taking another mouthful of bread and butter, Peter looked up and addressed Johnnie deliberately.

"Ah don't often say anything aboot who *you* go oot wi'," he remarked with great courage.

Razor King's grin vanished and his brows drew together in a savage scowl.

"Naw," he snarled. "You know better than that!"

Peter made no reply and would not be drawn even by the renewed giggling of his sisters. "Let them laugh," he thought furiously. "One day I'll show 'em. They'd think I was mad if I let on tae them noo whit I wis efter. Ay, but there's time yet."

When the evening meal was finished he went out before any of the others. He tugged his cap over his eyes and stalked out of the apartment.

Mrs Stark watched him go and sighed. Johnnie was standing close at her elbow, grinning derisively as the front door shut. Timidly she laid a hand upon his elbow.

"Johnnie," she whispered, "whit for dae ye go on at Peter? There's nae harm in the boy. Why canny ye let him alane?"

He looked down at her and frowned. To say that he loved his mother would be to stretch the meaning of the verb. She meant very little in his life. Her wishes did not exercise the slightest influence upon his conduct. And yet he felt a sort of tenderness for her. He would not let anyone worry her or say a word against her.

"Aw, don't worry yersel', Mither," he said with gruff gentleness. "Ah'm no' set tae hurt the boy. He's well enough wi' his skinny bit stuff. An' he's better aff than me an aw."

"Whit dae ye mean, Johnnie?" she asked anxiously.

"Naething. Only that I got paid aff the day. Ah, wheesht! There's nae need to greet. Ah'm no' carin'. Ah'm gled o' it. Ah've bin thinkin' it's kind of plummy for me to go to the toil."

But Peter had no hint of this conversation and would have been astonished to know that his elder brother thought of him with any kindness or consideration. He went along moodily to the local billiards hall and felt more cheerful after a game of snooker. At half-past seven he went to meet Isobel McGilvery and found her at the close-mouth waiting for him, in a brick-coloured coat and a red hat. Her face was pale beneath its freckles, but her brown eyes glowed a welcome.

"Were you waiting long?" he asked her casually.

"Naw," said she. "Ah'm jist this minute doon."

They understood each other so well that they did not waste time on those polite formalities and empty exchanges which are normally part of the routine of slum courtships. Nor was it their habit to linger very long at the close-mouth. That evening they walked at once towards Crown Street, Isobel taking the inside of the pavement like all other courting girls. She was deeply attached to Peter Stark. She never doubted his ability to do something and to be something above the ordinary level. She was proud of his looks and his high, intelligent forehead. It was she who had made him get a blue suit instead of a grey one. She told him simply that blue suited him and he smiled and promised to remember.

Nearing Crown Street itself, Peter hesitated and then suggested that they should dance instead of going to the pictures as previously arranged. The fact was that they had first met in one of the Gorbals dance halls where fighting was not encouraged and where dancing was looked upon as a serious and more or less respectable accomplishment.

Isobel didn't object to the change of plans but pointed out simply that the dancing would cost them more than the pictures. Peter shrugged his shoulders as much as to say: what did it matter for once? Bobbie Hurley and Lily McKay were leading off that night in the hall down the Paisley Road.

"Aw right, Peter," said Isobel smiling, "but I'll have to go back for ma shoes."

"Sure. Come along," said Peter cheerfully and they turned and went back to the close-mouth together.

Isobel lived in the top flat. She left Peter on the pavement, but she had rejoined him within eight minutes.

"Ah wasn't long, was Ah?" she asked happily.

"Naw," agreed Peter gaily, "you weren't. But waiting or no', Ah'm always confident when Ah'm alang wi' you; Ah don't know how it is!"

The girl coloured and laughed, but she did not loiter at the close-mouth. Instead she gave Peter her dance shoes to carry and they set off for the dance hall. Young as they were, they were both thinking of marriage. They were in love and there didn't seem any reason to wait. They were both convinced that they would be happy together and they were both prepared to make sacrifices in order to get on and live in a respectable home. Without having discussed the subject, they both felt that they must find their way out of Gorbals together. They didn't hope for luck, but they believed they could fight.

They were inclined to be snobbish. They tried to save all they could out of their meagre spending money. They didn't buy chocolates and Peter smoked very few cigarettes. There would be time for these indulgences later on, and meanwhile they felt happily superior to most of the Gorbals lads and lassies. They felt that if they couldn't succeed, then it wouldn't be much use for any other young couple even to try.

It was early for the dancing and they walked all the way to the hall, saying little, but well content in each other's company.

"Looks as if there's gaun tae be a crowd here," Peter surmised as they drew near the tall, yellowish building in which the nightly dancing had become so well organized as to draw big crowds all the six nights of the week.

"Looks like it," Isobel admitted. "Ah wonder whit's gaun on."

But there was no special attraction that night except for a poster in the lobby announcing that Bobbie Hurley and Lily McKay, the well-known speciality amateurs, were to lead off. Isobel handed Peter her shilling as a matter of course. He pocketed it with a nod and pulled out half a crown to pay for both at the doorway. They went at once to one of the forms against the wall and waited for the band to strike up. When it did, they were almost the first couple on the floor.

Others followed them quickly enough, for going to a dance hall means *dancing* in Glasgow, where the young people like to get full value for their money. Peter and Isobel were by no means in the star class but, like all the other dancers, they paid close attention to their steps and took their pleasure somewhat seriously on that account. Even in the cheapest "jiggings" the atmosphere is highly critical and technical skill greatly admired. That is why outstanding performers like Bobbie Hurley and Lily McKay can and do achieve a kind of fame in the slums.

The first exhibition dance by this already well-known pair was not given until the company had been warmed up by half an hour of general dancing. Then the manager of the hall, wearing evening dress, mounted a small platform at the far end of the building to announce the "champions", and there was something of a rush to get a good view from the side of the hall. Peter and Isobel scrummed their way to the front of the crush and stood unashamedly holding hands as Bobbie and Lily took the floor.

Apart from the manager, Bobbie was the only man there in evening dress. His dinner-jacket suit had been made to order and fitted him well, though the material was not of first quality. Lily, in a blue evening frock, moderately low necked, looked even more "professional" than he did. Her red lips were constantly parted and her rather prominent but regular and nicely shaped front teeth enhanced the effect of her cultivated smile.

The four-piece band on the platform struck up. There was no mechanism in that hall to dim the lighting, but even so, Bobbie and Lily showed up well under the travelling spot light. They understood each other instinctively as first-rate partners should do; their separate movements flowed harmoniously together. Not many stage partners could have rivalled them on that floor and in that setting. The audience was deeply appreciative. The lads and lassies clasped hands in admiring silence, their eyes following the dancers' every movement, never missing a step.

But as that dance was ending three young men began to edge their way through the crowd at the door towards the place where Peter and Isobel stood. One of the trio had recognized Peter as the brother of the now notorious "Razor King". He said very little; only: "Look across there! That'll be Peter Stark. Let's go talk to him."

The three young men came from the Plantation district of Glasgow and they were all in their early "twenties". They were gangsters of the second order – rank and file men, ready to join a riot, but not to lead it. They had not even been in the Masonic Hall during the big "rammy" in which Johnnie made his name and Gus MacLean was kicked into obscurity for ever. But they stood by their local "team"; they were against Gorbals when the chance occurred. And they were all three the worse for drink.

These young fellows had not come to that dance hall "looking for trouble". Perhaps there was a certain bravado in thus visiting outside their own district, but they were warmed with the drink inside them and each carried a bottle of beer in his hip pocket for refreshment during intervals. Their caps had been stuffed naturally enough into their jackets and they had found partners without difficulty among the surplus girls who always throng the halls.

It was because Peter was alone with his own girl and the crowd was evidently so respectable that the Plantation lads now recognized a special opportunity. Isobel was clearly a real "Jane bit o' stuff" – a girl of quality who wore a hat, without affectation, because she was accustomed to it. She wasn't likely to fight and it amused them to think that Razor King's brother should

79

be courting a lass of that kind so much above his proper class. Not gently, and yet not too conspicuously, they shouldered and elbowed their way towards the unsuspecting pair.

When they had come quite close, the leader of the Plantation lads launched his offensive.

"They always say," he shouted, with a grin, "that when ye *do* get a hiding it's up to you to pey somebody back for it!"

"Ay; even if it's only a brother o' the man ye might be lookin' for," agreed a companion, "it's still best tae take a chance tae square things."

The third of the trio, taller and tougher than his friends, whipped the bottle from his hip pocket.

"It might be a pity," he sneered, and this was loudly and clearly directed to Peter himself, "tae waste good beer an' aw, but at times it canny be helped!"

All this was the affair of a few moments, but the crowd, sensing trouble, had sheered away from Peter and Isobel as though by magic. The girl saw the danger just a flash before the boy. She gasped and tugged at his sleeve, drawing him towards the too-distant doorway. The tall lad from the Plantation stepped nimbly ahead of them and his companions closed in. All round about that group the other dancers had left a clear space.

Alive now to his danger, Peter pushed Isobel away from him with his free hand and side-stepped towards the wall. But his enemies anticipated him. For a moment his heart sank and then his eyes sparkled with a fighting glint. He did not wait to be attacked: he leaped at his nearest assailant, the tall one with the bottle in his hand, feinted and drove home a smashing left to the ear.

The big fellow staggered and swore, but one of his companions struck at Peter from behind, a blow that would have felled him had the bottle fallen full upon his unprotected skull instead of glancing off it. Peter reeled, and Isobel, screaming, ran to catch him.

In the same instant the third of the Plantation lads drew his bottle of beer and brought it down savagely on Peter's head. It broke with a loud report. Blood streamed down Peter's forehead and he sagged at the knees.

"That's wan for Razor King!" his opponent shouted. "Tell him Cameron did that tae ye! Cameron frae the Toll . . ."

But Isobel had flung herself in front of Peter's falling body. She saved him from the raised boot of an assailant, and, by that time – for this was a respectable hall and no gang rendezvous – there was a rush of young men to the rescue and the Plantation trio, cursing and swearing, were swept backwards by sheer weight of numbers.

The tallest, swinging his beer bottle, stood his ground until his feet were kicked from under him. The other two "flymen" made for the exit, but were overpowered before they reached it. The whole riot had scarcely lasted five minutes, and the manager of the hall, active and resolute for all the whisky that was in him, was in among the crowd with high, dominant voice and waving hands. The dancers fell back before him. The gangsters, overpowered and helpless, were tumbled into his office by many willing hands; the band, obedient to his gesture, struck up again and there were couples already dancing while Peter still lay stunned where he had fallen, with Isobel weeping and kneeling by his side.

Bobbie Hurley, obeying his natural instinct, ran over to his friend's brother. Lily followed close behind him. Her neat eyebrows were drawn together in a worried frown. She had nothing against Peter Stark. On the contrary, she knew that he was a steady young fellow of the sensible working-class type. And, of course, she knew perfectly well that he was quite blameless in this particular "rammy".

Knowing all this, she still wanted most particularly to keep out of all bother. She caught Bobbie's sleeve just as he was about to follow the young men who had picked Peter up and were carrying him into the office.

"Where are *you* gaun?" she whispered viciously. "I wish to Christ you wad be a little *manly*! Why can ye no' control yourself when anything happens?"

Bobbie turned angrily to face her.

"Hell!" said he, "it's young Peter Stark, Razor King's brother. I canny let him—"

"You canny do anything, Ah tell ye. Don't be plummy! You don't want to go and be a witness or anything like that, dae ye? Haven't we got enough tae look efter without being witnesses? Have some sense!"

Bobbie hesitated and his anger subsided.

"Maybe you're right," he conceded ungraciously, and allowed Lily to tug him to the other side of the hall.

They were dancing again to keep the diminished crowd together by the time the manager came back from the office and assured everybody that there was nothing to worry about. Police had arrived by this time. The bottles were taken away as evidence and the blood and glass swiftly cleaned from the floor. Peter was taken to the Royal Infirmary by ambulance, and Isobel went with him. He was not very badly hurt, though the surgeon put three stitches into his forehead, none too gently. The surgeon in the out-patient department was an overworked man with little sympathy to waste upon hooligans and their wounds.

Bobbie and Lily gave their second exhibition dance before the hall closed, and by that time the crowd was just as large and just as cheerfully in earnest as though nothing had happened. And Lily's smile was as dazzling as ever. It was not until the two of them were on their way home that she resumed her lecture.

"If I could only rely on you, Bobbie," she sighed, as they stood for a while on the stair-head in Bedford Street, "I'd be a happy dancer, believe me! It's things that crop up like they did tonight that test us. We've got to watch ourselves all the time or we'll never do any good."

He had his arm around her waist and their heads were close together, but he stood stiffly and sullenly away at this remonstrance.

"Tae hell!" he protested, "Ah did nothing out of place, Lily."

"No, Ah know you didn't, but if it hadny been for me, where wid ye have been now? That's what Ah'm askin' ye. Up in the Royal Infirmary likely, wi' your head split open. Or due to give evidence in court, wi' all the Plantation lads marking it up against you. That'd be a hellova fine advertisement for us! You're a grand dancer, Bobbie, and Ah'm hellova fond of ye, but you've got tae be more *manly*. That's all there is aboot it."

"Manly!" He knew what she meant well enough, and he grinned sourly. She meant that he had to put the dancing first all the time; that he had to assert himself; that he had to swallow scruples and, if necessary, cut adrift from old friends. And he knew that she was right. There was no other way to get on in the dancing world. His arm crept closer about her and his hand closed upon the thin silk that covered her firm young breast. She smiled and sighed and clung to him. Long and earnestly they talked of how they must stick together to get what they wanted out of life.

Both of them would have sworn – and so would young Peter – that they wanted something far different and better and finer than ever Razor King could aspire to. But, in fact, their individual ambitions were fundamentally common to every slummie who has any ambition at all. They wanted above everything else to escape; to live a little more cleanly and more spaciously; to dress better, to have more money to spend and to earn the consideration of their own world as being "out of the common", a cut above the crowd.

The affray in the dance hall had an influence, directly or indirectly, upon all their lives. It strengthened the determination of Bobbie and Lily to secure an engagement in one of the socially resplendent "palais de danse". It gratified Johnnie's sense of his own importance, since rival gangs do not wreak their vengeance on the brothers of unimportant men. And it set Peter definitely upon a new road.

He found, when he returned home with heavily bandaged head, that the report of the "rammy" had preceded him. His mother's concern was soon set at rest by his appearance; but Johnnie's attitude worried him a good deal. Razor King cared very little about Peter's broken head or his feelings. He was out to avenge the affront to himself. He would show the world that no-one could touch his brother and get away with it unscathed.

"Leave it tae me," he said loftily, "I'll pey the Plantation widoes (hooligans) for the smashing they gave ye."

Peter felt no gratitude for this assurance. On the contrary, he resented it and glowered at his brother, wanting to tell him so but afraid to do it. His one wish at that time was to avoid retaliations; to keep out of trouble, partly for his own sake and still more for Isobel's. Not that Peter was the kind of lad to take a bashing meekly; there was too much of his father's fighting blood in him for that, and, other things being equal, he would have lost no opportunity to get even with Cameron from the Toll. But he did *not* want to get involved in the gang feuds. Above all, he did not want to be known everywhere and always as Razor King's brother.

The McGilvery household seemed much better disposed to Peter after this affair. The old people knew that the fight was none of his making, and they felt that he had stood by "their Isa" as a good lad should, for she had made the most of the story and convinced them that Peter had saved her from a bashing. He began to go to tea with Isobel at her home and found himself made welcome. Being a little stand-offish and "superior", the McGilverys did not have many visitors and Peter brought a new interest to the house. But he knew very well that they would not have tolerated him there if they hadn't thought he was completely different from Razor King. Obviously, too, they were impressed because his employers kept his job open for him until he was able to return to work.

"It's just as well Ah could go back to them," he said one evening, "for a while, anyhow."

Isobel tossed her head and said she didn't know about that. She thought that there were jobs enough to be found for a clever fellow. Peter wasn't sure what she meant. It might be that she wanted him to be more ambitious, or it might be just a roundabout way of making her parents take his side. *They* hadn't any doubts about the matter. They thought it was all for the best that Peter still had his job in the big store near Glasgow Cross. And, being fairly shrewd, they knew that the firm must have thought well of his ability and keenness to get on. For workers are easy to get and employers don't go out of their way to keep a man unless he shows a profit.

Secretly they thought that even Peter would have found his place filled by another lad if the firm had realized that his brother was Razor King. All Gorbals knew it, of course, but outside the district Johnnie Stark was not yet notorious – nor even likely to be unless he committed a murder, and even the McGilverys did not rate Johnnie as a murderous type. But they wished Peter could escape his influence. If he was seriously courting their Isa, they thought they ought to help him to do so.

Isobel saw Peter down to the close-mouth that evening.

"You're feeling awright again noo?" she said.

"Ay, Ah'm feeling grand," he replied, "but Ah'll be marked on the crust aw the same. See!"

His fingers parted his thick hair to show an ugly scar. She nodded sympathetically.

"It doesny show if you keep your hair brushed over it that way," she consoled him, "an' maybe that's just as well. It's about the only thing we'll need tae take oot of Gorbals . . . in the end . . . when we're away thegither."

They smiled and kissed and parted. Peter went home triumphant and eager to take the first step towards the new career he was planning.

He found Johnnie at home.

"Hey, Peter," said Razor King, with unwonted amiability, "maybe it'll no' be sae lang before I get upsides with the Plantation widoes. There'll be naw screw-tops when *Ah* settle wi' them!"

He stuck his thumbs into his waistcoat with the words and Peter saw the weapons in his pockets. He frowned and made no reply. Soon he was left alone in the house with his mother.

"Ah've been thinking," he said to her, "that Ah might leave home for a while. Johnnie an' me don't get on thegither so awful well."

Then he told her that he and Isobel had been talking things over and that the McGilverys had suggested that he should come to them as a lodger.

Mrs Stark sighed and lifted the kettle with a hand that shook, for Peter was the favourite among all her children.

"If you think you're gaun to better yourself," she said in an expressionless voice, "you should go and stay wi' them. But you should be sure aw the same."

"Did ye hear what Johnnie said the noo, Mither?" he retorted. "Ah *am* sure. He's nae use to me. Ah'll have to go."

Mrs Stark got up from the table and bent above the stove. Her son could not see her face.

"Well, Peter," she said. "You'd better go."

CHAPTER VII

MARRIAGE AN' AW THAT

In work and out, the slum dwellers of Glasgow have always married young. In Gorbals, as elsewhere, girls are brought up in the belief that marriage is the natural destiny of woman. Moreover, any girl who remains single into the late twenties is classified automatically as one who "canny get a man". This is a reproach which few of them are strong-minded enough to ignore. Most of them feel their "inferiority" so acutely that they hasten to wed anybody obtainable, reckless of the consequences and definitely preferring a husband whom they despise or dislike to no husband at all. Even the street-walkers like to have a legal title to a wedding ring.

The young men can remain bachelors, if they choose, without any loss of respect, for obviously there is no whole man, drunkard, gangster, or shiftless idler though he be, who cannot find *some* lass ready to take him. But very few of them do remain single. They marry for love, or for the sake of a pretty face, or for social advancement, or, simply and crudely, to have a woman on the most economical terms.

Apart from all this, the lads and lasses alike are driven to marriage in the slums by sheer disgust of their own homes and desire to start afresh in a "hoose" of their own, roomy enough for two, though it be no better than a "single end". Married, they have babies in steady succession. If times are hard, they soon have to take in a lodger or two. In any event, before a dozen years have passed they have set up a home no whit different from the ones their parents made and soon their children begin to think of a similar escape from it.

Thus Razor King, proclaiming that he was "through with women", knew very well that before long he would be looking for a wife who would do him credit.

Thus Bobbie and Lily, dancing their way to affluence and public esteem, were delaying marriage only until their position seemed a little more secure. The delay was necessary because, once married, both took it for granted that a baby would arrive within the year and the dancing partnership would be necessarily interrupted for a while.

Thus Peter Stark and Isobel McGilvery, more soberly ambitious than any of their friends, better prepared to work and to save, considered only how long they would have to wait before they set up house together as man and wife.

And thus Gorbals, with its children swarming in and out of the tenements into the spacious streets that mock the squalor and the misery of the tall hives which line them!

Razor King began his courtship of Lizzie Ramsay some twelve months after his brother Peter had gone to live with the McGilverys. He was still out of work and still the acknowledged leader of the local gang. He had, indeed, added somewhat to his reputation as a fighter and, though he was drinking rather heavily, he kept in fair training and his muscles were hard and his body active and supple.

On that particular Thursday evening of 1924 Johnnie had left the open-air gymnasium in Glasgow Green and was on his way home when he met Lizzie Ramsay outside the "Coffin Building". Frazer's Hair Factory, which stands opposite St Luke's School and Chapel in Govan Street, Gorbals, is a brick building of three stories with a coffin-like bulge at the end nearest Commercial Road. Govan Street itself narrows into a bottle-neck to accommodate the bulge of the factory. Johnnie, walking along the street a few minutes after five o'clock, noticed that the red brick of the Coffin Building had warmed to a coppery glow in the sunset and the curved tramlines stretched ahead of him like streaks of gold. The rush of the tenement dwellers was over at that hour and, rounding the bulge, he overtook Lizzie Ramsay on her way home from work in a West End bakery.

By sight, at least, these two had known each other since childhood days, but socially there was something of a gap between them. Johnnie had always known that the Ramsays were "better class" than the Starks and he had not spoken to Lizzie more than half a dozen times since that evening, years before, when he rescued her and her fiddle from three young roughs in Cumberland Street.

Lizzie was well dressed for a working girl. She wore a hat and her green coat was of good material and fitted her well. A clean blouse was cut rather low at the neck and her long skirt concealed her legs that were her chief affliction in life. She could never forget her legs. Johnnie, leaving her after the rescue all those years before, had flung the one word "Bandy!" at her as he staggered away. She remembered them uncomfortably, but without bitterness because the taunt was so familiar.

He greeted her now with a cautious smile. His eyes appraised her and approved.

"Hullo, Lizzie!" said he.

"Hullo yourself," she laughed. "Are you no' in the jail yet?"

"Ah'm no' as well known as aw *that*, am I, Lizzie?"

He straightened himself and squared his shoulders as he asked the question. Far from being offended, he took her laughing enquiry as a compliment and hoped that she would make some further comment on his notoriety.

Lizzie pushed him playfully with her handbag.

"You're kidding you don't think so!" she laughed.

Johnnie wasn't sure how to take that. It might have been "cheek" or it might have been amiable banter. He glanced downwards at her skirt and she was instantly on the defensive. He laughed at her and she blushed hotly.

"You're no' trying to come it, are you?" said she. "Ah wasny expecting anything like that, Razor King."

The use of his "title" delighted him. It was significant. He took it as a tribute, coming from this girl who was, he felt, of superior stuff to himself though he would not have admitted it for the world.

"Ah wasny trying on anything," said he, flushing a little in his turn. "It was yoursel' that jumped to conclusions, so it was."

Both now felt more at their ease. To Lizzie the fact that Razor King was well made and straight of limb mattered even more than his notoriety in Gorbals. At that time she was definitely on the look out for a young man. She wanted to marry and, morbidly sensitive about her own legs, she was haunted by the fear of having many children who would have rickets and such misshapen limbs that they wouldn't be able to go about unaided.

"You'll be just getting home?" said Johnnie, breaking a silence and anxious to make conversation.

"Ay, that's right. I wasny working late or anything. Where were you making for? Home, too, eh?"

Johnnie nodded and fumbled with his muffler, wishing that he were better "togged up".

"I wear a collar and tie at night," said he, defiantly and truthfully. "Ay, an' Ah've got a brown suit, too – a new one wi' dee-bee lapels on the jacket . . ."

"That's right. Ah've seen you wi' it on."

"Have you, Lizzie? Well, where are ye gaun the night, eh? Out wi' some fellow likely? Or no. This is Thursday, winching night, is it no'?"

It was Thursday, and by immemorial tradition young Glasgow goes courting on that night of the week more than on any other. Lizzie glanced up at Razor King and considered him with a slow, half-shy scrutiny. She liked his square shoulders and she admired the jaunty arrogance of his carriage. She looked away and her long lashes drooped.

"Ah wis just gaun oot wi' ma china, Mary Halliday," she confessed. "You know her?"

He shook his head impatiently in a gesture which was not so much denial as rejection of an unimportant question.

"What about coming out wi' *me* the night?" he said softly. "We'll go to a place up the toon if you like?"

"A place? What place, Razor King?"

He hesitated. Glasgow bred and born, he knew very little of the city on the other side of the river. It was very seldom that he left Gorbals itself.

"Ah'm no' caring," he said. "Wherever you say."

Lizzie was minded to laugh at him, for she understood his difficulty. She knew Glasgow far better than he did and felt that this gave her a superiority, but she was tactful enough not to let this appear in her answer.

"I'll meet you at the Bank corner at half-past seven, then," she smiled, pointing with her handbag along to the corner of Govan Street and Crown Street. He knew the corner well enough but his glance followed her own to where a small knot of people waited on the pavement for a tramcar.

"I'll be there," he nodded, "an I'll have on a new tie!"

Lizzie thought his smile attractive; it was half apologetic and half defiant and wholly boyish for the moment.

"Ah'll have to tell my china Ah'll not be out with her the night, all the same," said she.

He shrugged his shoulders and his lips pursed into a silent whistle. They stood together for some moments longer, neither of them knowing what to say.

"Well," said Johnnie at length. "I'll away along to Crown Street now . . ."

"An' I'll away along to Mathieson Street . . ."

They parted with no other farewell, but looking back

91

at each other more than once with glances that were almost apprehensive.

Johnnie was no less nervous than Lizzie herself. He wasn't sure how he would get on with her. He was a little afraid that he would not do himself justice in some unfamiliar district of the city. But he was elated that she had promised to go with him and he began to swagger in his walk as he neared home and imagined the effect his announcement was likely to produce.

His mother and sisters were all in when he arrived and he did not keep them waiting for his news.

"Ah'm goin' out wi' a real toff the night, people!" he said importantly, throwing his cap on the open iron bed that now stood just behind the front door. "Ah'm going up the toon wi' Lizzie Ramsay from Mathieson Street, her that works in the bakery – the well-dressed one an' aw!"

There was a little chorus of exclamations from the sisters and even Mrs Stark sat forward in her chair with an air of pleased excitement.

"Ay," Johnnie continued. "Ah'm just efter meeting her at the Coffin Building yonder and I made it up that we're to go out thegither the night. Where's aw the good ties and aw that, Mither?"

"When have you to meet her?" asked one of his sisters with a note of envying admiration in her voice. She had a boy of her own, but her Angus had no class to recommend him nor even a reputation in the gangs.

"Half-past seven at the Bank corner," replied her brother briskly, and stepped across the room to where his mother was sorting the contents of a drawer for his ties.

All the family, with the exception of Mrs Stark, was getting ready to go out at this hour, but the girls interrupted their own preparations to watch Johnnie adorn himself. He shouldered them good-naturedly out of his way and drove his youngest sister from the sink before she had rinsed her face of soap. Washed, collared and tied, he put on the brown jacket with dee-bee lapels and then placed the razors ostentatiously in his waistcoat pockets. His sisters gazed at him with the frankest admiration, but Mrs Stark looked hastily away from his "weapons" and, walking across to the dingy window, stood there looking patiently down into the street, her wrinkled face expressionless and her mind busy with anxious, worried thoughts. She would have liked Johnnie to be out of the gangs and yet, living in that home in that society, even Mrs Stark had a kind of fearful pride in her son's reputation. He was a bad lad, but at least he was out of the ordinary; no rank-and-file gangster but a real "Razor King".

Satisfied at last with his own appearance and not a little gratified by the impression he had created in his family, Johnnie left the house at last to keep his tryst. A perfect shout of triumph went up as the front door closed behind him, for his sisters were elated to know that Johnnie was courting at last.

"Lizzie Ramsay, eh!" said the eldest girl. "Did you ever hear the like o' that, Mother? Her father's commissionaire at the Regal Palace. Three pounds a week he'll be getting – mebbe three pound ten – no less. It's grand news for us aw, an' it'll make a big stir."

"What like is this Lizzie Ramsay?" asked Mrs Stark. "I canny well mind the lassie."

"Yes, you do; you mind her well, Mother. Her that went to the schule wi' Cousin Maggie – wi' the pigtails and the bandy legs an' aw! Ay, an' I widny have Lizzie's legs not for aw the money her old man's making, so I wouldn't."

"She canna help her legs, poor lass," said Mrs Stark with a faint smile, "An' if Johnnie's no caring it's no' oor business. Away oot wi' ye aw: it's no' a night to stay ben wi' your boys waiting on ye and news tae tell them."

The news of the momentous rendezvous was received

with scarcely less excitement, though of a somewhat different kind, in Lizzie Ramsay's home in Mathieson Street. Well doing though the Ramsays were esteemed to be, their two rooms and kitchen housed a family of seven, and the picture palace commissionaire, then on duty, found it hard enough to provide for his large family and his chronic thirst without stinting either the one or the other. Lizzie's brief period of violin lessons had ended after her mother's fifth confinement and her wages from the bakery had become a considerable item in the total family budget.

Though the oldest of the family, she was neither the best-looking nor even the best "put on". Her second sister, Martha, was a distinctly pretty girl who spent all that she had to spend on clothes. Nevertheless Lizzie looked smart enough in her red dress, and her sisters, making their toilets in the back room, saw from her face that something unusual had happened. With seeming indifference they asked Lizzie whether she was going out with her friend Mary Halliday as usual, or whether the two of them would be joining the rest of the crowd of Mathieson Street and Adelphi Street girls.

Lizzie studied her own reflection in the swivel mirror over the dressing-chest by the window which looked out into the courtyard.

"At half-past seven," she said deliberately, "Ah'm gaun out wi' Razor King from Crown Street. I met him at the Coffin Building and we made it up to go up the toon. He doesn't know very much about the toon, but I'll show him about. An' we're gaun tae enjoy ourselves tae."

The sisters were too astonished to make any immediate comment. One of them asked what Mary Halliday would do about it and whether she knew.

"I'll let Mary know when she comes up and she can let the rest of them know," said Lizzie, trying to speak calmly. She was much more agitated and excited than she wished to appear, but, whatever her family might think, her mind was quite made up not to let slip this opportunity of going out with such a cavalier.

"You must be hard up," sneered Martha at supper, "for somebody to go out with if you have to pick up the likes of Johnnie Stark."

"Mebbe Ah am; mebbe Ah'm no', but Ah'm no' jealous of *your* boy friends, Matt, Ah can tell you that!"

Mary Halliday, a girl of twenty-two, sallow, but well-built and not ill-looking, called at a quarter-past seven and was immediately informed in chorus of Lizzie's date with Razor King.

"An' what wull I do?" she demanded indignantly. "Go out on my tod (alone)?"

"Be sensible, for Jesus' sake," retorted Lizzie sharply.

"Oh, sensible!" railed Mary, looking round for sympathy. "What do you make of that, eh?"

"Don't be daft awthegither, Merry. It's only just for this evening. Ah'll be seeing you again all right an' then we might baith manage to get a click somewhere, eh?"

With her hands clasped over her handbag in front of her, Mary looked at Lizzie suspiciously and Lizzie hurried on, hoping to escape argument and further protest.

"Come on an' see me away, Merry. I'll no keep you long."

Rather sullenly Mary nodded and followed Lizzie out on to the landing. Half-way down the stairs to the narrow close Lizzie paused, caught Mary by the elbow and spoke to her with earnest impressiveness.

"As sure as Ah'm going down they sterrs wi' you, Merry, I didn't know I was going out with Razor King until I met him at the Coffin Building alang there. I was all put about when I met him. I didn't know he was such a nice fella, Merry."

Mary became more cordial as she listened to this

explanation which was half an apology, and she began to think of Johnnie Stark with less resentment.

"Ah wull say," she agreed, "that he never uses the razors on lassies. Mebbe he's no sae bod. But better you than me, Lizzie, for aw that. Ah would take my time if I was you."

At the close-mouth they stood talking together for a few moments, and then Lizzie hurried off, waving a hand in farewell and looking quite pretty in her flushed excitement. Mary Halliday stared after her, and in her heart she was jealous of her friend's triumph.

That evening was the beginning of a curious court-ship, sedate and cautious in its early stages, never very romantic, and always calculating on both sides. Johnnie and Lizzie met on the Bank corner almost on the stroke of half-past seven, exchanged reserved greetings, and looked round about them uncomfortably at the other young people standing at the corner with them and waiting for someone or something to turn up. They felt that they were being watched and that their meeting would be talked about after they had gone on.

"What do you say if we cross over the street," said Johnnie, "and get a car up the toon, eh?"

"All right, then," Lizzie agreed, "whatever you say."

Both of them pretended not to be aware of the glances that followed them, but they were both flushed by the time they had climbed to the upper deck of a blue, Botanic Gardens tram.

"There are times," observed Johnnie, staring straight ahead of him, "when nobody'll look at anybody else at aw. When there's a rammy going on I've noticed there's hellova few people looking for anything. Ay, they're troubled to know where to look then."

Lizzie nodded. She understood that he meant to tell her that they had no cause to be worried about the curiosity of a mob of nobodies. She felt that they were nobodies in comparison with Razor King and herself.

She paid the fares happily for the Union Street and Argyle Street corner, the busiest crossing in all Glasgow.

"I like walking about here, do you no'?" smiled Johnnie as they strolled up Union Street.

"I like it the night, anyway," she said, returning his smile, and both of them felt much more at ease.

But they did not walk arm-in-arm. They were ashamed to do that because it was "low class". They passed other couples with linked arms and felt their own superiority. Entering Sauchiehall Street, Lizzie shot a glance at her companion and said primly: "You can take my arm when we become better acquainted, eh?"

"I wouldny mind," Johnnie replied, but he made no motion to anticipate this privilege. Indeed, he was well pleased with himself and Lizzie for behaving so much better than the ordinary "scruff" of Glasgow.

In Argyle Street they turned into a picture house and decided to take seats in the balcony. Lizzie handed Johnnie the money to pay for both. It looked better for him to pay but it did not occur to either of them that there was anything unusual in this arrangement. Nor was there. Among the poorer citizens of Glasgow there is no false shame in such matters. Man or girl, the one who has the money pays, and, since unemployment settled upon the city the girl's purse is often better filled than the man's pocket.

There was no love-making in the darkness of the kinema. Simply enough Lizzie slipped her own hand into Johnnie's and she shared a packet of hard sweets with him as the screen-play worked through to the inevitable close-up. They stopped until the programme ended at ten-thirty, and then walked back together towards Lizzie's home. It was dark by that time and the river was sombre and slow and quiet beneath the bridge. But they were not interested in the Clyde, though it had created the very city they lived in and spewed the slums from its bed like so much mud.

At last they came to Mathieson Street, walking very slowly and saying little.

"It's a fine quiet close this," said Johnnie appreciatively as they entered it. "Ours is more rory!"

"Oh, yours is no' so bad as aw that," Lizzie replied consolingly.

They had stopped at the foot of the stair, half-way through the close, that led up to her apartment.

"There's no use us going up the stair the first night, is there?" she pleaded softly.

"Well . . ." he hesitated, "whatever you say, Lizzie."

"Ah'll see you on Saturday night then at eight?"

Lizzie's tone was warm with relief and gratitude. She held out her right hand, her handbag under her arm. Johnnie took it with an embarrassed laugh.

"Ah hope you mean that, Liz," said he, "for Ah've took a fancy tae you."

"Of course I mean it . . . You can kiss me before you go, Razor King!"

But they shook hands first as though to seal a bargain. Then, unhurriedly, Johnnie took the girl into his embrace and kissed her lingeringly. He left her with a little laugh of satisfaction and excitement.

It never occurred to Johnnie, walking homewards with his hands deep in his pockets, that this new affair with Lizzie Ramsay could end like any of his other affairs. Though no word of love had passed between them he knew, and she knew, that marriage was to be the outcome of their friendship. Nothing else, he realized, would satisfy a girl of Lizzie's class, nor could he, for his part, hope to do better for himself. He thought deliberately that, except for her bandy legs, she was well enough for a wife, and he was glad that she had so good a job in the bakery. He hoped that when they set up house together they could make something of a show. And it occurred to him that it might be almost worth while to look for work again.

The courtship might have continued for a good many weeks on the basis of an undeclared understanding if events outside their calculations had not stirred both of them to decisions. Some weeks after their first evening out, Johnnie and Lizzie met again at the Bank corner, went up the town to a picture house once more, and emerged very happily, his arm about her waist.

He let go of her as they came into the lighted street, but bent to her ear and whispered: "Lizzie, it's been the best Saturday night Ah've had for a hellova long time!"

"It's the best Ah've had tae for a while an' aw!" she agreed smiling.

Loitering at the corner there was a group of young men hoping to get off with girls who might, or might not, have given them some encouragement in the darkness of the hall. Some of them had already "clicked", and three in particular, rather flash young fellows with their girls on their arms, stared at Johnnie and Lizzie in a somewhat marked and contemptuous way. Presumably they thought that he had picked her up in the cinema, just as they had picked up their own partners, and they glanced from Lizzie to Johnnie with smiles of unmistakable disparagement. Not a word was said, and yet no words could have expressed the sneer more clearly. For Lizzie was very smartly turned out in her green coat and Johnnie had neglected to put on his one whole suit that night, and wore a muffler instead of a collar and tie.

"Don't you bother with them," whispered Lizzie in an urgent undertone. "They're on about your paraffin (appearance) and aw that, but I don't want any battling, mind!"

Razor King was flushed with mortification. He knew that the three young men who were smiling so hatefully were no better class than himself even if they were a bit better "put on" and even if they did wear coloured collars. On the other hand, he did not really want to fight that evening for he was looking forward to having Lizzie all to himself on the stair-head in Mathieson Street. He scowled and quickened his pace.

"Aw right, Liz," he said. "Ah've the two weapons in my pockets, but if you're no' standing for it, Ah'll let them go."

If those three young men had known the reputation of their adversary they would have been glad enough to let him go on his way. They might have done so even now, thinking him just an ordinary fellow, but one of the three could not resist a final jeer.

"Got the crap on (wind up)?" he said, in a clear voice that ended on a laugh.

No sooner were the words uttered than Razor King wrenched himself free from Lizzie's detaining grasp. The slightest challenge to his courage was more than he could endure. His razors appeared in his hands as though by magic and the steel flashed under the electric lights of the picture-house doorway. He rushed at his three opponents with desperate ferocity. Their girl companions screamed and fled and the young men themselves hastily gave ground.

Lizzie Ramsay did not abide the issue of that fight. She ran towards Stockwell Street and then over Stockwell Bridge as fast as her legs would carry her.

But Johnnie was in the thick of the battle.

"Ah'm no mug!" he shouted, as his razor laid open the face of one of his opponents from cheekbone to chin. His movements were incredibly swift. He fought with two hands at once, slashing like lightning at faces, hands and necks.

No-one interfered. The small crowd broke up, each man and woman eager to escape an affray among hooligans.

Razor King had marked all three of his enemies before the fight had lasted two minutes. Their bare fists were no defence against the terrible weapons. They could not even use their feet effectively in their wild efforts to guard their faces. They shouted and cursed and the blood flowed in streams.

The tumult was becoming dangerous and the policemen came running with drawn batons. Johnnie leaped into his last attack and embedded one razor in the face of a young man who collapsed in the doorway of the picture house. He slashed out with the other razor and then threw the weapon away and ran like a hare between a double line of stationary trams. The police were pounding at his feet, but he turned into Glassford Street well ahead of them and, running easily, soon outdistanced all pursuit, dropping into a walk at last in the Candleriggs. He was unhurt and unmarked and almost bursting with exultation. For he had tackled three hooligans unaided and all three of them would have to go to the infirmary – stretcher cases he believed.

But his elation had subsided by the time he reached Mathieson Street and he was a little nervous as he turned into Lizzie's close.

She was waiting for him and ran to him with a little cry. He said nothing until she had satisfied herself that he himself was not hurt.

"Ah'm hellova glad you skinned out yon time," said he, at last. "There's naebody here anyway, Lizzie."

"What road did you come? Round by Glasgow Cross or what?"

"That's the way I came, all right . . . I don't know any other way any too well. But you can take it from me Ah'm gonny get in touch with this city. How did you get away yourself, Lizzie?"

"Over Stockwell Bridge. What did you do tae they three hooligans, Razor King?"

He told her, frankly and not without pride.

"They'll no' laugh so easy for a while," he concluded. "An' you'll see that this rammy'll go all over the Gorbals, Lizzie."

"How do you mean, 'go all over the Gorbals'?"

101

"I mean that there was bound to be some Gorbals people about yonder at the time and, although they hadn't the heart to say anything or do anything, they'll have the badness to spread it all right, so's to get my name up an' aw that."

"If any of them should spread it till it reaches the ears of some of them in the bakery where I work, it might be a bad day for me."

She spoke anxiously and Johnnie looked at her with a new concern. He did not think it at all likely that any of his victims either could or would give him away to the police, but the risk of Lizzie's reputation at the bakery being damaged by his notoriety was more serious.

"Aw, the hell!" he said at last consolingly. "Ah wouldnae worry for that, Lizzie. Come on up the stair for a while an' we'll talk it over."

Lizzie hesitated. She looked well round the close-mouth to see that they were alone and still hung back.

"Aw, come on, Liz! To-morrow's Sunday, isn't it? Well, then . . ."

"Well then . . . Ah'll come, but keep quiet, mind!"

They halted on a landing half-way up the stair and said no word until Johnnie had his arms round her waist and his face pressed closely to hers. Then they began to talk in whispers.

"It's no good kidding, Liz," he murmured. "This is sure to go all over the place, like I telt you. I lost the weapons, too. But it's you I'm thinking on. It would be hard lines if you're to lose your job through me, wouldn't it?"

"I should think it would. You're no working . . ."

"I haveny toiled for two years, but I wouldny mind going to the toil again if I was married to you, Liz. Do you like me well enough to marry me as soon as we could?"

He hugged her more tightly as he asked the question and she kissed him eagerly.

"You know I like you fine," said she, "but what about the dough? Ah've only got fifteen quid saved up."

"That's about all we'd need. Ah might get a job, too, through time. Ah'm no' sure that it isn't kind of plummy to go to the toil, but Ah would do it for you."

"Would you, Johnnie?" she said happily. "But Ah'm no' caring. Ah'll marry you whether or no . . . Aw the same, I would invite a lot of people to the wedding so as to let everybody see that we're not as hard up as aw that, eh?"

"Sure," he agreed enthusiastically. "We'll have about a hundred at it, Liz, and Ah'll leave you to look efter the money and aw that too . . ."

She laughed at that and they began to make arrangements for their next meeting and for Razor King to take her to Crown Street to meet his family. Soon they ceased to talk and were satisfied to cling and kiss.

On the Sunday, the day after this marriage had been arranged, a crowd of some fifty young men and women surrounded Johnnie and Lizzie in Adelphi Street and one among them, the spokesman of the party, formally presented Johnnie with a pair of new razors, sharp blades open and flashing.

He accepted them magnificently, brandishing them in the sunshine before he stuck them jauntily into his empty waistcoat pockets.

Loudly the crowd cheered the Razor King, who stood triumphantly among them with Lizzie, blushing and exalted, on his arm.

103

CHAPTER VIII

"THE LIKE OF THEM"

An understanding and reasoned contempt for one's
neighbours, together with a fiercely *un*reasoning conviction of personal superiority, is not an uncommon
phenomenon of the slum mind. Habit and custom may
blind a man to the squalor of his home, but they
may not prevent him from sniffing disdainfully when he
enters a friend's "hoose" no more sordid, dirty and over-
crowded than his own. Perhaps there is, all the time, a
subconscious rebellion against conditions which are outwardly taken for granted. And, as there is no escape from
these conditions except by imagination, many a tenement
dweller, particularly before the years have withered his
hopes, likes to think, and does, in fact, believe that he
has something in him – some special gift in mind or body
– to make him different from his fellows. He is always
hoping, like Micawber, for something to turn up. In face
of all evidence to the contrary, he is still confident that
the day will come when his superiority will compel
recognition.

It follows that society in the tenements is graded far
more narrowly than in the outside world. One street may
be definitely "better class" than another and not such
good class as a third. Families that have two rooms look
down upon those that live in a "single end". Immense
importance attaches to clothes, for, other things being
equal, young people who are "well put on" can always
command the envious admiration of the poorly dressed.
"Education" also counts for a great deal, but the word
is not given its proper meaning. In the Gorbals, for

instance, the tendency is to look up to people who do not habitually speak the broad Glasgow dialect. Their "education" consists in certain refinements of speech and avoidance of slang. Just as the uneducated Englishman is somewhat impressed by the superior "Oxford accent", so, but in much greater degree, is the slum dweller impressed by the refined speech of a fellow slummie.

The advent of Bolshevism in distant Russia has had many diverse and unexpected effects in other countries. It has, for instance, crystallized into a single word the tenement dwellers' vague aspirations to social advancement. "Bourgeois" is that word. In the Clyde Valley and in South Wales and in the Durham coalfields and in all densely populated areas of extreme poverty, Communism has spread like a contagion or a Holy War. But in Glasgow at all events it has spread chiefly from mouth to mouth as a grand, but ill-comprehended word. It is a slogan and not a faith, for there is no faith among the masses in the slums. Any revolutionary preaching the class war, promising, that is to say, the overthrow of the "haves" for the benefit of the "have-nots", is assured of an approving audience. But most of them do not care a damn for his politics and have scant faith in his sincerity. They may vote "Red", but that is because, whatever happens, *they* have nothing to lose. They may curse the "bourgeoisie", but their personal dream of heaven on earth is to be numbered in its ranks.

And so it happens that, except among the real "politicians" and enthusiasts, the secret ambition of the slums is to present a "bourgeois" front to the world.

Young Peter Stark, doing fairly well at his work and living now with the McGilverys, who were distinctly "better class" than his own family, would have declared himself a Communist without hesitation and yet nothing pleased him more than to be taken for a "bourgeois". He wore a soft felt hat and twisted the brim jauntily in the "bourgeois" manner. He was cultivating a small moustache chiefly because he thought it would give him the desired "bourgeois" appearance. He never went out without collar and tie. And, though he was really better educated and more widely read than most of his companions, he was not truly interested in any possible reorganization of society itself, but only in his own escape from the unsuccessful poverty-stricken masses of poor fools who constituted "the proletariat".

And he classed his elder brother among them although he knew that Johnnie was "ambitious" like himself. It was certainly better to be a "Razor King" than just one of the gang, but Peter felt sure that it wouldn't lead to anything worth while. It might, on the other hand, prejudice his own chances to have a brother who was too notorious, and so Peter kept out of Johnnie's way and seldom looked in upon his own family in Crown Street.

Thus it happened that he learned of Johnnie's official engagement to Lizzie Ramsay, not from his mother or sisters, but from Martha Ramsay, who met him by chance one Saturday evening in Argyle Street. Peter, very smart in brown coat and soft felt hat, stood on the kerb near the Central Station Bridge with an evening newspaper under his arm. From time to time his fingers went to his upper lip to caress the budding moustache. He was thinking that people might easily mistake him for a good class office worker, even a bank clerk.

Martha Ramsay herself, who knew him only by sight, was immediately impressed as she came towards him by his complete difference from Razor King. She thought that Peter, at all events, would be a brother-in-law to be proud of. She stopped for a moment to pat her hair and smooth her blouse. Then she came up to him. He did not see her and she lightly touched his arm.

"Excuse me," she murmured, "but I just wondered if you'd heard that your brother and our Lizzie are winchin' (courting)?"

Peter looked round in some surprise, straightened

himself, and then raised the downward-curving brim of his hat the merest trifle. Martha was further impressed by this cultured acknowledgement of her greeting.

Peter had not taken in what she said, but he recognized Martha at once, said "Hullo!" and smiled pleasantly.

"Ah was just asking you," Martha repeated, "whether you'd heard that your brother and our Lizzie are going with one another?"

He frowned and tried to hide his astonishment. For he was astonished. It had not occurred to him that Johnnie would ever fly so high, though he knew that he – Peter – was socially on a level with the Ramsays, he was equally well aware that Johnnie was not.

"No," he said after a moment's hesitation. "I hadn't heard. Since I went to live in Rutherglen Road, I don't often go to see them in Crown Street."

Martha searched his eyes and saw that he was telling the truth. She thought how well he spoke, and she didn't wonder in the least that he was inclined to keep away from his family.

"It's right enough all the same," she went on. "What's more, it looks as if they're going to get married soon and get a single apartment, somewhere in Govan Street, I think."

Her own English was now carefully studied and her manner a little prim. In spite of himself, Peter flushed and felt nervously in his coat pocket for a cigarette.

"I don't suppose," he said deliberately, "your family'll care too much for the like of Johnnie, eh?"

"Oh well—" Martha broke off and turned scarlet. He had completely spiked her guns by this frankness and now she was more embarrassed than he.

He lit a cigarette, broke the used match and threw it away. Then he looked at her and laughed sympathetically.

"Johnnie and I," he said, "don't see very much of each other, but he's well enough in his own way. You see, I'm

107

not getting on so badly where I am now and I'll soon be married myself, likely, and living outside the Gorbals."

Martha was pleased to hear that. Away from Razor King, Peter would not only make a most presentable brother-in-law, but she could already picture herself visiting him and his wife with her own young man.

"I like to hear of people getting on," she said with warm friendliness, "for I'm one of the lucky ones, too, that doesn't know what idle set (unemployment) is."

Peter was interested. He asked her where she was working and she told him volubly of her work in the big cigarette factory, of the bonus system there and of what some of the girls did with their few pounds in March and September of each year, leaving it to be understood that she didn't waste her money in the same way.

"I'm only getting thirty-five shillings a week in the meantime," said Peter, giving confidence for confidence, "but that's *only* for the meantime, believe me! Soon I'll be doing better than that."

He was doing better already. He was earning two pounds five, not one pound fifteen, but it was characteristic of him at that time to say he earned less than he did, where other young men of the working-class would usually boast of a few shillings more than their pay packets actually contained. For one thing, Peter didn't want anybody but his sweetheart, Isobel McGilvery, to know his private affairs. And, for another, he liked to feel he had something in reserve. Before they parted, Martha was much more reconciled to the prospect of her sister's marriage to Johnnie.

As Peter climbed the stairs to the McGilverys' room-and-kitchen flat his mind was busy, not with his brother's approaching marriage, but rather with the possibility of his own early marriage to Isobel. Without realizing it, he was jealous of Johnnie. It vexed him to think of his elder brother, living cheerfully on the rates and not hiding his opinion that most people who worked were fools for their pains, should be able to set up house with *his* girl just when he wanted to, while he, Peter, who was toiling and saving, had to wait to marry Isobel. But did they have to wait? Peter was resentfully saying "no" to his own question as he opened the door on the landing with the check key he was now entitled to use.

Isobel was in the kitchen with her father and mother, and Peter, just as pleased as any other "slummie" to be the bearer of tidings, good or ill, paused in the doorway to make his announcement effective.

"I heard from Martha Ramsay," he informed them all with an air of calm unconcern, "that that brother of mine is going to marry her sister, Lizzie – the one that works in the bakery."

There was a gasp of astonishment followed by an excited and gratifying buzz of questions. Peter retailed all that he had heard, offering no comment.

At length Mr John McGilvery, a slim man of medium height, whose baldness was emphasized by his black moustache, put down the newspaper he had been reading and looked over the top of his spectacles at his daughter's young man.

"Well," he said deliberately, "I hope it will be for the good of yon brother of yours if he does get married. In any case it canny do him much harm."

Isobel's father considered himself a politician and a staunch member of the Labour Party. Actually he took far more interest in football than in politics and knew vastly more about it, but he liked to talk about "improving the status" of the working man because that contributed to his own sense of superiority. Now he insisted on reading extracts from a speech by J. H. Thomas, declaring, moreover, that the railwaymen had never had an abler leader.

"Maist of the working men, Peter," he observed sententiously, "are no good for themselves withoot a good man tae speak for them and get them the best conditions, an' aw that. If you ever get into a good poseeshion, Peter, you'll find out that unless men are organized they're the lowest creatures on God's earth. You mebbe know that as it is?"

Now John McGilvery was no more than a working man himself and of working-class stock, but he was entirely without affectation in this contempt of his fellow-workers and of their mentality. He saw nothing odd about his attitude and neither did Peter. But the younger man was a little bored.

"Speaking for myself," he replied, sniffing a yawn, "I'm going to be my own leader. I'm no' goin' to wait for any man to help *me*: I'm goin' to help myself."

The brothers Stark did not meet until shortly before the wedding and then only by chance. Peter was paying one of his rare visits home, chiefly to see his mother. He did not expect to find any of the others indoors at three o'clock in the afternoon, and it was merely a business errand that had given him the opportunity to visit Crown Street at such an hour of a working day.

It happened, however, that Mrs Stark was away at a neighbour's house, called there urgently to lend a hand until the arrival of a midwife. And Peter found his brother in sole possession.

Johnnie, his waistcoat undone and his hair rumpled, was sprawling on the shake-down by the window. He had been drinking heavily that forenoon, and now, after his sleep, he was surly sober. Peter was oddly and suddenly embarrassed to know how to greet him, but he was spared the trouble of finding a conversational opening. His brother got up, scowled and nodded, and then walked without a word into the kitchen, there to sluice his head beneath the tap. He came back, towel in hand, and with something like a grin on his lips.

"So you're here, Pete," he began. "It's a pure treat for the likes of us to see ye these days. And how is it you're

110

no' toilin'? You'll be takin' a day off likely, or mebbe they've made you general manager by now and you c'n just please yourself?"

It was hard to tell, either from voice or manner, whether Johnnie was merely jesting or whether there was a sneer behind the jest. He stood there, very solid and strong, with the black hair still wet on his bullet head, the flannel shirt wide open at his bronzed throat, and that little half-grin on his lips. Peter stared back at him with the odd mixture of hatred, defiance and admiration which he had always felt for his elder brother. His hand rose to finger his tie, a trick of his when he was nervous, and he broke into a laugh that he hoped sounded natural.

"You're lookin' grand," Johnnie went on evenly, "collar and tie and aw! You should have said you were coming. The lassies wid have stayed in for ye, nae doot. And Ah wid have bin in ma paraffin, tae. Ah widnae be surprised if the Donaldson woman wid have put off bairnin' for a wee while so that Mither cud be here tae greet ye instead of helpin' to bring another breadsnapper intae the world."

"Aw, to hell with your kiddin', Johnnie! I was just out from the warehouse to see a customer for Mr Morgan, and being not far from here I thought I wid look in to see Mither before I went back. So she's away to the Donaldson woman? There's some will never learn sense. Eight of a family already and she forty-four or five if she's a day . . . She should ask some of the lassies what tae do to stop accidents, or mebbe how to poison that drunken old man of hers."

Johnnie began to rub his hair vigorously with his towel and he replied at jerky intervals.

"Education, Peter – we're no' aw so educated as you. You'll be for labour these days, mebbe – socialism by slow degrees – more schooling for the kids – an' less kids for the schools – what wey should the workin' classes have families they canny afford? I know – dumb brutes

111

like yon Donaldson – folk who havenae the sense or the guts tae hold a respectable job – only the one pleasure in life, breeding fodder for the capitalist cannons. Oh, ay! Ah've heard it aw. Ah can almost talk the language."

"If Ah'm anything," his brother retorted, "Ah'm a Communist, but Ah'm no' interested in politics at all. For all I care Donaldson and the like of him can go on havin' kids till he's played out. I'm only saying I wouldny be for having a big family myself."

"No? Well, wait till you're married and then we'll see."

"Sure. There's plenty time. No' sae much for you though, Johnnie, from what they tell me. I hear it's all fixed for you to marry Lizzie Ramsay in a week or two from now.'

"Who telt ye?" Johnnie asked the question with a scowl.

"I heard it first from Martha Ramsay a week last Saturday."

"Did you? An' she wid have been prood tae gi'e ye the glad news, mebbe. Her sister – one o' the Ramsays o' Mathieson Street – merrite tae Razor King! And what did ye say to her, Peter? Did ye tell her ye were no' seein' so much of the family nowadays? Did ye make it clear that there's two kinds of Starks – yours and mine?"

In spite of himself, Peter felt the colour rising to his cheeks, for the sneer came perilously near the truth.

"I told her," he said crisply, "that I was glad. I said it wid likely be a fine thing for you both and that she would do well to make up her mind to it."

"That was hellova nice of you. An' whit were you thinkin' yourself? Mebbe you were wunnerin' how such a fool as that brither o' yours ever came to get such a good-class bit stuff as Lizzie, eh? An' thinkin' it wid be like his bliddy nerve to set up hoose when he canny hope for a job? Ay, an' walkin' back to your fine friends, throwin' a chest an' saying, 'By Christ, Ah'm glad Ah'm no like him mysel'?"

"What's the good of talking that way, Johnnie? Is it my fault you an' me take different roads? Besides, you're wrong. Ah *am* glad you're tae be married. Ah'm no caring one way or the other whether you toil or whether you don't. An' I wid have telt Martha, if she hadny understood without the telling, that Lizzie is no' getting the worst o' the bargain."

"What does that mean?" said the other ominously.

"Nothing; except that Razor King could take his pick of many a lass in Gorbals."

"Mebbe that's what you meant. And mebbe it's no'. But let me tell *you* something, Peter lad. You think I'm Razor King and can never be anything else. You think you're hellova clever and I'm a mug. Well, there's more than one kind of mug. I've seen your kind before – plenty of them, likely fellas, goin' to toil every day, kissin' the boss's backside when he throws them a good word; readin' books and newspapers; winchin' brainy bit of stuffs wi' good clothes over a duff figure; keepin' aff the booze, talkin' and walkin' and dressin' and mebbe spewin' like a bliddy bourgeois, and dead sure, every one of them, that they're going to get on in the world.

"Ah'm no' blamin' you; Ah'm sorry for you. What happens to them aw? They get married and they have kids. An' the wages doesny grow with the family. An' they take to drink a little later instead of sooner. An' the shop shuts or the yard shuts down or there's a bliddy strike. An' there they go, back to the dung heap, haudin' up the street corners, drawin' their money from the parish, an' keepin' awa oot of the hoose all day, awa frae the auld wife's tongue and the kids that go crawlin' and messin' aroon the floor."

Johnnie paused for breath. He had spoken with a queer gathering passion not directed so much at his brother as at life itself, and Peter, who had never heard him so eloquent, was too surprised to interrupt.

113

"That's what all your toil will bring ye," the elder brother resumed. "That and nothing else. Ah may be a mug, Peter, but Ah'm no such a bliddy mug as that. The ones that win are no' the toilers. You c'n use your brains. Leave me my weapons an' I'll finish far ahead of you. You think you're daein' fine now with your two-three pound a week while I've nothing but the buroo. But let me tell you, Mither sees more o' my money than she does of yours!"

"That be damned!" shouted Peter angrily. "What you give her after you've paid for your booze widny pay for your keep."

"You're a liar, but that's because you've got no sense. A razor king doesny *have* to pay for his drinks. There's more ways of making money than toiling for it. Ask Mither yoursel' if you canny believe me. Whit's more, Ah'm gaun tae take a job mysel' for a while . . . Ah c'n toil as well as you or any other bliddy fellah when Ah think it's worth ma while. But I'll no forget Ah'm Razor King. That's somethin' more than any job."

"Oh far more, right enough!" sneered Peter in his turn. "A bliddy fine job, being Razor King – while it lasts! Wi' free holidays in Barlinnie an' aw! Christ! a great job for a gangster!"

Johnnie took a threatening step in his direction but checked himself.

"You mug!" he said bitterly. "You should still be at the schule. You and your 'gangsters'! Tell me this: are they no' *aw* gangsters who win in this stinkin' world? Look at Arthur Ross. Look at your own graftin' bliddy bosses! Look at the lousy politicians! What's jail worse than livin' outside it in Gorbals?

"You think yourself a hellova fellah," continued Johnnie, "but what about Bobbie Hurley? Mebbe you haveny heard that Bobbie and Lily are dancing at the Gaydom now, earnin' eight pound a week. And Bobbie was worse at school even than me!"

114

"That pimp! He can keep his bliddy money, the way he earns it!"

"Christ! Don't make me laugh! Whit's wrong with the dancing, then, that Mister . . . Peter . . . Stark widna soil his nice brown shoes by taking the floor?"

"An' the booking out?" retorted Peter. "*That's* a different kind of dancing, is it no'? Bobbie Hurley and Lily McKay! Whores, the pair of them, and booked to get married out of the profits! You can keep your pals."

"By God! Watch who you're calling my pals. Lily McKay might be worth more than that skinny bit stuff you're gaun wi'."

"To hell with you! She might be worth more than that bandy-legged tart you're going to marry!"

The elder brother leapt into action at that taunt, his razors flashing, but Peter kept him off for a moment with a raised chair.

"You couldn't . . . fight . . . even me, wi'oot your weapons," he gasped.

Johnnie uttered a furious oath and flung the razors across the room. Then he charged, head lowered and arms raised to guard it. The chair was dashed out of Peter's hands and his brother's fists drove home to chest and forehead, sending him spinning across the room.

At that instant the door opened and Mrs Stark stood on the threshold. She uttered one loud cry and her elder son staggered to check his run with the boot drive at the end of it. He lurched on top of Peter, caught him by the shoulders and jerked him to his feet.

"That's how I floored the Plantation widoe," he roared, "one punch and a kick, and he was oot!"

Peter was breathing very hard, but his lips parted in a wry smile.

"It was . . . quick work," he said. "I'd like fine to have seen you!"

They stared at each other for a long moment and the scowls relaxed and at last there was something almost friendly in their gaze. Johnnie turned on his heel and went to the window.

But Mrs Stark had sat down suddenly and her face was grey.

"So you're home, Mither," said Peter anxiously, matter-of-fact. "An' how did you leave them aw at the Donaldsons?"

"Baith doin' fine," she whispered. "It wis a boy. Ay, the poor soul; it wis a *boy*!"

CHAPTER IX

A WEDDING IS ARRANGED

Razor King was back to the coal lorry again.

If the people of Gorbals had ever questioned the truth of his coming marriage, the sight of Johnnie himself, in his coalman's clothes going the rounds with "Wull" McNeill, was enough to dispel their doubts. But it gave rise to doubts of a different kind. There were some who thought that he meant to reform; others who were maliciously pleased to suppose that he was "going soft" and might soon be "Razor King" no longer.

Nobody ventured to make any comment to Johnnie himself. He went on his own way disdainfully, accepting "toil" partly because he had half-promised Lizzie to do so; partly because he "cud dae wi' the money"; and partly – though he would not have admitted this – to show the world that he could work as well as the next man if he chose to do so.

Chance favoured him in this matter, for work of any kind was hard to come by. His old employer, who had paid him off more than two years before, was not in a big way of business and Johnnie knew that he had recently taken on an out-of-work brother-in-law to help him through the winter months. There was no hope in that quarter and Johnnie did not intend to broadcast the news that he was looking for a job.

One evening, however, he and Michael Briden and Pat O'Hara, a friend of theirs, stood in the bar of the pub at the corner of Shamrock Street and Rutherglen Road. Their caps were pushed back from their foreheads, the inevitable cigarettes were alight, and there was beer and the villainous "red wine" on the counter before them. They smoked and chatted cheerfully, making a little drink go a long way, for Briden was "haudin", and the other two had no money.

"The weather for the coal'll be comin' in," said Briden, apropos of nothing in particular, "an if Ah wisny working where Ah am, Ah'd be looking tae get in wi' Reilly. He'll be starting men next week maybe."

Razor King looked up with a flash of interest.

"Christ! That's right," said he. "Ah'll go down an' see 'm!"

Briden laughed, for he was working with Wilson, the demolition contractor, and his job "threw him" forty-eight shillings for the week of forty-eight hours – a shilling an hour, which was twopence better than some of the contractors paid for the hard and often dangerous toil of pulling down old buildings. Briden knew that he was a "lucky one" to have that wage in those days and his association with Razor King and the gangsters was merely to give an added spice to life.

"Till next February Ah'll be awright," he remarked complacently as he raised his glass of red wine. "We've got a hellova lot of work comin' on—"

"Ah'll go down to Reilly's alang wi' you, Razor King," interrupted O'Hara, paying no attention to Briden. "We might baith get startit."

"We'll go doon the morn's mornin', then," Johnnie agreed.

Early next morning both of them went round to Reilly's premises in South Wellington Street. Reilly was not in when they got to the stable at the rear of the tenement, but they had nothing to do and they sat and waited for him.

He came in at last, brisk and cheerful, a short, stout man, clean-shaven and full of ambition to be "something worth while", which meant, in his view, to acquire money and the respect that went with it. Already he was in a

118

fair way of doing that. Reilly's chief trouble was that his wife was much too fond of the drink; he and his two daughters had as much as they could do to keep the jovial Mrs Reilly from disgracing them in this way.

Great as is the gulf set between employer and working man, no-one attempts to bridge it in Glasgow by polite formalities and empty titles. Johnnie and O'Hara did not even get up when Reilly entered.

"Any chance of a job, Eric?" said Razor King bluntly, and wasting no time.

"The two o' us could be doin' wi' jobs," added O'Hara with a smile.

Eric Reilly hesitated for some moments. It happened that he did want men, but he was none too keen on the particular pair of young men in front of him.

"Ah don't want any trouble," said he, looking keenly at Razor King. "There's too much competition these days: too much other things tae mind withoot trouble wi' razors and aw that."

"Aw, there'll be nae trouble wi' us," Razor King assured him. "It's the dough Ah'm oot for and Ah don't mind workin' for it wi' you."

Three other young men now entered the stable, all of them looking for jobs. Reilly ran his eye over them, saw that they were all husky young fellows, and then spoke decisively to prevent further discussion. The coal was his chief business, but he was a more important figure in Gorbals than some people imagined. He controlled one of the smaller dance halls, in the poorer districts of Glasgow, and he also held a substantial interest in a local picture house. He would not be rushed into any decision.

"The five of you come in here after dinner-time," he said abruptly, "then Ah'll see what Ah can dae. Ah'm busy the noo."

They left him without further words, or at least with no more than a respectful concurrence in the fact that a man in his position must have very little time to spare.

And they *did* respect him, just as they respected all men who had got on and made money, no matter how.

He did not keep them waiting long when they returned after dinner and, though they had been joined by three more out-of-works by that time, Reilly was able to find work for all of them at twenty-seven shillings a week, plus Unemployment and National Health Insurance stamps.

"Ah'll have yon other stable in Errol Street next week," he explained, "alang wi' this one, and you can start then. An' as long as we've got no trouble, Ah think we'll come out o' it pretty well."

They assured him gratefully that there would be no trouble at all and Reilly, merely nodding, passed round a packet of "fags".

"Ah want you an' O'Hara," he said, pausing in front of Razor King, "to go oot wi' Wull. Wull's aw there wi' the money, mind, and if anything goes wrang, Ah'll hae a chynge without hesitation."

"Wull" – otherwise William McNeill, was one of Reilly's most loyal henchmen, one of the few men he trusted with the money – "the bag", as it was called. He was a well-known character in Gorbals, being huge of body and limb, but dwarfish of intellect. Indeed, he was little better than a half-wit outside his job with the coal. In that he was absolutely reliable. He knew all about the money he had to take for his coal and he was so strong and big that nobody thought of trying to "do him" for anything. Nobody but Reilly could "work" this simple giant and no other coalman would employ him, but he was an asset to the business when properly handled.

Razor King knew very well, just as all Gorbals knew, that Reilly got a tremendous amount of work out of "Wull", and that poor "Wull" himself paid all his wages over to his parents who gave him back no more than a few coppers for "sweeties". He also knew that if Reilly was attaching him to "Wull's" lorry it was because he meant to take no chances.

"Wull McNeill," he echoed simply. "Righto, Eric."

"That'll be the very thing!" O'Hara agreed, cheerfully acquiescent.

In fact they got on capitally with Willie McNeill. He was earning more money than either of them, but they did not envy him, because they knew he had to pay his wages over to his parents and could make no show with them. "Wull" did all the shouting from the lorry, and, such were his drawing-powers that Razor King and O'Hara were kept going all the time, swinging the sacks off the lorry on to their own shoulders and hefting them up the stairs to the purchaser's front door.

Scrupulously they handed over to Wullie all the money paid to them on the stair-heids. "Tick" was not at all common in the winter months and, if any credit were allowed at all, it was only to customers of long standing. Occasionally some wife would say that her man was out but that the money would be forthcoming the next morning. Then the coalmen would exercise their own discretion, but, if by chance one of them was ever "had" in this way, word would at once go round to all the others and the defaulter would be denied fuel altogether until the debt was paid. It is no joke to go fireless in a Glasgow winter and, consequently, the coalmen made few bad debts.

Within a few days Razor King was "well in" with Reilly. He did not hurry away directly work was finished. Instead he and the others were always ready to lend a hand for any odd job in the stable. There was no extra pay for this occasional and voluntary "overtime", but Reilly appreciated it all the same and was quite ready to pay for tea or fish suppers upon occasion. Often he would stand chatting with his workers at such times, smoking while they supped their tea or ate their fish. Then the

121

queer "equality" of man and "boss" would reassert itself and they would talk on level terms.

Razor King's coming marriage was naturally much discussed, but football was the staple topic of which none grew weary. Reilly himself used to fill in his "coupon" for the football pools on Friday evening and he did not disdain expert advice. Often, when they had threshed out the prospects of the coming match between the Rangers and the Celtic, they would talk of dancing or the latest pictures. Dancing would make them think of Bobbie and Lily, who were now on the highway to success in Glasgow's dancing world.

Everybody, Reilly included, agreed that Lily was a "grand bit stuff", and in the frankest possible way each of them would boast just "what he cud dae wi' her", if he could get her alone in a nice cavity bed with the curtains drawn. They wished they were in Bobbie Hurley's shoes just for a wee while, and none of them expressed the least contempt for him, though they knew well enough that any patron with a pound or two to fling away could hire either him or his pretty partner for "private lessons" under the "booking out" system.

Razor King took more kindly to the actual toil than might have been expected after his long period of idleness. The mere muscular effort of hefting the heavy sacks gave him a sort of satisfaction. He had kept in semi-training all along, but he felt the need of hard work. He throve on it physically and for the time being it made him actually happier. He seldom bothered to think that there was barely twelve shillings difference between his wages for a hard week's work and the money he could draw from the "buroo" for nothing. He was eager to have Lizzie all to himself, however, and would not much longer be satisfied with the privileges which were accorded to him on the stair-head of nights.

Several of the Starks' neighbours in Crown Street were very pleased to think of Razor King's getting married.

The prospect of an apartment in Govan Street had come to nothing for the tenants there had decided to stop on. But a "single end" in Crown Street, almost opposite his old home, was soon to be vacated and it was thanks to these same neighbours that the news was not allowed to get around. They may have wanted to do a good turn to Mrs Stark, who was always ready to help in any other house in times of trouble or sickness. Or they may have felt that queer admiration for a champion gangster which exists in the slums even among people who have nothing to do with the gangs. They were certainly curious to know how Razor King would make out as a married man. They were astonished that he had gone to work at all, and some of them fancied that he might settle down once he assumed the responsibilities of a householder.

Even to-day there are practically no small "houses" to let in Glasgow. In 1924 overcrowding was such that any empty apartment was immediately re-let. The Factor could pick and choose his tenants if he had a mind to. Actually it made little difference to him provided the rent were regularly forthcoming. Razor King wasted no time once he was given the hint about the "single end". At once he went round with Lizzie Ramsay to look at it and they immediately decided to take it.

The front door faced the stairs on the third-floor landing. Left and right of the "single end" were the usual two-roomed houses. But the one room of Razor King's new home was tolerably "large" by comparison with the kitchen or living-room of his own home. Of course, it had no lavatory and there was no bathroom in the whole of the long, grey, four-storied tenement, nor, for that matter, in the whole of Crown Street. And yet Johnnie and Lizzie agreed that the "single end" was a "pure treat". The rent was exceptionally low; only five and threepence a week.

"It's a great item, the rent," said Lizzie after the landing door had closed upon the dingy room still occupied by the family of four which was shortly to leave the district.

"Too true it is!" agreed Razor King feelingly, and then, as a sort of comment upon a thought which they had shared in silence, he added: "But we might get better through time aw the same, eh?"

Both of them knew that the opportunity to take this most advantageous dwelling had been engineered for them by the neighbours. They felt that it was a tribute to Razor King's local celebrity. Lizzie determined that they would do the place up in great style directly it was empty, and a day or two before they were married and moved in.

The news that the "single end" had been definitely secured for the Razor King and his wife-to-be made a big impression among the young people in Gorbals. It brought to a head more than a score of other love affairs, some of them of the "mixed" religious flavour too. Two of the young men who had been courting the elder Stark sisters now declared their matrimonial intentions as soon as homes could be found. Michael Briden, Mary Halliday's boy, who was a Catholic, said that he would turn "Prodisant" if she made a point of it. Talk of marriage was heard on every side.

The Ramsay household, following Martha's lead, was no longer opposing the match, but when Lizzie and Johnnie were out of the way, there was an undercurrent of sneering in all their comments. Lizzie knew this well enough, but nobody gave her an opportunity to retort. She became aggressive in her manners and deliberately rough in her talk. Because her family rather despised Johnnie for being a Razor King, she could never have enough to say about his prowess as a fighter. And there was a certain tension in Mathieson Street as a result of all this.

Towards the end of October the "single end" was vacated, and Johnnie and Lizzie went up to see it again that same evening. The empty room seemed grimier and drabber for its very emptiness. The dingy paper was peeling off the walls and two of the broken window-panes had been stopped with brown paper.

Lizzie drew her shawl about her shoulders and shivered. Determinedly she caught hold of Johnnie's arm and drew him over towards the recess for the cavity bed.

"It'll no' be so bad when we've got new paper on the wall and the windows mended and the furniture in," said she. "An' we'll have a bed in here as good as any bed you can get!"

She broke into a high-pitched laugh and Razor King laughed with her.

"Ay, an' we'll dae a hellova lot of work in it, Liz, eh?" He hugged her tightly as he asked the question, and the colour rose in her cheeks, though for a long while now she had denied him nothing. Johnnie had come straight from his coal lorry and was in his working clothes. They were alone in the empty room, and his eyes, rimmed by coal dust, were suddenly greedy.

"This is better than the stair-heid even now," he said.

When they came out of the close-mouth a little later and into the street they had the air of conspirators, happy but somewhat constrained. Lizzie was talking about Johnnie's luck in getting a job with Reilly, "temporary" though it was. Reilly was doing so well in Gorbals during the winter months that one of his "extra" lorries at least might be kept busy even through the summer.

"If Ah wisny suiting him, he widny be bothered wi' me," Johnnie agreed, "and anyway the summer's far enough away."

Later that same evening they met Lizzie's special friend, Mary Halliday, with Michael Briden, her young man. Many who knew them saw the four standing and talking on the pavement, but they did not venture to intrude upon such distinguished company.

"Come on up an' we'll have another look at the hoose," said Johnnie eagerly.

Mary Halliday looked at Lizzie and laughed significantly. "*Another!*" said she, "an' when was the first time the day?"

Johnnie hesitated, but only for a moment.

"We were up there the night," he smiled defiantly. "Liz and me. An' if you want to know, we didn't waste oor time, did we, Liz?"

"Mebbe we didn't," said she, half-relieved by his frankness, "but we're no' gaun again the night, Ah'm bliddy sure!"

They all laughed with her at that retort, but after they had had a drink or two at the corner pub they did, in fact, return to the "single end". Neighbours, watching them going up, took it for granted that they could be going for one purpose only. They were amused but indifferent, for what else could one expect of young people who were going to get married.

This time the gas was lit, and, although the jokes were crude enough, the four young people seriously discussed the decoration and furnishing, Mary offering suggestions with the most candid envy that she and Michael had not yet found a similar home for themselves.

The wedding was now definitely arranged for three days later, and in the interval the "single end" was freshly painted in green and the ceiling was whitewashed. The furniture, which Lizzie paid for out of her savings, was moved in. There were three of the usual plain wooden chairs and a plain table to go with them. Cheap crockery was displayed on the dresser shelves, and beneath them were hung the inevitable polished covers of different sizes. A grate costing thirty shillings was purchased and fitted into the fireplace. And, finally, amid the broadest jesting, Razor King and some of his friends carried up the mattress and bedding that were to fill the cavity bed.

This small business of paper-hanging, painting and

furnishing was all done by voluntary labour and, such was Razor King's status in the district, the bridal couple themselves did little more than look on and supervise. They did not hang even a single religious picture or text upon the walls and in this they were considered somewhat unusual, for Catholic and Protestant alike do not generally consider a home complete without some adornment of this kind.

"But what the hell are *we* wanting wi' such truck?" said Johnnie to Lizzie with an air of superiority.

"We're as well aff wi'oot it," she agreed, not too confidently, "but it's a good thing we're baith Prodisants, aw the same."

"Sure it is, Liz! But, between you an' me, none of us people here in Gorbals are anything in the religious line at all. We don't know anything at all about religion, do we now?"

"May be," she said uneasily, "but we've got to be *something*, aw the same. An' we're better to be what our old folks were, are we no'?"

This was one of their last conversations on the stair-head in Mathieson Street. Razor King dropped a used match on the landing and kicked it deftly down the stairs.

"Sure we are, Lizzie," he laughed. "We'll be Prodisants like they were, just as you say. There's no use of changing. But you an' me will be something better in the long run than our old folks were."

"So we wull, Johnnie," she agreed fervently.

They were married in a small church in Commercial Road on a cold Friday evening, and Briden and Halliday, as their two friends were commonly known, were the "best couple". Martha Ramsay and Angus Moir were also present at the church and Johnnie's eldest sister and her young man with them. There were some twenty other young people, drawn mostly from Razor King's own gang, but there was no other member of the respective families excepting old Mrs Stark herself, who went home immediately after the wedding.

Twenty-four couples were invited to the wedding tea-party, but there was no room for them all in the "single end" at once and the guests were therefore bidden to the first, or the second, or the third tea as the case might be. Martha Ramsay and Angus Moir, Johnnie's sister and her young man, and some others were included in the first party. Things had scarcely begun to get lively then, for these were guests in whose presence a certain restraint seemed advisable.

There was whisky and beer on the dresser, and the second tea-party was a merrier affair, with much loud laughter and broad jesting. But the real "party" did not begin until the privileged intimates of the third tea had the "hoose" to themselves. The drinks were flowing freely by this time and suddenly Razor King climbed onto the dresser in the bright gaslight and announced that: "Every couple that wants to stey for the dance c'n go the whole road here, or they're no use tae us."

He jumped to the floor again amid a chorus of laughter and cheers. The two musicians of the party got going with their accordions for a half set. They were self-taught, playing solely by ear, but they played well, and with table and chairs thrust back to the wall, the men and the girls began to dance, so closely packed in that small place that each couple was almost touching the next and the dancing was largely stationary.

The funds had not permitted a large supply of drink on this occasion and when the musicians grew tired of playing some other excitement had to be thought of. But there are not many games available to the tenement dweller and the "exciting" ones are various in detail, but similar in objective. A kind of "forfeits" – which is a guessing game with many traps for the unwary or for the predestined victims – grew noisier and more exciting as

Mary Halliday and her partner, Briden, lost forfeit after forfeit until they had to pay the final penalty.

"Aw, Ah don't think this is a good gemm!" shrilled Mary, her face hot with drink and embarrassment. "Ah widny mind goin' to bed wi' Michael, but Ah don't fancy strippin'."

They all knew that she was not shy of showing her body, but only of exhibiting cheap and much-mended underwear. Many a working girl adorned in outward finery had suffered a sickening "showing up" in the better class Glasgow dance halls by the accidental display of garments underneath the fine dress.

Michael Briden was scarcely less uneasy, for he had not had a bath for about three weeks. He was one of those who believed that it was "unlucky" to have too many baths and even that it was "lucky" to have some vermin in the house. But neither he nor Mary, nor any other in that company, was in any way shocked by the kind of "foolery" proper to such a party.

Razor King was sitting on the dresser swinging his legs and the victims appealed in vain to his leniency. He laughed and told them not to make such a fuss. Mary stepped out of her dress at last and her fine build gave her some reassurance.

"You should always go aboot like that, Mary!" shouted Razor King approvingly and then the company closed upon her and her lover and threw them, laughing and struggling and swearing and protesting, into the fine new bed with its green curtains.

But the party broke up at one in the morning because there was not enough liquor to keep it going. It was decided, however, that they would hold a better one and a bigger one later on with a real stock of whisky and beer to meet the occasion and Razor King promised that he would arrange a raid to secure supplies. When their last guests had gone the newly married husband and wife went somewhat drunkenly to bed.

"There's one thing, Liz," said Johnnie sleepily, "we'll no' retire on aw the presents we've got, anyway!"

"By Jeez, naw!" said the new Mrs Stark.

They counted up their presents on their first Sunday morning at home, pricing each one of them after much argument. Johnnie, with a pencil and paper, reckoned the total at £4 4s. 4½d.

'It's no' sae wonderful for a Razor King," he said.

"But they're no aw working," Lizzie laughed. "You should remember that."

"Naw; they're no' aw working! But *Ah'm* working!" – he banged his fist on the table in sudden fury – "an' before long they'll know Ah *can* work an' aw – wi' my weapons as well as the coal. Ah'm gaun tae show them that, Liz. If they think this is me finished, now Ah'm mairrit and at toil again, they've backed a bliddy loser, so they have!"

Lizzie made no reply. She did not know what to say and hardly knew what she thought. In a way she would have liked Johnnie to stick to work and drop out of the gang sooner or later. On the other hand she liked to know he was Razor King. She liked to feel that he was top dog among all the Gorbals fighting-men. She enjoyed the notoriety he had won. And she would never have forgiven him if he had just "gone plummy". Secretly she hoped that for a while nothing would happen one way or another.

"Ah'm gaun tae show 'em," he repeated sombrely. "Wait till I go to one of the dance halls . . ."

"You've forgotten one thing, Johnnie," she said, changing the conversation. "You've no' counted the pound note that Peter and Isobel sent. It was the best present we had, even though they didny come to oor weddin'."

"Peter and Isobel's aw right," he grunted. "All the others could have steyed away at the same price."

Actually Johnnie thought a little more of his younger

130

brother for his handsome gift. He did not resent the fact that Peter had not come to the wedding, for it was true that Peter and he were taking different roads. They wouldn't be likely to see much of each other. Peter was all right, but he just couldn't be bothered thinking about him.

"Come on out, Liz," said Johnnie. "Ah'm needin' a drink."

CHAPTER X

RAID AND A CHALLENGE

The dance hall in Cathedral Street was crowded on the Saturday night when Johnnie Stark and a dozen of his followers arrived noisily, looking for trouble. The man at the pay office would have refused their money had he dared, for there was something sinister about the sudden appearance of so large a party of young men late in the evening and unaccompanied by girls.

But the pay-box man was merely an employee of the hall, earning a pound a week, and it was not his business to argue with customers unless they were manifestly drunk and quarrelsome. These were not. They had been drinking, but they paid their money without dispute and they followed their leader briskly out of the lobby and on to the floor. The clerk shrugged his shoulders and took a nip at the flask of whisky that he kept beneath his desk, thinking vindictively that the manager could "bliddy well look after himsel' ", if anything happened, for his staff certainly didn't see much of the big profits he must be making.

Johnnie had just enough drink inside him that night to make him entirely reckless of consequences. To be a razor king is something like being a boxing champion: it isn't enough to win the title; one has to fight to hold it. Johnnie felt that he had been law-abiding too long. He wasn't sure what the Gorbals people thought about his sticking to his regular job with the coalman. He was afraid lest they should suppose that marriage had changed and softened him. He *had* to show them.

One dance had just ended and another – a "Ladies'

Choice" – was about to start when Johnnie led the way into the hall. Grouped together under the balcony at the entrance were all the young men who had been dancing already. There was nothing to distinguish them from Razor King and his followers. They were all of them working-class lads and they stood laughing and chatting and eyeing the girls, who were in little knots round the other sides of the hall. The lasses, giggling and whispering, were making up their minds which cavaliers they would choose when the music struck up, and they came fluttering towards the young men just as Razor King and his followers swept forward like invaders.

"Hey! Whit dance is this?" shouted Razor King as he thrust his way ahead. Nobody thought it necessary to answer him, for the words – "Ladies' Choice" – were posted, plain for all to see, on the notice-board to the left of the band platform. The nature of the dance was also obvious enough from the fact that the girls were even then crossing the floor towards the waiting men.

Razor King halted abruptly in front of a tall, red-haired fellow who had just joined his partner.

"Hey, Mac!" he asked loudly. "What dance is this that's on? Can you no' answer a fellow, eh?"

The tone of the voice more than the words themselves was an implicit challenge. It was loud enough to be heard by all. Men and girls suddenly stood still. Heads turned and all eyes were fixed on Razor King and the redhead. There was no working up to this climax; it happened in an instant and was so instantly sensed by all the company that the manager began running across the floor with a shout of "No fighting here!"

The big red-headed fellow stood transfixed with astonishment and gathering rage. Suddenly he came to life. He shook his girl from his arm and leapt at Razor King with a roar. Johnnie had no time to draw his weapons for the other's fist caught him a smashing blow between the eyes and felled him to the floor. That was the signal for the furious and bloody affray which followed immediately.

Johnnie's "division" was out of its own district in this hall, a favourite haunt of the crowd from Townhead. Razors flashed and bottles were grasped as the Gorbals lads charged indiscriminately into battle. McLatchie, the redhead, fought like a bull, but he was driven back from where Johnnie lay. The toe of an iron-shod boot laid open Johnnie's cheek, but he staggered drunkenly to his feet, only to be overwhelmed by the rush of Townhead lads to McLatchie's assistance.

Johnnie, knocked out completely, took no further part in that fight. He had barely regained consciousness when the police arrived at the urgent summons of the manager. The floor was cleared as though by magic. In a fighting, cursing stampede attackers and attacked broke through the lobby and into the street, the girls running with them, or cowering against the walls.

Eight men were taken to the Royal Infirmary by police ambulance, Johnnie among them. His face and head were covered with blood and his clothing half-torn off his body. His weapons had disappeared, but, by some lucky chance, he had escaped any serious body injuries. The surgeon put four stitches into the wound on his cheek and he was then allowed to go his way. Nor, as it happened, was it necessary to detain any of the other injured lads, though most of them had to call at the infirmary for treatment during the days which followed.

The police made only two arrests. McLatchie, who had been fighting at the far end of the hall with two of Razor King's men, broke free from them too late. He missed the stampede, which the police had been unable to stop, and was captured. With him was another Townhead lad, too dazed to know what had really happened and an entirely innocent victim of circumstance. Both of them duly appeared in the Sheriff Court and both were sentenced with strict impartiality to thirty days' imprisonment with hard labour. The police swore that they had been arrested as rioters and there was no evidence obtainable as to how the fight began or who began it. There seldom is. The code of the Glasgow hooligan may be elastic, but it does not permit telling tales to the police. Those who are neither hooligans nor gangsters take particular care to see nothing and to know nothing.

The tale of the big "rammy" had reached Crown Street long before Razor King, with his disfigured face and throbbing head, painfully climbed the stairs to his "single end". Lizzie was waiting for him and shrieked at his appearance.

"Haud your tongue!" he commanded angrily, "Ah'm no' much hurt, but there's gaun tae be somebody else hurt before long."

She would give him no peace until he had told all that he could of the evening's happenings. A strange pride stirred in her heart as she stared at her husband's wounded and bandaged face. The neighbours had already told her how Razor King had marched into the hall at the head of his "division" and deliberately sought out and challenged the biggest fighter in all the Townhead crowd. The story grew with the telling. Apparently McLatchie was the champion of all Townhead, with many legendary victories to his credit. Razor King had been unlucky, that was all; but his men had acquitted themselves well, for no less than six of the wounded were Townhead lads.

In actual fact Johnnie had neither known nor cared whom he chose for his adversary. He picked the first likely fellow in his path, and McLatchie's instant attack had taken him by surprise. He was secretly humiliated by his defeat and a little worried as to what reception he might receive when he went about again.

"Eh, well," said Lizzie at last, "you're well out of it that you're no' in jail alang wi' yon McLatchie. I don't

135

know whit for you have to be fighting, Johnnie, but the boys'll no' say you're finished efter this, Ah'm thinking!"

"They'd better no'," he retorted savagely, "for Ah'm hardly started. Ah'll need paying for this night's work."

On the Saturday evening he was drinking in the local pub again and he could sense the admiration of the company. Immediately, lest there should be any doubters whatever, he let it be known that he was determined to have a "fair fight" with McLatchie, who had "taken a liberty with him" in the dance hall. Someone bought another round of drinks and the company fell into joyful discussion of the day when Razor King would settle his accounts.

But Johnnie and two or three of the others who had been hurt were still attending the infirmary when McLatchie came out of prison. It wasn't long before they heard of him, for the big, red-headed fighter was burning for revenge and went about his own district, boasting, just as Razor King had done, that soon there would be a fight worth talking about, and "yon Razor King or whatever they ca' him", would have something better than "a broken heid" to remember him by!

Now Townhead lies north of the Clyde while Gorbals is on the south side, and there is little social commerce between the two districts, but excitement at the prospect of a formal challenge grew in both, spreading, indeed, throughout the tenements of the entire city. And the young men in either camp rallied strongly to their leaders. Soon, in Gorbals and in Townhead too, there was talk of little else and feeling ran high even among the great non-combatant majority.

One odd effect of this first "rammy" was that Razor King's wife began to wear a shawl when she was home from work and to stand, hatless, at the close-mouth, gossiping with the other wives. Those who do not know Glasgow may miss the significance of this social deterioration. But it amounted to nothing less, for Lizzie

Ramsay, before her marriage, would have scorned to wear a shawl – the very badge of "the hairy", the very uniform of the "poor class" woman slum dweller.

Lizzie had thought a good deal of herself in those pre-marriage days. Her father's regular work as a kinema attendant and his comparative affluence entitled him to some respect in Gorbals, and Mathieson Street, where they lived, was not one of the meanest thoroughfares. Moreover Lizzie herself, earning good money in the bakery, had always been "well put on". She had some pretensions to culture, too, with her violin-playing and certain refinements of speech and habit. In those days she despised the close-mouth gossips and would scarcely have run across the road without a hat on her head.

In Crown Street, however, hatted women were the exception rather than the rule and Lizzie felt somewhat isolated in her grandeur. At first this obvious social superiority was enjoyable, but she could not maintain the sense of it when she revisited her old home. True, the family had accepted her marriage to Razor King without too much obvious resentment, but, now that she was actually married, they were less tactful. They seemed, indeed, none too glad to see her, they made her furious with their scarcely veiled sneers at Johnnie and his new "respectability".

Soon she ceased to visit Mathieson Street. A perverse pride forced her more closely into the company of her own neighbours. If she had been able to put her thoughts into words, she might have said: "Johnnie and me are as well-doing as any of them at home and maybe making more money! Ay, an' there's more people has heard of Razor King than ever heard of the old man or any of them. They don't think Ah'm good enough for the likes of them in Mathieson Street! Well, Ah'll *show* them. Ah'll not put on any airs. But Ah'll go on making good money just the same, and Razor King'll not lose his reputation, not if I can help it!"

There was no hint of this attitude when she stood talking to her neighbours. On the contrary, she would declare, with a faintly condescending air, that it was no wish of *hers* that Razor King should still be looked upon as someone of importance in Gorbals. *She* didn't care about his fighting.

"Aw the same," she would conclude emphatically, "Razor King can beat that dirty big McLatchie any day in the week."

They listened to her with a new respect, for everybody in Crown Street admitted that they had never been so taken in in their lives about any man as they had been about Razor King. They didn't tell Lizzie so, of course, but they were immensely impressed by the fact that, on the one hand, Johnnie was sticking to his job, which they thought he would never do, and, on the other, that he seemed to have lost none of his fighting quality.

One old gossip, an elderly but still well-built woman, expressed the general feeling as she stood talking one evening in a little group at the corner of Thistle Street and Adelphi Street.

"Who the hell wid ha' thought," said she, "that he wid ha' worked awa' wi' a coalman, carryin' bags o' coal up aw they sterrs, an' him still attendin' the infirmary, eh? He must be hellova fond o' that yin, Lizzie Ramsay, in ma opeenion. Ay, an' he's no gonny drap oot! He's gaun tae cause mair trouble than the single yins by the looks o' things. He'll get a lot o' jail yet, the same Razor Keeng!"

It was true that Johnnie had gone doggedly back to work on the Monday morning. Reilly, who took an occasional "drunk" for granted and was secretly amazed that Johnnie had stayed the course so well, made not the slightest comment either upon his absence or his sadly battered appearance. And, oddly enough, Johnnie was driven towards respectability by just the same kind of pride that was making Lizzie shake it off. He knew very well what people were thinking, and he stuck to his work chiefly because they thought he never would.

It gave him immense satisfaction to spend part of the money he was earning on an entirely new rig-out – a blue suit, tony-red boots and a light-grey cap. In the evenings when he walked abroad, he was very conscious of his "paraffin". And he realized that he was winning more, instead of less, respect and support from the young, would-be flymen and gangsters of the South Side district of Glasgow. As long as he could fight, they liked the Razor King to cut a dash even though he "toiled" to find the means for it.

Older people in Gorbals would have paid little attention to this slight reciprocal change in husband and wife – this levelling down and up in social values – if it had not been that they looked upon Johnnie himself as a most uncertain quantity. They saw that he had more grit than they had at first supposed, but they also saw that he was by no means minded to become truly respectable. It seemed certain, for instance, that he intended to settle accounts with big McLatchie of the Townhead, and peaceful people were uneasy as to the possible developments and extensions of this feud.

"It all depends," was the general verdict. "He might settle down when they have some family. An' he might cause trouble if there's nothing to hold him."

During the last weeks of that year there was much tension in the air on both sides of the river, and, both in Gorbals and Townhead, the more responsible element of the population was fearful of some gang attack in force.

Johnnie's own men were getting restless and eager for action and "a big party" seemed to be called for to relieve their feelings. But a big party meant drink in large quantity and there seemed no way to obtain that except by a public-house raid.

Broadly speaking the Glasgow gangster is not a criminal; he is just a hooligan and a fighter, battling for

139

excitement and adventure and not for profit. But he has always held the publican to be fair game and the chance to steal drink attracts him far more than the chance to steal money.

Hitherto Johnnie Stark had not led his followers into anything but battle. Now, in the Christmas week of 1924, the circumstances drove him to plan an adventure on different lines. In the course of his coal rounds he had noticed a well-placed public house in Govan Street and gradually there dawned upon him what seemed to be the perfect scheme for obtaining a large quantity of much-needed whisky and possibly a little money into the bargain. He considered his plan from every angle before inviting three of his principal lieutenants home one evening to discuss it with them.

It never occurred to him to conceal this projected adventure from his wife. Actually he did not speak about it to her, but that was merely because his mind was not quite made up. To him it seemed just natural that Liz would stand by him in whatever he attempted. They were lovers still, but apart from that no slum woman ever gives her man away except for jealousy of another woman or love of another man, and then seldom, unless there has been outrageous provocation. This instinctive loyalty would hold good even if she violently disapproved of his proposed conduct, a possibility which Johnnie thought unlikely in the present instance.

The particular attraction which this one public house had for Johnnie lay in the fact that the pub stood at the entrance to a close, one of its side walls forming, indeed, the wall of the close-mouth itself. This blank wall, unrelieved even by the smallest window, curved inwards from the street, so that a man standing within the close-mouth some yards back would not be noticed by people passing on the pavement itself. This seemed to him to be the very key to the situation.

His three friends arriving at the appointed time,

Johnnie greeted them curtly and bade them sit down. Lizzie was leaning back in the one arm-chair reading a twopenny weekly. She scarcely troubled to acknowledge the visitors' awkward greetings, for she knew that they were there on business with Razor King.

When all four men were seated with their elbows on the table, and after the cigarettes were alight, Johnnie began deliberately to explain what he had in mind. The "single end", with its new green wall-paper, looked cosy in the bright gaslight. The inevitable polished metal covers on the dresser beneath the bottom shelf reflected the cheerful glow of the fire on the opposite side of the room. The window was tight shut and the atmosphere was close and heavy with tobacco smoke, but the night was cold and, by comparison with other houses, the newly cleaned and papered "hoose" was odourless.

Razor King was no great speechmaker and his black brows were knitted in a frown of concentration as he tried to explain clearly exactly what had to be done. His listeners did not interrupt him until he finished up at last with an abrupt: "That's all there's in it."

Then there was a chorus of delighted admiration. Lizzie was still reading, or pretending to read, her weekly. Johnnie shot a glance at her, but she did not look up. He was so pleased with the reception of his scheme by the other men and so proud of his own brains that he decided to go over it all again, briefly and emphatically.

"We canny go wrong," he insisted. "You three dress up as builders and you get a barrow out from Elliots' for the day. Then in the efternune, when the pub shuts, you take the barrow down to that close. And one of you has to carry a pair of steps as well. Then you go inside the close a bit beyond the bend of the wall and you stick the steps up and begin to dig a hole in the wall, high up. It's *got* to be high up, mind! They'll no' see you from the pavement and, if any of the neighbours pass in or out the close and ask you what's on, all you've got to say is

141

that there's an escape of gas and that you'll have it all right in an hour or two, see?"

"That's aw right, Razor King," interrupted one of the others, "and it's true enough nobody knows us down there, but how long wull it take us to get through the wall and what if they hear us workin' inside the pub?"

"Haven't I telt ye," said Johnnie impatiently, "that the boss'll be away hame at the time? The pub will be just empty while you're at work and, if you go to the job boldly wi' hammers and chisels, you'll be through in twenty minutes. Then, when the hole's through, two of you go into the pub and open the door from the inside and the one on the outside gives the tick-tack that there's no jailers about. First them that's inside empties the till and puts the dough into the bag you'll have with you. Then, when the coast is clear, you can all carry out as much whisky as should fill the barrow. I'll be passing with the old lorry now and again and I hope to see that barrow full of whisky, with maybe some bags and rubbish on the top of it to hide the bottles. When we've got that length, the rest's a meat ticket! You hide the barrow where we said until efter dark and then bring the stuff, or most of it, anyhow, right in here."

The other three young fellows gazed at Johnnie with the utmost admiration. "You're a marvel, Razor King!" exclaimed one of them enthusiastically.

Johnnie betrayed no pleasure at this compliment. He did not want too much enthusiasm until the job was what he would have termed "a thing of the past".

"It's got to be done to-morrow!" he grunted, "an' you'll not have to waste any time once it's started."

Lizzie, flushed and pretty in the gaslight, threw down her paper at that moment and the sound, slight though it was, immediately attracted the attention of the four men, who had been so absorbed that they had forgotten her very presence. She got up deliberately from the arm-chair, smoothed her blue skirt and white blouse and then patted her hair with conscious affectation.

"As for me," she said clearly, "Ah suppose Ah'm just to come home the morn's night as if nothing had happened?"

The question was addressed to no-one in particular and her tone was void of comment.

"*You* don't get here till efter six, Liz," said Johnnie tersely, "an it'll aw be a thing o' the past by then."

She stared at him and he met her gaze with eyes that had narrowed to a sudden challenge. Very deliberately he drew the packet of "fags" from his pocket, selected one, and lit it. His three followers did not move or speak.

Lizzie suddenly laughed. "Is there no' a fag for me?" she said.

Razor King's frown relaxed and his lieutenants began to laugh, excitedly, but with obvious relief. Two of them hurried to give Lizzie a cigarette.

She walked across to the press beneath the shuttered window.

"I would put most of the whisky under the bed," she advised. "And more in this press, eh?"

"It's all to go under the bed, Liz," said Johnnie, rising in his turn and pulling up the valance. "See! This should hold about twenty quid's worth of good whisky. Ay, twenty quid's worth, easy!"

Lizzie emerged from the press and stood with arms akimbo, her back to the window, and the others, Johnnie included, looked at her expectantly.

"You'll have it your own way, I can see, Razor King," she said, "and I'll not complain so long as you lay out that dirty big bastard McLatchie. That'll be worth more than all the whisky."

She threw her head back and began to laugh. Johnnie was puzzled and half-ashamed. He glanced rapidly at his friends, anxious to see whether they had remarked this patent deterioration in his wife's manners. They fidgeted uneasily.

But Lizzie stopped in mid-laugh, as it were. She did not notice the men's odd expressions and went on talking directly to Johnnie himself.

"Efter McLatchie gets his hiding," she said, "that'll be things squared up for another while, wull it no'?"

"Sure it wull!" agreed Johnnie uncomfortably. "An' we're gaun tae have a bliddy good party, aren't we, boys?"

He turned to them with forced cheerfulness, for he was suddenly aware that his wife was by no means the same Lizzie Ramsay he had married; no, not by a great deal.

"Sure thing!" they chorused eagerly.

Lizzie stretched her arms above her head and yawned.

"All right, then," she said, "but I'll be disappointed if there's no twenty quid's worth of whisky under that bed when I come home the morn's night. An' now I'll make some tea."

The three young men left soon afterwards and when they were gone Lizzie said nothing whatever about the coming raid. If Johnnie could have read her mind, he might have been no less puzzled, for there was conflict beneath the surface calm. Indeed, she wondered at herself. Instinctively she was frightened of the public house raid. She didn't want Johnnie to be mixed up in it. Above all, she didn't want him to get caught. But she did want him, desperately, to give this McLatchie, whom she had never seen, a thrashing. She had married Razor King, a fighting man, and, by God! she meant to be the wife of the greatest fighter in the tenements! She shivered and bit her lip. Suddenly she got up from her chair and ran to Johnnie where he sat, sullen-faced. She forced her way on to his reluctant knee, ran hot fingers upwards through the short thick hair at the back of his bullet head, tugged that same down against her breast – roused him at last to passionate response.

The raid on the following afternoon was a great success. The plan was carried through without a hitch in the space of ninety minutes all told. By four-thirty

Johnnie's three men were away with thirty-six pounds' worth of whisky and the contents of the till, some fifteen pounds in cash. The police were on the scene half an hour later, listening to the publican's frantic tale of loss and questioning the neighbours, but all to no purpose. Two women and one man admitted they had seen "three builder lads" at work on the wall "to stop a gas leak". But they had never seen them before. They were just "ordinary lads"; they hadn't paid any particular attention to them and could give nothing but the vaguest descriptions.

A big crowd had gathered outside the public house to gaze with delighted admiration at the pile of bricks and mortar and rubble which "the men had left in their hurry up at the last". But none among them could throw any light upon the robbery. The police took their notes resignedly and departed. The hole in the wall was blocked up and gradually the crowd dispersed.

Lizzie came home from the bakery just in time to lend a hand in stowing the whisky under the bed. In her relief that there had been no mishap, she laughed and talked excitedly and she spoke in the raw, undiluted dialect of the tenements, using those adjectives which the men employed habitually, but which the "better class" women avoided, at least in mixed company. In the general jubilation, none but Johnnie remarked the freedom of her speech. Two or three times he looked at her with a puzzled frown, shrugged his shoudlers, and turned to the business in hand.

"There's twenty quid's worth of whisky in here," he declared at last, "and almost as much again outside. That's all to the good, and everybody's to get a share of the dough. But, if anybody ever says a word about the night's work – a razor gets busy on them! Remember that!"

There were fourteen young men and women in the "single end" at the time. The fire was blazing, the window shuttered, and the atmosphere terribly close.

"Hey, Razor King!" shrilled one excited girl. "Nae-body wid think of saying anything to anybody out of the district."

"No bliddy fear!" chorused the rest of the party.

"Fine!" said Johnnie. "An' now we must get a good party made up as soon as we can. We'll kill one bottle at once to celebrate the occasion, but we'll keep the rest of the whisky for the big do."

And again the others joined in the clamour of assent.

The big party was actually held on New Year's night when the whole of Glasgow was celebrating after its fashion. There were many in Gorbals who feared that the Townhead contingent might choose that night of all others upon which to make an attack, but nothing of the kind happened, and the fearsome drinking orgy in Razor King's "single end" was remembered with awe and admiration for many months afterwards.

Thirty young people, men and girls, assembled in that single apartment and settled down to the solemnly deliberate business of drinking whisky until they could drink no more. When the party was finally broken up on the following morning, three-quarters of the whisky had been consumed and the "single end" stank like a sty. The drunks reeled away on their own legs or propped up by friends of greater physical endurance. One young girl lay half-naked and unconscious on a blanket under the dresser for an hour or two after the others had gone. At last two friends returned for her, soused her with water, clothed her, and more or less carried her home. She had a baby in the autumn of that year and never knew its father. Razor King and Lizzie were lying dead drunk in the cavity bed during all the time that she was revived and removed from the apartment.

But the "Gorbals United" – that is to say, all the shifting, shiftless mob of hooligans and reckless, excitement-craving young ruffians of both sexes – was thrilled and stimulated by this great exploit of the raid and the party, to a fanatic admiration of Razor King, and there were at least five hundred young men in the district now ready and eager to face "the armed strength of any other division in the city". A great gang battle seemed inevitable.

Within three days of that memorable party the last of the stolen whisky had been drunk, and Razor King and his men were planning openly to get into contact with the Townhead mob in general and big McLatchie in particular. But Johnnie missed only one day from his work. His iron constitution enabled him to throw off the effects of alcohol much sooner than most men. His eyes were red-rimmed and ugly in his grim face, blackened with coal dust, but he carried the sacks up the stairs like a giant, was sick now and again, and then, working the alcohol out of his system through the sweat of his toil, he would be back for more whisky in the evening, fit and fresh and dangerous.

A mass attack upon the Townhead mob was already closely planned when, one evening, a hatless girl, wearing a fur coat, walked boldly into that bar which served as Razor King's headquarters. Everybody there knew at once that this stranger to the district, with her air of quite special bravado, was a herald from the enemy camp, and she was received in polite silence.

She did not need to be told who was Razor King, for he stepped a little forward from the group of his supporters, and all eyes were focused upon him as he waited for the girl's message.

"Ah'm here tae tell you, Razor King," she said simply, "that big McLatchie is ready to meet you in a fair fight on the Glasgow Green on the Wednesday in a fortnight's time."

"You can tell him Ah'll be therr," said Johnnie simply. Thus the challenge was delivered and accepted and the "fair fight" settled.

The girl did not stay in the pub after she had had her

147

answer. She met Johnnie's gaze very squarely, suddenly smiled into his grim face, shook her curly hair and was gone. There was neither taunt nor comment from the crowd. Her status as a herald was strictly respected.

But, within an hour, all Gorbals was buzzing with the news of the coming fight. The respectable element was delighted to feel that the tension in the air had lessened and that the coming trouble – however big it might be – would be settled on the Green, which meant that peaceable folk could keep away from it if they chose. The gangsters and their girls were equally pleased, for there was no thrill quite like the matching of champion against champion, and they knew, from experience, that when the big fight was settled, there would be ample opportunity for general war.

Johnnie went home that evening and found Lizzie in a state of exalted enthusiasm. But he would not endure either her raptures or her caresses. The raided whisky was finished, but she had bought a flask specially to celebrate the great news.

"Ah'm no' drinking," said Johnnie curtly, "an' it wid dae ye nae harm yoursel', Liz, to give the drink a rest for a while."

"Whit's come over ye?" she gasped.

"Nothing; but Ah've a fight tae *win* in a fortnight's time and Ah'll be the better to do some training."

"Aw right," she agreed humbly. "Dae whit you think best, Razor King. But Ah'll be there on the Green that day and maybe a hundred women wi' me to see you paste hell out of yon McLatchie!"

Johnnie grunted and fell to on his supper.

"You're fair crazy about the fighting," he said suddenly, with his mouth full. "Well, it's as well you're pleased, seeing that you're married to a fighting man."

"Ay, Ah'm well pleased," retorted Lizzie defiantly.

CHAPTER XI

FAIR FIGHT

A crowd numbering close upon a thousand assembled on Glasgow Green to watch the fight between Razor King and big McLatchie. Lizzie, as good as her word, had mustered about a hundred young women from the Gorbals district, and the Townhead lasses were present in almost equal strength.

Johnnie was in good humour that afternoon immediately before the big fight of his career. For a fortnight he had been training hard, after his fashion, working on the coal lorry all day and exercising morning and evening in the open-air gym. During this period he had drunk nothing except an occasional glass of beer and smoked very little. He was clear-eyed and exuberantly fit. Without underestimating his opponent, he was confident of success, keyed up with excitement, the born fighter eager for action.

Deep in his heart there was another and a keener exhilaration. For he was Razor King, the leader of his imposing "division", a man outstanding among his fellows, someone totally different from the ordinary. Soon that crowd would be cheering him, yelling his title, mad with excitement to see him win. Ay, by God! He was different from the rest of them and he'd show them; he'd show them! He'd *show* them!

It is to be noted that a "fair fight" between gang champions is one in which nobody interferes, at least as long as both men are on their feet. But it is fighting, not boxing. There are no rules and no rounds and no weapons except fists and feet. It is sheer primitive battle that ends – and that can only end – when one man is battered into senselessness.

But there are certain formalities even upon these occasions. Each champion has two seconds to see that the fight continues "fair" and the crowd itself forms a solid ring to give them room.

It was a cold dry afternoon, grand fighting weather, when Johnnie and McLatchie, stripped naked to the waist, with belts about their trousers and wearing their working boots, entered the ring. The Townhead man was four inches taller than Razor King, but in weight there could not have been very much difference between the two. Both of them showed splendid muscles, but Johnnie's seemed closer knit and stockier than his enemy's. His bullet head was closely cropped and his short black hair shone sleekly. Red-headed McLatchie was bronzed to the elbows but his body colouring was lighter and the tangle of red hair on his chest was like a stain upon the white skin. Johnnie's body was hairless as a woman's, but very hard.

Now the ring was set not far from the gymnasium itself, where the grass slopes away a little towards the river. McLatchie, anxious to use his height advantage to the full, saw to it that he was looking down the slope. Johnnie's grim lips parted in a wolfish grin to show his strong and regular teeth; then his mouth snapped tight like a trap.

The seconds sprang back into a wall of spectators and the fight was on with no mockery of handshake. Razor King, bullet head tucked into his chest, rushed in to the attack. McLatchie, with some notions of "boxing", gave ground, careful to guard his body, waiting for a chance to use his left.

Johnnie had no science; he relied on his strength and ferocity and great capacity to take punishment. He got in with two lightning-quick jabs to McLatchie's body, left himself wide open, and received a smashing blow to the nose that set the blood flowing freely.

He shook his head and closed under a whirlwind of blows, locking his right arm round McLatchie's body and driving home a succession of savage punches to the stomach. One of his eyes was blackened and the salt taste of blood was in his mouth. He heard the deep roar of the men and the wild high shrieking of the women. And he smashed another half-arm jolt into flesh that gave to the blow.

Traffic had come to a standstill on Govan Street Bridge that overlooks the Green. The parapet was black with spectators, and the trams queued up one behind the other until there were five or six of them on the bridge itself. There were police, who saw and hurried away to fetch reinforcements. But the confused volume of sound from the bridge was lost in the frenzied yelling of the ring itself.

Groaning under the blow to the solar plexus, McLatchie broke out of the clinch and his left fist landed another punch to the head. Johnnie gave a bellow of laughter, rushed furiously into fists that flailed like a windmill, shot out a dexterous foot, and tripped McLatchie so that the big red-head fell backwards like a log. In an instant, while the shout that greeted that fall was still ringing, Razor King raised his right foot and brought the boot down hard on McLatchie's face between the eyes.

"Take that, yah red swine!" he roared.

McLatchie was out. The boot fell with such force that it not only smashed the bridge of his nose but actually ended his career as a fighting man. He was never again quoted "among the Townhead champions".

There is no appeal to Caesar in these gladiatorial combats. Johnnie took no chances. He kicked furiously at the fallen man's body and McLatchie's eyes closed in his mangled face.

Then the ring broke and the mob battle, which is the

151

almost certain sequel to these "fair fights", started. A Townhead man leapt at Johnnie, and Lizzie, screaming and cursing at the top of her voice, tried to reach his side, with his clothing in her arms.

Somebody struck her on the head with a bottle and she went down. Razor King had leapt aside from his new enemy and the sight of Lizzie, lying where she had fallen, drove him to a frenzy that was almost madness. Like a bull he drove through the mob, snatched at his waistcoat where it lay by his wife's side, and, an instant later, stood brandishing his weapons.

Men and women fell away from him. His eyes were glittering insanely and his bleeding lips were parted in an animal snarl. Like an animal he roared as he sprang at two young fellows who were battling with one of his own followers.

"The two of you," he screamed. "I'll get the two of you . . . !"

One furious slash laid open an enemy's face from cheekbone to jaw; another hideously gashed the second man's neck. Both collapsed, one of them with a thin, wild cry of anguish like a woman's. And the mob pressed back on itself still further, even against the thrust of fight and fury in its own core.

High above this turmoil and confusion there now came a shout of warning which swelled into a great chorus: "THE JAILERS!"

In fact a strong body of uniformed police was now coming up at the double and plain clothes men, too utterly outnumbered to interfere before, began to show up at Govan Street Bridge and at the Suspension Bridge and at McNeil Street.

"Rin for it, Razor King!" shouted some of his followers.

Johnnie, with a space cleared all round him even in the stampede that was starting, saw Lizzie stagger to her feet and heard her beginning to curse again. There was blood running from her head wound on to that same green coat she had worn when he had met her outside the Coffin Building for their first courting. A sudden fierce tenderness assailed him.

"Come on, Liz!" he yelled. "The 'Busies' are here!"

He flung his bloody razors one after the other over the heads of the running crowd and into the Clyde, raced to his wife, and thrust his arms into the jacket which she had dropped as she fell.

"Johnnie! Johnnie!" she gasped, clinging to him; worshipping him; adoring him.

The stalwarts of the "division" formed a close ring about the pair of them, and the police, already hovering on the fringe of that wild crowd, were none too anxious to rush the fighters on the Green, for that would have meant a riot far more desperate than any ordinary street "rammy".

"Thank Christ it's getting dark!" shrilled one of the Gorbals women who was holding Lizzie by the arm.

"Getting dark, is it?" she cried. "Then go give that bastard McLatchie another hit before it's right dark! That's whit I wid like tae see him getting – another hit!"

"I think he's had all he can stand," said Johnnie grimly, buttoning his jacket. "He'll be well out of it for a while if you ask me. Now hurry, Liz."

She put her right hand up to her head and drew it away with blood on it. She stared at the blood horrified; then screamed and fainted.

"Help me get her out of the Green, some of you!" said Razor King tersely. "Over the Suspension Bridge yonder. It's the safest way, I think."

The tumult and fighting all around them was still terrific, but Johnnie and his followers moved swiftly and compactly through it all, a very tide of Gorbals men and girls following in their wake.

"Jeez, I'm gled she's safe out of that," Johnnie exclaimed. "I don't know what I'd do without her; I don't, by Christ!"

He looked back at the battlefield from the Suspension Bridge as he spoke and was faintly annoyed to see that the Green had cleared of people like an overturned anthill of ants.

"Look at the bliddy busies!" he said contemptuously, "fair swarming on to the Green now there's naebody left to fight! Hell! There's wan or twa cripples or, mebbe, twa-three kids, they'll capture safely now as the ring-leaders of this 'riotous assembly!' Poliss . . . ! My arse!"

In fact only two arrests were made after this semi-historic battle. Both the captured ruffians turned out to be lads of under seventeen. They were brought up for trial the following day and, as everybody knew perfectly well that the boys had nothing whatever to do with the general battle, the court room was not even filled. The sentence upon each was thirty days' hard labour. One of the youngsters, taking this punishment very badly, was sentenced again two weeks later for a most ruffianly attack upon a warder. His old mother was in court at the time and he went back to his cell a confirmed, complete and utterly reckless enemy of society. Nobody cared.

There were twenty or more casualties conveyed by ambulance to the Royal Infirmary and big McLatchie was probably the most seriously hurt among the batch. The tenements generally were gossiping eagerly as to the possibility of his making a recovery and demanding a "revenge" from Razor King. They wasted their wonder, for McLatchie was "finished" as a gangster. His face was permanently disfigured, but, worse than that, his spirit was broken. It was commonly rumoured in Glasgow that the police had advised the infirmary surgeons not to be "too gentle" with this gangster chief. They must have known that if he ever came out of the infirmary as a whole man nothing would satisfy him but a return match with his enemy.

154

But he did not come out as a whole man. His face was marred for ever, with one eyebrow twisted into a sarcastic pointer at his broken nose-bridge. And he left the infirmary walking with a permanent limp as the final mark of some obscure body injury. Townhead gave its wretched ex-champion the cold shoulder. His girl deserted him for another, and fitter, fighter, and McLatchie – ugly and despairing and broken-nerved – fled from Glasgow and was lost forever from the city of his birth.

But the stock of Razor King rose steadily in the underworld of Glasgow. He, and Lizzie too, were both so "tough" that they went to work as usual on the morning after the fight. Reilly and all his men greeted Johnnie, without verbal comment, but with deeply marked new respect. His eyes were blackened and his face cut and scarred, but he could heft his coal sacks as lightly as ever and, when the day's toil was ended, Reilly himself asked the battered warrior into the corner pub for a drink.

"Ah'm holding, Johnnie," he said tersely. "Whit's it tae be? Whisky? Ay, you'll likely enjoy a tot of whisky *now*. They tell me the Townhead mob is hanging out black flags since McLatchie went inside? Ah'm right gled you're back to the lorry, Johnnie. There's naebody can argue wi' that!"

All Gorbals thought the more of Razor King because he was back at the toil after the fair fight.

But Lizzie was not so fortunate. Perhaps she would have been wiser to take two or three days off duty, but she would not do that. Instead, with big lint bandages round her head, she turned up at the bakery as usual. Neither her fellow-workers nor her employers made any comment, but she could *feel* that the forewomen were looking at her askance and she was aware that now, for the first time, she, Lizzie Ramsay, was definitely identified with the Gorbals Razor King. Defiantly she went about her job, as clever a cake-maker as any lass in the

155

factory. Nobody interfered; no forewoman ventured a criticism. But she left work that day alone. Her best friends had suddenly disappeared. Suddenly, overwhelmingly, she was aware that she was no longer the Lizzie Ramsay they had known, but, rather, the isolated, admired-despised and alarming wife of the Razor King.

In the spring of that year – that is to say by the end of March 1925 – Johnnie and Lizzie were both recovered from their injuries and were enjoying the fruits of their reputation as warriors in the district. They were constantly invited to parties and always their neighbours and friends were ready to buy them as much drink as they could afford.

It is true that there were households in many tenements, including some in Crown Street itself, which greeted them with reserve and stood carefully aloof from all festivities, but Razor King and his wife paid little attention to these "cautiously respectable" folk. They were well satisfied with the public consideration and respect which was displayed towards them in the streets when they walked abroad.

Moreover, not being called upon at that time to return the ever-lavish hospitality of the "division", Johnnie and Lizzie had all "the good time" they wanted and still contrived to put money away in the bank each week. Few people knew of this highly unusual thrift; none realized the swelling pride with which each fresh deposit was lodged at the Post Office. For Razor King and his wife were still in love and still confident that they would make their mark with or without their neighbours' help.

On the last Saturday evening of that month they sat alone in their clean, trim little apartment, wondering where they would go that evening, when there came a sudden knock on the door.

"Who the hell can that be, I wonder!" said Lizzie, yawning, as she rose from the arm-chair which she and

Johnnie had been sharing. She went to the door, looking domesticated enough in her blue frock and apron.

"Eh, Liz," murmured Johnnie contentedly. "Just tell them Ah'm gonny stick wi' you the night no matter what's on. Ah'm fed up wi' going out wi' yon mob from the corner."

She threw a brilliant smile at him over her shoulder and opened the door, only to fall back overwhelmed by a rush of strange young men.

Seven larrikens from the Townhead had taken this chance of making a name for themselves and evening the score a little with the Gorbals Razor King.

"Help! Murder! Poliss!" screamed Lizzie as she backed away from the door, but, almost in the same instant, one of the attackers struck her a tremendous blow between the eyes and she fell like a log, cutting her head against the corner of the chair.

Johnnie, his coat off, was lounging back in the arm-chair, but no cat could have been more quickly on its feet. His two razors were out of his vest pockets in a flash and he met the wave of the attack with answering fury.

One of the Townhead mob, slashed across the face, went down screaming and a second, intercepting a razor edge with driving fore-arm, cursed furiously as he hugged a crippled wrist.

"But we've *got* you, Razor King!" yelled a third assailant, hurling a small axe as he spoke. The blade twisted in mid air, but the heavy butt end of this formidable instrument caught Johnnie behind the ear and he dropped like a log. The enemy rushed upon him, hampered by their numbers in that small space, and kicked furiously at his prostrate body.

One among them, more brutal than the others, drew a weapon twice across the still face of the unconscious Razor King. Death was very close to Johnnie, then, but there came the sound of tumultuous feet up the stairway and instantly the Townhead mob turned at the yell of warning from one of its members still on the outer landing. Fighting like demons, the raiding gangsters smashed and fought their way down the crowded stairs and into the street. Then they took to their heels and ran, with none pursuing.

Johnnie lay very still, his face a mask of blood, and Lizzie was stretched unconscious by the door. The two razored men of the Townhead mob, one senseless and the other groaning as he kept his fingers pressed over the horrid gash in his wrist, were carried hastily down the stairs to be dumped into the nearest close-mouth. And Razor King and Lizzie were hurried to the infirmary for treatment.

The authorities never learned that there was any connection between the pair of double casualties admitted to the infirmary that day. Mr and Mrs Stark, when at last they had recovered enough to make a statement, could only swear that they had opened the door of their "hoose" to a gang of unknown assailants. And the two slashed Townhead lads were sullenly positive that they had been walking peaceably along the street when they were set upon by armed gangsters whom they had never seen before, and whom they could not possibly hope to identify.

Lizzie, stunned but not badly hurt, was able to return home the same day. Johnnie was naturally detained and the doctors marvelled that he had escaped any permanent or crippling injury. The whole affair caused a great stir in Gorbals. On the Sunday, indeed, the local papers published a sensational column, purporting to give the story of this gang attack. It was read with peculiar avidity by a score of men and women who knew that it was mistaken in every essential fact.

Johnnie came home in a fortnight's time, his scarred face hideous with plaster strapping. Lizzie met him and flung her arms round his neck ecstatically.

"I'll always be yours, Razor King," she sobbed, "I

widny care if you were as well marked again, so help me Christ, I widny! . . . You like me a wee bit, dain't you, Johnnie?"

He took her wrists in his hands and wrenched her arms apart with a kind of gentle violence.

"Can you no' see Ah've got someone wi' me?" he exclaimed, jerking his thumb over his shoulder towards the open door and the landing beyond. "Never mind, though, Liz. Sure I like you! I like you a hellova lot!"

CHAPTER XII

A HOUSE WITH A BATH

Just about the time of the "fair fight" on Glasgow
Green, Bobbie Hurley and Lily McKay moved into a
new home in Cathcart – a room-and-kitchen house
with a *bathroom*. They were inordinately proud of it.
True, they had travelled far since their first dancing
partnership of the "clabber jiggings". Then they were
just two little "slummies" with feet that tapped and
bodies that swayed instinctively to any musical rhythm.
Now they were true professionals, the recognized champions of the big Gaydom Palais de Danse, envied by
their fellow instructors and flattered and sought out
by the clients. They called the manager of the hall by,
his Christian name, and they still had thirty pounds
to their credit in the savings bank even after furnishing their new home. But the bathroom was the final
and tangible evidence of their success. The possession
of it placed them indisputably "far above the working
classes".

The slums of Glasgow have produced many gifted
dancers and some few of them have even attained
national celebrity. But these rare successes have never
been at all eager to advertise their origins, and, by the
time they have made names for themselves, they have
invariably invented a background outside the tenements.
At the first opportunity they have migrated from their
native slum to some better-class district, severing old
friendships and family ties ruthlessly for the sake of social
advancement. Glasgow men and women take this for
granted. For it is hard enough to win out of the slums at

all, and quite impossible to do so for those who try to carry their families on their backs.

Lily had never deceived herself about her own ambitions or the logical consequences of their fulfilment. But Bobbie was a sentimentalist. Mentally he despised his "ordinary" brothers and sisters and his squalid home, but his heart reproached him. For several years, too, after his father, old James Hurley, had been taken away to the madhouse, Bobbie was the only wage-earner in his family, and he was kept very much under the thumb of his mother, a dominant, managing body, who was nominally a Catholic but whose religion was "respectability".

Though old James had been a fervent dissenter, all the children of this particular mixed marriage were brought up in the Catholic faith, which meant at least that the boys doffed their caps to the priest when they couldn't keep out of his way. Mrs Hurley had been worried about Bobbie's passion for dancing from the very beginning, but in that one matter he rebelled, at first secretly and then more openly as his local reputation increased. But he went on working at the barber's shop long after Lily had broken definitely with her own family and had given ordinary work the go-by.

There were two versions current in the Gorbals of Lily's emancipation: one was that she had "walked oot", and the other that her father had thrown her into the street. In actual fact she left her employment as assistant in a fruiterer's shop because she was refused a week's leave for the New Year of 1923. By this time she and Bobbie were already earning small sums as leaders off in those minor halls which did not employ regular professionals. For that particular week they had an offer of four pounds between them for full-time work as exhibition dancers. Bobbie was lucky. His employer had a consumptive nephew stopping with him at the time, thrown out of work by his illness. Bobbie was granted the week off without pay simply because the consumptive was able to take his place in the shop – also without pay.

But Lily had no real claim to this holiday at the busiest time of the year.

"Ah'm sorry you canny let me off," she said simply, to her employer, "because Ah'll need tae be going just the same."

"Then you'll no' come back!" he retorted.

"That's what Ah wis meaning: Ah'll no' come back. You'll be better looking for another girl at once."

When she paid her mother the usual ten shillings out of her last week's pay she handed the money over with a defiant laugh.

"What Ah'm gaun tae dae *next* week," she observed, flippantly, "is more than Ah can tell you, for Ah took the sack at the fruit-shop this mornin'."

Her father was at home at the time and this announcement, or perhaps the manner of it, was the cause of the final quarrel.

"Whit's that ye say?" he shouted angrily. "You've ta'en the sack? An' what for, Ah wid like to know? Dae ye think ye're gaun out jazzin' wi' yon little pimp o' a Bobbie Hurley? No bliddy fears, you're no'! You'll find anither job, my lass, and until you've found one, you'll stop at home to help your mother, dae ye hear?"

"Ay," she said, "Ah'm no' deaf! But Ah'm no' gonny stop at home an' Ah'm no' asking you tae keep me. Bobbie an' me can look efter ourselves. An' Ah'm no' the *only* one who's no' toiling in this hoose."

Richard McKay had been out of work for two years and the taunt was more than he could endure. He took his daughter by the shoulders, shook her violently, and then hit her two or three times, flat-handed, on either cheek.

She broke away from him sobbing, but undaunted.

"Ah'll no' stay here to be struck," she shrieked, "by Christ! Ah willny!"

"You'll dae whit your telt, or Ah'll fling you oot, an' oot you'll stay."

"That'll suit me fine. Ah'll no' be wanting to come back . . ."

Then he sprang at her and knocked her down. He was not a man in the habit of hitting his women-folk about, and at heart he was proud of Lily's good looks, but her defiance and contempt drove him beside himself. He tugged his cap on his head and went out for a drink, swearing as he went. By the time he returned to the weeping and scolding of his wife, Lily had packed a battered suitcase and left her home for good. She was then barely seventeen and Bobbie a year her senior.

Lily, who had been saving money secretly for some time, was taken in as a lodger by a widow in Crown Street, whose two-roomed house was in the very tenement where, later, Johnnie and Lizzie found their "single end". Bobbie's face expressed such consternation when she told him of this decisive move that she broke into a vexed laugh.

"Ah *wish* you cud be a wee bit manly!" said she, galling him with that reproach which became the intermittent refrain of their married life. "Mebbe you'd be better aff yourself if you went my road. Sune the dancing will be worth far more than the barbering, Bobbie. You an' me are different from the working-class. One day we'll have to get right away from Gorbals and everything to do with it."

In his heart he knew she was right and that there was no other road by which he could attain his ambition. But he evaded the issue and talked instead of the long time he had been patient with her in not demanding his "rights". For at that time, though they often hugged and kissed, these two young people were not lovers in the physical sense, and they had discussed marriage only as a future prospect which would have to be considered when circumstances improved.

Their dancing during that holiday week was an unqualified success. The hall was crowded at every session, and there was an ovation for "the champions" after every exhibition number. Seeing Lily home one night, Bobbie became suddenly obstinate at the close-mouth.

"Well, we're here again, eh?" she said nervously, aware of his changed mood.

"Ay, we're here," he replied, "an' Ah'll see you up the sterrs."

"Don't be daft, Bobbie. You've hugged me plenty, I think, for one night. An' I'll tell you something: I'll no' keep you waiting long either."

"No? Well, Ah'll see you up the sterrs just the same."

She shrugged her shoulders mutinously, but they climbed the stairs to the top landing, his arm about her waist. She slipped from him then and stood smiling and flushed, taking her check key from her handbag.

"Ah'll be going in now, Bobbie," she said.

He made no answer, and she turned the key in the lock. As she opened the door one of the landlady's children, a girl of seven or eight, ran to greet her.

"Hullo!" said Lily eagerly, "you're up late, Minnie. See: I must away in, Bobbie. See you the morn, eh?"

He threw away his cigarette and moistened his lips.

"What about the night?" he demanded huskily.

"Nothing doing the night!" she said, and there was a note of panic in her voice.

He stepped very quickly into the open doorway.

"They'll all be thinking we're married anyway," said he.

"Not here, they won't. They know we're not!"

"Ach! Tae hell wi' them and what they think! Ah'm sticking here for the night."

He was "manly" enough to frighten her then, and she could see that nothing she could do would make him go quietly. Suddenly she knew that she did not want him to go.

"Away to bed wi' you!" she said, stooping to the wondering child. "He'll no' be a minute, but it's awful late."

The little girl obeyed at once, running through into the second room and closing the door behind her. Bobbie, his heart beating hard, closed the front door softly. She lit the gas and they stood facing each other under its light, two young people still in their 'teens, both desperately excited, both more than a little frightened.

Bobbie threw his hat on the bed in a gesture of challenge. His face was pale and drawn and there was a curious mixture of pleading and threatening as he appealed to his partner.

"I canny help it, Lily," he said, "I've got tae stick here the night."

"What will the woman say?" she demanded breathlessly, caring little what the woman said.

"I don't give a damn what she says! Ah'm sticking here."

He took off his coat, jacket and waistcoat all at once and threw them over a chair-back. It was a dextrous movement and the girl's eyes sparkled.

"This is a hellova way for us to start, aw the same!" she whispered, and then began to laugh.

Bobbie did not answer. He sat on the edge of the bed and began to pull off his shoes – those tony-red shoes which were part of the special "paraffin" which he had acquired since they had begun to make a success of the dancing. One shoe fell to the floor noisily.

"Be careful!" Lily protested. "Don't waken up the whole bliddy landing.'

He gave a low chuckle of delighted triumph.

"As long as they don't waken us up, that's the main thing. Aw, Lily, we've always gone well thegither."

"Ah'm not a bit afraid of you, if that's what you mean!"

"Who's saying you are?"

She took off her coat with trembling fingers that belied her words.

"Ah'm not afraid of anything," she said, "as long as I'm no' put into any trouble. It's all right for *you*, but—"

"I'll watch that, all right."

"You'll have to do more than watch, Bobbie. It's the jazzing Ah'm thinking of."

"I know. Ah'm not forgetting it myself."

Forcing herself to a composure she did not feel, Lily began deliberately to undress. Bobbie caught his breath in admiration as she struggled out of her frock.

"An' what will they be saying at your hoose the night, Bobbie?" she taunted him. "An' will you be going to work to-morrow?"

He silenced her with his kisses.

Later, when she lay close in his arms, her head against his shoulder, she said to him, half-fondly, half-reproachfully: "We're as well married as carrying on like this, Bobbie."

"We'll get married aw right, never fear!" he retorted. "And sune, too. Efter that we'll be dancing at the Gaydom. And then, one day, we'll be away out of all the scruff in a fine house wi' a bathroom an aw!"

"Eh, Bobbie," she gasped, "widn't that be fine?"

And now, in the winter of 1924, there they were, married, dancing at the Gaydom and settled into the new home with a bath.

At that time the Gaydom ranked high among Glasgow's public dancing halls. In the evenings the charge for admission was half a crown, for men and women alike. On Saturday evenings the admission was raised to three-and-sixpence: on Saturday afternoons it was lowered to two shillings. Two orchestras, each of six performers, discoursed the latest dance music in uninterrupted sequence, one taking up the task as soon as the other wearied. The great hall could accommodate five hundred couples without undue crowding. A fountain, illuminated by coloured lights, played in the centre of the building. From the gallery there were four points of coloured light which could concentrate their beams upon a single couple or sweep them over the floor in swiftly contrasting and blending hues. Twenty-four professionals, twelve men and twelve women, waited in their "pens" during the brief intervals between one dance and the next. Any one of them could be hired by any patron at sixpence a dance, or by arrangement, at an inclusive rate for the evening.

The Gaydom was no gangsters' hall. It was frequented by an essentially middle-class and prosperous clientele except on two "popular afternoons" a week. No caps protruded from jacket pockets in that exclusive domain. The boys paid their twopences for cloakroom fees with good-humoured resignation. The men professionals were all in dinner-jackets and the girls were in low-necked evening frocks. Sometimes, even among the patrons, there would be a couple in evening dress, who would, doubtless, attract attention, but who might dance without comment nevertheless.

Only on the afternoons of Tuesday and Saturday was the place at all invaded by the "working-class". The real mob – the "scruff" of Glasgow – was too overawed or too "broke" to seek admission. There had been no serious "rammy" – least of all a razor fight – at the Gaydom for over a year. Its atmosphere was so select that even the authentic dialect of the city was filtered into a studious refinement of "good English".

And yet, as all Glasgow knew, men and women with money could hire many of the professional dancing stars of this great dance hall for purposes far beyond the limit of professional instruction. Among the girl instructors there were few who could not be bought for the evening, provided the buyer were reasonably "decent" and his money reasonably adequate. The men, perhaps in less demand, were equally saleable. The system of "booking out" still prevailed. There were no dancers in the Gaydom who could afford to refuse such bookings except upon rare occasion or with legitimate excuse.

It is to be noted that, after the scandals which filled the Sunday newspapers in 1927, "booking out" as a recognized system was suppressed, first in Glasgow and then in Edinburgh, and, indeed, throughout Scotland. But it must not be supposed that the official discontinuance of this practice entirely ended it. On the contrary there are still some dance halls where it is understood by clients in the know that instructors of either sex can be hired for "instruction" off the premises. One does not now approach the management direct and pay, cash down, a "booking-out fee". "Booking out" is no longer spoken of under that name. The invitation is now made direct to the professional and involves the formality of consent. But, at least in some halls, that consent may almost be taken for granted.

When Bobbie and Lily accepted their first engagement at the Gaydom the question of "booking out" was not directly referred to. Neither the manager nor the young dancers themselves considered it necessary. For it is only fair to state that the professional dancer of that day – so far from resenting this system – counted upon it largely to supplement his or her income. The "champions" were in any case entitled to their own likes and dislikes within reason. They were *not* obliged to accept the invitation of any and every drunken or old or repulsive client. They were expected only to be reasonable and not to turn good money away for a mere whim.

In theory this toleration applied to all the professionals, even including the merely competent performers engaged more for their looks and good manners than for their actual talent. But the theory did not work out in practice for the simple reason that there were always a dozen men and girls eager for a trial and ready immediately to replace any professional who failed to give satisfaction.

It followed, naturally enough, that if wealthy patrons complained, the professionals whose squeamishness caused the protest simply lost their jobs. There was never any explanation; never a reproof that they had refused "bookings out". They were merely sacked, and their meagre two pounds a week went to the next applicant on the waiting list.

And yet, in spite of the fact that vicious people of both sexes visited the dance halls deliberately to pick up paid accomplices, dancing itself was so much in vogue and real talent was so highly appreciated that no successful hall could afford to be without a few star performers. Bobbie and Lily came into this category, for their fame had been noised abroad while they were still dancing at the second-rate Kingston Hall, and they had already shown up the Gaydom's professionals by a series of visits there as paying clients, when their dancing had held all eyes.

George Brass, the manager of the Gaydom, had wanted to engage them for some considerable time. He was, for all his "middle-aged spread", sufficiently expert himself to appraise their technical perfection. Above all, he saw in their youth and in their exceptional good looks the ideal qualification for his star pair. For the great majority of his patrons were just dancing enthusiasts, quick to admire talent, eager to learn and truly appreciative of youth and beauty, zest and romance.

At this period Bobbie and Lily were still sufficiently in love with one another and with dancing to look gay and happy and carefree and romantic. At times, during their exhibition numbers at the lesser hall, he had watched them and noticed that for minutes at a stretch they were so absorbed in each other, so entranced by the dance itself, that they were literally oblivious of the onlookers. They came to life, as it were, when the dance was over, flushed and laughing and naïvely delighted with the enthusiasm of their reception. That very *naïveté* – that superb quality of youth and enthusiasm –

always thrilled the crowd and provoked a storm of applause. Decidedly he had to have them for the Gaydom and he was prepared, if necessary, to pay them eight pounds a week, plus commission – one quarter of the instruction and partnering fees which they might earn.

Lily, far quicker than her partner in these matters, guessed that Mr George Brass wanted to make them an offer long before he had so much as spoken to them. She told Bobbie so and was furious at his scepticism. When he came across to them on that particular night and asked to have a word with them in his private office, she followed him demurely on Bobbie's arm, but her whispered aside was full of triumph and reproach.

"Whit did I *tell* ye?" she said. "He's had tae come tae us, not us tae him. Now be manly, Bobbie, for Christ's sake! Never let on you're pleased. Make him think we're no' sae keen to be dancing here in the Gaydom."

But Bobbie could not hide his jubilation as she could, and he hailed George Brass's offer of seven pounds a week, and commission, with a wide smile more eloquent than words. Lily was excited enough in her own way, though she would not show it, and afterwards reproached her partner for being so "saft". Actually even she did not realize that Mr Brass would have been quite willing to pay eight pounds had they held out for it. He was making three hundred pounds gross profit a week and believed that the "champions" might easily swell his takings by another hundred pounds or even more.

Everything was settled within a quarter of an hour, and, rising from his desk, the manager went to a cupboard and produced a bottle of whisky and three tumblers. At that time Lily, barely eighteen, was not used to raw spirits, and Bobbie scarcely more so. But both were eager to bind the contract in the traditional way.

Lily was given a smaller measure than her partner and she gulped it down at a draught. The fiery whisky burned her throat and set her coughing and choking in spite of

170

herself, but she kicked Bobbie furiously under the table
when he was about to apologize on her behalf.

"That's grand whisky," she said, throwing her head
back and laughing excitedly. "We'll show you a tango
after this, Mr Brass, better than you've ever seen before."

His eyes twinkled and he laughed at her gameness.

"Stick to the Gaydom," he said encouragingly, "and
we'll stick to you. I'll have a new frock for you the morn,
and I'll announce you to the crowd at the evening
session."

"But Ah'm telling you, Mr Brass," said Bobbie, with
sudden gravity, "Lily an' me'll do all you want *in* the
Gaydom, but we're no' promising tae dance for any
clients outside or anything like that. We've got to have
our freedom about that."

"Don't be saft!" said Lily bitterly. "Can you no' see
that Mr Brass will no' encourage any liberty-takers in
the Gaydom? We can count upon you, Mr Brass, and
you can count on us to be reasonable."

"I'm sure of that," he bowed. "You and me'll get on
fine."

Two months later Bobbie and Lily moved into the
house with the bath.

Their marriage had already estranged Bobbie from his
own family. That he should leave them sooner or later
was, of course, inevitable, but, in fact, Mrs Hurley had
taken a violent dislike to Lily from the start, accounting
her little better than a whore and believing, quite rightly,
that the girl was egging her son on to throw up his steady,
respectable job for the chancy, discreditable business of
the "jazzing".

After that, when Bobbie had begun to stay away from
home for nights at a time, there had been constant
reproaches, his mother's moral indignation being much
aggravated when she realized that she was getting little
benefit from Bobbie's increased earnings. After one

171

violent scene in the street between his mother and his girl, Lily had told him flatly that he must choose between them. And the marriage by declaration – the last shame in a Catholic household – had made the breach irrevocable.

"Whit's the use?" Bobbie had said to himself when he and his wife had first settled in a furnished room in Eglinton Street. "Mother canny see that Lily an' me's *different*. She canny understand – none of them can understand – that we've *got* to look after ourselves. Ay, poor old lady! She'll be grieving sore, but what cud Ah dae, what *cud* Ah dae?"

Then, very easily and very quickly, he put the family entirely out of his mind.

Even in the furnished room in Eglinton Street a bath had been a necessary purchase, though then it was no more than a zinc tub. At nights, when they came back weary from the dancing, they would bathe in it by turn in front of the fire, each rubbing the other down.

In the new house, which cost them the huge rent of fourteen and ninepence a week unfurnished, they stood lost in admiration of the bathroom with its gas geyser and its taps. They had furnished their two rooms somewhat sparsely to begin with out of their savings and Bobbie was suddenly frightened of the thought of all the money that was spent and the heavy expenses they would have to meet.

"I doubt," he said gloomily, after the first enthusiasm had evaporated, "we would have been better, maybe, to stick to the old room for a while. Fourteen and nine a week is a lot to pey even for a hoose like this."

"Will you stop grumbling?" Lily protested. "Are we no' daeing fine at the Gaydom? Didn't George and Mrs Brass theirselves find this place for us? Be a wee bit manly, for Christ's sake! Ah'm no' going to stop along wi' the riff-raff all my life, I can tell you. Whit's more, we'll be getting a girl in to look after the place when

172

"Ah'm oot. An' that'll cost another eight shillings a week for a good lassie."

"Twenty-two shillings and ninepence!" he calculated, frightened and yet elated. "Ah wisny making much more than that at the barber's shop for a week's toil."

"Too bliddy true! But we're making seven pounds a week the two of us for salary now – not to speak of the commissions."

His face clouded and he turned moodily away from her to light a cigarette.

"What's the manner now?' she asked fretfully. "Dae we have to have this all over again? Ach, the hell! Give me a whisky, Bobbie, and have a nip yourself and don't be so bliddy miserable. We can look efter ourselves, I suppose."

There was whisky in the press and he poured out two generous measures, making Lily's at least as stiff as his own. He was rather proud at that time of the way she had "come on at the drinking", for she could take her glass now as hardily as a man.

"That's good whisky," she exclaimed, brightening, "an' I wanted it bad. We're doing well enough maybe, but the Gaydom is getting a lot of work out of us, Bobbie."

"It wid no' be so bad if it was only the dancing," he grunted, "but it fair beats me to think of some clients."

The Gaydom, indeed, took full toll of the champions' physical energy. Bobbie and Lily had to be at the hall at ten every morning for practice and instruction work until noon. From twelve to one they were still on duty, giving special lessons to customers who would pay well for the privilege. Then they were free for rather more than an hour, but at two-thirty the afternoon session started and lasted until five o'clock. In the evening the Gaydom Palais de Danse was thronged from eight until nearly midnight and, often enough, there were parties to follow.

Lily lit a cigarette in her turn and then came over to sit on Bobbie's knee.

173

"Listen," she said persuasively. "What do we care about the bliddy toffs? They're different from us, are they no'? But you an' me are the goods, Bobbie. This is the life to live so long as we watch number one. Ah'm no' caring for anybody but you, and Ah'm no letting any of they dirty liberty-takers get away with it awthegither."

Bobbie grinned, in spite of himself.

"They can look, but they canny touch, eh, Lil?" said he. "Oh, I'll grant you can look efter yourself, but there's some of those big fat swine that paw you about I'll murder one day!"

"Ah'm no' made of glass," she said, "an' them that paws, peys."

"Too true," he laughed, but without real amusement. "Aw the same, there's some'll no' be satisfied wi' pawin'."

"What then? What if we dae go the whole road when the money's good. I tell you they're no' like us. It widny mean anything to *me*, Bobbie. Nor to you, Ah'm hoping. An' it's as well we're married an' aw. We've always got a grand excuse for no' going out by oorselves. When there's the two of us, they canny go very far."

"I know, but it's no' always the two of us. Ah'm no' jealous, Lil. We're artistes, I know that. But there's times I'd like fine to bash some of them that dance with you . . . when I see them sitting at the table wi' you . . . buying you drinks and getting a feel of your knee under the table. Yon bald-headed old bastard the ither night! Dae ye mind him? My fingers fair itched to tear the face aff him."

She laughed loudly and got up to pour more whisky.

"Have some sense, Bobbie," she protested. "Stop being daft about what canny be helped. We're the goods, you an' me. One day we'll run a dance hall of our own and we'll be well respected long efter Razor King's forgotten. We'll be toffs ourselves before we're through."

"By God! You're right, Lil!" he exclaimed excitedly,

carried away by her fierce ambition. "They canny stop us. We'll be the goods in Glasgow one day."

"Then drink to that," she laughed, handing him his glass. "Luck to us an' tae hell wi' the toffs! And now, Bobbie, it's two o'clock. What do you say? Wull we have oor baths?"

CHAPTER XIII

BIG BATTALIONS

If Matha Craig, a fighting man of sorts, had not laughed at the wrong time, the history of many people in Gorbals might have been greatly changed. But Matha was the lowest type of hooligan, one whose ignorance and brutality was unredeemed by any native intelligence. To him any demonstration of ordinary human affection was "saft" and he stared in sheer amazement at Lizzie's welcome of Razor King when he came back from the infirmary, his face disfigured by his recent bashing.

The front door was open, and Matha standing on the stair-head, when Lizzie flung her arms round her husband's neck. Johnnie, freeing himself, had not even sworn. Matha couldn't understand that and still less could he understand Razor King's smile and his "Sure, Liz, I like you a hellova lot."

Matha walked into the kitchen and they paid no attention to him. There were tears in Lizzie's eyes and Johnnie looked sheepish; there was no other word for it. Matha tugged his cap down on his head and swore derisively.

In a flash Johnnie had turned to face him, his eyes ablaze with anger. Before Matha realized his danger Johnnie leapt at him, drove a clenched fist to his nose and sent him toppling over a chair. Instantly, before the other had a chance to pick himself up, Johnnie kicked him savagely in the undefended stomach. Matha uttered a horrid groan, writhed convulsively, and passed into unconsciousness.

Lizzie had run screaming on the landing and half

a dozen neighbours rushed up the stairs to her help.

They found Johnnie completely unmoved. He prodded Matha's body with his toe and laughed evilly.

"He's well out," sneered the Razor King. "See the yellow he is? That's what comes to them that take liberties wi' me."

They actually laughed. One young man, loosely attached to Johnnie's own gang, looked down at Matha and then smirked at the company.

"What is it?" he said. "A half-caste or what?"

"Some kind of a mongrel, all right," Johnnie agreed, "but he might be liable to do us a good turn, for I've ta'en a fancy to him. He came oot o' the infirmary wi' me and I brought him along here for a cup o' tea. He'll be aw the better for a lesson."

Lizzie edged her way forward and gazed at Matha with much dislike.

"Dae you think he wid be a sticker, Razor King?" she demanded.

"He'll be put to the test aw right," Johnnie replied, with an ugly smile.

"Better get him up, eh?" suggested one of the young men.

"Ay. Get some water and wash him up. We don't want him to die on us all at once."

They poured water over his face, and, when he came to and began to blubber like a child in his pain, there was a chorus of sycophantic sniggers. But Matha was not seriously injured; he was merely suffering the agony of returning breath after being completely winded. When he had recovered himself he gazed at Johnnie with eyes like those of a dog which has been thrashed by his master. Gratefully and humbly he accepted a cup of tea. And he swore devotion to the Razor King before he left the house.

Nobody ever suspected that Johnnie had come home that day deeply pondering in his mind whether he should or should not pack up the razors for good. Nobody would have believed – Matha least of all – that he invited the unattached and unlovely hooligan to his home in a mood of rare sentiment. Walking along from the infirmary and exchanging curt remarks, Johnnie had seen in this other man a kind of frightening picture of himself.

Matha, unlike Johnnie, had bad teeth, broken and decayed and ugly. His eyes were small and his shock of straw-coloured hair grew low on his forehead. He could have been no beauty at his best; now, with his face worse marked than Johnnie's, one livid scar running from the temple to the slightly twisted upper lip, his appearance was truly repulsive. Johnnie, fingering the seam across his own cheek, shuddered inwardly. There came to him a moment of stark self-knowledge. He perceived, while the moment lasted, that, unless he gave up the gangs, he must fall inevitably to his companion's level. Even his notoriety could not last. Though he won fight after fight there would be no escape from other bashings and from ultimate defeat.

"Ah, Christ!" breathed the Razor King in a whisper that did not move his lips, "it's no' worth it! Ah'm through."

Of this softening, if softening it was, he betrayed no slightest sign until Lizzie threw her arms about his neck, pleading with shining eyes: "You like me a wee bit, dain't you, Johnnie?"

And it was then that Matha Craig laughed.

People speak too glibly of "turning points" in men's lives, for it may very well be that there is no incident, however seemingly decisive, which is really more than a link in the long chain of causation. All his life long, Johnnie was driven by passionate vanity, often ludicrous in its manifestations and yet not utterly ignoble. For beneath this vanity of the slums is anguish and protest and bewildered rebellion, the fierce and desperate long-ing to escape from the ruck. Perhaps, having no assets but his strength and physical courage, Johnnie would have drifted back to hooliganism in any case. But it is at least possible that, if Matha Craig had not laughed when he did, the Razor King of that day would have abdicated.

As it was, the assertion of his supremacy, the sycophancy of his neighbours and Lizzie's unaffected pride in his prowess combined to drive all thoughts of reformation from Johnnie's mind. It was curious that Lizzie, who did not like Matha Craig, now joined forces with that young ruffian to egg Razor King on to some fresh exploit.

The truth was that she always thrilled to the knowledge of her husband's sheer male strength and ferocity. It was for that that she had married him; for that that she had completely lost touch with her own better-class family; for that that she was always ready now to go one better than Johnnie himself. People at the bakery had looked down their noses at Lizzie when she had returned to work, bandaged for the second time, after the assault on the "single end" by the Townhead gang. There were no open sneers because it wasn't safe to offend the wife of a razor king. But she was vindictively aware of her fellow-workers' contempt. She knew that they thought she was "no class", and, perversely, she determined to show them just how tough she and Johnnie could be.

That was, primarily, the origin of the still remembered gang battle in Albion Street, which involved a crowd of more than two thousand "slummies", and led, indirectly, to the engagement of a servant for Razor King's single end.

Albion Street is normally a quiet enough turning off Trongate, but on that evening the opposing mobs surged down it from opposite ends in a tumult of shouting and yelling and cursing and defiance. Stones and bottles were thrown from one crowd to the other before the front ranks met. All traffic was held up, and scores of people who had intended to be no more than spectators found themselves swept into the riot by the pressure of an ever-increasing crowd.

Windows on either side of the street were magnificently smashed in the shock of the first meeting. Then, as the front rank hooligans joined battle, the high-pitched screams of the girls goaded them on until there were half a hundred furious fights in progress at once. The whole mob reeled and sprawled and swirled and eddied like a flooded river between narrow banks. At one point a group of young women yelling themselves hoarse were suddenly swept backwards by a great rush of sweating, pounding, cursing fighters and sent crashing through the plate-glass windows in their rear. And their screaming took on a new hysterical note of anguish.

Through all that battle Lizzie Ramsay, half-drunk on whisky and wholly drunk with excitement, fought at Johnnie's side. Razor King's bodyguard ringed them about, and Johnnie slashed and cut at blurred white faces that became streaked with red, kicked at stamping legs and tumbling bodies, lost first one weapon and then another as the falling victim wrenched them from his hand.

Matha Craig, reckless as a mad bull, charged blindly into a swirling mob of fighters too mixed to separate friend from foe, flailed about him with fists and feet, and fell stunned with a smashing blow from a brick to the back of his head. The crowd stamped over him and tramped him out of existence.

The battle had lasted fully thirty minutes before the police arrived in sufficient force to clear the street. Both sides fled before the onslaught of the jailers. Razor King, with Lizzie and his bodyguard, was safely away and over the Albert Bridge before the police, driving the melting crowd before them, had reached the end of Albion Street. Only ten arrests were made, but more than thirty casualties, including several girls who had been badly cut in the smashing of the plate-glass windows, were taken to the infirmary and some of them detained. Scores and scores of gangsters got home, badly marked, to dress their own wounds. But Razor King and Lizzie were practically unhurt.

Nobody bothered to attend Matha Craig's funeral.

The weeks passed uneventfully and the months slid away into the hinterland of past time. Bobbie and Lily were more and more in the city's dancing news. Peter Stark married his sweetheart, Isobel. Old Mrs Stark, with her lined face and wrinkled hands, was now keeping house for three daughters, a son-in-law and two lodgers, and worrying all the time about her eldest son. And, in the midst of these unperceived changes, Razor King's wife began to worry about a family.

There seems to be no logic in the philoprogenitive instinct. Lizzie had no particular fondness for children as such; she did not dream of baby hands that pulled and caressed. But she was humiliated because, after all those months, she was not pregnant to Razor King. Motherhood seemed somehow necessary to her self-respect.

Desperately, but without reasoning her longing even in her own mind, Lizzie wanted a son and heir. She felt that a baby boy would justify her even in the opinion of the neighbours.

But, curiously enough, neither she nor Johnnie seemed to care two straws for what the neighbours thought. They were never truly at home with their friends of the tenement. It was not so much that the neighbours were unwilling to be friendly and even intimate; it was rather that they were *afraid* to cultivate the Starks as they would have cultivated other dwellers on the same stair.

"Respectable" and steady folk never felt at home with Razor King and his wife, unless they were discussing football, or fighting, or horse-racing, or drinking-parties. They felt that their own small affairs – problems of schooling and difficulties with the rent and even questions of public politics – wouldn't interest Razor King.

181

And they were afraid, really, to start upon *any* general discussion because they knew that neither Johnnie nor Lizzie could endure contradiction. They would simply shout and get angry if they did no worse.

All the time, of course, everybody in their close, and almost everybody in the district, was polite to the acknowledged champions of the Gorbals. They were more than polite: they were positively respectful. But they would not mix; they were wary and guarded in their conversation; they remained aloof from all intimacy.

At the very height of this "splendid isolation" Johnnie took the fatal step of chucking up his job. It was late in the spring and the coal season was drawing to a close. Reilly, talking to nobody in particular, was always grumbling about the need for cutting down expenses. He was declaring, in audible asides, that he could save money with one lorry less at work. Suddenly he sacked two unimportant men. Gruffly he paid them what was due; as gruffly apologized for a disagreeable necessity. And his sidelong glance reached Johnnie like a blow.

Johnnie, honest at least with himself, knew that he was "fed up with the toil". He knew that he might go on for years carting sacks of coal up and down the tenement stairs and still get no further forward. He could not help remembering that one well-organized raid might bring him in more money than two months of solid work. Above all he took a deep satisfaction in the knowledge that he had shown all Gorbals how he *could* stick the toil if he had a mind to.

At that period of his career he did not need to worry about drinks and smokes. There was scarcely a bar in that district which had not a welcome for him. The youth of Gorbals was only too proud and eager to stand treat to the Razor King. The publicans, watching him warily, were still cautious not to rouse his resentment. He was a great figure in the district.

And it dawned upon him, with a remorseless logic not

182

to be contested, that he was slaving like a navvy for next to nothing a week. He knew that if he were sacked, he would go "on the dole" to draw, as of right – for he was an insured worker – almost two-thirds of his actual salary. Lizzie did not seem to mind much what he did. They were at that time living comfortably and actually saving money. She seemed to be much more concerned with his reputation as Razor King than with his uncertain renown as a worker.

Once he said to her, sullenly curious: "Ah'm thinkin' of chuckin' the toil, Liz!"

"Eh, well, Johnnie," she laughed carelessly, "there's the summer comin' along, and mebbe Reilly'll chuck you before you chuck him."

Towards the end of May, when he drew his week's pay one Saturday morning, he no longer pretended to misunderstand the comments of his employer.

"See here, Reilly," he said bluntly, "Ah'm no sae keen on sticking wi' the lorry if you've a mind to lay it up. It's for you to say though. You know I've got the Labour Exchange to satisfy."

Reilly's face cleared and his expression became friendly and almost grateful.

"Ah've got to dae *something*," he agreed eagerly, "an' so, if it's aw the same to you, it wid be better to end up and start again when the summer's over."

"Just whit you think," said Razor King dully. He took his pay and his dismissal with a surly nod and went at once to "put his books" on the Labour Exchange in Elgin Street.

When Lizzie came home in the evening, his news did not seem to upset her.

"Eh, well, Johnnie," she laughed, "Ah'm workin' yet an' we have some money in the bank an' aw. You'll have time noo to think of ither things."

"It's this face Ah'm thinkin' on more than anythin' else," said Johnnie sullenly, fingering his scarred cheek.

183

She broke into a laugh which disconcerted him.

"Who minds about your *face*," she said wickedly. "It's ither things worry me more than your wounds, Razor King. It's gettin' some family *I'm* thinkin' on."

"You're daft, Liz!" he replied. "But at any rate you're no' blamin' *me*, I hope. You couldny say I've neglected you."

From bantering they lapsed into serious discussion. Both of them agreed that children were, somehow, necessary for happiness, although there were not too many jobs going. They couldn't, in fact, decide *why* they were necessary; it was simply a shared conviction that marriage was not complete without a youngster or two.

"Johnnie," said Lizzie emphatically, "Ah tell you Ah wid *pray* for the power to get a breadsnapper if Ah thought it wid do any good."

"You can go ahead for me, Liz," he rejoined amiably. "You know more about it than I do, and prayers canny hurt, even if they do no good."

That afternoon he was wearing his best blue serge suit and a clean white collar. His scars did not show up very strongly under his tan. His black hair was sleek and his eyes sparkled. Lizzie appraised him earnestly and kissed him almost as though she were returning a verdict.

When opening time arrived, they left the single end and went to a public house in Rutherglen Road. There Johnnie ordered two bottles of beer and two half-gills of whisky, taking the drinks over to the small table where Lizzie was sitting.

The sun from the only window in the bar caught them in a shaft of light and touched Lizzie's rather sharp oval face to sudden beauty.

"Ah don't want you to be worryin' too much, Liz, aw the same," said Johnnie awkwardly.

"Whit wid I be worryin' for?" she laughed. "Ah'm happy enough as long as you don't let me down, Razor King."

"When I let you down, I'll be finished."

"Ah hope so!"

They looked into one another's eyes with an unspoken challenge.

"Aw, Johnnie," said Lizzie hurriedly, "wid ye no' like a wee son, eh?"

"Ah'm no' particular, Liz," he laughed. "A wee lassie wid dae me as well . . ."

Then they both laughed and raised their glasses in an unspoken toast. But the weeks went by and still there seemed no likelihood of Lizzie's ambition being realized.

Gradually her wish for a child became an obsession in her mind. She began to talk more and more frequently of the lack of a family. Johnnie lost patience with her. Never for a moment did it cross his mind that any reproach could be laid to his door. He was satisfied that he was, physically, the perfect partner. Time hung rather heavily upon his hands and he spent long hours at the open-air gym, exercising his splendid muscles with grave patience. Sometimes, having taken his exercise, he would return to the house, and wait there doing nothing in particular for hours at a time. There was nothing that seemed to him worth reading after he had completed his study of the day's racing. He betted very little, for lack of money and, like his father before him, he would always stake his threepence, or his rare sixpence, on a double or a treble. Naturally he hardly ever won. He and thousands like him, were a steady revenue to the new street bookie who was taking their bets in Arthur Ross's stead. Ross, as the Gorbals knew very well, financed the new man and took a big share of the profits. But he himself had moved right away from Gorbals and had opened a showy office in a main street, doing a big business by post. He was driving a car these days and rumour had it that he would be standing for the City Council before long. A very warm man, Arthur Ross, with money invested outside book-making altogether, in fish shops and kinemas and a dance hall, and, perhaps, in darker, underground activities the proceeds of which could never be shown on any income tax return.

Johnnie would lie on the bed and smoke cigarettes, brooding sullenly and vaguely about many things. Thoughts crossed his mind like insects that buzzed and stung. He would wonder, suddenly, what his mother was doing and whether she was still fretting about him.

"Ach, tae hell!" he would say, shrugging his shoulders as though he could really wriggle some small annoyance away from him. His mother was "well enough", he would console himself, keeping house for the family – what there was of it now.

And then he would dream of what he would do and what he would wear and of the dash he would make and the figure he would cut if only he had money "like yon clever devil o' a Ross!"

Sometimes, frowning blackly, he would ask himself whether "young Peter was in the right of it efter aw", working hard, living respectably, saving money and married now to his "skinny bit stuff". The thought of Peter always annoyed him, and yet he was fond of the lad. Isobel he couldn't stand at any price, with her stuck-up manners and her air of superiority.

Then Johnnie would get up and pace restlessly up and down the single end, planning new raids and new adventures and wondering at the same time why Lizzie had changed so much; why she didn't mind his being idle and was always encouraging him to some new adventure with the gang.

Always, in the end, he would tug on his cap, and stamp away out of it all to find men to talk to and a drink or two to cheer him up.

Lizzie, working away in the bakery, was brooding, too, but in a different way. There was a foreman there, Frank Smith by name, who was very cautiously trying to show her at that time that he had a liking for her. Or so she thought, for there was really very little to go on – no more than a smile now and again, the occasional exchange of two or three words that were not strictly necessary and, once, a very general conversation as he walked with her a piece up the road when they were leaving work.

Lizzie was excited about Frank Smith. She thought he would be about forty-five, more than twenty years her senior – but he was well preserved and had always looked after himself. There was something safe and dependable about him. He wasn't thrilling, like Johnnie, but there was nothing soft about him for all that. He was very much a man.

She knew that his wife had been an invalid for more than a year now and it wasn't natural for a man in the prime of life to do without a woman. She wondered, flushing a little at the thought, what he would be like as a lover. "Ah widn't be surprised," she thought deliberately, "if Frank cud get me a breadsnapper!"

And that was the beginning of a gradually deepening resentment against Johnnie. For in her heart she believed that it must be his fault that they had no family.

Neighbours on the same close in Crown Street all knew of Lizzie's longing for a baby and they hoped it would soon be satisfied. For they thought that if he had some family Razor King might settle down and even take to work again. His moody fits made them uneasy. They supposed that if he was spending so much time at home he must be thinking out new raids and fresh battles. That was all very well for the young ruffians, but it was uncomfortable for middle-aged neighbours on the same stair.

On a warm Thursday evening in June Lizzie leaned for a long while out of the front window watching three young mothers standing at the street corner gossiping. They wore dark shawls and each carried a child in her arms. They stood there, swaying gently from one foot to the other, very ordinary poor women without hats and, probably, without ambition. Their men were mere nobodies, away propping up some other street corner, likely enough. But Lizzie suddenly envied the young mothers acutely. She wanted to turn round and say something about this to Razor King, sitting back there in the arm-chair and drowsing over his paper. But if she did it would only give him another chance to sneer at her. That's what he had been doing lately; listening to her with a curl of the lips, saying nothing until she had finished and then looking her up and down with deliberate contempt.

"A family, eh," he would drawl. "Ah'll have to be the father o' some other wee lassie's kid some o' they days, so Ah wull!"

She sighed and turned away from the window.

"Ah wish the holidays were on," she began softly, "so as we could get down to Ayr as we've been plannin'."

"No' be long noo," he grunted, without looking up.

She went to him then and put her arms round his neck.

"Cripes! Have a heart!" said he, pushing them peevishly away. "Come on out; Ah'm fed up wi' stickin' in the hoose."

They went for a walk out Rutherglen way and many people looked at them as they passed by. Razor King was noticeable for his scars and his scowling face, and Lizzie's own face was drawn and pale, the face of a woman who was suppressing some outburst. They noticed that they were being looked at and secretly each blamed the other for it. In a public house they had several drinks for which Lizzie paid and they walked home in almost unbroken silence.

"Whit's the good of a wee home like this wi'oot a kid?" Lizzie began almost immediately they were indoors again.

"That's whit Ah wid like to know," he said savagely.

188

"Wull I fetch in another lassie and make one for you? Is that whit you're wantin'?"

Then she laughed. She did not say anything, but she stood there laughing at him – derisively. Johnnie swore and, for the first time in their marriage, struck her in the face.

Lizzie tottered and fell and Johnnie stood above her in a towering passion, dreadfully tempted to use his boot. She whimpered and clung to his knee.

"Ah'll let you off wi' that, *this* time," he said contemptuously, "but not the next time, mind ye, not the next time!" His eyes were glittering dangerously and the livid scar across his cheek was flushed.

"Aw right, Razor King," she whined, "Ah'll give you peace for a while, sure Ah will!"

He let her get up without another word and they went to bed together that night in silence, lying resentfully apart in that narrow space, thinking their own thoughts, dreaming their own dreams.

But the next day in the bakery, when Frank Smith smiled at Lizzie, she smiled back at him so definitely and so challengingly that he glanced round almost as though she had called aloud. They were in a corridor with nobody else in sight. He slipped his arm round her waist and kissed her on the lips. And she clung for a moment in that embrace.

CHAPTER XIV

A DEATH IN THE SLUMS

On a Saturday afternoon Mr and Mrs Peter Stark, impressively 'bourgeois' in dress and manner, set out to pay a call upon Peter's mother. Isobel made no fuss about this visit. She neither liked nor disliked old Mrs Stark, and, though she detested the home where Peter had been brought up, she drew a secret pleasure from appearing there, so very lady-like and elegant and prosperous, as his wife.

By pure chance they turned the corner into Norfolk Street and almost collided with Razor King and a young, red-headed girl who was clinging to his arm. Peter had not seen his brother since the Townhead gangsters had marked him and he was shocked by the disfiguring scars. Isobel, who had always hated Johnnie, kept a still face, but her eyes took in every detail of his appearance, the baggy flannel trousers, the old brown jacket over a dirty sweater, the muffler round his neck and the disreputable cap with the peak tugged over one ear. All this she saw with lowered lids, but she fixed a full gaze upon the red-haired girl, enveloped her in one contemptuous glance and turned her head.

Johnnie missed that look, though Agnes Massey did not. It happened that Razor King was in rare good humour, and he was actually pleased to see his younger brother looking so prosperous. He always had a grudging fondness for Peter, and, perhaps, at the back of his mind, it pleased him to feel that one of the Starks, at any rate, was getting on in the world. Of this there was nothing to be guessed from his manner or his greeting.

"Eh, Peter, lad," he said gruffly, "Ah was hearin' about you only the other day. They tell me you're turnin' politician? Well, well! You're lookin' fine. But we're a poor, uneducated lot round here. Ah widn't be bothered wi' talkin' to us if Ah wis you."

Isobel, her face expressionless, was angry at this sarcasm, but Peter understood that Johnnie was in friendly mood and the raillery did not disturb him.

"Ah'm no politician," he grinned, "though there's some wid like to make me one at the warehouse. Isobel an' me were just away to see Mother. Hoo is the auld lady?"

"They say she's no' so well," Johnnie replied, frowning. "Ah wid go along wi' you, but Mother's no' very gled tae see me these days. She's worried about my – reputation."

His hand went to the scar on his cheek, and he glared defiantly at his younger brother. Peter took no notice whatever. The red-haired girl was staring at him with a kind of hostile curiosity and Isobel was rigid at his side.

"Ah'll tell her we saw you," he said simply. "Have a fag?"

He extended a packet of cigarettes first to Johnnie and then, after an almost imperceptible hesitation, to the red-haired girl. She took a cigarette and laughed shrilly.

Johnnie turned and stared at her with an expression of warning disapproval.

"Whit dae you think of her, Peter," he said calmly, "a new wee bit stuff o' mine, Agnes Massey? Ah've been training this efternune down at the Green Gym. That's why Ah'm wearing these old clothes. Now Ah'm going home to put on ma paraffin, an' efter that we're awa' to the jazzin', are we no', Agnes?"

"Whatever you say, Razor King," she replied, looking up at him with an expression of devotion which she wanted Peter and Isobel to notice.

"Lizzie'll be awa' wi' friends, Ah'm thinkin'?" said Peter carefully casual.

"Ay, till Monday," his brother replied, "and Agnes will look efter me meanwhile. You're no' sae thin as you were, Isobel. An' no sae fat as you might be yet. But everything comes through time."

She flushed and bit back a retort.

"Peter and me can look efter ourselves," she said, as calmly as she could.

"Ah widn't be surprised. Eh, well, we won't be keepin' you. Ah'll bet Mother wull dust the chairs for you. They tell me she's takin' an awfu' lot of medicine, Peter. Ah wid tell her to take less o' yon chemist's trash. It's worse than the whisky an' it doesny taste so good. Away ye go, then!"

He threw a parting grin of amiable derision at Isobel, nodded to his brother and slouched away, the girl Agnes Massey still clinging to his arm but looking back over her shoulder maliciously.

Isobel was furious.

"The cheek o' yon red-haired tart!" she gasped. "Did ye no' see her laughin' at me, Peter? That's a fine bit stuff to keep your brither happy while his wife's away from home! A hellova fine bit!"

"Don't be silly, Isobel!" he said pacifically, "Johnnie means nae harm – tae *us*! Leave him and his lassies alone, can't you? There's no need for us to worry about him or them or Liz."

She looked up at him sharply and decided at that time to say no more. For a while she walked on in sulky silence. Then she sniffed and he heard her murmur: "Agnes Massey! . . . *She'll* be hellova fat an' aw before Razor King's through wi' her!"

Peter frowned, and then, suddenly, he laughed and laughed again. She thought he was laughing at her innuendo. She did not know that he was laughing at her and, amusedly, at all women. They walked on again restored to good humour.

But old Mrs Stark was not indoors when Peter's eldest sister, Mary, let them into the familiar "hoose".

"Ah don't know where she's gone," Mary informed them fretfully. "She wis here a while since, nursing wee Geordie. Ah thought she wid be back right away, for the kid's been sick an Ah'm hellova busy wi' cleaning up the kitchen an' aw, and there's nobody can keep Geordie quiet like Mother. She'll be having a crack wi' some o' the neighbours, likely. You'll better come in an' wait for her, only step quiet, for the kid's sleepin' noo."

When Mary was looking the other way Isobel wrinkled expressive nostrils and Peter grimaced understandingly, for the old familiar sour stench of the two-roomed house had not changed, and the reek of paraffin-oil that mingled with it told him that his mother was still busy with the unending battle to keep the vermin down. He stared uneasily at his sister in her slatternly house dress with its torn skirt hem and he thought: "My God! how soon women can change when they're merried and have a kid! An', by the looks of Mary, Ah widn't be surprised if she's starting another awready."

"How's Alfred, Mary?" he asked, making conversation by an enquiry after the brother-in-law whom he scarcely knew even by sight.

"Well enough, I suppose," she replied grumpily, "but they've put him on short time at the mill, and likely he'll be out awthegither before long. They tell me there's a depression these days! Cripes! Can you mind any time when there wis anything *but* a depression on?"

It was then between four and five o'clock and the child woke whimpering. Mary picked him up out of the padded soap-box which served as his cot and stood rocking him mechanically.

"May as well have wer tea," she said at length, not very cordially. "Wud you mind putting the kettle on, Isobel, and getting the things oot o' the press?"

Isobel, for all her good coat and skirt, was glad of the

occupation. But first she went across to the other and slightly older woman, and stood beside her looking down at the child. She thrust a finger into its small hand and felt a faint stir of mother impulse in her own heart at the baby's instinctive grip. But the child's forehead was ugly with a rash that even spread beneath the fluff of thin pale yellow hair and Isobel shuddered.

"What's wrong wi' him?" she asked, trying to be sympathetic.

"Naething. He's cutting his teeth and he's been worried wi' they dirty bugs. Mother canny get rid of them, try how she will. The whole bliddy house should be pulled doon, so it should! But the ithers are no' much better efter aw . . . The loaf an' the butter's in the kitchen. Ah'll get them."

For the time being Isobel and Peter had decided that they would wait awhile before they had any family. It was an unusual resolve for people of their class, for though there may be some primitive knowledge of birth control in the slums, contraceptives are very little used, partly because they cost too much money, partly because the tenement dwellers simply will not be bothered with them.

Presently the tea was ready and they sat down to table. Peter looked at the clock on the mantelpiece and noticed with a grim smile that it was the same old marble timepiece his father had pawned on the fatal occasion when the limit bet rolled up. His mother must have denied herself a lot to redeem it after she came out of hospital that time.

"We saw Johnnie when we were coming up here," he said to his sister, "an' he said Mother wis no' sae well an' taking a lot of medicine. What's the matter wi' her?"

"She's the same as aw the rest o' them at her age," said his sister wearily. "Something wrong wi' her stomach. Days at a time she canny get a movement. Then she takes terrible doses o' the stuff from the chemist's and she's better for a while. But we had the doctor to her three weeks ago an' *he* said she'd be the better to take a light nutritive diet instead o' so much o' the salts. 'Light' is a good word, is it no', Peter? Mother wis always light in her diet that Ah c'n mind so long as there wis one o' *us* wis hungry. But the doctor said 'light *an*' nutritive!' That's no' sae easy to arrange."

"Listen," retorted Peter angrily, "if the auld lady's needing something special, why could ye no' tell me before! We wid be gled to help her, wid we no', Isobel?"

"Sure!" she agreed, with no great enthusiasm.

But Mary shrugged her shoulders. "Mother's no' lacking anything, if that's what you mean," she said, "but you know well she'll no' always do whit she's telt. An' she will still worry about Razor King. Ever since she heard about yon fight he had wi' big McLatchie, and the bashing he got efterwards from the Townhead mob, she's made up her mind Johnnie's on the road to a bad end. An' she's about right an' aw!"

"Ach, tae hell wi' Johnnie!" was Peter's retort. "Ah wish Mother wid come in, aw the same. Ah'm wanting to see her and we canny wait long."

But at six o'clock Mrs Stark had still not returned, and Peter and Isobel took their departure, Peter reluctantly, but still more reluctant to annoy his wife, who had been very patient all that afternoon.

It was nearly midnight when a young girl came up from one of the single apartment homes in the close to empty the chamber she carried under her huge apron. Reaching the lavatory on the first-floor landing, she tried to open it with her key, but found that the key would not go into the lock.

"Anybody in?" she asked, not speaking too loudly. "There's somebody in wer ain doon in the close."

This was intended as an apology for her interruption, but it brought no answer. After waiting another few moments, the girl angrily tried once more to force her key into the lock. Failing again, she knocked loudly on the door with the key itself, but there was still no response. She swore plaintively, picked up the chamber, and climbed to the second floor. There the landing closet was empty and the girl emptied the utensil and returned to the close again.

"What the hell was keeping you?" her unemployed father demanded angrily. "Where the hell have you been at aw?"

"Ah couldny get in that one up the sterr," she complained, "an' Ah had to go the wan up the two sterrs."

"Ach, let me see to that bliddy chanty and away tae your bed, for God's sake! Ye gie me a sore heid every time Ah luck at ye."

Needing no second bidding the girl deposited her burden and was glad to go to her bed on the floor beside her two older sisters who slept on as though nothing had happened.

The door of the lavatory in the close slammed noisily to show that one at least was now vacant. Someone else went out to it almost immediately and he too slammed the door as he left, but the door of the lavatory up the first stair was not slammed and this seemed strange to the unemployed man who still lay awake.

His curiosity grew with his sleeplessness and at last he got up and put on his shirt – for he was lying nude in that warm weather. Then he shuffled into his trousers and, taking the lavatory key with him, mounted the stairs in his bare feet, carrying the chamber as his daughter had done a while before.

He, too, tried in vain to get the key in the lock, and then he hammered on the door so long and loud that other doors began to open, and presently Mary and her husband and Nellie Stark, Mary's youngest sister and the only unmarried one of the family, came out to the stair-head and demanded to know what all the noise was about.

196

"There must be something wrang wi' this door," said the disturber. "Ah've been tryin' tae get in for hauf an 'oor noo and . . ."

He was interrupted by a wild scream from Nellie Stark.

"It's Mother in there, Mary!" she cried. "Ah *telt* you she widny be stopping all this lang while with the Stevensons, even if their kid is sick. It's efter midnight . . ."

She ran across the landing and banged frantically with both hands on the locked door.

"Are you in there, Mother?" she cried. "It's Nellie."

People now came hurrying to the landing from floors above and from the close itself. Soon there was a jostling crowd of men and women, grotesquely clad and underclad. One of them, a burly, grey-haired fellow, turned and ran up to his own apartment. Soon he came down again, shouldering his way through the crowd.

"Whether it's auld Mrs Stark or some ither body," he said gruffly, "we'll have to open the door just the same. Oot o' ma wey a meenit an' Ah'll see whit Ah can dae."

The old fellow bent above the lock and produced a jemmy from beneath his jacket. A moment later there was a sharp crack and the door swung wide to his tug, the torn lock hanging loose. In the feeble moonlight that came through the dirty stair-head window the group outside the closet could just make out the figure of Mrs Stark huddled forward with her grey hair falling over her knees.

Nellie began to gulp and wail hysterically, but her older sister spoke calmly, though her face had gone chalk white.

"It's Mother right enough," said she. "Wull some of ye help me oot wi' her."

Two of the men pushed her gently out of the way. "Leave her tae us!" they said. "We'll bring her into the hoose."

They laid the old woman gently on the landing to see

if she could be revived. Small children edged to the front to look down at the still, sedate features of the woman who had been a kind of grannie to all of them. Then the body was carried from the landing into the house and laid upon the "shake-down" near the window.

At least a dozen neighbours had crowded into the room and, amid the general clamour, one of them mentioned the police.

"Ay," said the old fellow who had opened the lavatory door, "better get the jailers, tae be on the safe side." A few minutes later he had disappeared and was not to be found in the tenement when the police arrived.

But "the jailers" listened to the chorused story of the family and the neighbours with perfunctory interest. There was nothing they could do, for it was by no means the first time that some old body had died in similar circumstances. The only thing exceptional about this particular case was that so many hours had passed before the discovery was made. In buildings where one closet has to serve the needs of some thirty or more people, the chances were that the impatience of those who had to climb or descend unnecessary stairs would have resulted in earlier action. That the family had gone to bed with Mrs Stark out of the house was not surprising, for she was often out helping some neighbour in sickness or in childbirth and she had her check key.

A doctor paid a formal visit on the following morning and decided after a cursory examination that death was due to heart failure. It was not thought necessary to disturb Razor King or Peter or any others of the family until after daybreak, and when they arrived their mother was already lying in an open coffin.

Johnnie stood for a moment looking down at the quiet face. His brows were drawn together in a ferocious scowl and he turned away with a strangled oath, terrified lest any present should detect in him any sign of weakness or sentiment.

"It's as well," he said curtly, when he turned to face the family again, "that Mother was insured. We can bury the auld lady decently noo."

Peter did not hear him. He, too, had turned from the others and stood staring out of the window down into the wide street swarming with children. His face was working and his heart was filled with poignant remorse. He felt that ever since he had left home he had given his mother the go-by. She had been ill and he didn't even know it. And then to come round the very evening before and to sit there waiting when all the time she was "just ootside on the landing . . ." Little trivial incidents came back to his memory – how he had run to his mother for comfort when he was hurt; clung terrified to her skirts when his father was shouting the place down in drunken anger; besought her for pennies when the poor old soul was at her very wit's end for money. And for her to die alone – and like that! Suddenly he flamed into fury. He choked with hatred to the world and loathing of life.

"The bliddy bastards!" he muttered. "The bliddy bastards!"

He raised clenched fists that quivered in a passion of blind anguish and blinder wrath. And then, like Johnnie, he set his lips and faced the company with an air of dogged indifference.

The insurance money was enough to supply two coaches for the funeral and have the burial conducted in seemly fashion. There are many tenement dwellers like Mrs Stark, who contrive to maintain their premium payments through years of poverty so that, however miserably they may have lived, they can at least be buried respectably and to the credit of their families.

Johnnie and Peter went to the funeral together in the front coach with four unemployed men. It was all unemployed men that followed in the second coach and there were many neighbours who followed on foot. Most of them were unemployed, too, and they were not "too well put on", but it was definitely a respectable funeral for that locality. Mrs Stark's daughters, awaiting the men's return – for no women ever follow a funeral in Glasgow – were agreed that their mother would have been satisfied with the arrangements.

A true "Prodisant" clergyman took the burial service and the mourners and their friends trooped back to the "hoose" where an adequate supply of whisky and beer was ready for them.

"Eh, well, we aw go the same way home!" said Johnnie as he was leaving, slightly the worse for drink.

Peter scarcely heard him. "Ah'm gled," he said simply, "there was a clergyman. Mother would have wanted that."

Johnnie laughed.

"*Clergyman!*" he repeated with bitter irony. "Sure; they're grand when you're deid!"

CHAPTER XV

SERVANT AND MISTRESS

"So it's you, Liz! Eh, well, you're back home too sune."

Johnnie, lying nearer the front door, propped himself up on one elbow and grinned defiantly at his wife. She could see the red hair of Agnes Massey spread on the pillow, but the girl herself was hidden by Johnnie's upraised form.

Lizzie hesitated on the threshold of the single end with all kinds of angry and sarcastic comment rushing to her lips. She heard the girl lying behind Johnnie giggle and she herself swore luridly. Then she slammed the door of the apartment and walked away down the stairs.

"*That* little whore!" she whispered, as she ran down towards the street. "By Jesus! Ah wid have thought Johnnie wid have picked up something better than that!"

But when she came back home, much later that evening, Lizzie had made up her mind not to have any row with Johnnie about such an ordinary infidelity. In fact she knew that his affair with Agnes must have been going on for some time and she realized, most reasonably, that there was nothing else one could expect in the circumstances.

"Tae hell wi' the pair o' them," she thought. "Ah've bin a fule tae keep Frank Smith waiting."

Lizzie, walking furiously away from her own home with the picture in her mind of Johnnie grinning at her as she slammed the door, and the echo of the red-haired girl's giggle in her ears, suffered none of the ordinary jealousy that a middle-class woman would have felt in similar circumstances. For she knew very well that any husband in her set, out of work and lonely all day long, might quite naturally pick up some girl to amuse him while his wife was at "the toil". If the husband happened to be a razor king, as Johnnie was, it would merely be so much easier for him to find a girl to his liking. There would be dozens ready to oblige him and various neighbours had already taken occasion to warn her that Johnnie was always around "wi' yon red-haired bit stuff, Agnes Massey".

In Waddell Street a new fish shop had opened, for the tenements make their main meal of fried fish in the evenings and the supply has not yet overtaken the demand. Lizzie turned into this shop and ordered a helping of fish and chips. Eating ravenously after her day's work in the bakery, she considered the new position and gradually her first anger cooled off. She felt that, after all, Agnes Massey didn't matter very much. The girl was not in work and Razor King was far too dependent upon his wife at that time to want an open quarrel.

"As well yon red-haired bitch as any ither," thought Lizzie. "Onywey. Ah'm no' caring. Johnnie's well enough in his way, but Ah'm dead keen on Frank noo' and, efter this, Ah'll go all the road wi' him, so Ah wull! An' Johnnie'll no' try to stop me – not noo. He canny make a fuss; not wi' me working an' him on the dole."

She had, oddly enough, no resentment against him for his idleness. That she should be the wage-earner of the household seemed to her a very normal state of affairs, as, indeed, it was and still is in modern Glasgow. Her one real grievance against Johnnie was that he had failed to provide her with a "breadsnapper". She hoped, most cheerfully, that Frank Smith would succeed where Razor King had failed.

And so, after supper, she returned home amicably. Johnnie was out, but he came back alone half an hour later. He strolled over to Lizzie and kissed her challengingly without taking his hands out of his pockets. She laughed and contented herself with saying darkly that he "wis no' the only one who might be finding a new friend".

"Good luck tae ye, Liz!" he laughed. "Ah'm not grudgin' you a bit of fun!"

On the afternoon of the next day – a Saturday – Lizzie accepted Frank Smith's invitation to go along with him to his home in a long red-stone tenement in Trafalgar Street to meet the family. But they did not leave the bakery together; they met instead in a street some five minutes' distance away and then travelled the rest of the way by tram.

Even in Trafalgar Street, where the population was definitely of the "respectable" variety, conditions were not vastly different from those prevailing in Crown Street. True, Frank's two-room-and-kitchen house seemed more spacious than most, not only because of its extra room, but also because the whole family was only four in number, himself and his two grown-up daughters and his bedridden wife. The three women all slept in the living-room and Frank Smith had the "parlour" to himself. And the furniture was of better quality than in the lower-class slums. But the "hoose" opened upon a familiar stair-head with the front door facing a familiar closet. And the front window looked out upon a familiar, broad street, swarming with children. And the shawled women clustered in the close-mouth and the whole building hummed with the familiar clatter of talk and footsteps and children's noises.

Frank introduced Lizzie to his daughters with no obvious embarrassment. They were good-looking, fairly well-dressed girls, one of them soon to be married and the other already of marriageable age. They received Lizzie amiably enough, but with glances of shrewd appraisement as though they were considering whether she would be a suitable friend for their father.

Both these girls quite understood that their father, though still fond of his ailing wife, sought consolation outside the home from time to time. Things of that kind cannot be kept secret from the young people of the slums, who are thoroughly versed in all the problems of sex from the earliest childhood. They even discussed the matter with one another, considering gravely whether dad "wid no' be more contented wi' some nice steady lass than just going out to find whit he cud" when the mood was on him.

They considered Lizzie and approved of her. She was just sufficiently older than themselves to be suitable in that respect. She was pretty, but she had bandy legs and was "no' sae wonderful" in consequence. And she wore a wedding ring and was quite respectably dressed – an employed and married worker and therefore not likely to cause trouble. The Misses Smith felt, giving careful thought to the matter, that their father might do worse.

After tea, Margaret, the elder of the two, smiled broadly, and, looking from their visitor to her father, exclaimed frankly:

"Do you no' think Lizzie wid be the ideal housekeeper for you, Pa?"

"Have a heart!" smiled Lizzie, flushing a little, but not really much embarrassed, "Ah've a house of ma own tae look efter; don't forget that!"

Mrs Smith was with them at tea when this conversation occurred. She was a thin, shrunken woman, whose enormous black eyes shone from her sallow face with a wistful light. She sat at the table in an invalid-chair, but spent most of the day laying idly in her bed in the back room. The doctor thought she was suffering from a duodenal ulcer and spoke vaguely of an operation, but nothing was ever done about it. She read a great many paper-backed novels and was very grateful to her husband for his gentleness and consideration. She was just as much aware as her daughters that he had brought

Lizzie up for the family's approval, and she shared their good opinion of her.

"Nae doot you'll have enough tae do in your own home," she agreed mildly, "but you're no' tae stand on ceremony, an' this hoose is your ain when you've a mind to it."

"Ach, tae hell," interrupted Frank Smith a little awkwardly, "Lizzie an' me are only out for a bit companionship and aw that; naething more."

He winked solemnly at Lizzie, intending no-one else to see, but his elder daughter intercepted the message and laughed loudly.

"Companionship?" she jeered pleasantly. "Well, Peggy and me are gaun awa' oot the noo and we'll leave you tae your companionship and aw!"

"We're no' out to break any records," said Lizzie hastily, and this time the colour was high in her cheeks, "Ah've got to be gaun home myself in a few minutes."

But they only laughed at her the more. Frank saw her down the stairs, and in the close-mouth he begged her earnestly to return that evening.

"The wife'll be sleeping in her own room," he said, simply, "an' the two girls wull no' disturb us. You'll come back later on, wull you no', Lizzie? Ah've took an awful fancy to you, an' they all like you here, so they do."

"Ah'll come back, Frank," she said, "if Ah can get away. Ah wid like fine tae come, the night or any time."

Lizzie was home in time to get a meal ready for Razor King. He gave her a curt greeting when he returned to the single end and fell to ravenously. She studied his face as he ate, and at last decided that she would risk his reception of an announcement that was almost a challenge.

"Ah'm gaun oot in a wee while," she began, and there was a smile on her lips though her eyes were wary. "Ah'm gaun to dress myself and Ah might no' be in till late."

He looked up at her with a half-smile and a face she

could not read, but he only grunted without making any reply. Lizzie was exasperated by his silence.

"Ah'm gaun oot wi' somebody I know – somebody in the work!" she went on defiantly.

He greeted this information with a good-humoured but slightly mocking laugh.

"*Ah'm* gaun oot wi' somebody Ah know an' aw," he countered presently. "Likely we'll baith enjoy oorselves."

A little vexed that he should take her announcement so calmly, Lizzie was relieved, nevertheless, that it had provoked no storm. Above all, she was excited and deliciously thrilled at the prospect of being with Frank again – alone this time, with nobody to interfere.

"Aw right, Razor King," said she, "Ah'll put on an old hat for the night, as I want to be the way I used to be . . ."

"Good luck to you, Liz," he laughed. "You've been good to me; I'll admit that."

She dressed with more than usual care and took out of a drawer a hat she had worn before her marriage. Johnnie was leaning back in his chair reading an evening paper. She paused at the door, and then went back to put half a crown on the table in front of him. He pocketed it without the slightest embarrassment.

"Have a good time, Liz," he said cheerfully, "an' mind your feet on the stair!"

Johnnie did not really believe at that time that his wife was on her way to meet a lover. He thought she had found somebody ready to take her out and flirt with her, but even if he had known the full truth he would not have been particularly shocked. For the fact is that he was no longer in love with Lizzie and his outlook on affairs of this kind was not what he would have termed "hard". In his view a wife's first duty was to her own man – economically. If Lizzie had neglected the home or failed to see to his comfort, he would have been very quick to assert his rights. But, apart from that, he really did not much care how she amused herself. As long as she gave him a good shilling or two now and again so that he could have something to spend with Agnes when Lizzie was away from home, it seemed to him that he was getting a fair deal.

But he never bullied Lizzie for money. Every week he turned over to her all he drew from the Labour Exchange except an agreed two shillings for his own spending money. He left their financial affairs entirely in her hands once he had ceased to work himself. She was the bread-winner, and, with the curious simplicity common to men of his class, he felt it was only right that she should have the spending of the money she earned. On the other hand, if by any chance he did win a bet, or if he came into a little money through some gang activity, this unearned increment was his own to do what he liked with. Lizzie, without feeling herself generous in any way, fairly divided with him whatever was left over from the household expenses each week.

That night Lizzie did not come home until after one o'clock. Johnnie was in bed and heavily asleep with drink. She slipped in beside him, elated and triumphant. She almost wanted to tell him what a marvellous time she had had with Frank. But she was also a little afraid. In the morning he did not bother to ask her any questions. She was relieved and yet annoyed, for she wasn't quite sure whether she wanted him to be jealous or not. It was really difficult for her to keep her excited, jubilant thoughts to herself, and she wouldn't have done so if she could have been at all certain of his wickedly uncertain temper.

Surprisingly soon, however, the couple had slipped back into the ordinary comradeship of the household. Lizzie was scrupulously careful to prepare the evening meal as usual. On weekdays Johnnie knew that he couldn't expect her to come home from the bakery until work was finished. Usually he wanted no proper meal between breakfast and supper – a hunk of bread and some cheese taken in a pub was quite enough for him. But if he happened to feel hungry or had nothing much else to do, he didn't in the least mind going home to cook a meal for himself. For that matter, he could cook just as well as Lizzie could. Most working-class men can cook for themselves, and the unemployed habitually do when their wives are lucky enough to be at the toil. They often look after the house and the children, too – that is to say, as far as house and children are ever looked after in the slums.

By the end of that year Lizzie and Frank Smith were much in love with each other, but they kept their affair a secret from their fellow-workers, whom they did not trust. They never left the factory together and did not speak to each other while at work unless they were obliged to do so. Perhaps that air of "class" which she had never quite lost made the other women in the bakery less likely to suspect her. Perhaps they thought that, being married to a razor king, Lizzie wouldn't be likely to want any other man. At all events her intrigue with Frank was not suspected in the bakery at that time.

But they could not keep it secret from Johnnie. By the end of December 1926 he knew very well that Lizzie was engaged in something much more definite than a flirtation. Indeed, he was by then aware that she had become Frank Smith's mistress. One day, bluntly, he asked her who the man was. Without attempting any evasion, she told him all about Frank, stressing the fact that he was a foreman at the bakery, very "well doing", earning a good wage and with money in the bank. She admitted she liked him a lot, but she did not say in so many words that he was her lover.

It wasn't necessary. Johnnie listened to her with a sneering smile. He wasn't in the least jealous of middle-aged Frank Smith. As far as he was concerned, he still had Agnes Massey to go out with and to bring back to the house when Lizzie was away. He never for a moment dreamed that Frank could give Lizzie the baby she had been wanting. If anybody had suggested this to him he would have roared with laughter.

"What!" he would have cried, "Frank efter me? What a hope!"

But it would give a false idea of the curious moral outlook of Razor King and his mob if one were to suggest that he would, necessarily, have been jealous even in other circumstances. Among the gangster element of Glasgow, marriage is not held in great repute even by the women, and still less so by the men. Given her marriage lines, a woman can sue for maintenance, but this right is obviously of little value to the wife of an unemployed man. She would be far better off with the loosest unstatutory claim upon another man who was drawing a wage and had money to spend.

But that is not all. Even in extreme poverty these problems are not regulated solely by economics. There is a twisted sense of "fair play" among the lowest slum dwellers. The gangster who flaunts his mistresses *cannot* seriously blame his wife for taking a lover. He may cling to his rights; he may expect "service"; but he cannot and does not expect fidelity. Johnnie, for instance, knew that Lizzie knew, and all the neighbours also knew, of his undisguised affair with Agnes Massey. While that affair endured, he couldn't make much fuss about Frank Smith.

This situation of tolerant complacency on either side lasted well into the New Year. On New Year's Eve, Lizzie told Johnnie, half-defiantly, half-apologetically, that she meant to spend the holiday in the red-stone tenement in Trafalgar Street.

"That'll be just right," he replied aggressively. "Ah'm gaun tae have a party up here the night. An' there'll be plenty of whisky, too, if aw' goes well. You'll be missing a pure treat, Liz!"

She greeted this comment with a conciliatory laugh and suitable questions about his immediate plans. The questions were not perfunctory. She really wanted to know if there were any "big doings" arranged for the gangs. A new romance does *not* entirely destroy and change all old interests. The fiction-writers and the scenario experts may try to persuade us to the contrary, but they are wrong. Lizzie, very much in love with Frank Smith, was still keenly interested in Razor King and his doings. She *still* wanted her husband to cut a figure in their world. She still wanted – and was jealous of – the kudos which Razor King's wife would enjoy. More than that: she told Frank Smith so. She was constantly talking to him about her husband, and he listened to her with the most understanding interest.

Throughout the week-end of that New Year, Lizzie stayed with Frank Smith and his family and Johnnie held high festival with Agnes Massey and the young fellows and girls of the gang, either in their apartments or in his own single end.

Johnnie had scarcely begun to realize how necessary the booze had become to him. Drink mattered far more than the kisses of the red-haired girl. He liked to sleep with Agnes, but there were "plenty ither lassies", and, if it came to the bit, he could do without any of them. But his thirst was on him all the time. He didn't feel "right sleepy" until he had a belly-full of liquor. He drew a sort of pride from the knowledge that he could drink glass for glass with any of his gang, even the toughest among them, and see them all under. Drunk to the last limit, he could still find his own way home on his own feet. People couldn't tell when he was drunk. Sometimes he couldn't tell himself.

Occasionally in the afternoons, when he had reeled away from his pub companions to pull himself together with a walk until the pubs opened again, Johnnie would wonder hazily how much the drink cost him every week.

Often the common funds would not run to whisky and beer. Often the company fell back upon the iniquitous red wine, sour and poisonous and stunning, which all the public houses were beginning to sell at that time. A glass of red wine cost no more than a glass of beer, but it was twice as potent. Even if a man got sick on red wine, the fumes of it stayed in his head and he lived and moved and thought under its influence long after he had outwardly thrown off its effects. Johnnie did not like the taste of red wine. Some days it made him want to vomit when he drained the first glass. But he liked the feeling it gave him; he liked the drugged irresponsibility which it produced. Some of Johnnie's friends were already mixing their red wine with methylated spirits, but Johnnie himself had only tried "Red Biddy" once. That was in a brothel in his own tenement, and, hours later, he woke to a kind of dim consciousness under the cold stream from the tap above the sink.

A fat and blowsy girl was holding him there with an arm under his shoulder. She was squirting the tap water over his thick black hair and her puffy eyes were dark with anxiety.

"By Cripes!" she exclaimed, when he groaned and struggled in her grasp, "Ah thought you wis gaun tae die on me, Razor King! Ah widn't have known whit tae say to the jailers if they'd found you here like you are now, wi' your big smooth chest showing under your bit shirt and your heart fair stopped like a rin-doon clock! They wid sure have thought Ah'd killed you" – and here she giggled wildly. "Some hopes, eh, Johnnie? An' you so blind drunk you couldny send a wee kid greetin' to her ma, let alone dae her ony harm."

Johnnie had lurched away from her then to be desperately sick. She cursed him for "messing the fler". He gave her the loose change in his pockets and staggered away and up the stairs and so to his own bed. And since then he had drunk no more "Red Biddy".

But he was drinking very hard all the same. Mostly there were friends and followers ready to stand treat – yes, glad of the privilege. But nearly all the gang proper was out of work like himself. Sometimes he wondered how the hell they could afford to drink what they did "atween the lot of them". He knew that if he had to pay for all his own drinks the money he drew from the Labour Exchange and the shillings he had from Lizzie into the bargain wouldn't have been enough to meet the bill. Of course the others were a little different. There always seemed to be *somebody* in luck; somebody who had enough money to "haud" for the occasion. He supposed the poor devils had to go thirsty when their money was out. Well, that was the way of things. They weren't razor kings efter aw!

Another pub raid – but a smaller affair than the magnificent "hole in the wall" achievement – supplied the booze for the New Year celebrations. Johnnie had a party in the "single end" to celebrate this victory, with Agnes as his partner while Lizzie was away. He did not remember New Year's Day at all, and woke on January the second so doped and dazed that for a long while he stared at Agnes's red head, trying to make out how it was that Lizzie had changed all of a sudden to that extent.

He got up and washed and drank glass after glass of water. Then he went back to his bed and stood looking down at Agnes, who lay in a kind of stupor, breathing heavily through her wide-open mouth. Johnnie ripped the bedclothes off her and stared down unemotionally on her entirely nude young body.

"By God!" he muttered triumphantly, "if Ah canny click wi' Lizzie, Ah can click right enough wi' some of the ithers."

Then he tumbled into bed beside her to sleep off the remainder of that debauch.

Towards the end of January, Johnnie's restlessness, coupled with the perpetual restlessness of the younger hooligans in the gang, compelled him to plan another battle. He took Lizzie very little into his confidence on this occasion. Grumpily he told her that there was going to be a hellova lot doing pretty soon. In the ordinary way she would have been full of excited questions, but now she seemed satisfied to retort: "That's right, Razor King, it's time you should wauken them up, so it is!"

Already he was getting tired of Agnes and he knew that she was sharing her time with another lover – a plasterer in steady work. He told her nothing of the contemplated battle, and went across the Clyde finally at the head of his men while Lizzie was away with Frank Smith, and Agnes – he supposed – fooling about with "the ither fellow – guid luck tae him, the poor bastard!"

It was not an important battle in gang history. The Gorbals United was by no means at full strength and their raid had not been much advertised in advance. But a Townhead mob turned out in fair strength to oppose them and the fighting was bloody and ferocious while it lasted.

Something drove Johnnie that day to the wildest and most desperate extremes, some longing to impress his own followers if he could impress no-one else. He put three of the enemy out of action single-handed before the fight began to turn in favour of the Gorbals mob. His bodyguard surrounded him, and he could then have withdrawn with full credit. But the fumes of the red wine were in his brain, and he was more than drunk with the lust of battle. He broke away from his bodyguard and charged, cursing luridly, into the very thick of the Townhead retreat. They closed about him and his horrible red weapons flashed. One of them he lost as the blade stuck in the jacket of a fallen man. The other fell from his nerveless grasp when something hard – brick or bottle or paving-stone – hit him on the side of the head.

He knew no more of that fight until he came to himself under the surgeon's hands in the infirmary once more.

But this time, after they had patched up the fresh wound in his face and a fearful gash from neck to shoulder-blade, Johnnie was not discharged. Instead, he found himself handed over to the rough hands of the jailers who had picked him up on the field of battle and who were – two of them – prepared to swear that he had been a ringleader in the fight.

It was lucky for him that no "weapons" were found upon him and that it was impossible to prove that he had actually been using razors, although he had undoubtedly been wounded by one. A policeman, who had never seen him before – or so Johnnie confidently believed – swore that he recognized him as a notorious hooligan of the Gorbals district. Another officer gave evidence that he had seen Johnnie fall, battling furiously in the thick of the riot. And the sheriff, dealing with half a dozen ruffians brought before him on similar charges, made the usual remarks upon the necessity of suppressing this gang warfare, and sent all the accused to Barlinnie Jail for three months with hard labour.

Lizzie was not in court when sentence was passed, for it did not seem worth while to lose a day's work. But she could think of nothing but Johnnie all that day, imagining herself clinging to him, murmuring her assurance that she would be waiting for him when he came out. In her thoughts also – he shook her off, impatiently tolerant. He did not know that she was already pregnant to Frank Smith and wondering whether to confess this then, or after his discharge, when confession could be no longer delayed.

Johnnie left the court sullenly between his jailers and was driven away in the prison van with the other hooligans, two of them young fellows of his own mob who were respectfully sympathetic. They did not know, and he did not realize at all, that he had passed his zenith and that already his kingship was imperilled.

Agnes Massey was not present in court. On the day

214

that Johnnie was sentenced she and her plasterer lover were looking over a "wee hoose" that might be suitable for their forthcoming marriage. Agnes could not afford to *wait* for Johnnie, she was expecting a child and needed to find a father for it. The plasterer was well aware of this and it made no difference. His way of looking at it was that Agnes was "a fine bit stuff" and if he married her he would *gain* in general esteem by her "reputation". For Agnes had become a somebody in the Gorbals through her association with Razor King. And so the two of them went house-hunting and were married while Johnnie was still in Barlinnie.

Some weeks before he was likely to be released, Lizzie began to think anxiously about what arrangements she could make for that event. Now that she was spending so much of her time with Frank and expecting a baby into the bargain, she didn't want to be too much tied with household duties. But she wouldn't on any account allow Razor King to be neglected.

She therefore decided to install a young girl in the single end to act as housekeeper and lodger and – she hoped – to meet with Johnnie's approval as a mistress. All this was deliberately calculated and not at all unusual in the circumstances. Among the girls who followed the gang was a dark-haired, slimly well-built lass of nineteen named Minnie Ewing. Lizzie knew her tolerably well, and she had battled very creditably in the great Cathedral Street "rammy". Moreover, Minnie made no secret of her admiration for Razor King: she simply adored a "battler".

Minnie's own home was in one of the worst slums of the district and her family numbered eleven. She was working in a factory among five hundred other girls and cared for nothing at all except excitement. She was frankly delighted with the suggestion that she could come and live with Johnnie and Lizzie in the single end, paying only four shillings a week as "room money".

215

"Ah want Razor King to be well looked efter when he comes oot," Lizzie explained. "This is the end of March and he should be out before the end of next month."

Minnie, sitting in the arm-chair with her hands clasped on her crossed knees, cast an approving glance round the "kitchen". The one-roomed apartments in the tenements are always spoken of either as "kitchens" or "single ends". This one, she thought, was roomy enough for three. Besides, it had two good beds and it was clean and well kept.

"Ah wid wait for old Razor King in this wee single end till next *year*, Liz," she murmured with genuine feeling. "Ah feel that Ah'm the right woman to see you and him through."

Lizzie was sitting at the table, holding a cup of tea which she had made before Minnie's arrival.

"Ah hope you're right, Min," she said, a little doubtfully.

"Ah know Ah'm right, Liz."

They stared at each other for some moments and then Lizzie broke into a laugh.

"Everything is just what we make it," she observed, "an' awthough I don't exactly think as much of Razor King as Ah did at one time, Ah wouldn't hear a word against him aw the same."

"Ah believe that, Liz," replied the other, in a fluting voice and hiding a smile.

Lizzie knew she didn't believe it, and it amused her that the younger girl should think herself so "dead thick" (wide awake and knowing). For, in spite of her affair with Frank Smith, it was strictly and simply true.

"Eh, well," she went on. "Here you are, an' Ah'm leaving the hoose to you for the night, Min. You can have company in it if you like so long as you don't mess things about too much . . ."

"Whit! You're no' coming back here the night at all, then?" Minnie exclaimed, her eyes bright.

Lizzie shook her head and laughed again.

"Razor King knows aw about Frank Smith," she said simply, "but Razor King or nobody else knows him as well as I do, Min."

"Good luck tae you, then; that's whit I say."

Lizzie got up to leave, but she went on talking for several minutes, warning Minnie in particular about the trouble there would be with Razor King if he did not find the single end just the same as it had been before he was "carted". She repeated Minnie's name so often that the younger girl suddenly became irritable and interrupted her with a protest which she tried to make good-humoured.

"Not so much of the 'Minnie' for God's sake!" she cried. "It gets on my nerves, so it does!"

Her irritability amused Lizzie.

"Aw right," she said amiably. "Ah'll take your tip. But I like us two aw the same."

"Us two? Whit does that mean?"

"You an' me. I like to think us two will be aw right an' all that. What did you think Ah meant?"

"Ah just couldny make you out at all, Liz."

"Could you no'? Well, you're about the only one Ah've taken a likin' for, round about here, anyway. An' I don't know an' I don't care whit Razor King thought o' that yin, Agnes Massey, either – Minnie."

They both laughed at that.

"You can call me Minnie," said the dark-haired girl impetuously, "as much as you like, Liz. Ah'll no' say a word agin you."

"That's the stuff to give them, Minnie! We'll get on aw right."

Soon afterwards, Lizzie, dressed in her best, went out to meet Frank Smith, and Minnie was left to ecstatic contemplation of her new home and to dreams of wild romance when Razor King came back once more.

But it was a much changed Razor King who returned

from Barlinnie Jail to the single end, at the end of April. Johnnie had learned a lot while he was in prison. He had met men who seemed to have got a great deal more out of life than ever he had done – not just plain ruffians like himself, but real "flymen" who had been hooligans to some purpose and seemed at times to have made big money. And they weren't frightened of him. They took it for granted, readily enough, that he was a good "battler", and he was furious because they seemed to pity him for being no more than that. He tried in vain to assert himself by being insubordinate and unruly in the jail. That simply brought punishment, forfeited any chance of remission for good conduct and, above all, still seemed to evoke nothing but contemptuous pity. Brooding and sullen and tortured by his "thirst", Johnnie decided that when he came out he would go in for "something higher" – as he termed it – than just the ordinary "rammies" and raids. He felt that his marked face was rather against him, but he did not realize that his mind was no less scarred. He didn't understand that his naturally hasty temper had now become completely uncontrollable. Repeated bashings and concussions have a brutalizing effect upon their victims. Razor King *looked* like a desperate ruffian when he walked out of Barlinnie into freedom and bright sunshine. There was no-one to meet him at the gates and it took him an hour and a half to walk home across Glasgow. By the time he had reached the single end, his cheerfulness had evaporated. Lizzie and Minnie were both at work. He went out into the street to find old friends and a drink at last.

CHAPTER XVI

PETER AND ISOBEL

Peter Stark began to read a few popular books on Socialism, chiefly because his father-in-law *would* talk politics and he hated to be at a disadvantage in the arguments which he could not avoid. Peter was very sure of himself in those days, laughing at his wife's warning that no good ever came of too much reading. Reading, he thought, hadn't done old John McGilvery much good or much harm either for that matter, but then, he knew that the old man, much as he liked to talk of the need for "the solidarity of the working classes", wouldn't have risked his job or even a shilling of his weekly pay to save the very "cause" itself.

Peter didn't blame him for that. Considered in the mass, he despised his fellow-workers. It was only because he was getting on very well in the big store himself and was obviously singled out for promotion by the manager, that he enjoyed playing Socialist. To profess comradeship with them simply accentuated his own obvious superiority to his fellows. The more stale old slogans he learned, the more carefully he dressed and the more particularly he studied his manners and speech.

Originally, Isobel and he had intended not to get married until they could set up in a home of their own. Her parents, who approved this idea strongly in the beginning when Peter first made his home with them in Rutherglen Road, actually persuaded them later on that it would be a pity to wait so long. By that time, however, the McGilverys had come to the conclusion that Peter was an exceptionally promising young fellow. Already he was earning good money and they thought he was bound to make his way in the world. After that it seemed no more than prudent for Isobel to secure him safely as a husband without delay. The young people themselves, being very much in love, needed little persuading, and so they started their married life, as thousands of other couples do in Gorbals, by sharing the parental home. Comparatively speaking, they were well off, for they had the room to themselves at nights, thus enjoying a privacy few young married people could afford.

After some months had passed, however, Peter became restless for a true home of his own and he and Isobel made enquiries about several possible apartments, including one room and kitchen in Govanhill, which would have suited them splendidly. None of these enquiries led to anything, however, and one Saturday night, when the two were alone in the room, Peter had a brain-wave.

"Isobel," he said excitedly, "I've got a notion to ask the manager what he really thinks about me in that job of mine. I've been wanting to know how I stand there, and this might be a good test."

"That's what I was going to tell you myself!" – Isobel sat up on the couch in her eagerness and really believed that she *had* been going to make such a suggestion – "You should see your manager on Monday!"

"Monday, eh?" – Peter's tone was faintly dubious, but his wife's sparkling eyes encouraged him. "You're right. There's no use waiting. I don't know what I'd be daeing without you. It's a good job I've you to help me, an' I'm no kiddin'."

He threw the newspaper he had been reading onto the bed and got to his feet.

"I'm going out for a walk to think it over," he told Isobel. "I'll just take my time."

"I'll come wi' ye."

"No, ye'll no'!" Peter was suddenly irritated and

relapsed quite unconsciously into the Gorbals dialect. "You can have a night on yer own for a while."

Neither of them perceived the approach of crisis. Isobel got up and drew herself to her full height of five foot six. Peter stood two or three inches taller even in his socks and he was broader and stronger and far more active. The scar on his skull which he got in the dance hall could not be seen beneath his well brushed black hair. His lips were tight and Isobel was suddenly an antagonist. The white curtains at the two windows were fluttering in the light breeze and a slant of sunshine lit the room.

"Ah'm goin' to go wi' you!" said Isobel, stubbornly making for the dressing-chest.

He followed her swiftly.

"What's the idea? Have I *always* to have you runnin' efter me?"

That was too much for Isobel. She turned round instantly and, before she realized what she was doing, she slapped Peter violently on the right cheek. He went pale and drew back, his hand to his face. Then rage took hold of him. He leaped at Isobel and struck her on the forehead with his clenched fist. She screamed and staggered and he hit her again. The blow drove her backwards; she tripped over a chair and fell to the floor with a thud that sickened him.

"You asked for it and you got it!" he said, frightened, but still savage. He stooped to help her to her feet as Mrs McGilvery came running into the room.

She took in the situation at a glance.

"You're no better than that brother of yours!" she screamed. "Yon low, good-for-nothing hooligan, Razor King!"

"You shut up, Mother!" shouted Isobel from the floor. "Mind your own business and I'll mind mine!"

"It was an accident," said Peter, rather feebly, but Isobel would not have that either.

"It was *no* accident," she moaned.

"We'll have to see what *he'll* say when he comes in," said Mrs McGilvery vindictively, referring to her husband.

"Mind your own business!" repeated her daughter as Peter let go of her and began to adjust his tie with fingers that still trembled. "Away and leave us, for any sake, Mother!"

Mrs McGilvery hesitated, but then, unable to bear down her daughter's glance, flounced from the room.

"Right," said Peter, as though answering an unspoken question. "I'm away out for a while."

"You're no'! If you go out without me, you needn't come back or speak to me again!"

Isobel was shaken physically, but her spirit was indomitable. She clung to the press with one hand, but faced Peter undauntedly.

He laughed uncertainly. To him it seemed absurd for any married woman – even an intelligent, well-educated girl like Isobel – to make such a fuss over a mere blow in the face and one that she herself provoked.

He took his hat from the peg behind the door and turned towards her with a confident smile.

"That's the best one I've heard for a hellova long time!" he observed with a smile. "By Cripes! I've a good mind to let you come with me for that!"

"I mean what I'm saying . . . if you go out . . . without me . . . I don't want to see you here again. Or anywhere else either!"

Peter stared at her in sheer amazement. Her pale, pretty face was set. Her eyes were blazing. It dawned upon him, slowly and shockingly, that she meant what she said.

"Don't be daft, Isobel!" he whispered, and lit a cigarette.

"Daft or no' daft, Ah mean whit Ah say."

Peter blew smoke through his nostrils, frowning sullenly.

"All right," he said at length. "Ah'll wait till you're ready. Ah'll be down at the close-mouth till you come."

"You'll wait in *here* for me," she commanded, with her expression unchanged.

The crisis had passed. Peter felt a shamed relief.

"All right," he smiled. "I'll wait for you here."

An hour later they sat together in a teashop eagerly discussing the prospects of his interview with the warehouse manager. Isobel had a bruise on her forehead, but was otherwise unmarked. She held his hand under the table while they were waiting for the waitress to bring them some cakes. It seemed almost like their courting days.

Peter was given an unexpectedly cordial reception by the elderly manager of the department. He blurted out his questions with the tactlessness and defiance of a schoolboy. The manager's kindly, keen old eyes twinkled and his wrinkled fingers plucked at his chin.

"Ay," he said at length, "you should go in for a two-room and kitchen hoose wi' a bathroom. That's no' exactly a *big* hoose, but it will keep your wife occupied. It'll make her contented. An' when a man has a good contented home life, young Stark, especially a married man, I know I can rely on him!"

Peter was more thrilled and delighted than he dared to show. He held out his hand in his emotion, and the old manager clasped it with his own left hand, careless seeming, but cordially intentioned.

"You've small need tae worry," said he deliberately. "We need men – young men like you – when things are no' very bright. As long as you don't get any of the wild ideas in your head, Peter, you'll be all right here. Take that from me – an old war-horse! – an' I'll see what Ah can dae aboot the hoose."

Within the month their new house was found for them. It was on the third floor of a long tenement building in Govanhill. Most of the tenants were working-class people, but of a type much above the Gorbals average. They kept their homes cleaner and they did not use their sinks as latrines.

Here, too, the overcrowding was not so intense. The "wee kids" slept in their "shake-doons" just the same, but they were unaware of their parents' intimacies. In many of these households respectability was almost a fetish. The men even avoided going home too obviously under the influence of liquor, and priest or clergyman was a not infrequent figure on the stair. A cautious friendliness prevailed among the neighbours. They were less blatant in their curiosity than the neighbours of Rutherglen Road, and they were at least inclined to be kindly. In the long run, though, the difference from the Gorbals people was one of degree only.

Isobel, who gave up her laundry job once they were installed in their new home, told Peter frankly that she hoped it would last. That was on a Sunday morning when they were having their breakfast in the clean and cheerful kitchen.

"Ah don't want," she said emphatically, "ever to go back to the Gorbals as long as Ah'm living. Father and Mother's all right, but we're different even from them, are we no', Peter?"

"Sure we are," he replied absently, then added, with a touch of malice: "We're in a different class awthegither, Isobel! We're more in a class of Bobbie and Lily Hurley. They're in a hoose wi' a bath these days an' aw!"

"Ah wish you'd stop kiddin'," she protested rather crossly. "Ah know aw about Bobbie and Lily. But we're no' dancers, Peter, an' we've a right tae be living here."

Peter was reading an article on housing at the time. There was a new and precious bookcase at his elbow containing half a dozen volumes of the "literature" which he thought appropriate to a man of his standing and culture.

"You're right, Isobel," said he. "I hope it lasts an' aw!

An' although Ah'm gonny do a lot o' readin', Ah don't want to be a John MacLean or anything like that!"

"I should think no'! John MacLean was a fool – neither more nor less – to throw away everything for people that werny worth it!"

Peter did not agree with her, but he thought it wiser not to argue. *He* thought that MacLean was a saint and a martyr, but too unpractical for everyday life. And he himself had no instinct for martyrdom. He looked round his new home and studied his wife's happy face.

"We're all right," he thought contentedly. "Tae hell wi' every ither body!"

And it happened that Peter himself had a rise in salary only three or four weeks before the great firm which employed him thought it necessary to impose an all-round cut of 10 per cent in wages. The directors made a point of the fact that they were taking the same cut in their own fees. They produced impressive figures relating to the fall in prices and the keenness of competition. Peter and Isobel were very disappointed, but, even after the "cut", they were a shade better off than they had been before and considerably better off in comparison with Peter's fellow-workers. There was a lot of grumbling among the rank and file. Some of them tried to enlist Peter's sympathies. He was non-committal and avoided discussion as much as he possibly could. The reduction was gradually accepted as a matter of course. Many of the workers were members of large families and could exist on extraordinary little. A few work-girls, who might otherwise have remained chaste somewhat longer, grew desperate and looked for young men – or old ones – to help their budget. And business continued as usual.

It was not so very long after that that old Mrs Stark died. Isobel, though she was never unkind enough to say so, was inwardly glad that the last link had been severed between Peter and his old home. She could see no change in him, except, perhaps, an increasing tendency to read political books. Once or twice, lightly, she warned him about this. He dismissed her protests with a laugh. And she did not take them very seriously herself. She took an immense pride in her new home and enjoyed, now and then, playing hostess to her admiring parents. They were really most respectful to Peter when they came round to Govanhill of an evening. And the neighbours thought a good deal of him too.

"You never can tell," they said among themselves, sagely. "You widn't think tae look at him that Peter wis own brother to yon Razor King! A well-doing young man, so he is, an' his bit wife is a nice lass. But that's the way it goes wi' families – some good and some bliddy bad – you never can tell."

The second 10 per cent cut in the warehouse wages was announced in the week after Razor King had been sent to prison. And, upon this occasion, Peter and Isobel had received no compensating rise to make them take it easily.

When the notices were posted on all five floors of the great store, workers surrounded them with expressions of sheer consternation. Peter thrust his way to the front of one muttering group, read the announcement and stood there frowning darkly. A number of girls, several of them neatly and attractively dressed in spite of their low wages, stood close beside him, and even in that crisis, they looked at him admiringly, noting his clean, athletic figure, his neat blue suit and his general air of prosperity and importance. They thought he looked a "pure treat", giving him credit for his good taste, for which, had they but known it, Isobel was chiefly responsible.

Peter had a light raincoat over his arm and he stood there frowning without saying a word. He wasn't thinking of the others at all. He was just calculating that 10 per cent off his pay represented almost exactly what he and Isobel were still contriving to save every week.

"It needny make any *real* difference," he said to himself in a first access of relief. Then, resentfully, "Ay, but where'll we be if we canny save anything at all? Tae hell with the stingy bastards!"

Norah Grassey, a stout, pleasant-looking girl with red hair, who worked in the "household requisites department", was standing at his elbow.

"Whit dae *you* think of it, Mr Stark?" she asked respectfully.

Others heard her and crowded round, eagerly curious for his reply. They didn't say anything. As though of one accord they waited for Peter to speak.

He was flattered, and smiled even through his own annoyance.

"I think it's a liberty," he said, "taking 10 per cent off the wages at this time! A hellova liberty if you ask me."

There was a loud murmur of assent and approval.

"We wid be as well on the buroo, so we wid!" wailed Ina Gilmour, a small, dark, neatly built girl of nineteen.

Everybody looked at her and she coloured hotly. They all knew that Ina was more or less engaged to Robert Percy, a well-doing foreman carter, and most of them guessed that for months past she had denied him nothing.

"*You'll* be getting married onywey," said Norah, with a mixture of contempt and envy. "*You'll* no' need to kerr!"

"What aboot it if Ah am gaun tae get married?" she cried. "Have Ah no' got a right tae get married or what? An' whit's that got tae do wi' this cut, onywey?"

"It's not a case of marrying or not marrying," Peter put in with his best judicial manner. "It's a case of lowering the standard of life for everybody! It's a case of reducing the purchasing power of the people when there's a superabundance of all the necessaries of life everywhere. That's what it is!"

Everybody around him was obviously impressed. The girls looked at him with the most open admiration and

227

two or three men present waited respectfully for him to continue.

"That's what it is," Peter repeated, much gratified.

"An' it's serious enough, believe me. It should be made illegal."

He tried to draw out of the crowd, slipping his arms into the sleeves of his raincoat. Isobel, he remembered, would be waiting for him out at the entrance to the underground railway station at Glasgow Cross. The thought made him faintly uneasy. He wanted to get away while there was still time to think things over.

"But what wull we dae aboot it?" someone asked, and others took up the question.

"I think," replied Peter hastily, "we should call a meeting of all the workers some time next week and, if possible, discover and decide upon some plan of action. We ought to resist this 10 per cent reduction, because if we don't, another reduction is sure to come later on.'

He had not really intended to be so definite as that, but they were all looking to him for some suggestion and he couldn't disappoint them. There was a little clamour of approval, and some of the girls even began to laugh, so relieved at this prospect of doing something that they almost forgot for the moment that the meeting might have no result whatever.

"It's fine to be cheery," said Peter warningly, "but mebbe next week we'll have less to be cheerful about."

Their anger and fear returned to them with that reminder.

"They might ha gi'en us two weeks' warning," wailed a tall girl, whose neat dress and well-cared-for personal appearance were in striking contrast to her "common" accent. "One and sevenpence off sixteen shillings! Jesus! How can they expect us tae keep respectable if they don't pey us!"

This girl, like nearly all her fellow-workers, could speak good English when she took the trouble, but, in moments of stress or emotion, they all slipped back into their old way of speaking. Peter tried to be one of the exceptions to the general rule. He knew that too much of a Glasgow accent might be a fatal obstacle to advancement in that business.

"I'm away now," he announced, turning towards the tunnelled close that gave access to the side street. "See you later." There were many there who would have liked to have detained him for further argument, but he strode resolutely away, and Ina Gilmour and three or four others followed at his heels.

Ina did not like Norah Grassey, for she thought, quite wrongly, that the other girl tried to put on airs. As they walked towards the street, she realized contentedly that she was much better off than the others, and she thought that Norah, whose family was out of work, would be in a bad way. The thought pleased her a good deal, but she went on chattering complaints like the rest of them.

Peter shook the girls off once he had reached the main street, and hurried to meet Isobel. She was smiling when he came up to her and looked so different from the other lassies – so much more prosperous and secure – that he was instantly relieved, feeling quite illogically that the common misfortune could not really touch his wife and himself. But he told her the bad news immediately, nevertheless.

"We've got a 10 per cent reduction in the wages next week," he said bluntly. "The whole lot of us; everybody in the warehouse."

"Some hope!" laughed Isobel. She thought he was joking.

"But it's right enough," he protested. "Ah tell you the notice is posted all over the warehouse. They're all clamouring about it yet. Ah've just come away from them."

Even then it took him some few moments to convince her that he was serious, and, afterwards, she was too upset and worried to discuss the matter immediately. They took a tram to Jamaica Street, Isobel asking a question or two, but making no comment, and then they walked on arm-in-arm to Union Street, still full of this news and considering its implications.

"We'll go to the pictures for a while, eh?" suggested Peter nervously.

She nodded unhappily, and at last, in the friendly darkness and shelter of the kinema, she began at last to speak her mind. The burden of her advice was that, whatever happened, Peter must keep out of any fuss or trouble. Ten per cent, she reminded him, wouldn't really hurt *them* very much, and what happened to the rest of the workers was no concern of theirs. Uneasily he agreed with her and told her nothing of what he had said to the group in front of the notice-board.

"You needn't worry," he assured her. "Ah'm no' going tae interfere. Ah'll just need to wait and see what the rest are going to do about it."

They did not go straight home, but called instead upon Mr and Mrs McGilvery, both of whom took a gravely indignant view of their news. The elder man was particularly emphatic in warning Peter not to make himself conspicuous in any way. "The bosses," he said sententiously, "never forgive that. Stick wi' the crowd an' you'll mebbe no' come to much harm."

"You're a nice one tae warn him, Father," exclaimed Isobel bitterly. "If Peter's different from what he was it might be you that made him. He was all right till you started to educate him the wrong way."

Peter laughed reassuringly at that, but John McGilvery felt guilty and uneasy in his own mind. Like a lot more men of his class, he regarded himself as an "advanced thinker", but he went to ground like a rabbit at the least sign of danger.

Under the combined influence of his wife and her parents, Peter made up his mind that he would keep a very still tongue in his head when he went back to work on the Monday. Nevertheless he had no sooner arrived at the warehouse than eager fellow-workers begged him to attend the special meeting which was to be held that night on the first floor, by consent of the employers, to discuss the situation.

It was quite clear that they were looking to him for advice and guidance. They had been impressed by what he had said about "purchasing power" and "super-abundance". Very few of them had the faintest idea what he meant, but they weren't such fools as not to recognize politics when they heard them talked, and, clearly, young Peter Stark was a politician. They were none of them trade unionists in that warehouse and they needed a politician to help them. Uneasily Peter agreed to attend the meeting. He was flattered by their eagerness and obvious respect, but he wished he were well out of it all.

His promotions had freed him from routine duties by that time, and he spent most of the day canvassing in the better-class districts of the city. Shopkeepers treated him with some consideration as a smart young traveller likely to make his way. "Tae hell," thought Peter furiously, "wi' all they ithers! Ah'll be doing well enough sune, cut or no cut, if Ah keep out of trouble."

But he could not escape the meeting, nor, being once there, could he avoid the constant appeals to his judgement and the repeated requests for his advice. He tried to laugh things off, but the crowd would not be satisfied with evasions.

The directors, Peter was told, had given permission for the meeting after work was over. Nobody told him that his name had been mentioned as the originator of the idea, but there were several who reminded him now of what he had said on the Saturday, and in the general clamour of talk there were already voices raised calling for strike action.

The men seemed very bashful at this meeting. There

was only one of them on the trestle platform among half a dozen young women, and he seemed completely tongue-tied. Peter was practically forced to take his place on the platform and to state his views.

They cheered him as he moved reluctantly forward, and his vanity responded to this applause. When he faced his fellow-workers they all fell silent, listening expectantly.

"A lot of talking's no use," he began nervously. "*I* think we ought to ask the firm to reconsider their decision. We ought to petition them to postpone the 10 per cent reduction at least for another week . . ."

"Another *year*, you mean!" cried one girl, amid a chorus of laughter and approval.

Peter smiled, but took no other notice of this interruption.

"That's what we should do now," he went on, "and during the week we might be able to arrange for some other development. That'll do me, at any rate, but I don't want to keep anyone else back who can think of something better."

There was further applause when he had finished this short speech. He stepped down from the platform with a good deal of relief, but, before the meeting ended, he had to agree to sign the petition which was at once prepared. The meeting broke up at half-past eight, and Peter hurried away from the big building, refusing to be drawn into any further discussion with his fellow-workers. When he got home he told Isobel what had been decided, but did not say anything at all about his own part in the affair. The petition was presented on the following morning, and, a few hours later, fresh notices were posted, announcing that the firm had decided to postpone the cut for another week "in order to give all the employees time to realize its necessity".

This concession, far from conciliating the workers, tended to increase their indignation. The general public

– the countless customers of that big store – had seen the notices by this time, and some among them thought the wage reduction was probably necessary in those hard times, while others contended that it was an abominable imposition upon the workers. None among them was really much interested. The price of the goods was all that mattered to them.

During the days which followed, Peter found that, try as he would, he could not escape the unofficial leadership which had been forced upon him. All the other workers wanted to know what *he* was going to do. Often he heard them talking about him, declaring confidently that Peter Stark would never take an imposition like that lying down. He was half-frightened, and yet half-elated. When fear predominated he reminded himself of his friendship with the manager. He hoped that, whatever happened, his part in the whole affair would be overlooked.

On the Saturday morning the employees were informed – individually on this occasion – that the reduction would take effect on the following pay day. The firm deeply regretted the necessity, but necessity it was. Competition compelled them to reduce wages or to go out of business.

None of the employees believed that. Many of them, including Peter, knew that it was a lie. They knew that a cut might be necessary to maintain the high dividends then being paid, but they were certain that there was still a large margin of profit at the old rates.

And the meeting which was called for the second time displayed a different temper. There was no laughter on this occasion, no joking or jesting. The men's faces were grave and there were many girls on the edge of tears. If they had been organized: if they had had a Union at the back of them, strike action would have been unanimously acclaimed. Even as it was the great majority demanded an immediate stoppage of work. It was only the older hands and the employees in the better positions who were afraid and hesitant. They alone could see that a strike was foredoomed to failure.

And again the crowd clamoured for Peter. He was himself worked up into a fury of indignation and, in that mood, he really believed that a mass protest might convince the firm it had gone too far. Customers in the city had told him during the week that the reduction was scandalous. He felt that the public must be on the side of the workers and would support them by shopping elsewhere until the dispute was settled.

They yelled as he stepped on to the platform.

"I don't know what the rest of you are going to do," he shouted defiantly, "but I know what I'm going to do; I'm going to take a week off. You can call it going on strike, or call it what you like, but for a week you'll not see me here. This reduction is just overdoing it. Look at the profits the firm's making! It should not be so easy to impose reductions. We *must* make a protest."

There was a great outburst of cheering. Girls and men surrounded Peter and declared enthusiastically that they would follow his lead. But there were several in the company who slipped quietly away – one or two who were only too anxious to be the first to inform the management of this new development.

It was decided on a show of hands and by an overwhelming majority to adopt Peter's suggestion of this form of "silent protest". The word "strike" was not used, and the younger folk really believed that stopping away for a week was not actually striking.

Peter went home with drooping spirits. The excitement of the meeting evaporated like the fumes of alcohol and left him sick with apprehension. He told Isobel in the briefest terms of the decision which had been taken, again concealing the part he had himself played in the affair. She did not suspect him then, but, even so, she reproached him for not keeping out of it all. During the days which followed she and her parents learned the truth, and Peter's life became almost unbearable through their reproaches and lamentations.

On the Monday, the majority of the employees kept their word. They organized a demonstration in the streets, and marched through Glasgow cheering and singing. Peter refused absolutely to join in this procession, but the warehouse did not open that day, and even Peter had moments of excited hopefulness.

On Tuesday morning, however, the warehouse opened again with an almost entirely new staff. Some 10 per cent of the original employees had reported back for duty, and some 50 per cent of new hands had been engaged. Prices had been marked down and the shopping public thronged all five floors. In spite of the shortage of assistants a tremendous business was done.

Tuesday is early closing day, and on the following morning the "strikers" held an open-air meeting in Cathedral Square, but the numbers had fallen away and the public seemed to take no interest in their grievances.

Scores of the girls and several men went straight from that meeting to the warehouse and humbly begged to be taken back at the reduced figure. Among these early surrenders, the management took its choice, reinstating the cheaper hands who had taken no conspicuous part in the "protest". On the Thursday, the surrender was complete and the workers returned in a body. The management completed its necessary staff complement, but the blacklegs and the new employees were kept on, and so more than half of the "strikers" were told curtly that there was no vacancy. Peter was told to call again on the following Monday at 10 a.m. He left the warehouse dejectedly, and there were girls who cursed him as he passed out.

Isobel was waiting for him at home, white-faced.

"Do you think you'll get back?" she asked.

"I don't know," he confessed. "The manager might be

235

for me. But if I don't get back to the warehouse I'll find something else."

Isobel went with him on the fateful morning and squeezed his arm as he left her in the doorway.

"I'll wait here till you come out," she sighed.

He turned and smiled. "I might no' be too long!" said he.

Watching his retreating back, Isobel sighed deeply. She knew that she loved Peter and would have to go on loving him. But she did not think he would get his job back and a heavy desolation fell upon her.

She walked to the corner of the street, her handbag under her left arm. There was nothing "skinny" about her now. Her figure was still slim, but the angles had all been rounded off. Her dress was neat and well chosen, for, though she shared the general opinion of the slums that a married woman need not bother much about her appearance, Isobel had natural taste and spent her money cleverly. She stood patiently at the street corner – a pretty girl of obviously "superior class" – and was unaware of the heads that turned in her direction. She had no religion, but all her thoughts were a prayer.

Peter was shown at length into an office on the third floor, where he found the manager and two directors seated at a large desk. The directors' faces were expressionless, but the manager looked a little uncomfortable. He did not look at Peter when he spoke.

"We're disappointed," he began, "to hear that you took a prominent part in this strike, Stark. In your case, particularly, there was little excuse. You had been well treated and you had been warned."

"Does that mean," said Peter sullenly, "that I'm finished here?"

The manager hesitated, glanced for a moment at his impassive colleagues and then replied with a slight shrug of the shoulders.

"I'm afraid it does," said he.

Peter put on his hat.

"I'm sorry I cannot get back here," he said slowly, "but I cannot say I'm sorry for any action I took, for the wages paid to those . . . young ladies" (he stumbled over the two words, though he had chosen them deliberately) "were not enough to keep them reasonably respectable."

"That is for us to judge," put in one of the directors coldly.

Peter was suddenly furious.

"Maybe it is," he shouted, "but there might come a time when the like of you'll not be doing any judging; when the like of you'll be doing time in prison, where you should have been years ago!"

The manager half rose from his seat, sank back and pressed a bell. Peter felt a wild longing to dash forward and hit him in the face. Only the thought of Isobel restrained him. He did not wait to be shown out; he turned and slammed the door behind him.

He was shaking as he rejoined his wife on the pavement, and before he spoke she knew what had happened. He lit a cigarette and inhaled deeply. Then he tried to smile.

"I've got the push, Isobel," said he. "They don't want me back there. They think I'm a Bolshevik or something."

She tried to hide her dismay.

"All those books," she said softly. "I warned you about reading them. What are we going to do now?"

"It's all right, Isobel; I'll get another job. We're only starting the game, are we no'? If you think this is me finished, you're wrong! Damn them tae hell! We're no' gaun back to Gorbals! I can work!"

But the weeks passed and the months, and there was no work for Peter to do.

CHAPTER XVII

THE VANITY OF THE KING

When Johnnie returned to the "single end" for the second time on the day of his release from prison, he found his wife and Minnie at home and both eager to welcome him. He had been drinking a lot, but, even after the long period of enforced sobriety, he could carry his liquor well. He walked as steadily as ever, spoke distinctly and hugged Lizzie with rough good humour. Afterwards the scowl that had become habitual settled on his brow, but the two women had little idea that his nerves were on edge and that his always uncertain temper was dangerously inflamed. Indeed, he did not realize this himself. He was proud of his drinking capacity and quite unaware that alcohol was beginning to affect his mind while it still seemed powerless to damage his splendid constitution.

Both the women were excited and nervous themselves. Although Johnnie knew of her intimacy with Frank Smith, Lizzie was not at all sure what he would say – or do – when he learned that she was going to become a mother. That morning she had looked at herself in the glass, wondering whether he would notice, but her condition at that time was not very obvious. She hoped that she might get him really interested in Minnie before she told him about herself. All day long at her work she was rehearsing imaginary conversations with him.

In the middle of chatter that led nowhere, Johnnie himself gave her the opening she had been trying to make.

"Are you still gaun wi' that Frank Smith?" he asked her.

Minnie tittered, but fell silent as she met his swift and menacing gaze.

"Ah'm not only going wi' him," said Lizzie, desperately bold, "but Ah'm gaun tae have a breadsnapper. Did ye no' notice, Johnnie?"

He stared at her in speechless astonishment. He was not even indignant. He had got it so firmly into his mind that Lizzie would never have a baby that now he could scarcely believe she meant what she said. The truth dawned upon him by slow degrees and with it came a humiliation which quite bereft him of speech.

"It's aw right, Razor King," she hurried on. "Frank will look efter me an' pey for everything, no fear of that. And Minnie here is gaun tae look efter the hoose. So you'll no' need tae be lonely. And there's months to go yet, onywey."

Suddenly he began to laugh. It was a harsh, unnatural sound and both women were frightened.

"Eh, well," he said at last, "you've certainly got some news for me. You've no' been idle, the pair of you, Ah can see that."

Lizzie could not make him out at all that evening, but she was glad enough that he seemed to be taking her news so calmly. She went to the press and produced whisky and glasses. Johnnie nodded at her and drained a stiff measure.

"I had some news for you an' aw," he said at length. His vanity was aching like a tooth and he felt compelled to impress Lizzie and this new girl she had got in for him.

"When I was in Barlinnie," he went on, "I came into contact wi' some *real* flymen – fellows who can make money. An' I made up my mind I wid try for something big an' aw that myself. Ay, and sune too!"

Lizzie was eager to encourage him in this, though she did not really take his ambitions seriously. It was enough for her that he should talk and keep interested, but Minnie, who did not know him so well, made a grave blunder.

"Ah'm feart," said she, gazing at Johnnie with awe and admiration as the perfect ruffian of her dreams, "that the marks on your face wid keep you back, Razor King!"

There was dead silence for a moment. Johnnie's hand went to his scars. They stood out startlingly white against his flushed face. He was terribly conscious of them and his eyes blazed at the frightened girl who had been tactless enough to allude to them.

"Maybe they will," he said at last in a low voice, "an' the same marks will keep me back from *you* an' aw!"

"Whit . . . does that mean?" gasped Minnie, after another pause.

Her white face fascinated him. Something seemed to snap in his brain and he sprang at Minnie and his hands closed round her throat.

"It means that the marks won't keep me back from giving you a hellova good hiding and then chucking you out of here!" he roared. "That's whit it means!"

Lizzie ran to his side and put her hands on his shoulders.

"Don't lift your hand to her, Razor King," she implored. "I know she hurt your feelings and aw that, but I know she didn't mean it and that she's the one we both need to run this wee hoose . . ."

Minnie was almost choking in his grasp, but somehow she contrived a smile, raising her own hands to his wrists and trying to release his hold. But he did not look at her. His glazed stare fixed on Lizzie and the knowledge came back to him with fresh astonishment that she was going to have a child by this other man.

He loosed his hold of Minnie slowly, pushed her contemptuously away, and began to straighten his tie.

"All right, Liz," he said quietly. "Whatever you say. You know what's wanted."

He felt no anger against his wife and he didn't, after that first burst of rage, think about Minnie at all. His whole mood had changed to a sullen bewilderment.

Neighbours came in soon afterwards and their flattering congratulations upon his return and their interest in his plans for fresh gang activities restored him to something like good humour. They stayed until all the drink in the press was finished and, after they had gone, towards half-past nine, Johnnie sat in front of the empty fireplace smoking, with Minnie to his left and Lizzie standing with her back to the bed.

He seemed so calm that his wife began, much more hopefully, to discuss the whole position. He did not contest her right to get what enjoyment she could out of life and he only nodded when she reminded him that she had told him about Frank Smith and herself long before. She was fearful that he might try to get what some might call "his own back" on the father of her unborn child. Johnnie kept his thoughts to himself, but he made no threats. Actually, he was afraid to do so. His vanity tugged at him in two different directions at once. Earlier he had publicly scoffed at his wife's affair with the foreman baker. Now he couldn't be sure what the neighbours would think. His own impulse was to go out and give Frank Smith a "bashing". On the other hand, he felt that he might carry things off better by taking no notice whatever. It was Lizzie herself who puzzled him most.

It seemed to him that she had changed for the second time. Gradually, after their marriage, he had noticed that first change – her eagerness to be as "tough" as any of them; her deliberate discarding of those airs and adornments and refinements which she had valued as Lizzie Ramsay; and then, finally, her feverish anxiety to see him – her husband – live up to his title. Johnnie was no psychologist, but he began to understand now that his wife might have felt there was no other way to justify her position. With the acute social class-consciousness of his kind, he realized that she had married beneath her. None but the Glasgow born would have appreciated this: it was simply that the Ramsays were respectable folk and Johnnie and his family were pure "slummies". And so, knowing that her family despised her, she banked absolutely upon her husband's notoriety. He was the Razor King and she *plus royaliste que le roi*, or, as he would have put it, Liz was out to be more of a gangster than himself.

Almost up to the time when the affair with Frank Smith started, there was a double reason for Lizzie's inferiority complex. She wanted a baby, and no baby came. She fell in love with Johnnie, and decided to marry him chiefly because she thought him a perfect male. Morbidly self-conscious about her own bandy legs, Lizzie wanted a straight-limbed, well-built, husky fellow to be the father of her children. And, remaining childless, it was a long while before she even began to doubt that this sterility was an entirely personal curse.

Naturally Johnnie's thoughts were incoherent and confused. But he knew clearly enough that the second change – the change *back* – had come over Lizzie since he had been in Barlinnie. She was altogether prettier and more attractive than she had been. There are women who look their best as expectant mothers, and she was one of them. But what chiefly impressed Johnnie was his wife's new air of confidence and self-esteem.

"She's sae bliddy pleased wi' hersel'," he thought angrily. "Aw because she's gaun tae have a breadsnapper by yon old mug. Who wid ha' thought it? Who wid ha' thought it?"

Jealousy, as it is ordinarily understood, simply did not exist in Johnnie's mind. He was literally indifferent to her having a love affair, but that any other man should be able to give her a child was a keen humiliation to him. Never questioning her social superiority, he had always believed that he had better brains than Liz and a stronger personality. He wanted her to look up to him and respect him. Now he was uneasy lest she should despise him.

His thoughts went back some three or four years to the time when he was thinking of marrying Mary Hay, and he scowled more fiercely as he remembered the "sherricking". He could see Mary standing on the kerb, hysterical in her reproaches, denouncing him in that high-pitched wail. He had been afraid to give her a proper bashing because of the child – *his* unborn child. The scowl relaxed a little. Odd, he thought, that he had never seen Mary Hay from that day to this, nor yet the daughter she had borne so soon after she had married the crippled ex-service man. He had heard that the little girl had died since then. Still . . . *his* daughter! Agnes Massey too. She was another man's wife, but, again, the child was his own.

Johnnie began to feel happier. He began, for the first time, to take a contemptuous interest in Minnie. Lizzie, he thought sardonically, knew his tastes pretty well. The girl was "no' a bad bit stuff". She seemed frightened of him, but adoring. Her humility and eagerness soothed his vanity. He laughed and reached out for her and set her on his knees. The girl giggled, and Lizzie's smile showed her relief. Everything, she could see, was going to be most comfortably arranged after all.

There was little further discussion that evening. Johnnie now agreed amiably enough that Minnie was as nice-looking and sensible a girl as they could wish to have for a lodger and to look after the house. He only grunted when Lizzie announced, still with a trace of nervousness, that she was "awa' oot" to see Frank Smith again. His eyes smouldered for a moment as he watched her carefully putting on her hat. "Nane o' the hairy about Liz, noo!" he thought, "nae bliddy fears! She's got to be respectable for *him*!"

But Minnie had her arm round his neck and was fondling his cheek, and he had been in jail a long time.

"Away you go, Liz," he said. "Minnie and me can amuse ourselves." He kissed the girl on his lap to underline that, and his wife left them with a loud laugh.

She was given a warm welcome by Frank Smith, and she told him that everything had gone off splendidly. He may have been more relieved than he confessed. Neither of them really understood the strange workings of the mind of Razor King.

During the next couple of months, Johnnie and Minnie were constantly together and happy lovers in their way. The neighbours, in that tenement at all events, took little notice of an affair which nobody attempted to conceal. Their code was elastic in any case, and a razor king could only be expected to do as he chose. Lizzie seldom came back to the single end. When she did come it was usually in the day-time and Johnnie would be out. She had no complaints to make, for Minnie seemed to be looking well after the house. Besides, she was really happy with Frank and his family. One of the daughters had married in the meanwhile, but Frank's invalid wife and his unmarried daughter accepted her as one of the household quite without hostility.

Towards the end of June, however, she had to see Johnnie on business. Frank Smith had promised to pay her fifty pounds as "compensation for seduction". They were really fond of each other, and yet they discussed this matter in the most business-like way and actually used the word "compensation". Really it was merely a question of expenses and conventions. Both of them, and Johnnie not less than either, would have taken it for granted that the baby must be born in Lizzie's own home. Everybody who knew them – apart, that is to say, from the bakery workers – knew equally well that Frank was the father of Lizzie's child. Yet it would bear the name of Stark, and must, therefore, enter the world under Razor King's roof. Frank, a thrifty man earning a good wage, had more than £200 saved up in the bank.

Even so, fifty pounds was a generous payment. His own family thought he was only going to give Lizzie twenty-five. That was the amount which had been discussed in their presence and Lizzie had said frankly, "That'll do me". Privately, however, he gave her the whole fifty pounds in cash on the morning of Fair Friday, and it was decided that she was to accompany the Smith family to Troon for a holiday during that Glasgow Fair fortnight. Frank left her to make the necessary arrangements with her husband.

Lizzie found Johnnie and Minnie all dressed up to go out for the afternoon. In the simplest terms she told them what had been agreed between her and Frank, and produced the thick bundle of pound notes in confirmation.

"Whit's more," she added, "Ah'm gaun to Troon the morn an' aw!"

Razor King had the packet of notes in his hand and was counting them, his face somewhat flushed and his eyes greedy.

"Frank has played the game, onywey," remarked Minnie meaningly, with a smile and a nod at Lizzie over Razor King's bowed head.

Gently but firmly Lizzie took the notes back from Johnnie's hands. He did not attempt to keep them, but he looked up at her with a kind of guilty start. He was truly impressed by Frank Smith's munificence, and somewhat awed to think what an important position the foreman baker must hold.

"I will admit," he said, "that Frank seems a decent sort; but what do I get, Liz?"

There was a silence in the single end, though from the sunlit street there rose the strident, everlasting clamour of the children at play. Lizzie considered Johnnie appraisingly, and then laughed.

"I'll give you a fiver," said she, "an' you can take Minnie away with you somewhere, eh?"

She was excited and blushing, feeling that this was lavishly generous.

"You could have a week-end down at Ayr for the races," she went on recklessly.

Johnnie and Minnie were both overjoyed, for they, too, thought the offer very generous.

"You're a pure treat, Liz!" exclaimed Johnnie, taking the notes eagerly.

"Ah must give you a wee hug for that!" cried Minnie, suiting the action to the words.

They went out soon afterwards, elated as children who have been given an unexpected tip. Lizzie was also glowing with satisfaction and pride and importance. Before she returned to the Smiths', she looked in to see Mrs Grainger, a neighbour on the same stair, and asked her to arrange to get some food and drink in at the single end so that they could have a party on her return from Troon. It gave her intense pleasure to see the other woman's astonishment and envy – to be going to Troon for a holiday! To be wearing such clothes! To be arranging for a party on her return! Mrs Grainger was too deeply impressed for words.

"Aw right then," Lizzie concluded. "This quid should pay for all, eh?"

"Too true it will, Mrs Stark!" replied the other eagerly. "You can rely on me."

Well satisfied with the conduct of all that business, Lizzie counted her remaining notes carefully, and the following day she left Glasgow with the Smiths for Troon, where they had a four-apartment house which they rented out for the rest of the year.

Johnnie and Minnie did not leave Glasgow, but they and others of the gang had their notion of "a good time" with Lizzie's five pounds. They drank a good deal and they went to the pictures – Johnnie would not dance in these days, being too sensitive about his scarred face. The money did not last long, but, when it was all gone,

Minnie produced a couple of pounds of her own savings, and, what with that and the contributions of one or two other friends who happened to be in funds, parties of a kind continued until the end of Fair Week.

On a Saturday morning in August, after the holiday was over, Frank Smith, at Lizzie's urgent request, went with her to the single end in Crown Street. Her time was drawing near, and it seemed to her that everything would be more in order somehow if Frank showed himself. She felt, perhaps, that if that encounter between husband and acknowledged lover passed off smoothly, as she believed it would, Johnnie would be less likely to make any trouble later on. Not that she expected trouble: it was merely that she did not trust her husband's uncertain temper and could not calculate his dangerous moods or their possible causes.

It was nearly eleven o'clock as they climbed the tenement stairs. Frank was uneasy and uncomfortable. He had been brought up in just such a tenement, though he had not revisited one of that type for more than twenty years. He hadn't even thought about them, for his childhood memories were not happy ones. His spirit shrank within him as he climbed the stone stairs, and, though he did not lack courage, he could not help wondering rather anxiously what sort of a reception he would get from the man who was not only Lizzie's husband, but also Razor King.

Johnnie and Minnie were still in bed together when Lizzie opened the door of the "kitchen" and walked in with Frank close behind her. His nostrils twitched at the sour and horribly familiar smell of the single end. He closed the door behind him, lit a cigarette and stood rather awkwardly holding his soft hat in his hand.

Johnnie sat up in bed. He was wearing a coarse flannel day shirt and his thick black hair rose in an untidy shock upon his bullet head. The scars showed livid on the window-lighted cheek.

"Hullo, Liz!" he said. "Got back, eh? Minnie, here, has ta'en a dislike to work, an' she doesny care whether she goes back to the toil again or no'. Is that no' right, Minnie?"

The girl laughed and sat up in her turn. She put her bare and rather dirty arms round Johnnie's shoulders and pressed her face against his scarred one.

"As long as we've got a drink in the hoose, that's all I care," she said, and then began to sing in a ludicrous and tuneless way.

"For you are, rare Razory King," she sang. "An' I'm your Razory Queen; Queen of the Fair, the Fair, Fair, Fair – Fair Holidays of good old Glasgow Fair!"

"They're *still* half drunk," thought Frank Smith disgustedly. "The place stinks of booze and dirt." He exchanged glances with Lizzie and forced a smile.

"Well, as long as you're enjoying yourselves," said Lizzie, "that's all right. Ah'm gaun to give you another shilling or two, Razor King. Then I mean to go along to the bank in a wee while wi' rattling old Frank here, an' put the money away in case the rainy day comes along. What do you say, Frankie?"

Frank found it difficult to say anything at all. Razor King and Minnie, still sitting up in the bed, cheek to cheek, were watching him and he could not make out at all what Johnnie was thinking.

"You'll be doing the right thing all right, Lizzie," he said at last. "An' the sooner we get away the better, too, I'm thinking."

He was still trying to smile, but it was becoming increasingly difficult, for a kind of anger had come to him now in addition to his disgust and nervousness.

Lizzie took a pound out of her bag and handed it to her husband.

"Here you are. Another quid for you, Johnnie," said she. "An' don't say Ah'm no' good to you!"

Johnnie grunted and slipped the note beneath his pillow.

"Ah'll give you a hand to spend it, eh, Razor King?" cried Minnie. "You and me can go the pace, can't we? Not half!"

But he was staring at Frank Smith and did not trouble to answer her. He was thinking how well Frank looked in his newish grey flannel suit, which must have cost him at least four or five pounds. Johnnie supposed that the foreman baker would be earning six pounds a week or even more. He wasn't surprised that Lizzie had "taken up wi' a fellow like that". Envy almost choked him. If Frank Smith had been a man of his own class, Johnnie would have sprung out of bed and attacked him there and then. But he was over-awed by his gentility and importance. And yet he had to do something.

He turned to the young, coarsely pretty, rather stupid girl beside him, put his arms round her and began to kiss her. His lips were glued to hers in a long-drawn-out embrace like a "film close-up". In fact he was playing to his public. He wanted to show Frank Smith how little he cared about him and Lizzie. Only Frank; he didn't mind what his wife thought. He bore no grudge against her.

And Lizzie, whose mental processes were similar, grew uncomfortable on Frank's account, not her own. She took her lover's arm in an apparently natural way and fidgeted against his side. Frank stood very stiffly and the forced smile was frozen on his lips. The exhibition revolted him; he not only hated Johnnie, but, for the moment, he almost hated Lizzie, too. It sickened him to think that she was the wife of such a hooligan.

"Frank an' me are away oot now," said Lizzie, in a voice she tried to keep just ordinary.

Johnnie, nearer to them than his companion, ended his kiss slowly and then turned to face her.

"Please yourself, people," said he. "You know your way about an' aw that."

Minnie could not repress a snigger at the studied insolence of that reply. Her shoulders shook and the snigger became a loud laugh. Johnnie turned upon her furiously.

"Shut up that laugh of yours!" he snarled. "It gets on my nerves at times."

She held a corner of the dirty coverlet against her mouth, but her shoulders went on shaking.

Frank Smith put on his hat, eager to be off.

"Right; we'll away now," he said. "We'll have a meal in one of the restaurants in Bridge Street yonder, and Lizzie'll be back at dinner-time to arrange for everything else."

"So long, then, people!" said Minnie, giggling again.

Johnnie turned to her with such an expression upon his face as should have warned them all, particularly the two women, that danger threatened.

"Shut up, you!" he repeated softly. "Ah'm your boss."

Then he turned to Lizzie and Frank Smith who were making for the door.

"Enjoy yourselves now," said he, "when you've got the chance. Good luck tae you!"

The door had scarcely closed behind them before he had caught Minnie by the forearm and dragged her out of bed. She screamed in her surprise and fright and the pain of his grip upon her.

"You bitch!" said he. "I'll teach you to laugh out of turn!"

He struck her hard across the face and the suddenness of the blow drove her frantic. She hit back, cursing.

A frenzy near to madness came to him then. He dashed the girl to the floor, snatched an empty beer bottle from the table and smashed it over her head. She moaned and lay still with blood flowing fast from the wound. If the bottle had not broken, Johnnie would have hit her again. A murderous elation filled him. He felt as though he had "bashed" Frank Smith. He put on his coat

250

and trousers at once, moving quietly and quickly, though he longed to shout and go tearing down the stairs, his razors in his hand. He walked out of the "single end" and did not latch the door.

At that time there was not the faintest regret in his mind. He was all ruffian, with just enough sanity left to make him seek escape. He met nobody on the stairs, hurried into the street and walked on to a confectioner's shop and tea-room in Norfolk Street. He sat down at a table inside, lit a cigarette and waited for one of the girls to serve him. All this time his heart was hammering fast, but the frenzy was still on him. The tables in the shop were partitioned off from one another, so that each stood in a kind of cubicle. A pretty waitress came to his table at last and he ordered a large plate of custard tarts and iced cakes. He had had no breakfast and he felt hungry.

He laughed at the girl when she brought his order and fell to on the custard tarts.

"Will you eat *aw* the cakes on that plate?" she ventured, impudently coquettish.

"Sure thing! An' maybe some more an' aw! You can bring two or three more custards, in any case. They're the goods in here; the best stuff you make."

He put the pound note that Lizzie had given him on the table and began upon another custard. The girl was smiling and counting out the change from the first order. Then she looked into his eyes and something she saw in them frightened her. Until then she had not noticed the scars on his face. Johnnie saw that she drew back a little and that her smile had vanished. He saw, too, that she was blushing uncomfortably.

"Am Ah no good enough lookin' or *what*, eh?" he demanded in a fierce whisper.

The girl had recovered her confidence a little. She put her hands on her hips, tossed her head and answered saucily.

"Well," said she, "you're nothing very startlin', are you?"

He saw she was not afraid of him and concluded that she could not know who he was.

"Listen," he snarled. "If you weren't such a fine-lookin' bit stuff, I'd mark your face worse than mine is in a minute or two. But Ah'll let you off this time. Get some more custards. Bring another six good ones. Quick, for Ah've a good mind to give you a slap on the face even yet, an' report you over and above that an' aw, so you'll be on the 'buroo' for a while, where a hellova lot of fine people are just now."

She paled and ran, too terrified of the man and of his threat to make any comment.

Johnnie sat on at the restaurant until he had eaten all the custard tarts, and slowly his frenzy left him. Even then he felt no compassion for the wretched girl whom he had stunned and possibly killed. It seemed to him that she had "asked for it". In the morbid vanity of his mind he believed that she had been laughing at him and that she had made a mock of him in front of Frank Smith and Lizzie. He wondered sullenly whether she would "squeal", and decided that the only thing for him to do was to risk it and go home.

He left the restaurant and came out into bright sunshine. Absorbed in thought, he sauntered to Gorbals Cross, where he bought a racing paper. At a public house in Crown Street he ordered a glass of whisky and half a pint of beer to wash it down. Deliberately he entered into conversation with men he knew in the bar and also the barman. He invited two of the young chaps home with him, declaring that there was some bottled beer in the press which he was ready to share with them. They were flattered by Razor King's condescension, "seeing that they were not everybody".

But there was a crowd round the close-mouth when the trio arrived and several of the be-shawled women came running up excitedly to tell Razor King that "Minnie had been raided and nearly done in awthegither" while he was away out. Amid the clamour of many voices there were some raised to proclaim that this attack had probably been made by some of the Bridgeton gang.

Johnnie acted up to the part he had prepared. He roared out an oath and went pounding up the stairs with his companions at his heels. He yelled threats of what he would do to get vengeance of the Townhead mob. The single end was empty, for Minnie had been taken away to the infirmary. Neighbours crowded into the apartment after them. Nobody could tell a coherent story. The men were swearing and the women chattering in high, excited voices. It seemed that Minnie had been barely conscious when the ambulance arrived. She did not seem to know who had attacked her.

Johnnie breathed more freely and began to talk more loudly and luridly than ever of what he would do to the "bliddy flymen who had taken a liberty with his girl". He went to the press and produced the bottled beer, and soon it was all consumed. Again and again he told the company how he had been in a tea-room in Norfolk Street all the time the ruffians were "doing poor Minnie in". If he had been at home with his weapons there would have been a different story to tell!

After the beer was finished he insisted upon taking some of the company round to the tea-room so that they might hear his story confirmed. Half a dozen young men and women went with him, protesting that there was no need for Razor King to prove anything at all, but the frightened waitress was quite positive that Johnnie had been in there all the morning eating custards. She scarcely dared to look at him while she confirmed his story.

Johnnie and his friends went back to Crown Street triumphantly, talking of the big battle that would have to be arranged to square things up. Lizzie came home to find an excited company in possession with more drink supplied by its various members. It took her some time to find out exactly what had happened, and when at last she understood, her face paled and she began to talk of revenge more wildly than any of them, but she could scarcely keep her terrified eyes from Razor King's face.

Nobody ever learned the truth of that morning's brutal work. There were many neighbours, later on after the excitement had subsided, who began to wonder whether Razor King's alibi was any alibi at all. A little lad of eight told his father that he had seen Razor King walk out of the close soon after "Mrs Stark and yon ither man wi' the grand paraffin" had also come into the street. His father cuffed him unexpectedly and warned him with dire threats to keep a still tongue in his head.

Lizzie knew instinctively that Johnnie had done the "bashing", but never once did she betray that knowledge either to her husband or to Frank or to anybody else.

The police could obtain no evidence whatever.

And in the infirmary, where Minnie relapsed once into delirium before she got better, nobody paid any attention to her wild cries – "Oh, Razor King, don't bash me! Don't bash me, Razor King!"

Perhaps none of the nurses heard her. Even if they had, one couldn't expect them to take much notice of the ravings of a slum girl, whose mentality was probably as low as her morals.

Johnnie was half-drunk for days. The one thing he wanted now was to lead a great contingent into another battle.

CHAPTER XVIII

DOWNHILL WITHOUT BRAKES

Though it was not apparent either to his neighbours or even to his wife, Johnnie Stark, "Razor King" of the Gorbals, began to slip downhill, physically and mentally, from the time he "bashed" Minnie and escaped punishment. It may be that there are no absolute turning-points in any man's life. Every creature begins to die when it is born, and none can confidently declare when decay first sets in. But, sooner or later, it becomes visible. Frequent battles and repeated wounds had had their effect upon Johnnie; prison had hardened and coarsened him; heavy drinking had dulled his intellect, and unemployment, which he had made no serious effort to escape, had, nevertheless, lowered his morale. It always does and always must do. Glasgow, the second city in the Empire, with a third of its adult population idle, bears tragic witness to this indisputable *fact*.

But Johnnie underwent some subtle inner change when he stunned and wounded his foolish, vulgar, pathetically docile little mistress. He was half-drunk when he felled her to the ground and scarcely sober at any time in the days which followed. But once people had said of him that "Razor King never lifts his haund to a lass". They could say that no longer. It was true that he had struck Mary Hay down in the crisis of a public sherricking, and true that he had sometimes given Lizzie a cuff or two in the ordinary course of matrimonial dispute. No-one in the tenements would have held these things against him. To bash a girl with a beer bottle or to "use the weapons" on her was a different matter. His

255

neighbours and his fellow gangsters did not *know* that he had assaulted Minnie; on the contrary, they were eager for him to lead them against the Townhead mob. But Lizzie had guessed the truth, and, somehow, all Gorbals began to look on Razor King as an out-and-out hooligan, a ruffian no longer to be respected for anything *except* his ruffianism.

Johnnie himself began dimly to realize this changed atmosphere. The young men he talked to in the pubs or at the "gym" on Glasgow Green were as respectful as ever and as ready to pay for drinks. The neighbours were always polite to him and to Lizzie. They did not willingly converse, but, when they did, there was something almost abject in their agreement with everything he said. They would not even challenge his opinions on racing or football. In fact, he knew that they were afraid of him. They humoured him in much the same way that a cautious man will humour and gentle a savage dog. He could not tolerate opposition, and yet he was not satisfied with submission. "By God!" he would say to himself furiously, "I'll show them one day that Ah'm no' finished yet!" But he could think of no way to "show them" except by some new and more desperate ruffianism. Once, in a horrified moment of self-doubt, he asked himself whether he wasn't "ordinary" after all.

When Minnie was at last discharged from the infirmary she went back to live with the Starks in their "single end". Many things that would seem incredible outside Glasgow are commonplace in the tenements. Minnie, for instance, had parents living and several brothers and sisters, but her family lived like pigs in a sty and not one of them had even bothered to visit her when she lay ill and, perhaps, dying. She had broken away from them to live in Crown Street, and they had virtually forgotten her. And so she went back, humbly, to Razor King. Never, by look or word, did she refer to the "bashing".

She was simply more careful not to cross him; more anxious to please.

Lizzie needed a girl to help her in the house, and didn't much mind whether it was Minnie or another. Johnnie took Minnie back to board and bed with lordly disdain, but, in those days, he was strangely considerate of his wife, soon to become the mother of another man's child.

Very soon Lizzie knew that she would have to give up her work at the bakery. Financially that prospect did not greatly worry her because she still had the bulk of Frank Smith's fifty pounds safe in the bank. But she wanted to draw the usual maternity benefit and out-of-work pay from the Unemployment Exchange and she was a little nervous lest questions should be asked.

"Do you think anybody'll shop you at the buroo or anything like that, Razor King?" she asked him at breakfast one morning.

Johnnie was always "Razor King" even to his wife by this time. She scarcely ever called him by his Christian name after he came out of Barlinnie. He looked up at her with some suspicion and resentment. As far as the Exchange was concerned it didn't matter in the least whether the child was his or another man's. It would bear his name, and Lizzie's cards were stamped, and her legal right to assistance could not be challenged. He wasn't quite sure whether the authorities could do anything or withhold anything if they learned about Frank Smith's "seduction money", but he knew very well that his own prestige would have to be sorely on the decline before anybody in Gorbals would dare to give the "buroo" the least hint of his disadvantage.

"You know as well as me," he said curtly, "that I'm safe enough up at the buroo, Liz. You must be off form or something!"

"Maybe Ah am," she sighed. "Ah wis only wonderin', that wis all."

"Don't wonder too much; it's no' good for you. It's

257

this clash wi' the Townhead mob Ah'm wonderin' about."

She was glad enough to change the subject, for all working-class Glasgow was talking excitedly of the coming battle, and Lizzie was really glad that Johnnie had something to occupy his mind. In a queer, detached, almost motherly way, she was still fond of Johnnie. Perhaps she felt that she owed him something for being so reasonable about Frank and the "breadsnapper".

Minnie, who had been a silent listener to the conversation up to that point, now felt free to join in. She knew very well that the neighbours were talking spitefully about her, and yet she felt important because the great "battle" was to be fought on her account. Both women told Johnnie what great things they expected of him. The grotesqueness of that sham never occurred to him. He was even pleased by Minnie's flattery. He began to boast of what he would do to the Townhead flymen. And the two women, knowing all the truth, still listened to him admiringly.

But the big "clash" – or "raid" as some of them termed it – did not develop for many weeks. There were a few small "rammies" – running fights in the streets with bottles and stones exchanged as missiles by small contingents – and that was all.

Lizzie had to leave work during the third week in August, and her child, a boy, was born in the "single end" early in September. They had a midwife in for the occasion, but the baby only lived for two or three hours. Lizzie was heartbroken and Johnnie and Minnie genuinely shared her grief. Frank Smith came to see her the next day and did his best to comfort her, but she only cried weakly, and kept on saying over and over again that she wanted to leave that "unlucky hoose".

Johnnie was truly patient with her during the days which followed. The idea of moving to another apartment in a different street absorbed her, and Minnie diffidently agreed that it might be a good thing for them all.

"Aw right, Liz," Johnnie agreed. "Ah'll leave everything to you two. Get another hoose if you can, but wait a wee while until this fight is over. It's going to be a big one, and I've got to get well into it to keep my mind off that wee kid and aw that . . ."

There was a knock at the door as he spoke, and a moment later Minnie had admitted a woman neighbour, breathless with excitement.

"I've just heard now," she gasped, "that the trouble is to be next Sunday night."

"Who said that?" demanded Johnnie, displeased that he had not been consulted. "How did I no' know of it, Mrs Skee?"

"Ah've just heard from the close-mouth," she apologized hastily. "One of the Townhead flymen was over at Gorbals Cross only half an hour since. He just shouted, 'Tell your mob we'll be ready Sunday night!' an' they say he was away again. That wis aw."

Johnnie was still hurt in his vanity that the challenge had not been delivered to him personally, but there was no-one whom he could hold responsible for this except the Bridgeton contingent themselves.

"Sunday night'll do me aw right," he laughed unpleasantly, "an' Ah hope the fight is no' a hundred miles from Main Street, Bridgeton, an' aw!"

Lizzie's face paled. Frank Smith now lived in Main Street, Bridgeton, his family having effected a change of two-rooms-and-kitchen homes with a Main Street family who desired to be nearer Clydebank, where the head of the house had been re-started in one of the Clydebank "shipyerds". Lizzie was afraid for Frank Smith.

"What does – that mean, Razor King?" she asked in a low voice.

Mrs Skee was instantly all attention. She could feel that there was something hidden from her, something exciting and dangerous. But her curiosity was not to be gratified.

"That'll do *you*, Mrs Skee," said Johnnie peremptorily, and waited until the crestfallen neighbour had left the room. Actually he had merely wanted to frighten Lizzie; now, as his wife and Minnie both stood very still, waiting for him to explain, his vanity and his jealousy took hold of him again and he could not resist the temptation to heighten the effect he had caused.

"Smith is in the Main Street, isn't he?" he said, his thumbs and forefingers on the handles of the razors in his pockets. "Ah wis only thinkin' that if we did have the fight up there I might give him a call. And brand him, see? It wid be a hellova good chance. They'd think it wis just part of a gang-fight and nobody wid connect it wi' me by myself."

"You wouldn't do that, Razor King?" said Lizzie breathlessly. "Leave Frank out of it, for any sake."

"It's too risky, Razor King," said Minnie, in her turn. "Frank Smith is too respectable and aw that!" It did not matter to her personally whether Johnnie "branded" the baker or not, but she had a sort of affection for Lizzie, who had been good to her, and saw that she was in distress.

"Eh, it's aw right, Liz!" said Johnnie, laughing again. "Ah wis only kiddin' you. I'll leave Smith alone. He's well out of everything as far as Ah'm concerned."

"I should think he is!" she exclaimed, in mixed protest and relief. She sat down and the colour gradually returned to her cheeks. Johnnie had startled her badly for a moment, and even now, although she believed he *had* been "only kidding", she wanted to put the stupid notion right out of his head.

"Sune Ah'm goin' to try to get my job back again out where he is," she went on. "There's no-one else will help me at the bakery except Frank. An' Ah want to be working again, now Ah've got no breadsnapper efter aw."

"Smith might make you another one, eh, Liz?"

She winced under the sneer. "Ah never expected that – from you," she said quietly.

Johnnie was a little abashed, and Minnie chose that moment to giggle. She was not laughing at him. It was merely that her nervous tension demanded some relief. He hit her instantly in the face with his clenched fist, and she fell over the bed with a scream that must have been heard by all the neighbours on the landing.

Johnnie bent above her and his face was contorted. "Did Ah no' tell you," he said, "to watch what you laugh at? This time, though, Ah'll let you off."

The girl was not badly hurt. She got up whimpering and went to the sink to rinse the blood from her nose and lips. Johnnie paid no further attention to her, and Lizzie, much agitated, was still wise enough to ignore the whole incident.

"You can have all the battling you want," she went on, in a voice which she tried to keep calm, "without bringing Frank into anything. He and his family have been hellova good to me – an' to you and aw if it comes to the bit!"

"Sure! Ah told you Ah wis only kiddin'. Ah'll no' interfere with old Smith. In fact, Ah'm his pal if you only knew of everything."

"Well – I'm gled of it. He's a good pal to have, in my opinion."

"You can count on me, Liz," said Johnnie, getting his cap from the peg on the inside of the door. "Ah mean to go down to the corner now and see what it's all about. An' when the fight's over, then, maybe, we'll look for the new hoose."

The news was "right enough", and Johnnie found many friends eager to stand him drinks and hear him talk of his plans for the battle. But a restless mood was on him that day, and after half an hour or so he wearied of his friends and walked by himself to the Gallowgate. There, in the first public house he entered, Johnnie found

261

two men, one in brown plus-fours and the other in a decent blue suit, who had served time in Barlinnie Prison with him. These were two of those very "flymen" whom he so much admired, middle-aged fellows, not gangsters at all in the ordinary sense of the word, but professional criminals.

They hailed the Gorbals Razor King with assumed deference. Actually their view was that "only mugs" went in for gang fighting. In their eyes Johnnie was clearly a "mug", but they knew him for a desperate fighter, credulous and childishly vain. Such men could be useful upon occasion.

The flymen naturally had money, and, as naturally, paid for the drinks. Johnnie never understood how they got their "dough", for they were not on the dole and yet they certainly did no work. He found them uncommunicative, but very ready to listen to his own talk.

The red wine, though it was not laced with spirits on this occasion, was raw, heady stuff. Under its influence Johnnie began to brag about the coming "battle" and the thought of getting his own back on Frank Smith came into his mind. His friends displayed a more lively interest as he began to tell them how Lizzie and he had drifted apart, and how she was now "rinnin' round" with another fellow.

He felt that it was necessary to his vanity to explain that this other man was in an important position, with money – a foreman baker, no less.

"Ah wull say," he conceded tolerantly, "that this Smith is no' stingy wi' his dough. He paid fifty pounds' compensation when Liz had her kid by him, the one that died. Aw the same, an' though Liz an' me haven't been bothering about each other much for a hellova while, it was a liberty for Smith to go the whole road wi' her when I wis in jail. An' Ah've a good mind to give him a tannin' for that, one day, and to mark him, maybe, wi' these wee tools."

Johnnie fingered his razors with an evil smile, and the man in the plus-fours called for more red wine.

"Listen, Razor King," he said smoothly. "I know how you feel, and you could give this fellow a tanning aw right, of course, but what would be the use of it anyway – even if you brand him and get no dough out of it? Now, if it wis me, I wid rather give him no tanning at all – and get some dough out of him."

The blue-suited "flyman" nodded approvingly.

"There's a hellova lot of truth in that," he said. "We three could bash this guy easy enough, but it might be no' worth while if we lost money through doing it."

Johnnie, slightly fuddled, did not think at the time that the whole affair was nothing to do with his pals from Barlinnie. His one fear was that they should consider him stupid and slow-witted.

"Oh, Ah'll get the dough out of him some time or other, believe you me!" he retorted. "Ah've not been asleep awthegither, I can assure you!"

"I'll bet you haven't," agreed the man in plus-fours, "but listen a moment to what I've got to say and then pass your opinion on it. And if you don't like my idea, why, we can always go back to yours. Is that a bet?"

"Aw right," Johnnie nodded. "We're as well with the best ideas as with the worst. Go ahead with what you've got to say."

The two flymen exchanged quick glances. If Johnnie could have intercepted them and understood their meaning, there would have been savage trouble in that bar. But they thought him dead easy, and they were right. He listened like a "mug" to their crude scheme of blackmail and never even questioned their obvious intention to share the proceeds.

"Send this fellow a note and sign it with your wife's name," began the man in plus-fours. "Ask him to meet her at a pub in Gallowgate next Saturday night, say.

When he turns up, we three'll be there instead of your wife. We'll tell him we'll give him away to his firm unless he gives us about a fiver apiece. He's a foreman – is he no'? – an' the people in the work'll no' like a foreman who seduces other men's wives, puts them in the family way, gives them fifty quid, makes them chuck up their job, and still makes them go on the buroo to be kept by the rest of the public. An' that's not all. Your missus might get her job back in the bakery and he might still carry on wi' her from what you say. Then we could get some more dough out of him. Suppose I write the note out now? How's that for an idea?"

Johnnie not only fell in with this plan; he did so enthusiastically. But his outlook on life was crudely immoral. He had no strong enmity against Frank Smith, but it seemed to him only fair that he should "pey one way or the ither" for having "taken a liberty". The word "blackmail" did not occur to him; he would have been puzzled to define it if it had.

The three men adjourned at once from the public house to a dirty room and kitchen in the London Road, an illicit drinking-den frequented by criminals and prostitutes. There the note was written. The man in plus-fours was confident that he could write a woman's hand – as, indeed, he could – and Johnnie thought it unlikely that Lizzie had ever written to Frank. More drink was consumed, and then Johnnie parted from his new friends on the understanding that they would be waiting for him and Frank at the agreed public house on the Saturday evening, two days later.

Next morning it was all that Johnnie could do not to mention Frank to his wife. He was so much in the habit of telling Lizzie of his plans that he even wanted to talk over this one with her, though that was impossible, of course. But he could not keep quiet. His excitement and the drink that he had had the night before compelled him to chatter, and so he strode up and down the kitchen, flourishing his razors and describing how he would use them in the great battle on Sunday.

Lizzie answered him rather wearily. She had not seen Frank except once since the baby was born. Now that she was feeling better he was constantly in her thoughts. She wanted badly to be with him again, and at last she interrupted Johnnie and said that it was time she was thinking of getting her job back again at the bakery.

"If Ah wis you, Liz," protested Johnnie hastily, his face grown suddenly cunning, "Ah wid no' bother about working for a good month yet. You're no' strong enough for a while."

"But we might no' get another hoose unless one of us is working."

"We'll get another hoose in time enough. There's no' all that hurry, is there?"

She thought he was being considerate of her and smiled.

"Aw right, Razor King," said she, "we'll see efter this fight. *You* might be gled to get out of this hoose by then!"

"Ah might an' aw!" he agreed, laughing because of the load lifted from his mind. "We'll see about everything next week after the fight. Then you can try and get your job back again an' Ah might get some kind of a job myself some day."

That consolation was too much for Lizzie, for she knew in her heart that Johnnie would never go to the toil again. She threw back her head in that wailing laugh of the slum woman. Johnnie, who would have assaulted Minnie for a snigger, gazed at his wife in angry perplexity and let her be.

On the Saturday night he arrived early at the rendez-vous and found the two flymen already waiting for him. They went into the bar and had a preliminary drink, for it had been decided that Johnnie was to meet Frank outside and the other two to wait in the bar. Their chief anxiety was lest their victim should suspect the genuineness of the note and keep away.

In fact, Frank Smith had suspected. He didn't know Lizzie's hand-writing, but the phrasing of the note, short though it was, seemed strange to him. Besides he could not understand why – if she needed to see him so much – she hadn't come to his house as usual. Unfortunately for the foreman baker, he reached a wrong explanation of this problem. He supposed that Lizzie had had trouble with Razor King; that perhaps he had menaced her; and that she had asked a neighbour to write to him in her name. It was only for her sake that he refrained from going round at once to see her in Crown Street, for Frank did not lack courage. As it was, he arrived at the Gallowgate public house punctually, a well-dressed, respectable working man, middle-aged, but evidently prosperous.

Johnnie was lounging at the side door. When he saw Frank arrive, the older man's clothes and general air of well-being filled him with envy. He stepped out of his shelter to meet him.

"So you *have* turned up, eh?" he sneered. "But Ah'll bet you thought it was the Missus you were going to meet instead of me!"

Frank Smith looked into Johnnie's eyes with bitter contempt. He did not condescend to answer; he merely turned on his heel and began to walk away rapidly in the direction of Glasgow Cross. His hand was in his coat pocket crumpling the forged note.

Wrath almost choked Johnnie.

"The cheeky bastard!" he gasped, feeling the two razors in his waistcoat pocket, "he thinks Ah'm no' good enough to speak to, by God!"

He had completely forgotten the blackmail plot and the two flymen who were waiting for him in the bar. He began running after Frank Smith before he was fully conscious of the fact. His weapons were in his hands and

266

his scarred face was hideous with rage. The Gallowgate was crowded, and Johnnie had just enough sense to drop his hands and hold the razors concealed. Even then, men and women turned and stared after him as he dodged after his enemy, slipping in and out of the throng.

Smith turned into a dark side street, and Johnnie was on him in a bound. His razors were out and open again now, and he slashed the baker twice across the face and head. Smith screamed and staggered back against the wall, his hands making futile movements against the glittering weapons.

There were scores of people coming and going, and though it was too dark in that gloomy passageway to recognize faces, several of them shouted and began to run. But those who were nearest to the Razor King stood still, hesitating for a fatal moment.

Nothing would have stopped Johnnie then. He toppled Smith over with a furious blow, kicked again and again at his head and body, and then slashed the keen blades through coat and underclothing so fiercely that they stayed in their billets. Then he turned and ran.

When Frank Smith regained consciousness he was lying in a clean infirmary bed, his head and shoulder and back swathed in bandages. The razor wounds did not hurt him much, but he was suffering great pain from internal injuries caused by Johnnie's boots. The night sister had tried to make him comfortable and the house surgeon had administered an opiate, but he was still dazedly awake. He hoped that no arrest would be made. He had powerful friends in the baking world and he was not afraid of losing his job even if his wounds did keep him in hospital for some weeks. But he did not want his affair with Lizzie to become generally known. He knew that if his firm heard the full story of his affair with the wife of a razor king, even his friends might find it difficult to save him. Then, in his pain and weakness, he began to whimper. He longed to have Lizzie beside him to

267

comfort him. He wanted to tell *her* what had happened, but no-one else. At last he, too, fell asleep.

It was not until towards noon of the following day, Sunday, that Frank's unmarried daughter brought news of the assault to Lizzie in Crown Street. Her father had asked her to do that, and she told Lizzie that he didn't know in the least who the hooligan was who had attacked him, or why.

"Dad says," the girl concluded, "that the poliss have been worrying him already, all for nothing. He would like it fine if you could get round to see him this efternune."

Although she was friendly enough with her father's mistress, Elsie Smith did not linger in the single end. The smell of the place revolted her, and even her curiosity to see Razor King, still sleeping in the cavity bed, did not induce her to remain a minute longer than was necessary.

Lizzie was shrill in her exclamations of grief and horror. She talked about the attack upon "poor Frankie" incessantly as she and Minnie got ready the midday meal.

"Who cud have done it?" she wailed. "Frank's such a fine chap, there's naebody wid want to hurt him."

Johnnie had been sitting up in bed for some time. His eyes were red-rimmed and he felt sick and very confused in his mind. But when he heard what his wife was saying he got up at last to question her further.

"Aw, Johnnie!" cried Lizzie excitedly. "Are you wauken at last? There's been some hooligan who has razored poor Frank and very near done him in aw-thegither. Last night, it was, in the Gallowgate. Ah'm away to the infirmary to see him sune. By Jeez, Ah wish Ah knew who did it!"

Lizzie turned to the stove again as she spoke, and Johnnie stood where he was with a foolish, embarrassed grin on his face. Minnie stared at him. She was a slow-witted, rather stupid girl, and the idea that came into her head then was so sudden and unexpected and – to her – so wildly funny, that she burst into laughter. Johnnie's face had, in fact, betrayed him. He looked guilty as a schoolboy caught in the act. Minnie found exquisite delight in the idea that Lizzie was asking for sympathy for Frank when, as she now felt certain, Johnnie himself had razored his wife's lover. Her laugh became a shriek.

Completely bewildered by this sudden outburst, Lizzie turned from the stove in time to see Johnnie dash furiously at the almost hysterical girl.

"You stupid laughing bitch!" he shouted, and hit her across the mouth. She fell, but he struck her again and again, hitting with fists clenched, blackening her eyes. Now she was screaming in real earnest, raising a hic-coughing, sobbing yell of "Murder!"

Johnnie grabbed her at last by the shoulders and ran her to the door and down the first flight of stairs.

"It's lucky you're *no'* murdered!" he shouted. "You're oot of the hoose now and oot you stay, you bliddy, daft little idiot. If ever I catch sight o' you on they sterrs again, Ah'll fling you right doon tae the bottom, so Ah wull!"

He was still in a towering passion when he returned to the kitchen, but Lizzie had collapsed into the arm-chair and was weeping noisily. Johnnie's anger vanished. Suddenly, just as he used to feel sometimes with his old mother, he felt torn now between pity and repentance. He wanted to comfort Liz and so to comfort himself.

He knelt beside his wife and put his arms round her shoulders, his cheek against her cheek.

"Don't cry, Liz," he said. "Minnie's *no'* worth it. I wis finished wi' her, anyway. She's away now and she'll *no'* be back here again, Ah'm thinking. We'll get someone else in her place; someone wi' more sense. Listen, Liz – it's the big fight the night. I'll go to battle wi' a big heart if you'll only say you're *no'* angry wi' me!"

Lizzie did not want to say that she was weeping more

for Frank than for anything else. Except for the shock and surprise of the attack, she was not really very distressed that he had given Minnie a hiding. She was even a little touched by Johnnie's new mood, for she was still very fond of him at heart.

"It's aw right, Razor King," she sobbed. "See that your razors are in good order, an' although Ah'll no be at the battle, Ah'll be here waiting for you and having everything ready when you come back."

Johnnie got to his feet and turned away.

"Ah'll need to get a couple o' new weapons," he muttered, in an altered voice. "Ah wis half-canned last night and Ah was showing my razors to a fellah, and he has them yet for aw I know."

Lizzie stopped weeping. She was frightened and cried out what was in her mind.

"*You* didn't have anything to do wi' what happened to Frank, Razor King?"

"Don't be daft! What the hell do I care about him, Liz?"

The reply sounded natural enough, and Lizzie laughed in her relief.

"Ah think Ah'm worryin' too much," she explained. "What wi' Frankie and the battle that's coming. Never mind that. Ah'm away oot, noo, an' before Ah go to the infirmary Ah'll tell some o' them at the corner that you'll be needing new weapons the night."

"Ay, that's right," he agreed. "An' Ah'll away doon and find some nice wee lassie to put in Minnie's place. Ah'll no' be that long, an Ah'll see what's doin' an' aw while Ah'm at it, eh, Liz?"

She nodded and looked at the clock. "Ah'll be back likely, and have the table spread for tea," she said.

"Spread it for four then, Liz," he replied, and tugged on his cap. His wife followed him down the stairs some minutes later.

But they did not meet again that day. Johnnie was soon

back in the single end with two young girls, Margaret Bannerman and Jennie McLaughlin, both blondes, both slender, both passably good-looking. They lived only a little way down the street, and, as they were both working, they were able to come out in good "paraffin" on Sundays. They were painted and powdered and they carried neat handbags. Neither of them was yet eighteen, but they were lassies of the real gangster class, who followed the mob and fought with it too. Both of them meant to be in the battle that night.

They went back with Johnnie simply because he *was* Razor King. They were thrilled by his exploits; proud to be noticed by the greatest fighting man in the Gorbals. They liked him all the better for being married to a good-class quiet young woman like Lizzie, for whom everybody felt rather sorry since her child had died.

Their cheap perfume filled the kitchen, though it could not quite shut out the other odours. Laughingly they took off their hats and put them on the dresser beside their handbags. Johnnie told them that Lizzie would be back soon enough. He felt sure that whichever he chose was his for the asking, though actually the girl would come to live with them, like Minnie had done, as a lodger, paying a small price in consideration for helping in the house. He did not bother to flirt with either of them. There was time enough for that: meanwhile he was content to laugh at their pert conversation and to join in their speculations about the coming "clash".

A deputation of young men and women mounted the stairs some time after Lizzie should have returned. They brought with them three different pairs of razors of which the Razor King could make his choice.

Johnnie took this presentation as a matter of course. He inspected the weapons carefully, tried their weight, flourished each in turn, tested the edges with his thumbs.

He asked Margaret Bannerman which she preferred,

thereby marking his preference for her. She declared instantly for two large razors with black handles.

"Ay, there're the right ones," said Johnnie, condescendingly shutting them and slipping them into his waistcoat pockets. "Ah'll take these, people, and thanks. Hell knows where they'll be this time to-morrow!"

That met with a chorus of laughter. There was still some drink in the press and bottles and glasses were produced. Johnnie found that the first swallow of whisky made him feel sick again, but another gulp steadied him and put fresh heart into him. Presently, since Lizzie had not returned and all the drink was finished, the whole company trooped down the stairs and into one of those drinking "clubs" which slake the thirst of Glasgow when the public houses are closed. There they awaited their "zero hour".

272

CHAPTER XIX

CRIME AND PUNISHMENT

Broken bottles and glass from smashed windows were strewn so thickly in Main Street, Townhead, that the driver of the Corporation cart and his mate grumbled and swore continually all through the Monday morning after the great "clash". And the cart was piled high before their job was finished.

"Holy Mother of Heaven!" said the driver, as he climbed to his seat before taking his full load to the dump, "there's no' been such a battle in Glasgow for two years at least. Ah wid like fine tae ha'e seen it, wid ye no', Alan?"

"Ah did see it, an' if you'd no' been drunk you *wid* ha'e seen it, tae," retorted his mate. "True enough, the big clash started here in Main Street, but there was fifty rammies all over Glasgow before it all ended. Ay, an' there's twenty-nine battlers up at the infirmary the day, not counting scores and scores of lads and lassies that are home i' bed wi' sore heids, or hiding away for the coppers not tae see them wi' their bandages and plastered faces."

"Wis there no poliss hurt in the battle, then?" asked the driver.

"Two or three wi' cuts an' bashes, but they wereny detained. From my window I could see maybe fifty, maybe a hundred, coppers in Main Street, but they were just lost in the mob. Yon Razor King from Gorbals came along right up the tram-lines at the heid o' his division. There must have been nearly two thousand o' them yelling and shouting, wi' a hundred or more lassies

273

among them. Razor King was whirling his weapons like a drum-major wi' his bodyguard o' hooligans close behind him."

"Yon must ha'e been a fine sight!" sighed the driver, an Irish-Catholic. "But did the poliss no' interfere?"

His mate puffed at his cigarette and then spat contemptuously.

"What for wid they interfere?" he retorted. "The Townhead mob was well over two thousand strong, an' if the coppers had got caught between the two armies they wid ha'e been drooned i' the tide. They wis scrum three-quarters, the poliss – blowing their whistles and dancing wi' rage on the edge o' the battle, an' being terrible rough wi' the wee yins that wid come rollin' out of the big rammy like washed-up pebbles! Mind ye, the poliss was holding the side streets, and, in the end, when the heat of the clash wis spent, they cleared Main Street. But the mob was rinning away by hundreds, an' they carried the fightin' aw over the toon. Ay! We'll be readin' in the papers o' the 'grand baton charge', but they didny charge at all until the two divisions wis gaun away of their own accord. There wis no traffic for half an oor. Ye saw yon tram wi'oot a whole pane o' glass in it, yourself, did ye no'? There was three or four women an' as many kids cut and hurt wi' broken glass who had nothin' to do wi' the clash itself. An' you should have heard the women screeching and the men swearing oot o' the windows – heids stickin' oot like brambleberries in a hedge all doon the street. An' some wis so excited that they drank all the liquor in the press quick as they could so as to have the empties to fling doon intae the mob. It wis a hellova battle! I never seen a better."

The driver picked up his reins and set the horse in motion with a click of the tongue.

"It was my brither home frae his last voyage," he explained regretfully, "that got me so full Ah missed the fight. He's in bed yet, Ah'm thinkin', for aw they stewards

274

swank aboot holding liquor . . . They say yon Razor King was hurtit badly!"

"Ay, he'll be lucky if he's no' deid. He laid oot half a dozen Townhead lads before he lost his weapons, they tell me, an' then he got hit on the heid wi' a bottle. Efter that they just kicked him intae unconsciousness and his bodyguard couldny save him. The battlers on both sides stamped over him, an' it wis two lassies who dragged him oot to the pavement in the end. Stark, his name is – Johnnie Stark – an' I remember his old man. He wis a terror, too, specially in drink. Hey, hey! Fightin' rins in families as well as ither things. But this bashin' will be the finish for Razor King, Ah'm thinkin', even if he doesny die. He wis no' very strong i' the heid tae begin wi', and when he comes oot o' Barlinnie next time he'll likely have no intellect left at aw."

"A razor king's no great loss, onywey," observed the driver philosophically. "Mind ye, a young fellow is aw the better for a bit o' fighting, but it's just plummy to go wi' the mobs efter you're a grown man. Do ye no' think so, Alan?"

"Too bliddy true, it is!" agreed the other. "An' if it wisny for the razor kings we widny have a kert full o' broken bottles the day."

The cart passed on. The driver's mate had, in fact, given a reasonably accurate account of that great Sunday night battle which many in Glasgow still remember.

In the last week of October 1927, Johnnie and the three other men, described as "ringleaders", were sentenced to twelve months' imprisonment with hard labour. A dozen other young fellows were sent down for periods varying from one to three months, and the only girl arrested was cautioned and bound over.

Meanwhile, for Peter there had been an endless search for work. For six weeks he had been unable to draw any money from the Labour Exchange because of the "report" which had been put in by his firm to the effect that he was himself to blame for being out of work.

Ultimately, when he did begin to draw relief to which he was entitled, their savings were exhausted, for Isobel and he had spent a good deal in furnishing the new house. Soon they began to go for their meals to Isobel's old home in Rutherglen Road. That was a bitter blow to Peter's pride, but there was nothing for it, and, to give Mr and Mrs McGilvery their due he had to admit that they had not thrown his failure in his teeth.

Day after day, week after week, month after month, and still no work. Peter had kept away from the Gorbals through it all. He knew that his family must have heard about his "come down", and he realized that, though they might be sorry for him in a way, every one of them – except, perhaps, Razor King – would have a secret satisfaction in it, if only because he had always tried to be superior to them. There was no work to be had. Three or four times, when he did hear of a vacancy and actually secured an interview, the prospective employer had always found out or seemed to know already that he had lost his previous job through "politics", and that ended the matter. Nobody had any use for "agitators".

Wearying at last of this useless search for work, Peter went on the drink for a little while. That was long after he and Isobel had given up their own house and sold the furniture and were living with the McGilverys again.

One night he came home very drunk and vomited on the floor. Isobel came in then – a frightened Isobel, angry and disgusted.

"God, I never thought to see *you* this way, Peter!" she cried. "Nae wonder your family'll no' look near you! Ah don't blame them. The way you're going on now, you're little better than yon brither of yours."

The quarrel that followed ended in Isobel's declaring that she was going out to look for a job for herself. Somehow that seemed to Peter the final admission of his own defeat. Thousands of men in Glasgow, and many real good fellows among them, had grown used to being idle while their wives were at the toil, but Peter knew he would never grow used to it.

"If you take a job," he declared passionately, "Ah'll do maself in, so Ah wull! Ah'll no' ha'e that, Isobel!"

The same argument was renewed again and again. One day Isobel went out without telling him and found a job at the first attempt. It wasn't a very good job – merely that of waitress in a restaurant to "a model" in Gallow-gate – one of those buildings which are ironically termed "Working Men's Hotels". None of the inmates in a "model" do any regular work, but Isobel toiled all day to serve them with "pennyworths of black and white", which means tea and sugar. She earned enough money to clothe herself and even to put a little away for the paying of the debts that had accumulated.

The total wages she was paid came to only a shilling or two more than Peter was drawing at the "buroo" for the two of them. If he had reported her employment, the relief money would have been immediately reduced in proportion. So he kept quiet – with the result that he appeared in the dock one day and was sentenced to three months' imprisonment for what the magistrate described as a "contemptible fraud".

Isobel who, of course, had been sacked when he was arrested, was waiting for him on his release, with a welcome which should have put new heart into any man. Peter tried to respond to her eagerness; tried to smile at hopeful words which seemed to him only pathetic and futile. But he could not be convincing. She was chilled and disappointed, frightened at some queer change in him which she could not understand.

The next morning Peter went round to the warehouse and asked to see the manager. Other workers, who had known him when "young Mr Stark" was looked upon as a coming man in the business, saw him waiting there, nodded awkwardly and passed on. At last he was

277

admitted to the manager's office, and there, forcing himself to humility, he told him everything, not even omitting the prison sentence just completed.

The manager heard him in silence. After their last interview it was only natural that he should feel a certain satisfaction in having this young man coming to him now and begging for a job. And yet he felt sorry for Peter, having once liked him much.

He resisted the temptation to tell him that he had only his own folly to thank for his present situation.

"All I can do for you, Peter," he said simply, stroking his own bald head with a pudgy hand in a gesture which was really nervous, though Peter thought it complacent, "is to offer you the porter's job which just happens to be vacant. It's only twenty-five shillings a week and you know what the work is. But, with your record, I'm afraid that's the best we can do."

"Ah'll take the job, Mr Booth," said Peter eagerly. "I don't mind what the work is. I want to be something that that wife of mine will like. An' I mean to stick in, too, and maybe through time I might—"

"Good for you, Peter," the manager interrupted. He was a kindly man at heart and he did not want this young fellow to build false hopes. In his own mind he was certain that the directors would never allow Peter Stark to hold any more important post.

"When will I start?" asked Peter anxiously.

"Start on Monday next at nine o'clock."

"Thank you, Mr Booth. I'm going to work well—"

"Yes, yes. I'm sure you are."

The manager nodded and rang a desk bell. The interview was at an end. Peter went home at a fast walk, breaking sometimes into a jog-trot. He was bursting to tell Isobel the news. And being still so young, it seemed to him that perhaps the worst of their troubles were over and that here at last was a new chance in life. He did not stop to think then, that there was never any rush for the porter's job at twenty-five shillings. The wage was too near the dole level and the work too hard. In fact, it was not easy to get a steady man to take the post and keep it.

Peter kept it. Isobel and her parents were overjoyed when they first heard that he had got taken on again by his old firm. When they learned what the new job was and what wages he would be getting, however, their enthusiasm was a good deal damped, but they were still pleased and hopeful. In the course of a month or two young Mr and Mrs Stark even managed to move into a house of their own once more. But this time it was a single end in one of the poorest side streets in the Anderston district.

"It's far better than no hoose of our own at all," said Isobel, when first she saw it.

Peter looked into her face and read the bitterness behind the eyes that tried to smile.

"Ay, it's no' sae bad at all!" he said defiantly, and then, suddenly tender. "Never mind, Isobel. Maybe – maybe we'll do better through time, and it's pretty near the West End—"

"Through time . . ." All the young people in the tenements of Glasgow cling to the vague, vain hope that things will be better for them "through time"; that there may be work to do and money enough to move into a better home, or, at the very least, a chance to bring the kids up respectably and give them a better start in life.

Even Lizzie, waiting with very mixed feelings for Razor King's release from jail, still believed that things would turn out better for Frank and for Johnnie and for herself "through time". But Lizzie passed through a strange crisis before the knowledge that she was to become a mother again somewhat reconciled her to difficult conditions.

On the evening of "the big battle" Frank Smith had told her the truth of how he came by his injuries. She sat

279

by his cot in the infirmary and tried to hide from her lover the shock she experienced at his ghastly appearance. Frank's face was partly hidden by bandages, but his lips were bloodless and one exposed cheek was a dirty yellow beneath the stubble. He was still feeling very sick from the kicks to the body.

In a steady, undemonstrative, cautious and limited way, Frank Smith loved Lizzie. It never occurred to him as necessary or even reasonable that he should abandon his own invalid wife or his home on her account. Nor had he any intention of endangering his own position at the bakery by letting it be known that Lizzie was his mistress. But he was very happy with her and his eyes lit up when she came to him and he held her hand tightly and whispered: "God, Liz! How glad I am to see you!"

"An' Ah'm gled to see *you*, Frank," she said, "but *no' in here*! Ah couldny believe it when they telt me you wis hurt, an' Ah canny understand it even now!"

Under his pillow Frank had the note which had been written to him by the Barlinnie "flyman" in Lizzie's name. He handed it to her and watched her puzzled, frightened expression as she read it.

"Don't fret, Liz," he said quietly. "Ah'm sorry to tell you what happened, but it's as well you should know. It wis that little letter caused all the trouble. Though I could see you hadn't written it yourself, Ah kept the appointment, thinking you might be needing me through trouble with Razor King. An' he wis there to meet me! We didny speak a single word. Ah walked away, an' he came up wi' me in a side street an' that's why Ah'm here the day."

"It wis Johnnie that laid you oot, then?" she gasped. "Ah never thought he could be so rotten!"

Frank chuckled.

"Ah can't help being gled to hear you say that," he said, "for though Ah'm a wee bit sorry for Razor King, Ah wid like fine to know he wis in the next cot to me

280

for a while. But we'll no' talk of him any more. Ah suppose you'll be lookin' for that job of yours back, pretty soon now, Liz? You're lookin' fine efter all you've gone through. And you know Ah'm almost sorry as you aboot the kid, don't you, Liz?"

She nodded, but could not speak.

"Listen," he went on. "Ah've managed to write a wee note to the bakery. You can take it round as soon as you like, an' everything'll be all right. An' sune Ah hope Ah'll be back there myself, and we'll be having a good time thegither again. Ah would burn that ither note at the first chance. There's no-one else should see it but us."

She stayed with him after that until one of the nurses told her that she must stay no longer. Then they kissed and parted, and Lizzie walked quietly out of the big spacious ward and sat for a while in a little teashop, and went back to the single end in Crown Street, nervous and ill at ease.

News of the great battle came to her before she had passed Gorbals Cross, and, at her own close-mouth, she was at once surrounded by eager neighbours who told her in a shrill and excited chorus of the mighty "clash" there had been and of the great part Razor King played in it.

"And Ah doot," said Mrs Skee, with immense satisfaction, ill-hidden by the whining sympathy of her tone, "whether Razor King'll ever properly get over the bashing he had the night! They tell me he was fair covered wi' blood when the ambulance picked him up. He'll maybe no' live tae go to court at aw."

"He'll live as long as *you* will, likely, Mrs Skee," said Lizzie furiously. "Ay, an' he'll be back up they sterrs one day ready tae lead the division again an' well able tae mind his own business – which is more than some folks can do. An' so good night tae ye, Mrs Skee."

Back in the single end at last, Lizzie was astonished at

281

her own rage; still more astonished that, hating Johnnie as she did for his brutality to Frank, she must still be eager to defend his name and reputation.

She crept into the empty bed and drew the blankets to her chin. She thought of Frank, and began to cry weakly. And then, in the darkness, she could see nothing but Johnnie, with his bullet head and his thick, closely cropped hair and the sudden boyish grin which would sometimes transform his whole expression. The tips of her fingers tingled as though she had just run them gently up the back of Johnnie's neck in a favourite caress of their first courting days.

"Ah *hate* him!" she whispered viciously, in the darkness. And she knew that it was not true; knew that somehow, in spite of everything, in spite of Frank and in spite of Minnie and the other "wee bits stuff", something held her to Johnnie still; some queer, distorted loyalty that was not physical at all.

"That Mrs Skee and the ithers!" thought Lizzie Stark. "They widny dare to stand in old Razor King's path if he came home again. Ay, an' whatever he's done, Ah'll no' let *them* forget that Ah'm Johnnie's wife. There's no' a man in the Gorbals can stand up to him. Whit was it Frankie said? . . . 'Ah'm a wee bit sorry for Razor King!' . . . *Him sorry!* . . . Me an' Razor King an' Frankie. Jesus! Ah wid laugh masel' if I wis some ither body!"

But Lizzie did not see her husband again until full twelve months later. He was removed from the infirmary in custody before she could bring herself to visiting him, for his injuries were not so serious as they appeared. In the jail he behaved throughout his sentence with sullen ferocity, refusing as a point of pride to conciliate any warder or to obey any order cheerfully. Constant breaches of the prison discipline and a stubborn recalcitrance that never softened led, as it had done before, to the forfeiture of all possible remission and to many periods of special punishment. Johnnie smiled evilly at every remonstrance. He knew that the officials were all wary of him. He saw that even his fellow-prisoners kept cautiously out of his way. And his vanity was comforted in the knowledge that he was different from the rest of them – tougher, stronger, more brutal – "a hopeless case". Ay, a razor king still, even in Barlinnie!

Early in that year, Lizzie moved out of the house in Crown Street into another single-end in Hallside Street. There was little obvious advantage in this change, for the one "kitchen" was much like the other and the "new" tenement just as definitely a "low-class" slum. But at least the neighbours were new and Lizzie could not tolerate the slight change of atmosphere on the old stair. Not that any of the old neighbours tried to offend her. They would not have done that with Johnnie due to come home again about Christmas or the New Year. No; she felt that they were almost *too* friendly, and the faint trace of patronage in their manner infuriated her. "They think it's Johnnie an' me finished!" she raged, "but, by God! he'll show them when he comes oot!"

Frank, who laughed at her anger on this score, encouraged her to move nevertheless. He said that she would be better off up a new stair, but actually he wanted her to be free from the old associations. And he was devoutly thankful when she came to him at last, from the new address, and told him, somewhat timidly, that a new youngster was on the way.

"Lizzie," he said simply. "Ah'm just as pleased as if we wis married. You needny bother aboot anything. Ah'll look efter you. An' this yin'll be safe an' happy in its cot before ever Razor King comes back again. He'll be all right wi' a wean, Ah'm thinking. Change your hoose, Liz, an' you'll be the better for it. An' get yourself in some nice girl – any easy wee lass you can find – tae help you through. I'll stand by ye whatever happens."

Poor Frank; he was ready enough to stand by Lizzie at that or any other time, but he had never recovered his

283

health after his bashing. He was always liable to sudden fits of unaccountable sickness and to violent pains that twisted his somewhat shrunken body. Lizzie knew that he was thinner and that his face had never regained its normal colour, but she did not suspect, fortunately for her, that her lover was suffering from some internal malady from which he would never be free. In those days she looked upon Frank almost as her husband. Most of her spare time she spent in his company. His younger daughter was now so busy courting that she was scarcely ever at home, and a queer uncertain friendship had arisen between Lizzie and the invalid Mrs Smith herself. Of course, Mrs Smith was not exactly pleased that Frank had taken a mistress, but she was very glad that he had found so nice and reasonable a woman as his special friend. In all humility she realized that she couldn't give her husband proper satisfaction, and she was really rather grateful to Lizzie because she was always so considerate and friendly and never failed to treat her – the real Mrs Smith – with kindness and respect. It was for that reason that she stilled the pang of envy in her heart when she learned that Lizzie was going to have another baby by her man.

All this time, Lizzie continued to work at the bakery, earning more money than she actually spent, not because of Frank's influence, but because she was in fact, a superlatively good mixer of beatings, and a first-class table-hand. Lizzie lived very simply in her new home. When she wasn't with Frank she drank a good deal of "red wine", and sometimes went to bed rather fuddled. But she was always at work in the bakery dead on time, and often enough she had to chivvy Mary Allen, her lodger help, out of bed in the morning so that she would be punctual for her job in the shoe factory.

Lizzie thought a good deal of Mary Allen. She was only a small lass of about twenty, but she was earning nearly twenty-five shillings a week at her work in

Maxwell Street, and she was extraordinarily deft and quick in the single end. Lizzie was quite ready to do her own share of the work, but Mary Allen generally got ahead of her. For one thing, she used to get home somewhat earlier. And for another she seemed really anxious that her hostess should not be too burdened with household cares. She knew Lizzie was "expecting", and she treated her with special consideration on that account.

"She's a good lass, yon Mary Allen," said Lizzie to Frank one evening. "Ah can leave aw the work o' the hoose in her hands an' be certain she'll no' let me doon. It's true she's moving a bit wi' the gangs, an' there's a young lad, named John Gray, who comes round tae see her a lot these days, but Mary's a safe friend to have in the kitchen for aw that. Ah'm a little worried what will happen when Razor King comes oot of jail, but oor wee kid'll be here before then, Frankie, an' Mary'll just have to look efter herself, Ah'm thinking."

"Onywey," said Frank cautiously, "Razor King willny be oot much before Christmas or New Year an' he may be changed by then. Meantime you've not to worry, an' Ah'm gled this Mary Allen is there to look efter ye."

All through that year life in the Gorbals was relatively featureless. Now and again a steady working-man lost his job when some fresh yard closed down or some fresh factory went out of business. But the street bookmaker still did a good trade at the street corner, and the pubs were often busy. Once in a while there was a little "raid" and the young men met at the "Green Gym" and exercised their muscles. There was no big "rammy" in the city, for want of leaders, and, though the younger set was now inclined to follow John Gray and give deference to his opinions, nobody questioned the ultimate return of Razor King and nobody – as yet – was at all inclined to challenge his supremacy.

The ordinary life of Glasgow flowed on just as usual.

The ministers and the priests and the social reformers and the politicians were all talking rather vehemently about housing reform and "the abolition of the slums". And a few Council houses were going up, and some of them were already being transformed, slowly but relentlessly, into fresh slums. There were even tenants in some of the grand new homes who complained that they were verminous before they were occupied, and the story was spread abroad that certain contractors had made great profits by building anew with ancient and condemned material.

Be that as it may, the removal of some few hundred families made no visible difference in the tenements. Idle men still propped up the street corners and the young hooligans still gathered together in restless knots. And the Factor came and went up the foul stairs collecting his rents. The children swarmed in the broad streets between the grey cliffs of the teeming tenements, and a priest, lashing himself to frenzy outside a drinking-den, called the curse of heaven down upon the unknown landlords and the wrath of God upon their ragged, drunken, lazy and immoral tenants. They stood and laughed at him. A young woman, who held a blanket loosely about her dirty nakedness, tipped a bottle of "red biddy" to her mouth to drink the priest's health, and staggered back to the brothel from which she had emerged. There her lover of that evening, who was a Catholic and even drunker than she was, beat her most brutally for mocking the church. And all the neighbourhood chuckled over the quaintly unimportant episode.

At the beginning of August, Frank Smith was taken suddenly ill and died in hospital a few days later from ulceration of the stomach. His married daughter happened to be home at the time, and Lizzie, though she knew he must be sick, preferred not to visit him just then. Towards the end he became unconscious, and, though he spoke of Lizzie in his ramblings, nobody sent for her.

The news of his death took her utterly by surprise. It was conveyed to her by the married daughter, who spoke without sympathy and declared in so many words that the family wanted to see her no more.

She looked Lizzie up and down with a hard stare.

"It'll be a shock tae you, nae doot," she said, "but *we're* no' responsible for your condition, though Ah'm no' so sure yon husband o' yours was no' responsible for the bashing that dad got that has helped to kill him now."

It was a shot in the dark, but it went home. Lizzie turned away, white-faced, to hide her grief and despair.

Her child, a girl, was born in the following October and wailed most lustily. Mary Allen took the baby and clothed it in warm flannel, and sat before the kitchen stove smiling gently down upon it. And while Lizzie lay, scarcely conscious, in the cavity bed, John Gray came up the stairs and tiptoed into the room and admired the child in whispers as he stood with his hand about Mary's shoulders.

And the year drew slowly to a close in a grey and forbidding autumn that presaged bleak weather for the winter release of the Gorbals Razor King.

CHAPTER XX

CHECKMATE

Johnnie walked out of prison on a raw December morning and hurried to the new home he had not seen, and to his wife, who had become the mother of another man's child. Lizzie had told him about these things in short and matter-of-fact letters. He was glad her baby had lived this time and thought she would be happier with the child to look after. And he really wanted to see Lizzie again because she seemed somehow to be a necessary part of his existence.

When she opened the door to his knock he took her in his arms and hugged her with much the same delight that a schoolboy might hug his elder sister when returning home for the holidays. There was no passion left between these two.

"By Christ, Liz, I'm *hellova* gled to be back wi' you again," said he. "I wis sorry to hear old Frank Smith had snuffed it. Where's the kid, Liz? Let's have a look at it. Ah mean to do something worth while now Ah'm oot again. Let me just get hold of a couple o' good razors an' *Ah'll make such a butcher's shop as naebody'll ever in creation forget!*"

Lizzie looked into the eyes that glittered in his horribly scarred face and she knew then that Johnnie was not quite sane. She didn't exactly put it in that way even in her own thoughts. She would have said, if she had tried to explain her feelings at all, that Razor King was still "half-daft from the jail".

It was barely ten o'clock in the morning when Johnnie came home and the baby was in the bed beside Mary

Allen. He went over to look at the child and laughed. Then he looked for the first time at Mary, who flushed and drew the red bed covering closer about her.

"Are you hungry?" murmured Lizzie, going to the stove. "We've no' had anything to eat yet, have we, Merry?"

"No, that's right," the girl replied.

Johnnie had been in jail twelve months and the sight of Mary's bare arm outside the blankets excited him.

"You're a fine-looking wee bit stuff," he muttered thickly. "Ah'm gaun tae have some fun wi' you, amn't Ah?"

He laid hold of the coverlet as though to drag it away, and the girl screamed.

"Oh! Mind the wean, for Jesus' sake!" cried Lizzie, making a rush for the child.

She snatched the baby from Mary Allen's arms, disarranging the coverlet as she did so. Johnnie did not attempt to interfere. He waited to see the baby safe with Lizzie, and then, just as Mary Allen was trying to scramble out of bed, he caught her by one bare shoulder and thrust her back again.

"Let go of me!" she shouted. "Ah'm no' dressed an' Ah want tae—"

"Ah like you better wi' naething on," he said hotly. "Ah know it's a hellova cauld day, but Ah'll soon warm the two of us."

He made a snatch at the bedclothes and tore them right away. Mary Allen had gone to bed in a night-gown, and again, screaming loudly this time, she tried to scramble to her feet. Johnnie ripped the gown from her shoulders and then struck her across the mouth. There was the sound of running feet on the stairs and then a knocking at the front door.

"Haud your row, *you*!' said Johnnie furiously to the terrified girl. "And you, Liz, tell they silly bastards

289

outside that Razor King's home again. And keep the inside door shut an' you'll see nothing at all in here."

Lizzie was too terrified to do anything but obey orders. She ran into the lobby and drew the door to behind her, crying to the neighbours on the landing that Johnnie was home again and there was nothing but a bit of a row going on. They dispersed, reluctantly, but the screams had stopped.

In the kitchen itself, Mary Allen had ceased to struggle in Johnnie's arms.

"Chuck fighting," he snarled, "or, by God, Ah'll brand you! Those who live in my hoose'll dae what Ah wish."

She gulped and sobbed and her face was ugly with blood running from a cut lip. Lizzie waited in the lobby outside for nearly ten minutes. When she came back into the kitchen Johnnie and Mary were in bed together with the red cover over them both.

It was not until later in the morning that Mary Allen, dry-eyed and furious now, dressed and left the single end. She did not complain to any neighbours on the stair, but she ran like the wind to find her own lover, John Gray. He was standing at the corner of Thistle Street and Rutherglen Road, and she gasped out the story of what had happened.

His face changed as he listened to her. There was nothing in the least pathetic about Mary Allen in that moment. It was rage that choked her, not shame.

"Can you no' *say* something?" she shrieked. "Are you *crappy* or what, John Gray? Are you no' man enough to go an' take on that dirty bastard, Razor King, efter what he's done tae *me*?"

He glowered at her as though in some way she were to blame for forcing him to this ordeal.

"You go back," he said slowly, "an' tell Lizzie or somebody to tell Razor King that Ah'll have a fair fight wi' him over on the Green on Sunday without ony weapons at aw."

Mary Allen sobbed with sheer relief and threw her arms round his neck.

Sullenly he freed himself.

"Ah'll fight," he said, "but Ah'm finished wi' you aw the same, Mary, efter what you've just telt me. You can easily get some other fellow to marry you, an' Ah hope you'll be hellova happy an' aw that."

She stepped back from him and faced him with blazing eyes.

"We'll see aboot that!" she shouted.

"Ah'll beat Razor King for you," he repeated stubbornly, "but that'll be me well oot o' a good thing. Ah'm finished wi' you, Mary Allen."

He turned and walked deliberately away. Tears welled into Mary's eyes and she stood where he had left her. But he never went back to her.

And Mary never went back to the "single end". She gave Lizzie the challenge as her lover had bidden her, and then found a new lodging. Before the day was out the news was all over Gorbals. Razor King accepted the fight with sheer delight. He was training on the Green gymnasium that same evening, and, physically, he was in hard condition after his prison sentence. There were only two days to wait and by a desperate effort of will he contrived to keep sober until the Sunday.

More than three hundred men and women turned out to see the fight. Some of them believed, and many of them hoped, that young John Gray would defeat the old Razor King. If he had done so, almost the entire crowd would have been eager to acclaim the victor. For Gray was already a coming champion in the Gorbals division. He had been the leader in two successful public-house raids and in several minor "rammies", and there were lads who had been speaking of him openly as the new Razor King.

Lizzie herself could not keep away from that fight. She felt a little sorry for Mary Allen and a little indignant with Johnnie, not for what he had done to the girl, but for his quite brutal contempt of herself on the morning of his release. Apart from that, she didn't exactly blame her husband. Mary had come to help in the house knowing perfectly well what Razor King would expect from her. She had been prepared to be his mistress in the first place. Lizzie knew that, and knew that it was only Mary's affair with John Gray which had made her become "so particular all of a sudden".

But, dominant above all other considerations in Lizzie's mind, was the eagerness for Razor King to reassert himself in the eyes of the neighbours, and, indeed, of all Gorbals. Since Frank Smith had died, Lizzie knew that she had fallen out of esteem. People were actually rather sorry for her. It made her blood boil to be looked down on by "the scum" that hadn't dared to argue when Johnnie was home. *They* thought he was finished – Razor King and his wife, too.

The fighters stripped to the waist, and Lizzie's anger grew when she saw how the young men hung back when Razor King asked for someone to look after his clothes. One of them did come forward in the end, but there were half a dozen eager to help John Gray.

In an impressive silence the fight began. Lizzie saw at once that Johnnie was heavier than his opponent. His muscles were magnificent as ever. As he stood with his back to her, so that his scarred grim face was hidden, he seemed scarcely changed; only a little more solid and compact than on the day of his first fight. His bullet head was bent low and he waited for Gray's attack.

The younger man leaped in with great fury, but Johnnie met him with a rushing, two-fisted, counter-attack that drove Gray back and instantly set the crowd yelling. The fighters flailed blows at each other with hatred but without science. It seemed useless to hit Johnnie. He took punishment and didn't even seem to notice it. But Gray staggered under a fearful blow to the body, and, before he could recover, Johnnie hit him between the eyes, grunting himself with the sledge-hammer force of that punch.

"Razor King!" yelled the crowd. "Good old RAZOR KING!"

They danced and shrieked with excitement. Gray was down and Johnnie bending above him.

"Get up, damn you!" he snarled.

Gray rose to one knee, and Johnnie, nothing more now than a savage, murderous ruffian, kicked him in the forehead, and then used his heavy boots upon the fallen body while the onlookers became almost delirious. The King had come into his own again and the mob roared its applause.

From the front of the ring Mary Allen threw the empty beer bottle she had hidden under her shawl. It struck Razor King on the back of the head with a thud that was heard by many in spite of the tumult. Perhaps it saved Gray's life. Johnnie raised both hands to his head and went staggering across the ring. Lizzie, uttering an un-earthly scream, rushed at Mary Allen, sank clawed fingers into her hair, hit with her free hand, and kicked like a wild cat. They had to tear Mary away from her in the end, and they made a path to allow the weeping and dishevelled girl to escape. Many young men hurried to help Razor King on with his clothes, and a clamorous bodyguard escorted him and Lizzie to the nearest public house, where soon the drinks were flowing more freely than they had done for many a day.

The King had come into his own again. The whole Gorbals "division" was his to a man. They had forgotten about Gray. When he came out of the infirmary a month later he dared not face the contempt of his former friends. He left the district and did not come back. Mary Allen also left the Gorbals, but she left it alone. Gray was "*finished*". Even if she had been able to find him, he would not have been worth a "sherricking".

But Johnnie had a new and docile little mistress in the "single end" before the week was out.

By Christmas of that year – 1928 – the large gangster elements of Gorbals had settled down, as it were, to the old routine. No big adventure was attempted without the approval of the Razor King. Under Johnnie's direction two public houses were successfully raided. The tills had little money, but there was a large stock of whisky in the tenements for the New Year's celebrations. No big battles were then in contemplation, and the "division" saw the Old Year out with a series of drunken parties that had never a single casualty to remember them by.

Peter Stark and his wife, Isobel, passed that New Year's Eve in the McGilverys' home none too joyously. Peter was still holding down his porter's job, but he and his wife were finding life much harder owing to the unexpected and quite unwanted arrival of a son. They reproached each other for that accident. Isobel, unlike her sister-in-law, had no wish for children at all unless she could bring them up in the world with "a decent chance". She and Peter had often discussed this subject, and agreed that they would be "as well to wait". Their son, a healthy youngster, was born in the first week of December, and Isobel's mother, hastily summoned, ushered the boy into the world before even the midwife arrived. Isobel herself never recovered properly from that birth. She loved her baby in spite of everything, and wanted to call him "Thomas", after her father's brother, who had held a good position in a Greenock shipyard and was now retired, a childless widower.

Peter, very seldom obstinate in those days, proved unyielding in the matter of the baby's name. "Ah don't care what you say," he declared stubbornly. "We'll christen the boy 'John'. He's a 'Stark', is he no'? Right; then he shall be 'John Stark', like my father was before me and *his* father before that."

"Ay!" said old Mrs McGilvery bitterly, "an' like yon

brither o' yours – him they call Razor King! Fresh oot of jail, they tell me, an' a worse hooligan than before!"

Peter swore under his breath, and Isobel, lying in the bed with the baby in her arms, began to weep fretfully.

"Ah'm no' caring about Johnnie," said Peter vehemently, "an' Ah haveny seen him since Mither wis buried; but my son shall be named 'John', or there'll be hell to pey. An' so Ah'm telling ye."

The child was christened John, and it seemed to thrive in the dirty, airless, verminous "single end" where its father and mother now lived, in Anderston – "near the West End!"

Razor king himself did not even know he had a nephew. He had long since given up even thinking about Peter or his sisters. He was back on the "parish" again and money was very short in his own household. Polly Moran, the seventeen-year-old, black-eyed, black-haired, wild lass who was now his lodger and his mistress too, was in steady work in a factory, and she paid seven and sixpence a week towards the household expenses and often "treated" Johnnie to the pictures or to a fish supper and a drink into the bargain. Polly was really in love with Johnnie at that time. His brutality thrilled her: his terrible reputation gained her respect among her own friends. And she had no other "boy" of her own. She got on well enough with Lizzie, who seemed always fretfully busy with her baby.

It certainly did not occur either to Lizzie or to Polly that Razor King would ever take a job again. During the spring of that year he spent endless hours walking round Glasgow. In the evenings when the pubs were open there was always company to be found in the bars, and, nearly always, some young fellow, either in work or temporarily in funds, ready to buy a gill of red wine and a bottle of beer for him. But, in the long afternoons, Johnnie was desperately lonely. Once, sauntering aimlessly towards Reilly's office, he met the coal merchant, his former employer, and bade him good day, remarking in a surly voice that he "widny mind going out wi' the kerrt again".

Reilly, more prosperous and "bourgeois" than before, stared into Johnnie's face and broke into a nervous laugh.

"You're kidding, Razor King!" he said defensively, "here's the winter finished an' sune Ah'll be taking men off, let alone giving new jobs. Besides the coal trade's gaun aw tae hell, onywey . . . But ye wereny serious, of course? *You'll* no' want to gae to the toil again, Ah'm thinking."

"You're dead right," said Johnnie savagely. "Ah wis only kidding."

But he hadn't been kidding. He walked gloomily across the river with his battered old hat pulled down over his face. Johnnie was always nervous of strangers seeing him in those days. He never forgot his scars, and rage and fear and hatred filled his heart if ever he caught a glance that quailed at the sight of his face.

He had fallen by this time into the prison habit of muttering to himself as he walked abroad. Slowly he slouched up the great thoroughfare of Sauchiehall Street, gazing into the rich shop windows, watching the cars that drew up outside the hotel entrances, and observing with fascinated wonder and envy the well-dressed men and women who hurried or sauntered by.

"Ah might as well no' know my way aboot at aw," he muttered aloud. "Whit can Ah do wi' knowing the streets o' Glasgow? Damn aw! This is no' Glasgow onywey! It's full o' bliddy Englishmen and high-class tarts an' Jews stinking of money. There's none in this part can tell the difference between me an' any common hooligan. By God! whit am Ah doing out o' Gorbals?"

It was then nearly five o'clock and he wanted some tea and some food, but he felt in his pockets and there was only twopence there. Sullenly and dejectedly he walked home again. Polly started and finished her work early. She was already at home and the kettle was on the fire. He found her sitting in the solitary arm-chair reading a twopenny weekly with Lizzie's baby in her lap. She smiled at him and got up to make tea.

Johnnie threw his cap on the dresser and obediently took the child in his arms while Polly busied herself with the kettle.

"Where's Liz?" he asked dully.

"Do you no' mind? She's away the day looking for anither job."

"Ah doot she'll no' find one," Johnnie grunted; "not now Frank Smith is dead. Still – some folk are lucky . . . D'you know, Polly, Ah wis away for a walk aboot the city, an' Ah wish to God anither fight or something wid start, because Ah could see when Ah was walking that you've got to make a stir or something before people'll look at you. Did you no' notice that, Polly?"

"Ah've noticed a hellova lot of things lately," she agreed, "and that's one o' them. We're getting stale these days, are we no'?"

The little girl baby in Johnnie's arms screwed up its small face and sneezed. He loked down at it with a smile and drew his sleeve gently across its nose.

"Ah mean tae get up a *big* rammy one o' these days, Polly," he continued, "a battle that will give all Glasgow something tae talk aboot and to remember me by . . . This is the good weather for a rammy like that, and if we *do* get the jail, well, what the hell of it? It just means we spend the winter on holiday, eh, Polly?"

She laughed, set tea and bread and butter on the table before him, and took the baby from him again.

"Ah'm wi' you, Razor King," said she. "Anything for a change!"

"There wis a time once," said Johnnie, drawing up a chair, "when Ah had an idea we should try to *be* something, Lizzie an' me. Efter the first year in Barlinnie, Ah wis thinking that more than ever. There wis some flymen Ah met in the old Gallowgate, but they thought

Ah wisny good enough to work wi' them. And Ah wis not! Ah can fight, Polly, but it seems Ah can do damn aw else. Now Ah've just chucked up trying to *be* something an' Ah'm going tae *do* something instead."

"Well," smiled the girl comfortingly, "you can be something by doing it, can you no', Razor King?"

"Ay," he agreed doubtfully, "in a way you can . . . Ah, Liz, you're back at last then? Did ye hae any luck?"

Lizzie was wearing a hat again with a coat and skirt. She had never looked so well-dressed nor so animated and pretty since the time of Frank Smith's death. Now she hurried to her baby before answering any questions. Then, satisfied that the child was well and happy, she smiled at the two others and told them pridefully that she had found a job at thirty shillings a week in another bakery where she had never worked before.

"That's fine for you, Liz," said Razor King simply, "an' Ah'm gled you'll have the toil to go to if onything should happen tae me. Ah wis just telling Polly here that Ah'm fed up. Ah mean tae start a big rammy again pretty sune, and noo you'll be aw right if Ah should get the jail again."

Lizzie had a few shillings hidden away in an old shoe beneath the dresser, and presently she sent Polly out to buy two bottles of red wine with which to celebrate her new job. Johnnie stopped at home that evening to share the drink with the two women. By two o'clock in the morning Lizzie joined her baby in the shake-down by the window, and Johnnie and Polly fell fast asleep together in the cavity bed.

That fearful sense of being "fed up" with life – that frustration of the spirit which comes at times to every healthy unemployed man – held Johnnie in its thrall during the weeks that followed, and not all Polly's love-making nor the extra money that Lizzie now brought home could coax him back to a better humour.

It added to his exasperation because there seemed to be absolutely "nothing doing" in the gangs. There seemed to be no feuds in progress, no injuries to avenge. Each mob kept to its own territory, and in Gorbals itself the Razor King could find no taunts which would provoke a single one of his followers into rebellion.

News reached him at this period that Bobbie Hurley and Lily McKay had broken their partnership and left the "Gaydom". At first he would not believe it, but at once there were a dozen voices to confirm the rumour.

"You'll mind Arthur Ross, him that was the bookie here?" began Kenneth Blain, one of Johnnie's chief lieutenants in those days, and a young man of some consequence because he held a job as a mechanic in a motor garage. "Well, everybody knows Ross has got on in the world wi' his offices in the city and doing a great business by post wi' London. He's the one that's caused it aw."

"Whit do ye mean?" growled Razor King. "Whit the hell wid Ross be doing to make the champions leave the 'Gaydom'?"

"Ross wisny doing anything. It wisny like that at aw. But he's been dead keen on the dancing this past two-three years an' it seems he wis always booking Lily oot an' getting her tae teach him the tango – ay, an' plenty ither steps, nae doot! The champions wis living in a big hoose wi' a bath an' making a lot of money. Lily had a baby aboot a year ago last Fair Week, but she wis well over that an' back at the dancing again wi' a good lass to look efter the kid an' help in the hoose. Do you mind, Razor King, she wis always telling Bobbie Hurley to be 'manly'? He must ha'e took her by surprise wi' that kid unless it wis some ither body wis the father."

There was a loud laugh at this comment, and Blain, much gratified, paused to finish his drink before resuming his narrative.

"Onywey," he went on, "long efter Ross came along the champions wis still going strong at the 'Gaydom', and, for that matter, there's nae better pair i' aw Glasgow the day – or widny be if Lily had no' left Bobbie and chucked the dancing awthegither."

"Lily McKay could no more chuck the birlin'," sneered Razor King, "than Ah could give up ma weapons. Ah mind her when she wis a wee kid dancin' wi' Bobbie Hurley i' the clabber jiggings. She thought o' nothing else."

"That's right, Razor King," agreed Blain pacifically. "Ah'm no' saying she willny sune be dancing again, but she's no' dancing noo, for she has anither breadsnapper on the way, by aw accounts. An' that's whit finished Bobbie wi' Lily, an' finished the pair o' them with the 'Gaydom'. He wis making a lot o' dough himself through a Mrs Gorman, a widow woman whose husband left her very well off. An' the two o' them wis *always* booked out, not tae speak of being away for week-ends and days at a time. At last the management wouldny stand it ony longer an' they tell me there was clients stopping away from the 'Gaydom' and aw because o' the scandal. Ay, ye may laugh, but there's plenty respectable people go there an' they didny like the wey things wis going on, the champions being married an' aw that."

"Whit happened then?" asked Razor King, interested in spite of himself.

"Well, Bobbie was aw for breakin' the two friendships wi' Ross and this Mrs Gorman, but Lily told him to be manly, for Christ's sake, an' tae mind his own business. And, they say – but Ah widny be sure it's true – that he forgot himself for once and hit yon Arthur Ross a hellova punch i' the jaw. That wis in the ballroom tae, an' Ross gave him a hiding, an' Bobbie wis left there crying like a wean . . . Lily went away efter that tae live in a wee hoose that Ross took for her, and she took the baby away wi' her an aw. As for Bobbie, he's found anither girl who's not nearly sae good as Lily, and they'll be dancing thegither likely in some other hall through time."

Johnnie drank the fresh drink that somebody had set on the counter before him.

"Bobbie Hurley an' me," he said defiantly, "wis at school thegither. An' whatever else he is or isn't, he's a grand dancer. He'll be better off wi'oot yon daft missis o' his, an' maybe she'll no' find it sae easy to get anither job for hersel' when Ross gives her the go-by."

Nobody seemed inclined to challenge this opinion, and a little later Johnnie left the bar. Talk of the Hurleys and of dancing had given him a fresh idea. It happened that he had a few shillings in his pocket, and he walked at once to a big dance hall in the East End. The booking-clerk scarcely looked up as he paid his admission money, and, in the shaded lighting of the hall itself, his scars were not noticeable.

The place was crowded. There might have been some four hundred couples there, or even more. Johnnie waited until one dance had ended and, deliberately choosing a blonde girl in a group of young men and women, strode across to her and asked for the next dance. Not too willingly she took his arm. The band had only just restarted and there was no excuse for giving him the deliberate affront of a refusal. But two young men in that group looked after them resentfully and followed them with their eyes as they took the floor.

Johnnie made no effort to please his partner. The hair on his bullet head had been sleeked with water and there was something aggressive and defiant in the very cut of his square shoulders.

"Good crowd here the night," said the girl nervously.

"It's aw the bliddy same tae me," said Razor King loudly, "who's here and who's no' here. As long as there's no man here can beat me, what the hell should Ah care?"

"Maybe you fancy yourself!" she sniggered.

Johnnie stood suddenly still and pushed the girl away from him contemptuously.

301

"Ah don't fancy *you*," he said violently, "an Ah wid like tae see if there's onybody got anything tae say aboot that."

The girl went off into an hysterical and frightened laugh, and the two young men whom she had left standing by one of the pillars came running towards her. Round about Johnnie the floor cleared as though by magic. His razors were out in an instant and his lips parted in a devilish grin of battle.

Before anybody could stop him he had slashed the blonde girl across the lips, and his other weapon laid open the cheek of the nearest of her champions. The second young fellow hesitated for a fatal second and was "branded" in his turn. Then a roaring tide of angry men swept down upon Johnnie, and, while the band still played, a wild mêlée developed in that corner of the hall.

It chanced that three or four of Razor King's own "division" were present that night and they fought by his side long after he had lost his razors, hustling him to the door. The little knot of furious men broke through the doorway into the outer lobby. For an instant Razor King shook himself free of friend and foe alike.

"Ah'll have an *army* wi' me when Ah come back here again!" he shouted. "You people don't know what a good razoring is! But Ah'll come back two-thousand-handed, so Ah wull – and then you'll learn."

He ran into the street and was lost in the darkness. The grin never left his lips as he walked home.

"By God!" he muttered to himself. "If this doesny start a good battle, Ah don't know what will."

Now, though this utterly unprovoked assault took place in the East End, there must have been many present in the dance hall who could have sworn to Johnnie Stark as the aggressor. The fact remains, however, that the police were once again powerless to obtain any evidence whatever.

The only sequel to this affray was the tremendous

302

street battle which raged a week later through all the streets near Dennistoun and spread to cover the entire East End of Glasgow. Razor King was among the scores of injured in that battle. He kept his feet for a full hour of desperate fighting, but he was felled at last by a bottle blow from behind.

And two weeks later, still heavily bandaged, he was sentenced for the third time to a year's imprisonment.

There were a dozen other men and two girls sent to prison that day, but none with a record so bad as Johnnie's. His scars and bandages bore out the police evidence of his persistent ruffianism.

Lizzie and Polly were both in court to see Johnnie sentenced, and when they were sitting at the fireside in the "single end" that evening they talked for a long while about the whole proceedings, and both were emphatic that there must be something seriously wrong with the mentality and outlook of the "heid yins", among whom they included the magistrature, the police and the City Council.

"If the last sentence didny dae any good to old Razor King," said Polly, sitting with Lizzie's child on her knees, "how the hell with *this* yin dae him any? Specially seeing he's a damn sight worse now than he was the last time."

Lizzie stared into the fire, and there was a long pause before she replied.

"Polly, you're no' kidding yourself that they're trying to dae anybody any *good*, are ye? If there wis no jail, God knows where or when the fighting wid stop . . . But Ah'm afraid Razor King'll no' be up to hellova much when he comes oot this time. He's lucky, in a way, to be whole wi' aw the bashing and abuse he's had. An' aw for damn aw when you think of it, Polly!"

"Ay, that's right enough," the girl laughed. "Barring a pound or two efter a raid now and again, and far more whisky than ever did him any good, he's got little enough to show for being Razor King o' Gorbals."

"Nought but his scars. An' his reputation, in a way, but Ah'm thinking he'll be forgotten by the time he comes oot."

"Ah'll no' forget him, though!" said Polly hotly.

Lizzie shrugged her shoulders with a faint smile of disbelief.

"There's a lot o' them has forgotten him awready," said she.

"Sure. Because they're aw jealous of him. There's half a dozen fellows just dying to be the next Razor King i' the Gorbals. You know that, Lizzie, eh? Well – good luck to them; that's whit Ah say. They have to pey for aw they get sune or late."

"Too bliddy true, they do!" said Lizzie bitterly. "Johnnie has come through a hellova lot, when you think of it. He was no' a well-educated fellah or anything like that, but, aw the same, the crowd of mugs that have ministers and priests and aw that looking efter them, wid have had *naebody* looking efter them at aw if it wisny for the likes o' Razor King. Whit does it matter to the heid yins what happens in Gorbals or Bridgeton or Garngad or Anderston, or in any ither bliddy slum in Glasgow for that matter, so long as we keep quiet? Do they care hoo we live or whit we dae or whit kind of derrty hoose we have? No bliddy fears! They need wakin' up once in a while, and it's fellows like Razor King that makes them remember we're alive."

And that was a very long speech for Lizzie. She sighed and then laughed.

"There's the half of a bottle o' 'red biddy' still in the press," she said. "We'll drink it tae Razor King."

However much mistaken she may have been in her philosophy, it is simply a matter of Glasgow history that the big movement to establish working men's clubs in all the slum districts of the city was a sequel to the great gang battles which may be said to have reached their peak in 1929. Ministers and priests now became loud in their denunciation of what they termed "the razor-slashing menace". From the pulpits and the press the fiat went forth that something must be done, not so much to suppress the gangs, as to give the hooligan youth of the city a different outlet for its excitement and its energy.

By the time of the Glasgow Fair of that year something was done. The first of the clubs and recreation halls which now play an important part in tenement life were opened. Young people flocked to them, interested but derisive. They at least provided better and cheaper meeting-places than the pubs and the street corners. The workless who were not gangsters found them an enormous boon. Some of the worst gangs were broken up or fell into disorganization. Bigger, but less desperate, gangs not known by that name, began to form at the various centres. The reformers and the preachers and the social workers were jubilant. For a while, at all events, it seemed that the tide of violence had been stemmed. Razors and broken bottles were a little out of fashion, and the "rammies" were neither so numerous nor so dangerous as they had been.

But of all this, Johnnie Stark, sullenly serving his time in Barlinnie, was scarcely aware. His sleep was troubled in those days and he suffered from terrible headaches. He muttered to himself at work and exercise and in the solitude of his cell. The prison officers watched him warily, but almost with a touch of pity. Sometimes he had a letter from his wife, and once from Polly. Polly did not write again, for, a month after he was jailed, she found another young man, and when he offered to marry her, she thought it better to give Johnnie the go-by entirely. She left Lizzie with some regret, but the elder woman took her departure philosophically and immediately replaced her with another lodger.

Lizzie was herself beginning an affair by then with a fellow-worker in the new bakery, Harry Hay, a foreman like Frank had been, and, like him, a married man with a family. She was not in love with Harry as she had been with Frank, but he was good to her and she was a lonely woman, still young. He visited her often in her own home and took her out in the evenings whenever he could. But he was more tied to his own family than Frank had been, and didn't want them to hear about Lizzie at all. She found him open-handed with his money, and on the days when he could not visit her she became more and more inclined to take a few drinks in the neighbouring public houses and, often, to take half a bottle of whisky or a bottle of red wine home with her. Sadie Bell, the new girl who had taken Polly's place, was glad enough to drink with her on these occasions and to listen to her confidences, which were apt to become tearful as the hour grew late and the bottle emptied.

Secretly Sadie rather despised Lizzie, but she was far too glad to share the single end with her and the child ever to betray this feeling. Sadie's own family, nine of them all told, lived in a sunless room-and-kitchen in the "back lands" of a tenement within a tenement. She had "a boy" of her own with whom she had long been on intimate terms, but he was out of work like the rest of them and marriage seemed a distant prospect. The girl was barely twenty, small and sallow and under-nourished, but her figure was trim and she had fine eyes and a mass of dark hair. She had never spoken to Razor King and scarcely knew him by sight, but his reputation was glamorous, and Sadie looked forward to his release, believing that an adventure with him would probably rather enhance her value in her own boy's eyes.

Lizzie, who would have nothing to do with the neighbours on her own stair, had to unburden herself to somebody, and Sadie was a patient listener. Sometimes, when the older woman was out with Harry Hay, the girl had her own lover up to visit her, and they laughed together as she mimicked Lizzie's tedious stories over the red wine.

"Ah canny see," said the girl spitefully, "what Razor King could ever have seen in Lizzie. Maybe she's no' ill-looking, but the way she's drinking these days, she'll no' keep her looks. An' she hasny telt Razor King aboot yon Harry Hay. Likely he'll find there's anither bread-snapper on the road when he comes oot o' the jail."

"Likely he winny care," retorted the boy. "The love-making has been finished between old Razor King and Lizzie for a hellova long while, from what you tell me."

"Ay, that's right," Sadie agreed, "but you widny think so tae hear the wey she's forever talkin' o' him and his great 'reputation'. They must think a lot of each ither still, aw the same."

Perhaps they did. When Johnnie came out of prison for the last time on a June morning in 1930, he found Sadie Bell at home with the child, and, scarcely looking at either of them, he asked when Lizzie would be home.

Sadie told him that she was expecting her back in the evening, but not before. She spoke in an unusually timid voice for, now that she actually saw him again, his whole appearance terrified her.

"You'll be the new 'servant'?" he said, apparently without much interest.

"Ah'm a new one, aw right," she replied meekly. "An' Ah hope I'll be here for a while yet, too, eh?"

Johnnie threw his cap on the dresser and walked over to the sink, where he looked at his face in the wall mirror.

"You can be here as long as you bliddy well like, for aw Ah care," he said gloomily over his shoulder. "Ah'll likely be in jail again before hellish long, and, as long as you look efter that missus of mine the wey she wants, that'll be aw right. Ah'm away oot noo. Tell Lizzie Ah'll be looking tae see her the night."

For all her fright of Razor King, Sadie was piqued by his complete indifference to her.

"Maybe," she ventured, "you'll find things changed in

Gorbals. There's been clubs opened this past year and things are quieter."

"Ah heard something of it in Barlinnie. Ah know they've forgotten about *me*, aw right. When the ministers and the priests look into things, Ah suppose everybody is well satisfied – till the likes of me comes along an' wakens them up again."

He spoke so quietly and yet bitterly withal that Sadie began to get over her first fear of him. She thought the jail must have made a great change in him. To her he looked old and battered and very worn.

"Are you no' gettin' too old to be gaun aboot with razors looking for the jail, eh?" she said boldly.

Johnnie took two quick steps towards her, his black brows meeting in a ferocious scowl. His eyes were blazing and his face so menacing that she shrank away from him, all her first terror revived and accentuated.

"Too old?" he said in a whisper. "How dae you mean, 'too old'?"

"Ah didny mean anything at aw," she said in a voice that was almost a scream.

"Did ye no'?" He whispered still, but his whole body was quivering and the girl was in greater peril than she knew. She escaped it for her ignorance and for no other reason.

Johnnie suddenly relaxed, and his scowl became a sneer.

"Ah can see you're not so well advanced after aw," he said contemptuously. "Ah'll away for my walk. Don't forget to tell Lizzie Ah'll be back."

The outside door slammed behind him, and he went clattering down the stair and out into the street. Presently he met two of the men who had fought with him in the last battle. They hailed him cheerfully, took him into a pub, and regaled him with whisky and beer. The drink cheered him so much that he scarcely noticed a subtle difference in his companions' manner. They called him

"Good old Razor King", and willingly bought more whisky and more beer. But there was a sort of wariness in their manner, a faint unease as they listened to his eager talk of what they would all do now that he was out of the jail again.

"Ah wid no' be in a hurry, Razor King," said one of them cautiously. "Conditions in Gorbals is no' exactly like they was a year back. There's plenty time."

"By God! There's no time for me!" he shouted. "Ah'm gaun tae waken up the toon, that's whit Ah'm gaun tae do! As sune as Ah've got ma weapons, Ah'll show them aw that Razor King is back home again!"

The raw whisky was a fire in his parched throat that the bottled beer would not quench. When he saw that his friends would buy no more drink because, they said, their money was all spent, he gave them a nod and stalked out of the bar. What he had drunk would not have been enough to have the slightest effect on him in the old days. Now he was exhilarated and did not realize the cause.

The three men had been standing in the bar for perhaps an hour and a half, and, during that interval, the news of Johnnie's release had spread all over the district. Many watched him leave the public house, and there were some who saw his thumbs go into his waistcoat pocket, feeling for the weapons that were not there.

Johnnie determined he would go home and wait for Lizzie and see if she had any money to spare. He felt uncomfortable without his weapons and wanted to buy a pair of razors at once.

"The sooner Ah get them, the better," he reflected, as he walked along Rutherglen Road alone, with his head bent and his eyes on the pavement.

From the windows of the dirty grey tenements the faces of men and women looked down, blobs of white on the lichened rock. Knots of young men and of old lounged as ever at the street corners. Children were kicking a large rubber ball from pavement to pavement and high up against the cliffs of masonry. There was a huddle of card-players in the shelter of a doorway. And the whisper ran among them all – the tireless watchers at the windows, the shuffling loiterers, the gamblers and the children: "Look over yon! That'll be Razor King oot o' the jail!"

The priests and the ministers and the social workers had not toiled wholly in vain. They had denounced the gangs and hooligans were a little out of favour. They had poured scorn upon the "razor kings" and some believed that it was the like of them that caused trouble in the tenements.

The whispers became hostile. Young men wearying for the diversion of a fight – young men of Johnnie's own gang – repeated them more loudly: "There he goes: Razor King, the bliddy swanker!"

Until they were close upon him he did not hear the running feet of the young hooligans who had formed a pack to hunt the old Razor King. Some of them had fought under his leadership; now, at a mere suggestion from a new club leader, they joined as eagerly as any in his pursuit.

The pack of twenty or more young fellows were almost at his heels as Johnnie turned into Crown Street, head still bent, hands deep in his trousers pockets.

"There he is!" they yelled. "On the bastard!"

They pounded after him in a mad rush. Johnnie looked up with their yells in his ears, and in a moment they were close upon him.

"Ma weapons!" he groaned, then turned and ran so that he might at least have a wall to his back.

Two men were walking together down Crown Street when the chase swept by them. One of them was Peter Stark and the other was Bobbie Hurley, the dancer.

It sometimes happens that the separate threads of individual destiny are suddenly caught together in a tangle of coincidence. Peter had been sent out from the warehouse that day to deliver a parcel, and, just as years before he had once visited his mother on a similar occasion, so now, after he had fulfilled his errand in a familiar neighbourhood, the whim took him to call at Johnnie's house to see if his brother was yet out of jail.

Peter fell in with Bobbie Hurley as he was crossing the river. They had not met for some years, and Peter, in his shabby blue jacket and dirty grey flannels, would have been glad to pass with a nod. But Bobbie stopped him. He was still well dressed, with collar and tie and polished shoes, but it seemed to Peter that his suit was a little shiny at the elbows; that his manner was almost too jaunty; and that his surprising affability hid a certain nervousness.

Stalling off Bobbie's enquiries about himself, Peter explained reluctantly that he had just happened to be in the neighbourhood and thought that he would take "a bit walk" through Gorbals "tae see what the old place looked like".

"Ah'll steppit wi' you," said Bobbie surprisingly. "Being summer an' aw that, Ah'm taking a kind of holiday. By September Ah expect Ah'll be opening a hall of my own."

Peter did not believe him. He knew he had quarrelled with Lily and that his new partner had since left him. There were pouches under Bobbie's eyes and his waistcoat was buttoned too tightly.

"He'll be lucky," thought Peter, with more satisfaction than pity, "tae find a job as one of the ordinary professionals in any hall – let alone the 'Gaydom', or one of his own – by next season. It's him finished as a champion, Ah'm thinking."

Bobbie, who had heard nothing of Peter for a very long time, walked beside him now, disparaging his companion in the same way and drawing a similar conclusion from the disparagement.

"Hey, hey," he thought. "Young Peter's looking in a bad way. For all his brains and his ambitions, he's just low-class like the rest of them. Ah would say he's no better off than his brither."

And then, in Crown Street, these two came suddenly upon the wild pack that hunted Razor King, saw the quarry turn at last, his back against a wall, and fell his foremost pursuer with one smashing blow to the chin. Then the others closed upon him in a struggling mass.

"By God!" shouted Peter. "It's my brither. It's Johnnie over there! Johnnie! Hey – JOHNNIE! Ah'm wi' you! Come on, Bobbie! . . . Rin like hell. Come on an' rescue RAZOR KING!"

He was into the thick of the fight while he still shouted. He had forgotten his wife and his home and his child and his job. He was full of a wild fierce joy that he had not known since boyhood. His fists whirled and his boots stamped and kicked. Blows rained upon him and he knew no pain. He was through the mob and standing for a moment over Johnnie's fallen body. Then something crashed down on the back of his head and the boots rose and fell and the gang stamped over the fallen Razor King and his last bodyguard.

Bobbie Hurley did not stop to see the end of that fight. He ran like hell, but he ran the other way. There was some excuse for him. It would have done no good to a dancer out of work to get mixed up in a gang fight. And Bobbie was never very manly.

The brothers Stark were taken to the infirmary in the same ambulance. Peter was detained for only two days, but Johnnie was so brutally kicked in the head that he never regained consciousness and died the following morning.

Lizzie sat by his bed, weeping as though her heart were breaking. She died in the August of that year when she brought a dead son into the world, and they buried her beside Razor King in the Necropolis in the Caledonia

312

Road, thousands turning out to see the funeral. Her daughter was adopted by Lizzie's parents, who thought it only right that they should see to its upbringing.

Peter was at both funerals, his brother's and Lizzie's. He had plenty of time to spare, for the warehouse dismissed him from the porter's job when it was learned that he had taken to hooliganism as well as "politics".

And Gorbals life goes on its way – just as if nobody could help it.

THE END

APPENDIX

Though all the characters in *No Mean City* are imaginary and the book itself merely fiction, the authors maintain that they have not drawn an exaggerated picture of conditions in the Glasgow tenements or of life as it is lived amongst the gangster element of the slum population.

General readers, some of whom may find it difficult to believe this, may be interested in the following quotations:

"It is not uncommon for eight, ten, or twelve persons to be herded together in a single room. There are (in Glasgow) 175,000 'houses' without baths, and 105,000 'houses' have no internal sanitation." – *News of the World*, 29/4/34.

"Glasgow's infantile death rate, which was mainly caused by tenement congestion, was 112 in the thousand in 1932 compared with 67 per thousand in London and Birmingham. The infantile death rate in tenement wards is four to six times greater than in residential areas where there are few tenements." – *Daily Herald*, 16/8/34.

"John R—, 22, leader of the Billy Boys Gang, *and known as the Razor King*, was sent to prison for eighteen months at the High Court in Glasgow yesterday for having assaulted William R— and seriously injured him." – Glasgow *Daily Record*, 17/12/30.

"The spear of a swordfish and a wicked-looking Gurkha knife were among the number of weapons taken possession of by the police following an alleged gang fight in Kerr Street, Bridgeton, yesterday afternoon. The 'battlefield' was strewn with weapons after the fight . . . a piece of copper tubing . . . a brass-headed poker . . . a cudgel two feet long with a knob of wood as thick as the head of a drumstick . . . a wooden baton . . . an axe weighing 1½ lb . . . a steel file two feet long . . . a bayonet-like knife . . . and an iron rod three feet long with a hook at each end. Many of these articles, it is stated, were thrown away by the alleged gangsters in their flight from the police." – Glasgow *Evening Times*, 17/6/31.

"A gang disturbance in the East End of Glasgow, arising out of jealousy on the part of a sister of one of the gangsters, led to the appearance of four young men . . . at Glasgow Sheriff Court to-day. Accused, all unemployed . . . were stated to be members of a gang known as the 'Eminent Gang' which frequented the Calton district . . ." (This report goes on to describe how the jealous girl threatened her fickle lover that she would bring her brother round to "cut off his head".) When one of the accused was arrested, *"he said he thought it was a fighting man they had to deal with and there would be no court case . . . In many cases no complaint was made because those who ought to be the complainers were afraid."* – *Evening Times*, 26/12/29.

"RAZOR SLASHING." – Sir, It is depressing nowadays to take up one's paper and read the daily catalogue of assaults and murders with knives, razors and other lethal weapons. Indeed, razor slashing and stabbing are becoming so common that they appear to be accepted as part of our modern youth's recreation, etc., etc. – Letter to Editor, Glasgow *Evening Times*, 14/3/30.

"RIOT IN CITY PICTURE HOUSE.
GANG WARFARE HELD RESPONSIBLE.
WOMEN FAINT.
SEVEN YOUTHS CHARGED IN COURT."

Headings to report of Glasgow police court case. – *Evening Times*, 4/12/29.

"PANIC IN GLASGOW CINEMA.
VICTIMIZED BY GANGS OF YOUTHS."

"Superintendent Cameron stated that this outbreak was a particularly serious one. The picture house had been singled out latterly by various gangs who deliberately wrecked the performances. Every member of the audience on this occasion was in a state of panic." Headings and extract from report of another police court case. – Glasgow *Evening Times*, 17/12/29.

"During the past ten years, in Glasgow alone, gangsterdom has been responsible for at least four slayings and the serious injuring and maiming of many others who have incurred the savage wrath of the different cliques of young hooligans who terrorize the poorer districts of the city . . .

"The true trysting places of the gangsters are the cheap dance halls, dens of obscene immorality, that exist in many parts of the city . . .

"In true Chicago style the Glasgow gangster has his 'Moll', and in these dance halls she is frequently the cause of the trouble that leads to razor-slashed faces and bottle-crowned heads . . . There is, indeed, a rivalry among the girls connected with the gangs as to how many fights they can get their 'bloke' to engage in." – *The Sunday Mail*, 3/2/35.

"The gangsters *have* come to Britain. Glasgow, second city of the Empire . . . frankly acknowledges their reign of terror. A thousand young men – not forty are more than thirty-five – rule the poorer class districts. Their insignia of office are the broken bottle, the razor blade, the 'cosh', the knife, and – newest and most effective of all – the bayonet. – *Sunday Express*, 3/3/35.

"GLASGOW'S NAME A BY-WORD." – Under this heading

the Glasgow *Evening Citizen*, of 26 August 1935, reported a case before Bailie M'Lean in which two young gangsters were charged with committing a breach of the peace. Police evidence was that one of the accused emerged from a dance hall, drunk and shouting. When he was arrested his friend drew a bottle from his pocket and threw it at the police.

"This was the signal for a general assault on the police by the large crowd which had gathered, mostly young men from the dance hall, and bottles were thrown at the police. One of the bottles struck their prisoner on the head and he was knocked unconscious . . . from 200 to 2,000 were the estimates of the number of persons in the crowd."

The *Citizen*'s report added that a tenant in that district protested that rows of that kind had been going on for thirteen years. Another witness said that the particular dance hall was the meeting-place every Friday night of a well-known gang called the "Beehives".

Bailie M'Lean, passing sentence, said: 'The Magistrates are determined to put down these gang fights."

Extracts of the same kind could be quoted *ad nauseam* from the Glasgow and national papers of recent years.

A. McA.
H. K. L.

Autumn 1935.

BRIDGE ACROSS MY SORROWS
by Christina Noble
with Robert Coram

'A record of grief and courage that would take a tear from a stone'
Dervla Murphy

Christina Noble's story is one of bravery and resilience in the face of deprivation and abuse on a scale most would find unimaginable. Her childhood in the Dublin slums barely merits the name: after the early death of her mother the family is split apart, their alcoholic father unable to care for them. Christina is sexually abused and later escapes from an orphanage only to become destitute on the streets of Dublin. At sixteen she is pulled into a car by four men and raped repeatedly. Later, driven to near insanity by overwork and a violent husband, she finds in a dream the will to fight back. Yet this is no vision of luxury and self-indulgence; instead Christina's hope lies in a determination to work among the *bui doi*, the street children of Vietnam.

And here the most extraordinary part of her story begins, on the streets of Ho Chi Minh City, where destitute children swarm and the rich turn a blind eye. To these needy children 'Mama Tina' became, and remains to this day, an irrepressible, unorthodox and staunch champion.

Outspoken, often angry, yet profoundly moving, *Bridge Across My Sorrows* is one of the most inspirational stories ever told.

'An extraordinarily moving story . . . Both heart-rending and inspirational'
Cameron Mackintosh, producer of *Miss Saigon*

'We see a human spirit of shining dignity, courage and resilience – it is not a surprise when she ultimately turns her life into a magnificent act of love and generosity'
Mia Farrow

'Christina Noble's story is heartbreaking but finally inspiring because of her own indomitable courage in the face of violence, neglect and abuse. Her spirit blazes across the page in this unforgettable book'
Sinead Cusack

0 552 14288 3

A SELECTED LIST OF RELATED TITLES
AVAILABLE FROM CORGI AND BLACK SWAN

☐	99065 5	THE PAST IS MYSELF	Christabel Bielenberg	£7.99
☐	13407 4	LET ME MAKE MYSELF PLAIN	Catherine Cookson	£5.99
☐	14093 7	OUR KATE	Catherine Cookson	£5.99
☐	14384 7	PLAINER STILL	Catherine Cookson	£5.99
☐	99926 1	DEAR TOM	Tom Courtenay	£7.99
☐	15027 4	THE GOD SQUAD	Paddy Doyle	£6.99
☐	14239 5	MY FEUDAL LORD	Tehmina Durrani	£6.99
☐	99802 8	DON'T WALK IN THE LONG GRASS	Tenniel Evans	£6.99
☐	13928 9	DAUGHTER OF PERSIA	Sattareh Farman Farmaian	£6.99
☐	12833 3	THE HOUSE BY THE DVINA	Eugenie Fraser	£8.99
☐	14185 2	FINDING PEGGY: A GLASGOW CHILDHOOD	Meg Henderson	£7.99
☐	14164 X	EMPTY CRADLES	Margaret Humphreys	£8.99
☐	13943 2	LOST FOR WORDS	Deric Longden	£5.99
☐	13822 3	THE CAT WHO CAME IN FROM THE COLD	Deric Longden	£5.99
☐	14544 0	FAMILY LIFE	Elisabeth Luard	£7.99
☐	13356 6	NOT WITHOUT MY DAUGHTER	Betty Mahmoody	£6.99
☐	13953 X	SOME OTHER RAINBOW	John McCarthy & Jill Morrell	£7.99
☐	14137 2	A KENTISH LAD	Frank Muir	£7.99
☐	14288 3	BRIDGE ACROSS MY SORROWS	Christina Noble	£6.99
☐	14632 3	MAMA TINA	Christina Noble	£5.99

FINDING PEGGY:
A Glasgow Childhood
by Meg Henderson

Scottish journalist Meg Henderson grew up in Glasgow during the fifties and sixties as part of a large and often troubled family. The tenement block in which they lived collapsed and they were moved to the notorious Blackhill district, where religious sectarianism, gang warfare and struggles with hostile bureaucrats were part of daily life for the people. Meg was born into a mixed-religion family, where there was warmth and laughter as well as conflict. She had a close relationship with her mother, Nan, and her mother's sister, Meg's Aunt Peggy, two idealistic, emotional women who took on the troubles of the world. Together they shaped Meg's life, shielded her from the effects of her father's heavy drinking and helped her to move on, eventually, from the slums of Glasgow.

A hopeless romantic, Peggy searched for a husband until late in her life and then endured a harsh, unhappy marriage until she died tragically in childbirth. Her death devastated the family and destroyed Meg's childhood, but it was only as an adult, after the death of her own mother, that Meg was able to discover the shocking facts behind Peggy's untimely demise.

'Beautifully written and immensely enjoyable. Captures Glasgow perfectly with no rose-tinted glass'
Alan Taylor

0 552 14185 2